Second Grave
on the Left

Also by Darynda Jones

First Grave on the Right

Second Grave
on the Left

Darynda Jones

ST. MARTIN'S PRESS ✥ NEW YORK

SECOND GRAVE ON THE LEFT. Copyright © 2011 by Darynda Jones. All rights reserved. Printed in the United States of America. For information, address St. Martin's Press, 175 Fifth Avenue, New York, N.Y. 10010.

www.stmartins.com

Library of Congress Cataloging-in-Publication Data

Jones, Darynda.
    Second grave on the left / Darynda Jones. — 1st ed.
        p. cm.
    ISBN 978-0-312-36081-8
    1. Women private investigators—Fiction.   2. Women mediums—Fiction.   I. Title.
    PS3610.O6236S43 2011
    813'.6—dc22

                                                                            2011011243

First Edition: August 2011

10   9   8   7   6   5   4   3   2   1

For the Mighty, Mighty Jones Boys,
Danny, Jerrdan, and Casey.

You are the reason I breathe.

Acknowledgments

Even in my wildest dreams, I never thought I would get an agent like Alexandra Machinist or an editor like Jennifer Enderlin. I've said this before, but it bears repeating. I'm not sure what I did to deserve you. Maybe it was that stretch as a volunteer at the local nursing home. Or the time I pulled that kid out of a burning building. No, wait, I never pulled a kid out of a burning building.

'Kay, I'm going to keep working on that. In the meantime, thank you so much to Jen, my spectacular editor, and everyone at St. Martin's Press and Macmillan. You guys rock so hard.

To Alexandra, my own personal Superwoman, and everyone at the Linda Chester Literary Agency.

To the wonderful Whitney Lee at the Fielding Agency and the super-savvy Josie Freedman at ICM. Thank you guys so very much.

To the super-talented Liz Bemis at Bemis Promotions. Just, wow.

To my very own Charley Davidson, Danielle Tanner.

To my family—you know who you are—and my friends. Thank you for liking me. Or pretending to like me. I appreciate the effort either way.

To the goddesses of LERA and the Ruby Slippered Sisterhood, my other family.

To Bria Quinlan, Gabi Stephens, and Samira Stephan for help with translations.

To Commander Murray Conrad. Thank you for letting me bug you on a continual basis without arresting me.

And a special thank-you to my readers, especially those readers who stayed up the night before this book was due to give me feedback: Danielle Swopes, Tammy Baumann, and Kit Carson. I totally owe you guys a mocha latte. Or a small island.

Second Grave
on the Left

Chapter One

GRIM REAPERS ARE TO DIE FOR.

—T-SHIRT OFTEN SEEN ON CHARLOTTE JEAN DAVIDSON,

GRIM REAPER EXTRAORDINAIRE

"Charley, hurry, wake up."

Fingers with pointy nails bit into my shoulders, doing their darnedest to vanquish the fog of sleep I'd been marinating in. They shook me hard enough to cause a small earthquake in Oklahoma. Since I lived in New Mexico, this was a problem.

Judging by the quality and pitch of the intruder's voice, I was fairly certain the person accosting me was my best friend, Cookie. I let an annoyed sigh slip through my lips, resigning myself to the fact that my life was a series of interruptions and demands. Mostly demands. Probably because I was the only grim reaper this side of Mars, the only portal to the other side the departed could cross through. At least, those who hadn't crossed right after they died and were stuck on Earth. Which was a freaking lot. Having been born the grim reaper, I couldn't remember a time when dead people weren't knocking on my door—metaphorically, as dead people rarely knocked—asking for my assistance with some unfinished business. It amazed me how many of the dearly departed forgot to turn off the stove.

For the most part, those who cross through me simply feel they've been on Earth long enough. Enter the reaper. Aka, *moi*. The departed can see me from anywhere in the world and can cross to the other side through me. I've been told I'm like a beacon as bright as a thousand suns, which would suck for a departed with a martini hangover.

I'm Charlotte Davidson: private investigator, police consultant, all-around badass. Or I could've been a badass, had I stuck with those lessons in mixed martial arts. I was only in that class to learn how to kill people with paper. And—oh, yes—let us not forget grim reaper. Admittedly, being the reaper wasn't all bad. I had a handful of friends I'd kill for—some alive, some not so much—a family of which I was quite grateful some were alive, some not so much, and an *in* with one of the most powerful beings in the universe, Reyes Alexander Farrow, the part-human, part-supermodel son of Satan.

Thus, as the grim reaper, I understood dead people. Their sense of timing pretty much sucked. Not a problem. But this being woken up in the middle of the night by a living, breathing being who had her nails sharpened regularly at World of Knives was just wrong.

I slapped at the hands like a boy in a girl fight, then continued to slap air when my intruder rushed away to invade my closet. Apparently, in high school, Cookie had been voted Person Most Likely to Die Any Second Now. Despite an overwhelming desire to scowl at her, I couldn't quite muster the courage to pry open my eyes. Harsh light filtered through my lids anyway. I had such a serious wattage issue.

"Charley . . ."

Then again, maybe *I'd* died. Maybe I'd bit it and was floating haplessly toward the light like in the movies.

". . . I'm not kidding. . . ."

I didn't feel particularly floaty, but experience had taught me never to underestimate the inconvenience of death's timing.

". . . for real, get up."

I ground my teeth together and used all my energy to anchor myself to Earth. Mustn't . . . go into . . . the light.

"Are you even listening to me?"

Cookie's voice was muffled now as she rummaged through my personal effects. She was so lucky my killer instincts hadn't kicked in and pummeled her ass to the ground. Left her a bruised and broken woman. Groaning in agony. Twitching occasionally.

"Charley, for heaven's sake!"

Darkness suddenly enveloped me as an article of clothing smacked me in the face. Which was completely uncalled for. "For heaven's sake back," I said in a groggy voice, wrestling the growing pile of clothes off my head. "What are you doing?"

"Getting you dressed."

"I'm already as dressed as I want to be at—" I glanced at the digits glowing atop my nightstand. "—two o'clock in the freaking morning. Seriously?"

"Seriously." She threw something else. Her aim being what it was, the lamp on my nightstand went flying. The lampshade landed at my feet. "Put that on."

"The lampshade?"

But she was gone. It was weird. She rushed out the door, leaving an eerie silence in her wake. The kind that makes one's lids grow heavy, one's breathing rhythmic, deep, and steady.

"Charley!"

I jumped out of my skin at the sound of Cookie's screeching and, having flailed, almost fell out of bed. Man, she had a set of lungs. She'd yelled from her apartment across the hall.

"You're going to wake the dead!" I yelled back. I didn't deal well with the dead at two in the morning. Who did?

"I'm going to do more than that if you don't get your ass out of bed."

For a best-friend-slash-neighbor-slash-dirt-cheap-receptionist, Cookie was getting pushy. We'd both moved into our respective apartments across the hall from each other three years ago. I was fresh out of the Peace Corps, and she was fresh out of divorce court with one kid in tow. We were like those people who meet and just seem to know each other. When I opened my PI business, she offered to answer the phone until I could find someone more permanent, and the rest is history. She's been my slave ever since.

I examined the articles of clothing strewn across my bedroom and lifted a couple in doubt. "Bunny slippers and a leather miniskirt?" I called out to her. "Together? Like an ensemble?"

She stormed back into the room, hands on hips, her cropped black hair sticking every direction but down, and then she glared at me, the same glare my stepmother used to give me when I gave her the Nazi salute. That woman was so touchy about her resemblance to Hitler.

I sighed in annoyance. "Are we going to one of those kinky parties where everyone dresses like stuffed animals? 'Cause those people freak me out."

She spotted a pair of sweats and hurled them at me along with a T-shirt that proclaimed GRIM REAPERS ARE TO DIE FOR. Then she rushed back out again.

"Is that a negatory?" I asked no one in particular.

Throwing back my Bugs Bunny comforter with a dramatic flair, I swung out of bed and struggled to get my feet into the sweats—as humans are wont to do when dressing at two o'clock in the morning—before donning one of those lacey push-up bras I'd grown fond of. My girls deserved all the support I could give them.

I realized Cookie had come back as I was shimmying into the bra and glanced up at her in question.

"Are your double-Ds secure?" she asked as she shook out the T-shirt and crammed it over my head. Then she shoved a jacket I hadn't worn since high school into my hands, scooped up a pair of house slippers, and dragged me out of the room by my arm.

Cookie was a lot like orange juice on white pants. She could be either grating or funny, depending on who was wearing the white pants. I hopped into the bunny slippers as she dragged me down the stairs and struggled into the jacket as she pushed me out the entryway. My protests of "Wait," "Ouch," and "Pinkie toe!" did little good. She just barely eased her grip when I asked, "Are you wearing razor blades on your fingertips?"

The crisp, black night enveloped us as we hurried to her car. It had been a week since we'd solved one of the highest-profile cases ever to hit Albuquerque—the murder of three lawyers in connection to a human trafficking ring—and I had been quite enjoying the calm after the storm. Apparently, that was all about to end.

Trying hard to find her erratic behavior humorous, I tolerated Cookie's manhandling until—for reasons I had yet to acquire—she tried to stuff me into the trunk of her Taurus. Two problems surfaced right off the bat: First, my hair caught in the locking mechanisms. Second, there was a departed guy already there, his ghostly image monochrome in the low light. I considered telling Cookie she had a dead guy in her trunk but thought better of it. Her behavior was erratic enough without throwing a dead stowaway into the mix. Thank goodness she couldn't see dead people. But no way was I climbing into the trunk with him.

"Stop," I said, holding up a hand in surrender while I fished long strands of chestnut hair out of the trunk latch with the other one. "Aren't you forgetting someone?"

She screeched to a halt, metaphorically, and leveled a puzzled expression on me. It was funny.

I had yet to be a mother, but I would have thought it difficult to forget something it took thirty-seven hours of excruciating pain to push out from between my legs. I decided to give her a hint. "She starts with an *A* and ends with an *mmm–ber*."

Cookie blinked and thought for a moment.

I tried again. "Um, the fruit of your loins?"

"Oh, Amber's with her dad. Get in the trunk."

I smoothed my abused hair and scanned the interior of the trunk. The dead guy looked as though he'd been homeless when he was alive. He lay huddled in an embryonic position, not paying attention to either of us as we stood over him. Which was odd, since I was supposed to be bright and sparkly. Light of a thousand suns and all. My presence, at the very least, should have elicited a nod of acknowledgment. But he was giving me nothing. Zero. Zip. Zilch. I sucked at the whole grim reaper thing. I totally needed a scythe.

"This is not going to work," I said as I tried to figure out where one bought farming equipment. "And where could we possibly be going at two o'clock in the morning that requires me to ride in the trunk of a car?"

She reached through the dead guy and snatched a blanket then slammed the lid closed. "Fine, get in the back, but keep your head down and cover up."

"Cookie," I said, taking a firm hold of her shoulders to slow her down, "what is going on?"

Then I saw them. Tears welling in her blue eyes. Only two things made Cookie cry: Humphrey Bogart movies and someone close to her getting hurt. Her breaths grew quick and panicked, and fear rolled off her like mist off a lake.

Now that I had her attention, I asked again. "What is going on?"

After a shaky sigh, she said, "My friend Mimi disappeared five days ago."

My jaw fell open before I caught it. "And you're just now telling me?"

"I just found out." Her bottom lip started to tremble, causing a tightness inside my chest. I didn't like seeing my best friend in pain.

"Get in," I ordered softly. I took the keys from her and slid into the driver's seat while she walked around and climbed into the passenger's side. "Now, tell me what happened."

She closed the door and wiped the wetness from her eyes before starting. "Mimi called me last week. She seemed terrified, and she asked me all kinds of questions about you."

"Me?" I asked in surprise.

"She wanted to know if you could . . . make her disappear."

This had *bad* written all over it. In bold font. All caps. I gritted my teeth. The last time I'd tried to help someone disappear, which was pretty much last week, it ended in the worst way possible.

"I told her whatever her problem was, you could help."

Sweet but sadly overstated. "Why didn't you tell me she'd called?" I asked.

"You were in the middle of a case with your uncle and people kept trying to kill you and you were just really busy."

Cookie had a point. People had been trying to kill me. Repeatedly. Thank goodness they didn't succeed. I could be sitting there dead.

"She said she would come in and talk to you herself, but she never showed. Then I got this text a little while ago." She handed me her phone.

Cookie, please meet me at our coffee shop as soon as
you get this message.
Come alone. M

"I didn't even know she was missing."

"You own a coffee shop?" I asked.

"How could I not know?" Her breath hitched in her chest with emotion.

"Wait, how do you know she's missing now?"

"I tried calling her cell when I got the message, but she didn't pick up, so I called her house. Her husband answered."

"Well, I guess he would know."

"He freaked. He wanted to know what was going on, where his wife was, but the message said come alone. So, I told him I would call him as soon as I knew something." She bit her lower lip. "He was not a happy camper."

"I'll bet. There aren't many reasons a woman wants to disappear."

She blinked at me in thought before inhaling so sharply, she had to cough a few moments. When she recovered, she said, "Oh, no, you don't understand. She is very happily married. Warren worships the ground she walks on."

"Cookie, are you sure? I mean—"

"I'm positive. Trust me, if there was any abuse in that relationship, it was to Warren's bank account. He dotes on that woman like you wouldn't believe. And those kids."

"They have kids?"

"Yes, two," she said, her voice suddenly despondent.

I decided not to argue with her about the possibility of abuse until I knew more. "So, he has no idea where she is?"

"Not a single one."

"And she didn't tell you what was going on? Why she wanted to disappear?"

"No, but she was scared."

"Well, hopefully we'll have some answers soon." I started the car and drove to the Chocolate Coffee Café, which Cookie did not own,

unfortunately. Because, really? Chocolate and coffee? Together? Whoever came up with that combination should have won a Nobel Peace
Prize. Or at least a subscription to *Reader's Digest*.

After pulling into the parking lot, we drove to a darkened corner
so we could observe for a few moments without being observed. I wasn't
sure how Mimi would take to my presence, especially since she told
Cookie to come alone. Making a mental list of who could be after her
based on what little I knew, her husband was at the top. Statistics were
hard to dismiss.

"Why don't you wait here?" Cookie asked as she reached for her
door handle.

"Because we have a lot of paperwork back at the office, and that
paperwork's not going to file itself, missy. No way can I risk losing you
now."

She glanced back at me. "Charley, it'll be okay. She's not going to
attack me or anything. I mean, I'm not *you*. I don't get attacked and
almost killed every other day."

"Well, I never," I said, trying to look offended. "But whoever's after her might beg to differ. I'm going. Sorry, kiddo." I stepped out of
the car and tossed her the keys when she got out. After scanning the
near-empty lot once more, we strolled into the diner. I felt only slightly
self-conscious in my bunny slippers.

"Do you see her?" I asked. I had no idea what the woman looked
like.

Cookie looked around. There were exactly two people inside: one
male and one female. I wasn't surprised it was so slow, considering the
freaking time. The man wore a fedora and a trench coat and looked
like a movie star from the forties, and the woman looked like a hooker
after a rough night at work. But neither really counted, since they were
both deceased. The man noticed me immediately. Damn my brightness. The woman never looked over.

"Of course I don't see her," Cookie said. "There's no one in here. Where could she be? Maybe I took too long. Maybe I shouldn't have called her husband or taken the time to drag your skinny ass out of bed."

"Excuse me?"

"Oh man, this is bad. I know it. I can feel it."

"Cookie, you have to calm down. Seriously. Let's do a little investigative work before we call in the National Guard, okay?"

"Right. Got it." She placed a hand over her chest and forced herself to relax.

"Are you good?" I asked, unable to resist teasing her just a little. "Do you need a Valium?"

"No, I'm good," she said, practicing the deep-breathing techniques we'd learned when we watched that documentary on babies being born underwater. "Smart-ass."

That was uncalled for. "Speaking of my ass, we need to have a long talk about your impression of it." We walked to the counter. "Skinny? Really?" The retro diner was decorated with round turquoise barstools and pink countertops. The server strolled toward us. Her uniform matched the light turquoise on the stools. "I'll have you know—"

"Hey, there."

I turned back to the server and smiled. Her name badge said NORMA.

"Would you girls like some coffee?"

Cookie and I glanced at each other. That was like asking the sun if it would like to shine. We each took a barstool at the counter and nodded like two bobbleheads on the dash of a VW van. And she called us *girls,* which was just cute.

"Then you're in luck," she said with a grin, "because I happen to make the best coffee this side of the Rio Grande."

At that point, I fell in love. Just a little. Trying not to drool as the rich aroma wafted toward me, I said, "We're actually looking for someone. Have you been on duty long?"

She finished pouring and sat the pot aside. "My goodness," she said, blinking in surprise. "Your eyes are the most beautiful color I've ever seen. They're—"

"Gold," I said with another smile. "I get that a lot." Apparently, gold eyes were a rarity. They certainly got a lot of comments. "So—"

"Oh, no, I haven't been on duty long. You're my first customers. But my cook has been here all night. He might be able to help. Brad!" She called back to the cook as only a diner waitress could.

Brad leaned through the pass-out window behind her. I'd expected to see a scruffy older gentleman in desperate need of a shave. Instead, I was met with a kid who looked no older than nineteen with a mischievous gaze and the flirty grin of youth as he appraised the older waitress.

"You called?" he said, putting as much purr into his voice as he could muster.

She rolled her eyes and gave him a motherly glare. "These women are looking for someone."

His gaze wandered toward me, and the interest in his expression was nowhere near subtle. "Well, thank God they found me."

Oh, brother. I tried not to chuckle. It would only encourage him.

"Have you seen a woman," Cookie asked, her tone all business, "late thirties with short brown hair and light skin?"

He arched a brow in amusement. "Every night, lady. You gotta give me more than that."

"Do you have a picture?" I asked her.

Her shoulders fell in disappointment. "I didn't even think of that. I have one at my apartment, I'm sure. Why didn't I think to bring it?"

"Don't start flogging yourself just yet." I turned to the kid. "Can I get your name and number?" I asked him. "And that of the server on duty before you as well," I said, looking at Norma.

She tilted her head, hesitant. "I think I'd have to check with her before giving out that information, honey."

Normally I had a totally-for-real laminated private investigator's license that I could flash to help loosen people's tongues, but Cookie dragged me out of my apartment so fast, I hadn't thought to bring it. I hated it when I couldn't flash people.

"I can tell you the server's name," the kid said, an evil twinkle in his eyes. "It's Izzy. Her number's in the men's bathroom, second stall, right under a moving poem about the tragedy of man boobs."

That kid missed his calling. "Breasts on men are tragic. How 'bout I come back tomorrow night? Will you be on duty?"

He spread his arms, indicating his surroundings. "Just living the dream, baby. Wouldn't miss it for the world."

I took a few moments to scan the area. The diner sat on the corner of a busy intersection downtown. Or it would be busy during business hours. The dead silver screen star with the fedora kept staring at me, and I kept ignoring. Now was not the time to have a conversation with a guy nobody could see but me. After a few hefty gulps of some of the best coffee I'd ever had—Norma wasn't kidding—I turned to Cookie. "Let's look around a bit."

She almost choked on her java. "Of course. I didn't even think of that. Looking around. I knew I brought you for a reason." She jumped off her stool and, well, looked around. It took every ounce of strength I had not to giggle.

"How about we try the restroom, Magnum," I suggested before my willpower waned.

"Right," she said, making a beeline for the storeroom. Oh well, we could start there.

A few moments later, we entered the women's restroom. Thankfully, Norma had only raised her brows when we began searching the place. Some people might've gotten annoyed, especially when we checked out the men's room, it being primarily for men, but Norma was a trouper.

She kept busy filling sugar jars and watching us out of the corner of her eye. But after a thorough check of the entire place, we realized Elvis just wasn't in the building. Nor was Cookie's friend Mimi.

"Why isn't she here?" Cookie asked. "What do you think happened?" She was starting to panic again.

"Look at the writing on the wall."

"I can't!" she yelled in full-blown panic mode.

"Use your inside voice."

"I'm not like you. I don't think like you or have your abilities," she said, her arms flailing. "I couldn't investigate publicly, much less privately. My friend is asking for my help, and I can't even follow her one simple direction, I can't . . . Blah, blah, blah."

I considered slapping her as I studied the crisp, fresh letters decorating one wall of the women's restroom, but she was on a roll. I hated to interrupt.

After a moment, she stopped on her own and glanced at the wall herself. "Oh," she said, her tone sheepish, "you meant that literally."

"Do you know who Janelle York is?" I asked.

That name was written in a hand much too nice to belong to a teen intent on defacing public property. Underneath it were the letters *HANA L2-S3-R27* written in the same crisp style. It was not graffiti. It was a message. I tore off a paper towel and borrowed a pen from Cookie to write down the info.

"No, I don't know a Janelle," she said. "Do you think Mimi wrote this?"

I looked in the trash can and brought out a recently opened permanent marker package. "I'd say there's a better-than-average chance."

"But why would she tell me to meet her here if she was just going to leave a message on a wall? Why not just text it to me?"

"I don't know, hon." I grabbed another paper towel to search the garbage again but found nothing of interest. "I suspect she had every intention of being here and something or someone changed her mind."

"Oh my gosh. So what should we do now?" Cookie asked, her panic rising again. "What should we do now?"

"First," I said, washing my hands, "we are going to stop repeating ourselves. We sound ridiculous."

"Right." She nodded her head in agreement. "Sorry."

"Next, you are going to find out as much as you can about the company Mimi works for. Owners. Board. CEOs. Blueprints of the building . . . just in case. And check out that name," I said, pointing over my shoulder to the name on the wall.

Her gaze darted along the floor in thought, and I could almost see the wheels spinning in her head, her mind going in a thousand different directions as she slid her purse onto her shoulder.

"I'll call Uncle Bob when he gets in and find out who has been as-signed to Mimi's case." Uncle Bob was my dad's brother and a detective for the Albuquerque Police Department, just as my dad was, and my work with him as a consultant for APD accounted for a large part of my income. I'd solved many a case for that man, as I had for my dad before him. It was easier to solve crimes when you could ask the departed who did them in. "I'm not sure who does missing persons at the station. And we'll need to talk to the husband as well. What was his name?"

"Warren," she said, following me out.

I made a mental list as we exited the restroom. After we paid for our coffee, I tossed Brad a smile and headed out the door. Unfortunately, an irate man with a gun pushed us back inside. It was probably too much to hope he was just there to rob the place.

Cookie stopped short behind me then gasped. "Warren," she said in astonishment.

"Is she here?" he asked, anger and fear twisting his benign features.

Even the toughest cop alive grew weak in the knees when standing on the business end of a snub-nosed .38. Apparently, Cookie wasn't graced with the sense God gave a squirrel.

"Warren Jacobs," she said, slapping him upside the head.

"Ouch." He rubbed the spot where Cookie hit him as she took the gun and crammed it into her purse.

"Do you want to get someone killed?"

He lifted his shoulders like a child being scolded by his favorite aunt.

"What are you doing here?" she asked.

"I went to your apartment complex after you called then followed you here and waited to see if Mimi would come out. When she didn't, I decided to come in."

He looked ragged and a little starved from days of worry. And he was about as guilty of his wife's disappearance as I was. I could read people's emotions like nobody's business, and innocence wafted off him. He felt bad about something, but it had nothing to do with illegal activity. He probably felt guilty for some imagined offense that he believed made his wife leave. Whatever was going on, I had serious doubts any of it had to do with him.

"Come on," I said, ushering them both back into the diner. "Brad," I called out.

His head popped through the opening, an evil grin shimmering on his face. "Miss me already?"

"We're about to see what you're made of, handsome."

He raised his brows, clearly up to the challenge, and twirled a spatula like a drummer in a rock band. "You just sit back and watch," he said before ducking back and rolling up his sleeves. That kid was going to break more than his share of hearts. I shuddered to think of the carnage he would leave in his wake.

Three *mucho grande* breakfast burritos and seven cups of coffee later—only four of them mine—I sat with a man so sick with worry and doubt, my synapses were taking bets on how long he could keep his breakfast down. The odds were not in his favor.

He'd been telling me about the recent changes in Mimi's behavior. "When did you notice this drastic change?" I asked, the question approximately my 112th. Give or take.

"I don't know. I get so wrapped up. Sometimes I doubt I'd notice if my own children caught fire. I think about three weeks ago."

"Speaking of which," I said, looking up, "where are your kids?"

"What?" he asked, steering back to me. "Oh, they're at my sister's."

A definite plus. This guy was a mess. Thanks to Norma, I'd graduated from taking notes on napkins to taking notes on an order pad. "And your wife didn't say anything? Ask anything out of the ordinary? Tell you she was worried or felt like someone was following her?"

"She burned a rump roast," he said, brightening a little since he could answer one of my questions. "After that, everything went to hell."

"So, she takes her cooking very seriously."

He nodded then shook his head. "No, that's not what I meant. She never burns her roast. Especially her rumps."

Cookie pinched me under the table when she saw me contemplating whether I should giggle or not. I flashed a quick glare then returned to my expression of concern and understanding.

"You're a professional investigator, right?" Warren asked.

I squinted. "Define *professional.*" When he only stared, still deep in thought, I said, "No, seriously, I'm not like the other PIs on the playground. I have no ethics, no code of conduct, no taste in gun cleansers."

"I want to hire you," he said, unfazed by my gun-cleanser admission.

I was already planning to do the gig for Cookie pro bono—especially since I barely paid her enough to eat people food—but money would come in downright handy when the bill collectors showed up. "I'm very expensive," I said, trying to sound a bit like a tavern wench.

He leaned in. "I'm very rich."

I glanced at Cookie for confirmation. She raised her brows and nodded her head.

"Oh. Well, then, I guess we can do business. Wait a minute," I said, my thoughts tumbling over themselves, "how rich?"

"Rich enough, I guess." If his answers got any more vague, they'd resemble the food in school cafeterias everywhere.

"I mean, has anyone asked you for money lately?"

"Just my cousin Harry. But he always asks me for money."

Maybe Cousin Harry was getting more desperate. Or more brazen. I took down Harry's info, then asked, "Can you think of anything else? Anything that might explain her behavior?"

"Not really," he said after handing his credit card to Norma. Neither Cookie nor I had enough to cover our extra coffees, much less our *mucho grandes,* and since I doubted they would take my bunny slippers in trade . . .

"Mr. Jacobs," I said, putting on my big-girl panties, "I have a confession to make. I'm very adept at reading people, and no offense, but you're holding out on me."

He worked his lower lip, a remorseful guilt oozing out of his pores. Not so much an I-killed-my-wife-and-buried-her-lifeless-body-in-the-backyard kind of guilt but more of an I-know-something-but-I-don't-want-to-tell kind of guilt.

With a loud sigh, he lowered his head into his palms. "I thought she was having an affair."

Bingo. "Well, that's something. Can you explain why you thought that?"

Too exhausted to put much effort into it, he lifted his shoulders into the slightest hint of a shrug. "Just her behavior. She'd grown so distant. I asked her about it, and she laughed, told me I was the only man in her life because she was not about to put up with another."

In the grand scheme of things, it was quite natural for him to sus-pect adultery, considering how much Mimi had apparently changed.

"Oh, and a friend of hers died recently," he said in afterthought. His brow crinkled as he tried to remember the details. "I'd completely for-gotten. Mimi said she was murdered."

"Murdered? How?" I asked.

"I'm sorry, I just don't remember." Another wave of guilt wafted off him.

"They were close?"

"That's just it. They'd went to high school together, but they hadn't kept in touch. Mimi never even mentioned her name until she died, so I was surprised at how much it affected her. She was devastated, and yet . . ."

"And yet?" I asked when he lost himself in thought again. This was just getting interesting. He couldn't stop now.

"I don't know. She was torn up, but not really upset about losing her friend. It was different." His jaw worked as he rifled through his memories. "I really didn't think much about it at the time, but quite frankly, she didn't seem all that surprised that her friend was mur-dered. Then I asked her if she wanted to go to the funeral, and my god, the look on her face. You'd think I'd asked her to drown the neighbor's cat."

Admittedly, drowning the neighbor's cat didn't really clue me in as much as I would've liked. "So, she was angry?"

He blinked back to me and stared. Like a long time. Long enough to have me sliding my tongue over my teeth to make sure I didn't have anything in them.

"She was horrified," he said at last.

Damn, I wished he could've remembered the woman's name. And why Mimi wasn't surprised when the woman was murdered. Murder is usually quite the surprise to everyone involved.

Speaking of names, I decided to ask about the one on the bathroom wall. Having found no foreign objects in my teeth, I asked, "Did Mimi ever mention a Janelle York?"

"That's her," he said in surprise. "That's Mimi's friend who was murdered. How did you know?"

I didn't, but his thinking I did made me look good.

Chapter Two

DON'T CROSS THE STREAMS. NEVER CROSS THE STREAMS.
—BUMPER STICKER

"What are you listening to?" I asked, reaching over and turning down the radio as Cookie drove home. "This Little Light of Mine" was just way too happy for the current atmospheric conditions.

She hit the SCAN button. "I don't know. It's supposed to be classic rock."

"Oh. So, did you buy this car used?" I asked, thinking back to the dead guy in her trunk and wondering how he got there. I still needed to figure out if Cookie had been a black widow before she met me. She did have black hair. And she'd recently cut it. A disguise, mayhap? Not to mention her early-morning, pre-coffee mean streak that made road rage a practical alternative for a healthier, happier Cookie. The departed rarely just hung out on Earth for no particular reason. Dead Trunk Guy most likely died violently, and if I was ever going to get him to cross, I'd have to figure out how and why.

"Yeah," she said absently. "At least we know where to start with Janelle York. Should I call your uncle on this one? And maybe the medical examiner?"

"Absolutely," I said supernonchalantly. "So, then, where did you buy it?"

She looked over at me, her brows knitting. "Buy what?"

I shrugged and looked out the window. "Your car."

"At Domino Ford. Why?"

I flipped my palms up. "Just wondering. One of those weird things you think about on the way home from investigating a missing persons case."

Her eyes widened in horror. "Oh my god! There's a dead person in my backseat, isn't there?"

"Wait, what?" I said in stuttering astonishment. "Not even. Why would you assume such a thing?"

She fixed a knowing gaze on me a heartbeat before she pulled into a gas station, tires screeching.

"Cook, we're five seconds from home."

"Tell me the truth," she insisted after nearly throwing me through the windshield. She had really good brakes. "I mean it, Charley. Dead people follow you everywhere, but I don't want them in my car. And you suck at lying."

"I do not." I felt oddly appalled by her statement. "I'm an excellent liar. Ask my dentist. He swears I floss regularly."

She threw the car into park and glared. Hard. She would do well in a prison setting.

After transforming a sigh into a Broadway production, I said, "I promise, Cook, there's not a dead person in your backseat."

"Then it's in the trunk. There's a body in the trunk, isn't there?" The panic in her voice was funny. Until she flew out of the car.

"What?" I said, climbing out after her. "Of course not."

She pointed to her white Taurus and stared at me accusingly. "There is a dead body in that trunk," she said. Really loud. Loud enough for the cop sitting next to us with his window down to hear.

I rolled my eyes. It was late October. Why the hell was his window down? When he opened his car door and unfolded to his full height, I dropped my head into a palm. Thankfully it was my own. This was so not happening. If I had to call my uncle Bob, an Albuquerque Police detective, in the middle of the night one more time to get me out of one of these ridiculous altercations I tended to have with random cops, he was going to kill me. He told me so himself. With an orange peeler. Not sure why.

"Is there a problem here, ladies?" the officer asked.

Cookie scowled at me. "Why don't you tell him there's not a dead body in that trunk? Hmmm?"

"Cook, really?"

She threw her hands on her hips, waiting for an answer.

I turned back to Dirty Harry. "Look, Officer O. Vaughn," I said, glancing at his name badge. "I know what Cookie said sounded bad, but she was speaking metaphorically. We would never really h-have . . ." I'd looked back at his face, at the almost contemptuous expression lining his mouth, and a vague familiarity tingled along my spine. In a Stephen King's *It* sort of way. "You wouldn't happen to be related to Owen Vaughn?"

His mouth thinned. "I *am* Owen Vaughn."

No way. For reasons known only to him, Owen Vaughn tried to kill me in high school. With an SUV. Though he later told the police he was only trying to maim me, he refused to tell them why. I'd apparently rained buckets on his parade, but for the life of me, I never figured out what I'd done.

I decided to play it cool. No need to throw past criminal activity in his face. Time to let bygones be bygones. Mostly 'cause he had a gun and I didn't.

I smiled and socked him in the arm like we were old friends. "Long time, no see, Vaughn."

It didn't work. He tensed, took a moment to examine the place where my fist had made contact, then let his gaze wander back to me, zero in on my eyes like he wanted nothing more than to strangle the life out of them.

Awkward.

Then I remembered he'd been friends with Neil Gossett in high school. I'd recently become reacquainted with Neil, and decided to use that bit of info to break the block of ice Vaughn was encased in. "Oh, hey, I just saw Neil the other day. He's the deputy warden at the prison in Santa Fe."

"I know where Neil Gossett is," he said, the contempt in his voice undiluted. "I know where all of you are." He leaned toward me. "Don't ever doubt that."

I stood in shock a solid minute as he turned and walked to his patrol car. Cookie stared, too, her jaw slightly ajar as she watched him drive away.

"He didn't even check the trunk," she said.

"Is it just me," I asked, gazing at his disappearing taillights, "or was that a really stalkery kind of thing to say?"

"What the hell did you do to him?"

"Me?" I placed a hand over my chest to demonstrate how much her words hurt. "Why do you always assume it's my fault?"

"Because it always is."

"I'll have you know that man tried to maim me in high school. With an SUV."

She turned to me then, her expression incredulous. "Have you ever considered moving to another country?"

"Oddly, yes."

"Trunk. Dead body." She walked to the car and unlocked the trunk lid.

I dived toward her, closing the lid before the dead guy could see me.

"I knew it," she said, backing away from the car again. "There's a dead body in the trunk."

Trying to shush her with an index finger slamming against my mouth repeatedly, I whispered, loudly, like drunks do in a singles bar, "It's not a dead body. It's a dead *guy*. There's a difference. And if he realizes I can see him, he'll be all up in my face, trying to get me to solve his murder and crap."

Suddenly her expression turned accusing. "You were going to let me drive around with that guy in my trunk forever."

"What?" I said with a snort. "No way. Well, not forever. Just a few days, until I figured out who he was."

She stepped forward until we stood toe to toe. "That is wrong on so many levels." Then she turned and started walking home.

Darn it. I jogged up behind her, marveling at how much ground a large pissed-off woman could cover in so short a time. "Cookie, you can't walk home. It's still dark. And we're on Central."

"I would rather meet ten bad guys in a dozen dark alleys than ride in that car." She pointed behind her without missing a step.

After doing the math in my head, I asked, "What about dark parking lots? Or dark breezeways? That would be scary, too, huh?"

She trod onward, continuing her noble quest to avoid the departed by getting herself knifed for the five dollars in her back pocket. While I couldn't quite see the logic, I did understand the fear. Wait—no, I didn't.

"Cookie, I have dead people around me all the time. They're always in the office, sitting in the waiting room, hanging by the coffeepot. Why is it suddenly a problem now?"

"That's just it. *You* have dead people around you all the time. Not me. And not my car."

"I probably shouldn't tell you about the little boy in your apartment, then, huh?"

She skidded to a halt, an astonished expression on her face.

"No. Right. Forget I mentioned it."

"There's a dead boy in my apartment?"

"Not all the time."

She shook her head, then took off again, and I found myself struggling to keep up with her in my bunny slippers. With a sigh, I realized I was getting way too much exercise. I'd just have to counteract it later with cake.

"I can't believe I have a dead boy in my apartment and you never told me."

"I didn't want to alarm you. I think he has a crush on Amber."

"Oh, my god," she said.

"Look," I said, grabbing her jacket and pulling her to a stop, "let's just get your car home, then I'll deal with this. We can't leave it there. Someone will steal it."

Her eyes lit up. "You think? No, wait, maybe I should go back and put the keys in it. You know, make it easier for them."

"Um, well, there's an idea."

She took off toward her car, a new purpose driving her. I was only a little worried. At least she was going in the right direction.

"If you don't count that time I went skinny-dipping with the chess club," I said, only a little out of breath, "this has been the busiest night of my life." I looked up in thought, tripped, stumbled, caught myself, then glanced around like I'd meant to do that, before saying, "No, I take that back. I think the busiest night of my life was the time I'd helped my dad solve the mystery of a gas explosion in which thirty-two people died. Once the case was solved, they all wanted to cross. At the same time. All those emotions swirling inside me simultaneously took all night to get over."

Cookie slowed her stride but had yet to look my way again. I could hardly blame her. I should've told her about the little boy long ago. It wasn't fair to blindside her with that kind of information.

"If it hadn't been for that man who saw a college student vandalize the gas pipes, that case may never have been solved. But I was only seven," I explained, hoping to distract Cookie with small talk. "I had a hard time understanding it all. Hey, at least your car's safe." I pointed to it.

She strode to her Taurus then turned toward me. "I'm sorry, Charley," she said.

I paused and offered a suspicious glower. "Are you about to make a tuna joke? 'Cause I had my fill of those by the time I was twelve."

"Here I am freaking out over a dead body in my trunk—"

"A dead guy. Guy."

"—and you're just doing the best you can. You never told me that story."

"What story?" I asked, still suspicious. "The explosion story? That was nothing." I'd just told her about it to take her mind off all the dead people running amok.

"Nothing? You're like a superhero without the cape."

"Aw, that's really sweet. What's the catch?"

She chuckled. "No catch. Just tell me there's not a dead body in my trunk."

Reluctantly, I took the key and lifted the trunk lid. "There's not a dead body in your trunk."

"Charley, you can be honest. It's okay."

I blinked in surprise. He was gone. "No, really," I said, scanning the area. I took a step back for a better look and ran into something cold and unmoving. The temperature around me dropped, sending a chill down my spine. It was like walking into a freezer, but I didn't want to alarm Cookie. Again.

"Nope," I said, shrugging my shoulders, "no dead guy in there."

Her mouth thinned knowingly. I stepped to the side and looked around as if searching the area. From the corner of my periphery, I studied the tower standing beside me. Dead Trunk Guy was staring down at me yet not seeing, his face completely void of emotion. I resisted the urge to wave a hand, to snap my fingers. It would probably only irk him anyway.

"Is he standing beside you?" Cookie asked.

I must have looked at him too intently, because she'd picked up on my façade of nonchalance. With a sigh of guilty resignation, I nodded.

"Hurry." She snatched the keys and rushed to the driver's-side door. "Charley, hurry, before he gets back in."

"Oh." I booked it to the passenger's side and slid in. Cookie still thought it was possible to outrun the departed. I let her believe it as she started the engine and tore out of the parking lot like a banshee hell-bent on doing whatever banshees do.

"Did we ditch him?" she asked.

I was torn. On one hand, she needed to know, to understand how the other world worked. On the other, I had a burning desire to make it home alive with little to no car parts protruding from my head or torso or both.

"Sure did," I said, trying really hard not to stare. The situation reminded me of the time in college when I was headed to class, turned a corner, and came face-to-face with the resident streaker. It was hard not to stare, then or now, mostly 'cause Dead Trunk Guy had taken up residence in her lap.

"Brrr," she said. She leaned forward and turned up the heat even though we were already pulling into the parking lot of our apartment building.

"I'm going to take a shower, then find out what happened to Janelle York," she said when we reached our second-floor apartments. It was barely four thirty. "Why don't you get some more sleep?"

"Cook," I said, inching to the left, as Dead Trunk Guy was invading my personal bubble. I had a thing about my bubble. "I've had three-plus cups of coffee. There is no way I can go back to sleep at this point in my life."

"At least try. I'll wake you up in a couple of hours."

"Are you going to throw clothes at my face again?"

"No."

"Okay, but I'm telling you, I will never be able to get back to sleep."

I awoke two hours later, according to my clock. Almost seven. Just enough time to shower, make some coffee, and look at hot guys on the Internet for a few. Apparently, Dead Trunk Guy needed a shower as well.

Chapter Three

"This is one Froot Loop beyond certifiable."

I stood in the shower, the water as hot as I could get it, and still goose bumps textured every inch of my body. That tended to happen when dead people showered with me. I looked up into the unseeing eyes of the departed homeless guy from Cookie's trunk. He had shoulder-length hair, mop-water brown, a matted, ragged beard, and hazel green eyes. I was such a magnet for these types.

My breath fogged in the air, and vapor bounced off the shower walls. I resisted the urge to look toward the heavens and raise my arms slowly while steam rolled up around us in waves, but pretending to be an oceanic goddess would have been cool. I could totally have thrown in some opera for effect.

"Come here often?" I asked instead, humoring no one but myself. So it was totally worth it.

When he didn't answer, I tested his lucidity by poking his chest with an index finger. The tip pressed into his tattered coat, as solid to me as the shower walls around us, yet the water dripping from my finger went straight through him to splash with all the others on the shower floor. My prodding didn't elicit a reaction. His unseeing eyes stared straight through me. Which was odd. He'd seemed so sane huddled in Cookie's trunk.

Reluctantly, I leaned back to rinse the conditioner from my hair, forcing my eyes to stay open, watching him watch me. Sort of. "Have you ever had one of those days that starts out like crazy on whole wheat and goes downhill from there?"

Obviously the insane silent type, he didn't answer. I wondered how long he'd been dead. Maybe he'd been walking the Earth so long, he lost his mind. That happened in a movie once. Of course, if he was really homeless when he died, mental illness could've already played a big role in his life.

Just as I turned off the water, he looked up. I looked up, too. Mostly 'cause he did. "What is it, big guy?" When I glanced back, he was gone. Just disappeared as dead people are wont to do. No good-bye. No catch ya on the flip side. Just gone. "Go get 'em, boy." Hopefully he'd stay that way. Freaking dead people.

I reached past the curtain for a towel and noticed droplets of crimson sliding down my arm. I looked back up at a dark red circle on my ceiling, slowly spreading like the bloodstain of someone who was still bleeding. Before I had time to say "What the f—," someone fell through. Someone large. And heavy. And he landed pretty much right on top of me.

We tumbled to the shower floor, a heap of torsos and limbs. Unfortunately, I found myself plastered underneath a person made of solid steel, but I recognized one thing immediately. I recognized his heat, like a signature, like a harbinger announcing his arrival. I struggled out from under one of the most powerful beings in the universe, Reyes Farrow, and realized I was covered in blood from head to toe. His blood.

"Reyes," I called out in alarm. He was unconscious, dressed in a blood-soaked T-shirt and jeans. "Reyes," I said, clutching on to his head. His dark hair was dripping wet. Large scratches slashed across his face and neck as if something had been clawing at him, but most of the blood stemmed from wounds, deep and mortal, on his chest, back, and arms. He had been defending himself, but against what?

My heart thundered against my chest. "Reyes, please," I said. I patted his face, and his lashes, now dark crimson and spiked with blood, fluttered. In an instant, he turned on me. With a growl, his black robe materialized around him, around us, and a hand thrust out and locked on to my throat. In the time it took my heart to beat again, I was thrown against the shower wall with a razor-sharp blade glistening in front of my face.

"Reyes," I said weakly, already losing consciousness, the pressure around my throat so precise, so exact. I could no longer see his face, just blackness, the undulating robe that was so much a part of him protecting his identity even from me. The world blurred then spun. I fought his hold, his grip like a metal brace, and as much as I wanted to believe I fought the good fight, I felt my limbs going limp almost immediately, too weak to hold their own weight.

I felt him press against me as a total eclipse crept in. I heard him speak, his voice winding around me like smoke. "Beware the wounded animal."

Then he was gone and gravity took hold and I collapsed onto the shower floor once again, this time face-first, and somewhere in the back of my mind, I knew it was going to suck.

———

The strangest thing happened on the day I was born. A dark figure was waiting for me just outside my mother's womb. He wore a hooded cloak. It undulated around him, filling the entire delivery room with rolling black waves, like smoke in a soft breeze. Though I couldn't see his face, I knew he was watching when the doctor cut the cord. Though I couldn't feel his fingers, I knew he touched me when the nurses cleaned my skin. Though I couldn't hear his voice, I knew he whispered my name, the sound deep and husky.

He was so powerful, his mere presence weakened me, made air difficult to draw into my lungs, and I was afraid of him. As I grew older, I realized he was the only thing I was afraid of. I'd never been plagued with the normal phobias of childhood, probably a good thing, since dead people gathered around me en masse. But him, I was afraid of. And yet he showed himself only in times of dire need. He'd saved me, saved my life more than once. So why was I afraid? Why had I dubbed him the Big Bad growing up when he seemed anything but?

Perhaps it was the power that radiated off him, that seemed to absorb a part of me when he was near.

Jump ahead fifteen years to a frigid night on the streets of Albuquerque, the first time I'd seen Reyes Farrow. My older sister, Gemma, and I had been on recon for a school project in a rather bad part of town when we noticed movement in the window of a small apartment. We realized in horror that a man was beating a teenaged boy. At that moment, my only thought was to save him. Some way. Somehow. Out of desperation, I threw a brick through the man's window. It worked. He stopped hitting the boy. Unfortunately, he came after us. We tore down a dark alley and were searching for an opening along a fence when we realized the boy had escaped as well. We saw him doubled over behind the apartment building.

We went back. Blood streaked down his face, dripped from his incredible mouth. We found out his name was Reyes and tried to help, but he refused our offer, even going so far as to threaten us if we didn't leave. That was my first lesson in the absurdities of the male mind. But because of that incident, I wasn't completely surprised when I found out more than a decade later that Reyes had spent the last ten years in prison for killing that very man.

That was only one of several truths I'd recently found out about him, not the least of which was the fact that Reyes and the Big Bad, the dark being that had been following me, watching over me since the day of my birth, were one and the same. He had been the thing that saved my life over and over. The thing that studied me from the shadows, a mere shadow himself, and protected me from afar. The thing I was most afraid of growing up. Hell, the only thing I was afraid of growing up.

It was mind numbing to realize the smoky being from my childhood was a man made of flesh and blood. Yet he could leave his physical body and travel through space and time as an incorporeal presence, one that could dematerialize in the span of a heartbeat. One that could draw a sword and sever a man's spinal column within the blink of an eye. One that could melt the polar ice caps with a single glance from underneath his dark lashes.

And yet every revelation brought more questions. Only a week ago, I found out where his supernatural abilities stemmed from. I saw into his world when his fingertips brushed down my arm, when his mouth scorched flames over my skin, and when he sank inside me, causing the surge of orgasm to unlock his past and pull back the curtains for me to see. I watched the birth of the universe unfold before my eyes as his father—his real father, the most beautiful angel ever created—was thrown from the halls of heaven. Lucifer fought back, his army vast, and in this time of great turmoil, Reyes was born. Forged from the heat of a supernova, he rose quickly through the ranks to become a respected leader. Second only to his father, he commanded millions of soldiers, a general among thieves, even more beautiful and powerful than his father, with the key to the gates of hell scored into his body.

But his father's pride would not be subdued. He wanted the heavens. He wanted complete control over every living thing in the universe. He wanted God's throne.

Reyes followed his father's every command, waited and watched for a portal to be born upon the Earth, a direct passage to heaven, a way out of hell. A tracker of flawless stealth and skill, he negotiated his way through the gates of the underworld and found the portals in the farthest reaches of the universe, a thousand lights identical in shape and form. A thousand reapers hoping for the privilege to serve on Earth.

But Reyes looked harder and saw one made of spun gold, a daughter of the sun, shimmering and glistening. Me. I turned and saw him and smiled. And Reyes was lost.

He defied his father's wishes for him to return to hell with our location, waited centuries for me to be sent, and was born upon the Earth himself, forsaking all that he knew for me. Because the day he was born in human form was the day he forgot who he was, what he was. And more important, what he was capable of. He gave up everything to be with me, but a cruel twist in fate sent him into the arms of a monster, and Reyes grew up with his every move dictated by a predator of the worst kind. Slowly, he began to remember his past. Who he was. What he was. But by that time, he'd been sent to prison for killing the man who raised him.

I awoke with a start on the floor of my bathtub and bolted upright. The hard slippery surface being what it was, mostly hard and slippery, I dropped just as quickly, my palms sliding out from under me. I hit hard. Thus, on my second attempt, I took it a bit slower, glancing around for Reyes and swearing to get some nonslip bath appliqués.

There was no blood. No signs of a struggle. And no Reyes. What had happened to him? Why was he so mutilated? I fought the image of him in my mind. Mostly because I grew faint the moment it appeared. Queasy.

Then I remembered what he said to me: *Beware the wounded animal.* Only he'd spoken in Aramaic—one of the thousands of languages I'd known inherently from the moment of my birth. His voice had been a low, pain-filled growl. I had to find him.

After hustling into a pair of jeans and a sweater, I threw on some boots and gathered my hair into a ponytail. I had so many questions. So many concerns. For the last month, Reyes had been in a coma. He'd been shot by a prison guard firing warning shots near a gathering of inmates who looked like they were going to riot. The day the state was going to disconnect life support, Reyes seemed to magically wake up, and he strolled out of the long-term-care unit in Santa Fe like he didn't have a care in the world. That was a week ago, and nobody had seen or heard from him since. Not even me. Not until today.

Was he still alive? What had attacked him? What could? He was the son of Satan, for fuck's sake. Who would mess with that? I had a couple of resources I could check out, but as I was leaving my apartment, my landline rang.

"Make it quick," I said when I picked up.

"Okay. Two men from the FBI are here," Cookie said. Quickly.

Crap. "Men in black are at the office?"

"Well, yes, but they're actually in more of a navy."

Crapola. I so didn't have time for men. In any color. "Okay, two questions. Do they look mad, and are they hot?"

After a long, long pause, Cookie said, "One, not really. Two, no comment at this time. And three, you're on speakerphone."

After another long, long pause, I said, "Okie dokie then. Be there in a jiff."

Before I could do it myself, a long arm reached over my shoulder and disconnected the call. Reyes stood behind me. The heat that forever radiated off him soaked into my clothes, saturated me in warmth. He eased closer, allowing the length of his body to press into my backside. I responded to his nearness with a flush of adrenaline, and when he bent his head, his breath fanning across my cheek, my knees almost gave beneath my weight.

"Nice catch, Dutch," he said softly, his voice like a caress.

A rush of delight rippled down my spine and pooled in my abdomen. Reyes had been calling me Dutch since the day I was born, and I had yet to find out why. He was like the desert, stark and beautiful, harsh and unforgiving, with the promise of treasure behind every dune, the allure of water hidden just beneath the surface.

I twisted around to face him. He refused to give up any ground he'd gained, and I had to lean back to look at him, to drink him in. His dark hair curled over an ear and hung slightly mussed over his forehead. His lashes—so thick, he always looked like he'd just woken up—shadowed liquid brown eyes. They sparkled with mischief nonetheless. He let his gaze wander at will, let it slow when it reached my mouth, dip when it reached the valley between Danger and Will Robinson. Then it rose and locked with mine, and I knew in that moment the true meaning of perfection.

"You look better," I said, my tone airy. The wounds that had been so deep, so potentially fatal, had all but vanished. My head spun with a mixture of relief and concern.

He lifted my chin and brushed his fingers over my throat where it was still swollen from his momentary lapse of reason in the shower. He had a strong grip. "Sorry about that."

"Care to explain?"

He lowered his head. "I thought you were someone else."

"Who else?"

In lieu of an answer, he put his fingertips on a pulse point. He seemed to revel in the feel of it, the proof of life flowing through my veins.

"Is it the demons you told me about?" I asked.

"Yes." He said it so matter-of-fact, so casually, one would think demons tried to kill him on a regular basis. He'd told me about them only last week, when I found out who he really was. He'd said they were after me, but to get to me, they'd have to go through him. I thought he was speaking metaphorically. Apparently not.

"Are they—" I stopped midsentence and swallowed hard. "—are you okay?"

"I'm unconscious," he said, edging closer, his tongue wetting his full mouth.

My stomach somersaulted, but only in part because of the tongue. "You're unconscious? What do you mean?"

He had braced a hand against the countertop on either side of me, imprisoning me within his sinewy arms. "I mean, I'm not awake," he said a heartbeat before nipping my earlobe with his teeth, just hard enough to send a quake skimming over the surface of my skin.

The deep tenor of his voice reverberated through my bones, lique-fying them from the inside out. I fought hard to focus on his words instead of the turmoil each syllable generated, each touch. He was like chocolate-covered heroin, and I was an addict through and through.

I'd had him inside me before. I'd known heaven for a brief period of time, the experience so surreal, so earth-shattering, I was certain he'd ruined me to all other men forever. Seriously, who could compete with a being created from beauty and sin and fused together with the blis-tering heat of sensuality? He was a god among men. Damn it.

"Why aren't you awake?" I asked, struggling to redirect my thoughts. "Reyes, what happened?"

He'd been busy nibbling his way to my collarbone, his hot mouth evoking seismic activity at each point of contact.

I really hated to interrupt, but . . . "Reyes, are you listening to me?"

He raised his head, a sensual grin playing at the corners of his mouth, and said, "I'm listening."

"To what? The sound of blood rushing to your nether regions?"

"No," he said with a husky chuckle that made me tingle everywhere. "To your heartbeat." He leaned in again, began the aerial assault again.

"Seriously, Reyes, how did you get hurt?"

"Painfully," he whispered into my ear.

My chest constricted with his answer. "Time-out," I said, grabbing the wrist of a hand that was doing the most amazing things to my girl parts.

He twisted his hand around and wound his fingers into mine. "You're putting me in time-out?"

"Yes," I said as a shaky sigh slid through my lips.

"If I don't go, do I get a spanking?"

A burst of laughter escaped before I could stop it. "Reyes," I said in admonishment. "We need to talk."

"So talk," he said, stroking my wrist with his thumb.

I placed an index finger on his shoulder and nudged. "Let me rephrase that. You need to talk. Please tell me what happened. Why are you unconscious?"

He let out a slow breath and leaned back to focus his liquid brown eyes on mine. "I told you last week, they found me."

"The demons."

"Yes."

"What do they want?"

"The same thing I want," he said, his eyes raking over my body, "but perhaps for different reasons."

He'd explained before that they wanted me, the portal, a way into heaven. I had no idea they would go to such lengths. "Are you still alive?"

"My corporeal body is like yours. It's harder to kill, much harder, than most humans'."

Relief flooded every cell in my body. I took a deep breath and said, "Tell me what's going on. Exactly."

"Exactly. Okay, they're waiting for *exactly* one of two things to happen."

"Which are?"

"For my body to die so they can take me back to hell or for you to find me. One would give them access to the key," he said, indicating the smooth, flowing lines of his tattoos with a nod. Amazingly, his tattoos were a map to the gates of hell. Without it, the hazardous journey through the void of eternity rarely ended well for any entities trying to escape. "And the other would give them access to heaven." He looked at me point-blank. "Either would make them exceedingly happy."

"Then tell me where your physical form is, and we can . . . I don't know, hide you."

He shook his head in regret. "Afraid I can't do that."

My brows shot together. "What do you mean, you can't do that? Reyes, where are you?"

A humorless grin tipped one corner of his mouth. "In a safe place."

"You're safe from the demons?" I asked, my voice full of hope.

"No," he answered. "You're safe from the demons."

When he went for a jugular again, I pulled back. "So, they know where you are? They're trying to kill you?" What he was proposing sounded like my worst nightmare. Injured and helpless somewhere, with a madman trying to kill me. I'd never considered the culprit to be demonic, but now that I had new fodder, surely my reoccurring nightmare would update its software to reflect an evil presence. Wonderful.

With a loud sigh, he stepped back and sank into the chair at my computer desk, propping his feet up and crossing them at the ankles. "Do we really have to do this now? I may not have much time."

My heart stumbled in my chest. I wondered how much time he had. How much time *we* had. I didn't have a table and chairs, but I had a snack bar with a couple of barstools. I sat at one and turned to him. "Why won't you tell me where you are?"

"Lots of different reasons." His gaze slid over me like a veil of fire. He could ignite my deepest desires with a single glance. I decided right then and there no more reading romance novels by candlelight.

"Can you tell me what those reasons are, or should I guess?"

"Since I probably can't stay all day, I'll tell you."

"At least we're getting somewhere."

"The first one is because it's a trap, Dutch. Set for you and you alone. Why do you think they haven't killed me yet? They want you to look for me, to find me. Remember, you don't see them, they don't see you." He'd mentioned that before, but the truth was difficult to comprehend. Not to mention disturbing.

"And if I see them?" I asked.

He let his gaze travel over me once more. "Let's just say, you're hard to miss."

"So, we'll do this incognito. You know, like Navy SEALs or SWAT or something."

"It doesn't work that way."

"That's not good enough for me." My hands curled into fists. "We have to try. We can't just let them kill you."

"You haven't heard the second reason."

That sounded foreboding. "Okay, so tell me." I crossed my arms and waited.

"You won't like it."

"I'm a big girl," I said, raising my chin a notch. "I can handle it."

"Fair enough. I'm going to let my corporeal body pass away."

Every muscle in my body stilled.

"It's not like I need it," he continued with a callous shrug. "It slows me down and, as you have witnessed yourself, makes me vulnerable to attack."

"But in the camera, when you woke up from the coma, you disappeared. You dematerialized your human body."

"Dutch," he said, casting me a chastising gaze from underneath his dark lashes, "not even I can do that."

"Then how did you just disappear? I saw the tape."

"I can interfere with electrical devices anytime I want to. So can you, if you concentrate."

I never knew that. "I just thought—"

"Wrong," he said, his tone absolute. He was so testy when he was being tortured.

"Fine. I was wrong. It's not like being a supernatural entity came with a manual."

"True."

"But that's no reason to let your corporeal body pass away. I mean, what will happen to you? You just said that if you die, they'll take you back to hell."

"Even they don't know if they can take me back to hell or not. That's simply what they're hoping for. There's one surefire way to find out, I guess," he said, raising his brows at the challenge.

"Wait, you don't know what will happen? If they can take you back?"

He shrugged. "Not a clue. But it's doubtful."

"But what if they can? What if you're sent back?"

"That's not likely to happen," he insisted. "Who would do the sending?"

"Oh, my god. I can't believe you're willing to take such a risk."

"It's riskier being alive here on Earth, Dutch," he said, an angry edge to his voice. "And it's a risk I am no longer willing to take."

"Riskier for who?"

"Riskier for you."

His answer frustrated me even more. "I don't understand. Why is it riskier for me?"

He raked both hands through his dark hair. The gesture left it more mussed, sexy, and it took me a moment to refocus. "They're demons, Dutch. And there is only one thing in this universe they want more than human souls."

"The breakfast burritos at Macho Taco?"

He rose and stood in front of me, towering over me. "They want you, Dutch. They want the portal. Do you know what will happen if they find you?"

I bit my lower lip and offered a one-shouldered shrug. "They'll have a way into heaven."

"I can't let that happen."

"Right," I said sadly. "I forgot, you'll have to kill me."

He stepped closer and lowered his voice. "And I will, Dutch. In a heartbeat."

Great. It was nice to know he had my back.

"You're hurt?" he asked, lifting my chin with his fingers.

"Stop reading my mind," I said defensively.

"I can't read your mind. I'm like you: I read emotions, feelings. And you're hurt."

"How did a demon find its way onto this plane in the first place?" I asked, pulling away from him. I stood and started pacing. He sat back down, propped his feet again. For the first time I noticed the boots he was wearing. They were black, part cowboy and part motorcycle. I liked them. "I thought it was almost impossible for demons to get through the gate."

"Yes, *almost* impossible. Every once in a while, a demon braves the void and searches for a way through the maze. It's hazardous and they rarely make it. Most are lost in the oblivion of eternity." He nudged my mouse and my computer came alive. Which meant my wallpaper popped up. Which meant Reyes's picture popped up, his mug shot, the only picture I had of him. He frowned.

I resisted the urge to crawl under the barstool. He could probably still have seen me anyway. "You were saying?"

"Right." He refocused on me. "If one miraculously makes it through the gate, it still isn't really here. It has to piggyback onto the soul of a newborn. It's the only way for them to gain access to this plane. The plane that you and I happen to be on," he reminded me.

"But that's not what you did when you escaped from hell. You didn't have to piggyback."

"I was different. Once I escaped, I could navigate between the planes as easily as you walk through a doorway."

"How is that possible?"

"It just is," he said evasively. "I was made different. I was created for a reason. When the fallen were thrown from heaven, they were banished from the light, thus the need for me. I was a tool. A means to an end. But being born on Earth was perhaps not the wisest decision I've ever made. My corporeal body has made me too vulnerable and should be destroyed. The physical evidence of the key hidden."

When Reyes was born in human form, the key, the map to hell that was imprinted on his body when he was created, appeared on his human body as well. I wondered what his human parents had thought of it. What the doctors had thought. A tattoo on a newborn. I wasn't sure how it all worked, but apparently the tattoo was the means for Satan to escape from hell. He didn't want to escape, to render himself vulnerable, until a portal was born. And he sent his son to this plane to wait for one. Reyes was supposed to retrieve Satan and all his armies the minute I was born. Instead, he was born upon the Earth as well. To be with me. To grow up with me. But he was kidnapped from his birth parents long before his dream could come to fruition.

"If those demons make it back through the gate," he continued, "they'll have the key and my father can escape. Which is exactly what he'll do." He leaned back in the chair and clasped his hands behind his head. "You know how people have prophesied about the end of time since pretty much the beginning of time?"

"Yes," I said, knowing instinctively his anecdote would end badly.

"They have no idea what hell awaits them if my father gets this key." He dropped his hands and leaned forward. "And the first thing he would do is come after you."

"I don't care."

He fixed a dubious scowl on me. "Of course you do."

"No. I don't. You can't just let your body die. We don't know what'll happen. They could get you either way."

"Let's say, for argument's sake, they were no longer a threat, that you were able to vanquish them all."

"Me?"

"There's still this one little problem I have called *life behind bars.* I'm not going back to prison, Dutch."

What? He was worried about that? "I don't understand. You can leave your body anytime you want. It's not like those bars can hold you."

"It's not that simple."

He was being evasive again, holding something back. "Reyes, please tell me."

"It's not important." He reached up and turned my computer screen off as if it suddenly bothered him.

"Reyes." I placed a hand on his arm, coaxed him back to me. "Why isn't it that simple?"

He worked his jaw and glanced down at his boots. "There's . . . a side effect."

"When you leave your body?"

"Yes. When I leave, my body mimics a seizurelike state. If I do it too often, the prison doctors put me on drugs that keep me from seizing. Drugs that have an unacceptable side effect." His gaze traveled back to mine. "They keep me from separating. I'm stuck in prison and you are completely vulnerable."

Oh. "Well, then keep running. I'll help you. But let me get you medical attention for now. I have a friend who's a doctor, and I know a couple of nurses. They would see you for me. They wouldn't turn us in, I promise. Let me find you and we can worry about prison later."

"Because if you find me, he finds me. And I go back to prison no matter who you know."

That again? "Who finds you?"

"The guy your uncle has glued to your tail."

That took me by surprise. "What are you talking about?"

"Your uncle put a tail on you, probably in the hopes that I'd show up."

"Uncle Bob put a tail on me?" I asked, appalled.

"Aren't you supposed to notice those types of things? You know, to detect them?" He winked teasingly.

"You're changing the subject," I said, trying to recover from the wink.

"Sorry." He sobered. "Okay, so you want me to stay alive because there is a slight possibility I could be sent back to hell. Does that about sum it up?"

"Reyes, you escaped from there. The same being that was created with the map to the gates of hell on his body. You're the key to their freedom, and you absconded with it. You were their general, their most powerful warrior, and you betrayed them. What do you think will happen to you if you're sent back? Not to mention the fact that if you are sent back, your father—who just happens to be Satan, by the way—will have the key to escape from hell himself."

"If."

"And it's an *if* I'm not willing to risk. Hell has to be torturous enough without being public enemy number one. And to risk Satan getting out?" I crossed my arms. "Tell me where you are."

"Dutch, you can't just come after me. Even if you could vanquish them all—"

"Why do you keep saying that?" I asked, exasperated. "I'm a bright light that lures the departed in so they can cross through me. I'm kind of like one of those bug zappers, if you think about it. And I'm fairly certain Vanquisher of Demons is not in my job description."

A soft grin slipped across his handsome face and somehow managed to melt my kneecaps. "If you had even an inkling of what you were capable of, the world would be a dangerous place indeed."

That wasn't the first time I'd heard such a thing, and worded just as vaguely. "Okay, why don't you tell me, then?" I asked, knowing he wouldn't.

"If I told you what you were capable of, you would have the advantage. That's a risk I can't take."

"What on planet Earth could I do to you?"

With a growl he stood and pulled me to him. "God, the things you ask, Dutch."

He wrapped his long fingers around my neck and tilted my chin up with his thumb a split second before he captured my mouth with his own. The kiss skyrocketed from hesitant to demanding instantly. His tongue dived inside my mouth, and I reveled in the taste of him, the earthy smell of him. I leaned into his embrace, tilted my head to allow the kiss to deepen, then held on to his wide shoulders for dear life.

One hand wound around the nape of my neck while the other held me to him as he walked me back, pressed me against the wall. Taking both my hands into one of his, he fastened them against the wall above my head as his other hand explored at will. He cupped Danger, brushed over her peak until it hardened beneath him and I couldn't stop a soft moan from escaping my lips.

He grinned, dipped his head, and pressed his hot mouth against my pulse. Molten lava swirled in my abdomen, causing sensual quakes to shudder through me. I fought for the strength to stop him. Seriously, this was ridiculous. My utter lack of control where Reyes was concerned bordered on deplorable. So what if he was the son of Satan, reportedly the most beautiful being ever to have walked the paths of heaven? So what if he was formed from the heat of a thousand stars? So what if he made my insides gooey?

I had to get a grip. And it needed to be on something other than Reyes's manly parts.

"Wait," I said when his tongue sent a shiver straight to my core. "I have to give you fair warning."

"Oh?" He leaned back and leveled a lazy, sensual gaze on me.

"I'm not going to allow you to let your corporeal body die."

"And you're going to stop me?" he asked, his voice skeptical.

I pushed him away, picked up my bag, and headed out the door. Just before I closed it, I looked back at him and said, "I'm going to find you."

Chapter Four

IF IT HAS TIRES OR TESTICLES, IT'S GONNA GIVE YOU TROUBLE.
—BUMPER STICKER

I locked the door behind me, essentially leaving the son of Satan in my apartment. Alone. Annoyed. And quite possibly sexually frustrated. A niggling in the back of my mind had me hoping I didn't make him angry. I would hate for him to catch my bachelorette pad on hellfire.

But really, he was being ridiculous. Utterly ridiculous. The whole thing reminded me of my elementary school days when my best friend said, "Boys are yucky and we should throw rocks at them."

I stomped across the parking lot, allowing the cool breeze to calm my shaking desire, and cut through my dad's bar to get to the interior set of stairs. My dad was an Albuquerque cop who, like my uncle Bob, skyrocketed through promotion after promotion until they both made detective. With my help, naturally. I'd been solving crimes for them since I was five, though *solving* might be a strong word. I'd been relaying information from the departed to help them solve crimes since I was five. Better. While my uncle was still on the APD payroll, my dad retired a few years ago and bought the bar I now worked out of. My office was on the second floor. I also lived about two feet from the back door. It was all very convenient.

Dad was in early. A light from his office filtered into the dark lounge, so I wound around bistro tables, cornered the bar, and ducked my head inside.

"Hey, Dad," I said, startling him. He jerked at the sound of my voice and turned toward me. He had been studying a picture on the far wall, his long thin frame resembling a Popsicle stick clothed in wrinkled Ken-wear. Cleary he'd been working all night. A bottle of Crown Royal sat open on his desk, and he held a near-empty goblet in his hand.

The emotion radiating off him took me by surprise. It was wrong somehow, like when a server once brought me iced tea after I'd ordered a diet soda. The normally mundane task of taking that first sip sent a shock to my system, the flavor unexpected. While Dad had his occasional off days, his flavor was different. Unexpected. A deep sorrow mixed with the overwhelming weight of hopelessness barreled toward me to steal the breath from my lungs.

I straightened in alarm. "Dad, what's wrong?"

He forced a weathered smile across his face. "Nothing, hon, just getting some paperwork done," he lied, the deception like a sour note in my ear. But I'd play along. If he didn't want to talk about what was bothering him, I'd let it slide. For now.

"Have you been home?" I asked.

He put down the glass and lifted a tan jacket off the back of his chair. "Headed that way right now. Did you need anything?"

God, he was a bad liar. Maybe that's where I got it from. "Nope, I'm good. Tell Denise hey for me."

"Charley," he said, a warning tone leveling his voice.

"What? I can't say hey to my favorite stepmother?"

With a weary sigh, he shrugged into his jacket. "I need a shower before the lunch crowd descends. Sammy should be here soon if you want some breakfast."

Sammy, Dad's cook, made huevos rancheros to die for. "I may get something later."

He was in a hurry to get out of there. Or, possibly, to get away from me. He slid past without making eye contact, despair rolling off him like a thick, muddy vapor. "Be back in a few," he said, as cheerful as a mental patient on suicide watch.

" 'Kay," I said back, just as cheerfully. He smelled like honey-lemon cough drops, the scent lingering in his office. When he was gone, I strolled inside it and glanced at the picture he'd been looking at. It was a photo of me around the age of six. My bangs were crooked and both of my front teeth were missing. I was eating watermelon nonetheless. Juice dripped from my fingers and off my chin, but what caught my attention, what had caught my dad's attention, was the dark shadow hovering just over my shoulder. A smudged fingerprint on the glass gave proof that Dad had been examining that same spot.

I glanced down to the top of a bookshelf housed underneath his montage of humorous family moments. He'd set out several photographs of me, each one featuring a dark shadow somewhere in the background, each one smudged with a fingerprint in that exact same spot. And I couldn't help but wonder what Dad was doing. Well, that and what the dark shadow meant, 'cause even I didn't know that one. Was it a by-product of grim reaperism? Or maybe, just maybe, it was Reyes, his dark robe almost visible, almost capturable. The thought intrigued me. Growing up, I'd seen him only a handful of times. Had he been there more often? Watching over me? Protecting me?

————

When I arrived at my office, sure enough, two men in crisp navy suits sat waiting. They stood, each offering a hand.

"Ms. Davidson," one said. He showed his ID then tucked it away inside his jacket. Just like on TV. It was wicked cool, and I realized I needed a jacket with an inside pocket if I were ever to be taken seriously. I usually kept my laminated PI license in the back pocket of my jeans, where it got bent and crinkled and thoroughly mutilated.

The other agent did the same, taking my hand in one of his and flashing his ID with the other simultaneously. They were very coordinated. And they looked like brothers. Though one had a few years on the other, both sported light blond crews and transparent blue eyes that, in any other situation, wouldn't have been nearly so creepy as I was finding it.

"I'm Agent Foster," the first one said, "and this is Special Agent Powers. We're investigating the disappearance of Mimi Jacobs."

At the mention of Mimi's name, Cookie knocked over a pencil cup. That wasn't so bad until she tried to grab it and sideswiped a lamp in the process. While pencils and other writing paraphernalia went flying, the lamp fell halfway to the floor, stopping to crash against the front of her desk when she grabbed the cord. Reacting to the sound, she pulled too hard, and the lamp ricocheted back up, crashing into the back of her computer monitor and knocking off the ceramic wiener dog Amber had given her for Christmas.

Subtle.

After a five-minute trailer of *The Young and the Accident Prone*—one that would give me the giggles for months to come—I turned back to our guests. "Would you like to step into my office?"

"Certainly," Agent Foster said, eyeing Cookie like she needed to be locked up.

As I led the way, I flashed her my best incredulous look. She lowered her eyes. Thankfully, the wiener dog landed in the trash can atop a cushion of papers and didn't break. She fished it out, keeping her gaze averted.

"I'm sorry, but I'm not sure I've ever heard of a Mimi Jacobs," I said, pouring myself a cup of coffee as they took a seat in front of my desk. Cookie was excellent at keeping the coffee fresh and the hugs warm. Or maybe it was the coffee warm and the hugs fresh. Either way, it was a win–win.

"Are you sure?" Foster asked. He seemed like the young cocky type. I wasn't particularly fond of the young cocky type, but I was trying really hard to get past my first impression. "She's been missing for almost a week, and a notepad with your name and number scribbled on it was the only thing on her desk when she disappeared."

She must have written my name and number down when she talked to Cookie. I turned back to them, stirring my coffee in doe-eyed innocence. "If Mimi Jacobs has been missing for almost a week, why are you just now coming to me?"

The older one, Powers, chafed, probably because I'd answered a question with a question. He was clearly used to getting answers with his questions. Silly rabbit. "We didn't think much of the note until we realized you were a private investigator. We thought she might have hired you."

"Hired me for what?" I asked, fishing.

He shifted in his chair. "That's what we're here to find out."

"So, she wasn't in trouble? Maybe with the company she works for?"

The men glanced at each other. In any other situation, I would have shouted eureka. Internally, anyway. But I felt as though I had just handed them the perfect scapegoat. They knew more and were not about to tell me. "We've considered that, Ms. Davidson, but we would appreciate it if that information were kept between us."

So, not the company. One possibility down, twenty-seven thousand to go.

Apparently satisfied, they both stood. Foster handed me a business card. "We need to insist that you contact us if she tries to get in touch with you." His tone held the slightest hint of warning. I tried not to giggle.

"Absolutely," I said, leading them back out. I stopped before opening the door that separated Cookie's office and mine. "Sorry I couldn't be of more help, and you have to leave now."

Foster cleared his throat uncomfortably when I hesitated a moment more. "Right, okay. We'll be in touch if we need anything else."

As they stood waiting behind me, I turned the knob slowly, jiggled it a little, then opened the door. Cookie was typing away at her computer. If I knew her, she'd been listening in on our conversation through the speakerphone.

"Ms. Davidson," Foster said, tipping an invisible hat as they walked past.

After the agents left, Cookie turned an exasperated expression on me. "Jiggling the knob? That was subtle."

"Oh, yeah, grace. Could you have knocked anything else over?"

She cringed at the reminder. "Do you think they suspected anything?"

So many possibilities came to mind: *Duh. Ya think? Only if they weren't complete idiots.* "Yes," I said instead, the lack of inflection in my voice insinuating all of the above.

"But, shouldn't we be working with them instead of against them?" she asked.

"Not at this precise moment in time."

"Why not?"

"Mostly 'cause they're not FBI agents."

She sucked in a soft breath. "How do you know?"

"Really?" I asked. The last thing I wanted to explain was how I could tell when someone was lying. For the thousandth time.

"Right," she said, shaking her head, "sorry." Then she gasped. "You knew they weren't real FBI agents?"

"I had my suspicions."

"And you led them into your office anyway? Alone?"

"My suspicions don't always pan out."

She thought about that a moment and calmed. "True. Remember that time you tackled the mailman and—"

I held up a hand to stop her. Some things were just better left unsaid. "Cancel looking into the business stuff," I said, thinking out loud. "I'd bet my virtual farm that's a dead end. Concentrate on finding a connection between Mimi and Janelle York."

"Besides the fact that they went to high school together?" she asked.

"No. Let's start there. Dig into both their backgrounds, see if anything stands out."

Just then, Uncle Bob walked into the office. Or, well, stormed into the office. He was always so stressed. It was probably time for us to have *the talk*. He needed a girlfriend before he stroked. Or maybe a blowup doll.

"If you're going to be a grumpy bear," I said, pointing to the door, "you can just leave the same way you came in, Mr. Man." I twirled my finger in circles, motioning for him to do an about-face, make like a sheep, and get the flock outta there.

He stopped short, eyeing me with a mixture of confusion and annoyance. "I'm not grumpy." He sounded offended. It was funny. "I just want to know what you've gotten yourself into now."

It was my turn to be offended. "What?" I asked. "Why I never—"

"No time for your theatrics," he said, shaking a finger. That'd teach me. "How do you know Warren Jacobs?"

What the heck? Word traveled fast in the crime-fighting world. "I just met him this morning. Why?"

"Because he's asking for you. Not only is his wife missing, but a car dealer he stalked and threatened to kill was found dead last night. Call me crazy, but I think there might be a connection."

Son of a bitch, I thought with a heavy sigh. "Instead of plain old Crazy, can I call you Crazy Bob?"

"No."

"CB for short?" When I only got a glare, I asked, "Then can I see him?"

"He's being questioned right now and he'll probably lawyer up any second. What's going on?"

Cookie and I glanced at each other then spilled our guts like frogs in biology lab.

We told Uncle Bob everything, even the writing-on-the-wall thing. He took out his phone and ordered one of his minions to check out the diner. "You should have told me," he said after hanging up, his tone scolding.

"Like I've had a chance. But since we're on the subject, there are two men posing as FBI agents to get to her. And they want her bad."

Alarmed, Uncle Bob—or Ubie as I liked to call him, though rarely to his face—took down their description. "This is serious stuff," he said.

"Tell me about it. We have to find Mimi before they do."

"I'll get a hold of the local feds and let them know they have a couple of impersonators. But you should have called me when this whole thing started."

"Well, I didn't think I would need to, since you're having me tailed and all."

His jaw clamped down, totally busted. With a heavy sigh, he stepped closer, towering over me, and lifted my chin gently. "Reyes Farrow is a convicted murderer, Charley. This is for your own protection. If he contacts you, will you please let me know?"

"Will you call off the tail?" I asked in turn. When he hesitated then shook his head, I added, "Then may the best detective win."

I strode out the door, realizing what a ridiculous statement that was, as Uncle Bob, a veteran detective for the Albuquerque Police Department, was the ace of spades when it came to investigations. I was kind of like a three of hearts.

As I walked down the block to my friend Pari's tattoo parlor, I scanned the street for the shadow Ubie'd assigned to me, with no luck. It had to be someone good. Uncle Bob wouldn't send a rookie to watch over me.

I stopped in front of Pari's shop, not because I particularly needed a tattoo, but because Pari could see auras. I could see auras as well, but I figured maybe I'd missed something over the years. How could I see auras and dead people and sons of Satan and yet in all my days never see a demon? Heck, I didn't even know demons existed until Reyes told me, much less that they would be fighting tooth and nail to get to me. To get through me. My breath caught as another realization dawned. If demons existed, heck, if Satan himself existed, then angels surely existed as well. Seriously, how could I be so out of the loop?

Hopefully, Pari knew something I didn't, other than the correct timing for a 1970 Plymouth Duster with a supercharged 440 big block. I didn't even know cars had timing issues—speaking of which, it was still early in tattoo parlor time, so I was surprised to see Pari's front door open. I stepped inside.

"I need some light," I heard her call out from the back.

"On it," came a male voice.

Then I heard scrambling in the back room as I walked up behind Pari. She was bent under a refurbished dentist's chair, electrical wires in a heap at her knees.

"Thanks," she said, quietly deciphering the wires.

"What?" the guy in the back room called out.

Startled, Pari jolted upright and hit her head on the seat of the chair before turning back to me. "Charley, damn it," she said, raising one hand to shield her eyes and the other to rub the sting from her head. "You can't just walk up behind me. You're like one of those floodlights shining from a cop car in the middle of the night."

I chuckled as she fumbled for her sunglasses. "You said you needed light."

Pari was a graphic designer who'd turned to body art to keep the bill collectors at bay. Luckily, she'd found her calling, and she did the profession proud with full sleeves of sleek lines, tiger lilies and fleur-de-lis. And a couple of skulls thrown in to impress the clientele.

She'd designed the grim reaper I now sported on my left shoulder blade. It was a tiny being with huge, innocent eyes and a fluid robe that looked like smoke. How she managed that with tattoo ink was beyond me.

She slipped her shades on, then looked back at me with a sigh. "I said I needed light, not a starburst. I swear you're going to permanently blind me one day." As I said, Pari could see auras; mine was just really bright.

She grabbed a bottle of water off the counter and sat on the broken dentist's chair, propping her hiking boots onto two crates on either side of her and resting her elbows on her knees. I grabbed a water out of a small fridge and turned back to her, struggling not to crack up at her indelicate position.

"So, what's up, Reaper?"

"I can't find the flashlight!" the guy yelled from the back room.

"Never mind," she called back before grinning at me. "All beauty, no brains, that one."

I nodded. She liked beauty. Who didn't?

"Okay, so you're pretending to be all cool and collected," she said, studying me with a practiced eye, "but you're about as serene as a chicken on the chopping block. What's going on?"

Dang, she was good. I decided to get right to the point. "Have you ever seen a demon?"

Her breathing slowed as she absorbed my question. "You mean like a hellfire and brimstone demon?"

"Yes."

"Like a minion of hell demon?"

"Yes," I said again.

"Like—"

"Yes," I repeated for the third time. The subject made my stomach queasy. And the thought of one torturing Reyes . . . not that the little shit didn't deserve to be tortured just a tad, but still.

"So, they're real?"

"I'm going to take that as a no," I said, my hopes evaporating. "It's just, I think I have a few after me, and I was hoping you might know something I didn't."

"Damn." She glanced at the floor in thought then refocused on me. At least I think she did. It was hard to tell with her shades on. "Wait, there are demons after you?"

"Sort of."

After she stared a long time, long enough to be considered culturally insensitive, she bowed her head. "I've never seen one," she said, her voice quiet, "but I know there are things out there, things that go bump in the night. And not just the prostitute next door. Scary things. Things that are impossible to forget."

I tilted my head in question. "What do you mean?"

"When I was fourteen, a group of friends and I were having a slumber party, and like most fourteen-year-olds do eventually, we decided to have a séance."

"Okay." This was going nowhere good.

"So, we went down into my basement and were all séancing and chanting and conjuring a spirit from beyond when I felt something. Like a presence."

"Like a departed?"

"No." She shook her head, thinking back. "At least I don't think so. They're cold. This being was just sort of there. I felt it brush up against me like a dog." One hand gripped the opposite arm in remembrance, a soft shiver echoing through her body. "No one else felt it, of course, until I said something." She glanced up at me, a dire warning in her eyes. "Never tell a group of fourteen-year-old girls having a séance in a dark basement that you felt something brush up against you. For your own safety."

I chuckled. "I promise. What happened?"

"They jumped up screaming and ran for the stairs. It freaked me out so, naturally, I ran, too."

"Naturally."

"I just wanted away from whatever had materialized in my basement, so I ran like I had a reason to live despite my suicidal tendencies."

Pari had been Goth when Goth wasn't cool. Kinda like now.

"I thought I was in the clear when I reached the top stair. Then I heard a growl, deep, guttural. Before I knew what was happening, I fell halfway down the stairs, spraining a wrist and bruising my ribs. I scrambled up and out of there without looking back. It took a while for me to realize I didn't fall. My legs were pulled out from under me and I was dragged." She lifted her pant leg and unzipped her knee-high boots to show me a jagged scar on her calf. It looked like claw marks. "I've never been so scared."

"Holy crap, Par. What happened then?"

"When my dad found out why we were all screaming, he laughed and went down into the basement to prove to us nothing was there."

"And?"

"Nothing was there," she said with a shrug.

"Did you show him the wound?"

"Oh, hell no." She shook her head like I'd just asked her if she ate children for breakfast. "They'd already filed me in the *F*'s for 'freak of nature.' I wasn't about to confirm their suspicions."

"Holy crap, Par," I repeated.

"Tell me about it."

"So, what makes you think it was a demon?"

"I don't. It wasn't a demon. Or, well, I don't think it was. It was something more."

"How do you know?"

She twisted the leather straps at her wrist. "Mostly because I knew its name."

I froze for a moment before saying, "Come again?"

"Do you remember what I told you about my accident?" She glanced at me, her brows drawn together.

"Sure I do." Pari had died when she was six in a car accident. Thankfully, an industrious EMT brought her back. After that, she could see auras, including those of the departed. She'd learned that if she saw an aura with a particularly grayish tint and no body attached, it was the soul of someone who'd passed. It was a ghost.

"When I died, my grandfather was waiting for me."

"I remember," I said, "and thankfully he sent you back. I owe him a fruit basket when I get to heaven."

She reached over and squeezed my hand in a rare moment of appreciation. Awkward. "I'd met him only once," she said, wrapping both hands around her water. "The only thing I remembered about him was that he had Great Danes taller than I was, yet I knew beyond a shadow of a doubt he was my grandfather. And when he told me it wasn't my time, that I had to go back, the last thing I wanted to do was leave him."

"Well, I for one am glad he sent your ass packing. You would have been hell on wheels in heaven."

She smiled. "You're probably right. But I never told you the strange part."

"Most people find near-death experiences pretty strange."

"True," she said with a grin.

"So it gets stranger?"

"A lot stranger." She hesitated, drew in a long breath, then rested her gaze on me. "On the way back, you know, to Earth, I heard things."

That was new. "What kinds of things?"

"Voices. I heard a conversation."

"You eavesdropped?" I asked, a little amazed such a thing was possible. "On celestial beings?"

"I guess you could call it that, but I didn't do it on purpose. I heard an entire conversation in an instant, like it just appeared in my head. Yet I knew I wasn't supposed to hear it. I knew the information was dangerous. I learned the name of a being powerful enough to bring about the end of the world."

"The end of the world?" I asked, gulping when I did so.

"I know how it sounds, believe me. But they were talking about this being that had escaped from hell and was born on Earth."

My pulse accelerated by a hairsbreadth, just enough to cause a tingling flutter in my stomach.

"They said that he could destroy the world, he could bring on the apocalypse if he so chose."

I knew of only one being who had escaped from hell. Only one being who had been born on Earth. And while I knew he was powerful, I couldn't imagine him powerful enough to bring about the freaking apocalypse. Then again, what was? I totally should have paid attention in catechism.

"And so the night of the séance, in all my teenaged wisdom, I decided to summon him."

I gaped, but only a little. "Right. Because that's what we want to do. Summon the very being who can destroy every living thing on Earth."

"Exactly," she said, spacing my sarcasm. "I thought I might convince him not to. You know, talk some sense into him."

"And how did that work out for you?"

She stopped and pursed her lips at me. "I was fourteen, smart-ass."

I tried to laugh, but it didn't quite make it past the lump in my throat. "So, for real? This being is going to bring on the apocalypse?"

"No, you're not listening." She pressed her lips together before explaining. "I said he is powerful enough to bring on the apocalypse."

Okay, well, that was a plus. No prophecies of mass destruction.

"And so that night during the séance, I summoned him. By name."

Goose bumps crept up my legs and over my arms in anticipation. Either that or Dead Trunk Guy had found me again. I glanced around just in case.

"But, like I said," she continued, "he's not what you think. He's not a demon."

"Well, that's taking a frown and turning it upside down."

"From the gist of the conversation, he is something so very much more."

He was more, all right. "Pari," I said, growing impatient, "what's its name?"

"No way am I telling you," she said with a teasing sparkle in her eyes.

"Pari."

"No, really." She turned serious again. "I don't say it aloud. Ever. Not since that day."

"Oh, right. Well—"

Before I could say anything else, she grabbed a piece of paper and scribbled onto it. "This is it, but don't say it out loud. I get the feeling he doesn't like being summoned."

I took the paper, my hand shaking more than I'd have liked, and gasped softly when I read the name. *Rey'aziel*. Rey'az . . . Reyes. The son of Satan.

"It means 'the beautiful one,'" she said as I read it over and over again. "I don't know what he is," she continued, unaware of my stupor, "but he caused quite a stir on the other side, if you know what I mean. Chaos. Upheaval. Panic."

Yep. That would be Reyes. Damn it.

Chapter Five

WHAT HAPPENS IF YOU GET SCARED HALF TO DEATH, TWICE?

—T-SHIRT

My head reeling, I left Pari's shop stunned, wandering aimlessly toward home before I remembered I had a job to do. And a job I would do. Time to pull the curtains back on my shadow. Whomever Uncle Bob had assigned to follow me was about to have a very bad day.

I opened my cell phone and answered as if it had been ringing. I stopped, incredulous. I looked around. Gestured wildly. "Meet? Now? Well, darn it, okay. You're in the alley to my right? You're that close? Are you crazy? You'll be caught. Surely someone will suspect you might get in touch with me. Surely . . . Okay, fine." I closed the phone, scanned the area, then eased between two buildings, the passageway leading to an alley, all the while throwing furtive glances over my shoulder.

After my production of *Casablanca* meets *Mission: Impossible,* I high-tailed it toward a Dumpster and ducked behind it, waiting for my shadow to appear. As I sat scrunched, feeling oddly ridiculous, I played with Reyes's name in my head, let it shape and slide over my tongue. Rey'aziel. The beautiful one. Boy did they have that right.

But why would he hurt Pari? I calculated ages. If Pari had been fourteen when she performed her little séance, then Reyes could have been no more than eight. Nine at the most. And he attacked her? Maybe it wasn't him. Maybe she summoned something else accidently, something evil.

"Whatcha doin'?"

I started at the voice behind me and—having flailed a bit—fell back, my palms and ass landing in an illegally dumped oil slick. Wonderful. I ground my teeth together and looked up at a grinning departed gang-banger with more attitude than was socially acceptable.

"Angel, you little shit."

He laughed aloud as I examined my filthy hands. "That was awesome."

Freaking thirteen-year-olds. "I knew I should have exorcised your ass when I had the chance." Angel died when his best friend decided to take out the *puta* bitch *vatos* who'd invaded their turf by utilizing the drive-by technique of execution so popular with the kids today. Angel tried to stop him and paid the ultimate price. Much to my eternal chagrin.

"You couldn't exorcise a cat, much less a bad-to-the-bone Chicano with gunpowder in his blood. Besides, you hate exercise."

Chuckling at his own joke, he took my outstretched hand and pulled me onto the balls of my feet. I needed to stay squatted behind the Dumpster, the prime tactical position for an ambush. "You don't have any blood," I pointed out helpfully.

"Sure I do," he said, looking down at himself. He wore a dirty white T-shirt with jeans hanging low on his hips, worn-out sneakers, and a wide leather wristband. His inky black hair was cropped short over his ears, but he still had a baby face and a smile so genuine, it could melt my heart on contact. "It's just kind of see-through now."

I scraped my hands down the side of the Dumpster to no avail, wondering how many germs were hitching a ride in the process. "Do you have a reason for being here?" I asked, now swiping my hands at my pants. The oil was obviously going to remain stuck until I found some water and a professional-grade degreaser.

"I heard we got a case," he said. While Angel had been a constant companion since my freshman days of high school, he agreed to become my lead investigator when I opened my PI business three years ago. Having an incorporeal being as an investigator was kind of like cheating on college entrance exams—nerve-racking yet oddly effective. And we'd solved many a case together.

Facing no such quandaries with the oil slick, he sat down in front of me, his back against the Dumpster, his eyes suddenly drawn to my hand as I knocked the rocks and soil off my left butt cheek. "Can I help?" he asked, indicating my ass with a nod. Thirteen-year-olds were so hormonal. Even dead ones.

"No, you can't help, and we suddenly have not one, but two cases." While Mimi was my professional priority, Reyes was my personal one. Neither was expendable, and I pondered which case I should put him on. I opted for Reyes because I simply didn't have any other resources in that area. But Angel wasn't going to like it.

"How much do you know about Reyes?" I asked, hoping he wouldn't disappear. Or pull a nine-millimeter and gank me.

He eyed me a moment, shifted uncomfortably, then rested his elbows on his knees and looked off into the distance. Or, well, into a warehouse. After a long while, he said, "Rey'aziel isn't our case."

I sucked in a soft breath with the mention of Reyes's otherworldly name. How did he know it? Better yet, how long had he known it?

"Angel, do you know what Reyes is?"

He shrugged. "I know what he isn't." He leveled an intent gaze on me. "He isn't our case."

With a sigh, I sat on the pavement, slick or no slick, and leaned against the trash bin beside him. I needed Angel with me on this. I needed his help, his particular talents. After placing a dirty hand on his, I said, "If I don't find him, he's going to die."

A dubious chuckle shook his chest, and in that instant, he seemed so much older than the thirteen years he'd accumulated before he passed. "If only it were that easy."

"Angel," I said, my tone admonishing. "You can't mean that."

The look he stabbed me with was one of such anger, such incredulity, I fought the urge to lean away from him. "You can't be serious," he said as if I'd suddenly lost my marbles. Little did he know, I'd lost my marbles eons ago.

I knew Angel didn't like the guy, but I had no idea he felt such malevolence toward him.

"Is there a reason you're sitting in a puddle of oil talking to yourself?"

I looked up to find Garrett Swopes standing over me, a dark-skinned, silvery-eyed skiptracer who knew just enough about me to be dangerous; then I glanced back at Angel. He was gone. Naturally. When the going gets tough, the tough refuse to talk about it and insist on running away to stew in their own crabby insecurities.

I struggled to my feet and realized my jeans would never be the same again. "What are you doing here, Swopes?" I asked, swiping at my ass for the second time that morning.

As skiptracers went, Garrett was one of the best. We'd been fairly decent friends for a while until Uncle Bob, in a moment of weakness brought on by one-too-many brewskis, told him what I did for a living. Not the PI part—Garrett already knew that—but the Charley-sees-dead-people part. After that, our slightly flirtatious relationship took a left turn into hostile territory, as though he were angry that I would try to pull off such a scheme. A month later, Garrett was slowly but surely—and quite reluctantly—beginning to believe in what I could do, having seen the evidence firsthand. Not that I gave a shit if he believed me or not, especially after his behavior over the last month, but Garrett was good at his job. He came in handy from time to time. As for the skeptic in him, he could bite my ass.

At the moment, he seemed to be contemplating that very thing. He'd tilted his head and was eyeing the general vicinity of my lower half as I knocked dirt and rock chips off it when he asked, "Can I help?"

"No, you can't help." Didn't I just have this conversation? "Stop channeling Angel and answer my question. Wait." Reality sank in slowly but surely. My jaw dropped for a moment before I caught it and turned on him. "Oh, my god, you're the tail."

"What?" He stepped back, his brows drawn sharply together in denial.

"Son of a bitch." After staring aghast for a solid minute—thank goodness I'd recently practiced aghast in the mirror—I watched him try to disguise the guilt so plainly on his features. Then I threw a punch that landed on his shoulder with a solid thud.

"Ouch." He covered his shoulder protectively. "What the hell was that for?"

"Like you don't know," I said, stalking away. I couldn't believe it. I simply could *not* believe it. Well, I could, but still. Uncle Bob had actually put Garrett Swopes on my tail. Garrett Swopes! The same man who'd been taunting and badgering me about my ability for the last month, swearing to have me locked away or, at the very least, burned as a witch. Skeptics were such drama queens. And Uncle Bob put *him* on my tail?

The injustice of it all. The indignation. The . . . wait. I stopped short and considered all the possibilities. All the wonderful, glorious possibilities.

Garrett had been trailing behind me when I stopped and, his reaction time being what it was, almost ran me down. "Did you go off your meds again, Charles?" he asked, sidestepping around me while trying to change the subject. He'd taken to calling me Charles recently. Probably to annoy me, so I didn't let it. And my meds were none of his concern.

I turned, planted my best death stare on him, and said, "Oh, no, you don't."

"What?"

He stepped back. I stepped forward.

"You aren't getting off that easy, buddy boy," I said, stabbing him with an index finger.

The confused expression on his face would have been comical had I not felt so blindsided that my uncle put him, of all people, on my tail. And I was in dire need of an investigator who was on Albuquerque's finest's payroll. Free labor.

"Did you just call me buddy boy?"

"Damn straight I did, and if you know what's good for you," I said, taking another step toward him, "you won't insult me for not coming up with anything better on such short notice."

"Okay." He held up his hands in surrender. "No insults, I swear."

I trusted him about as far as I could throw him. He was totally going to insult me the first chance he got. Damn it. "How long have you been tailing me?"

"Charles," he said, trying to come up with a good story.

"Don't even." I poked him again for good measure. "How long?"

"First . . ." He took hold of my shoulders and led me back toward the building as a car passed through the alley.

When we were out of harm's way, I crossed my arms and waited.

With an acquiescent sigh, he admitted, "Since the day Farrow disappeared from the long-term-care unit."

I sucked in a sharp breath of indignation. "That was a week ago. You've been following me for a week? I can't believe Uncle Bob did this to me."

"Charley," Garrett began, his voice sympathetic. I didn't need his sympathy.

"Don't. Ubie is so not getting a Christmas card this year." When he spread his hands as if I were overreacting, I added, "And you can mark your name off the list as well."

"What did I do?" he asked, following me as I cut across a parking lot toward the street.

"Stalking isn't pretty, Swopes."

"It's not stalking when you're being paid for it."

I stopped and scowled at him.

"Well, when PD is paying you, anyway. And your uncle Bob didn't do anything *to* you. He figured there was a possibility Farrow would try to contact you, and for some unexplainable reason, he didn't want a convicted murderer hanging with his niece."

Always with the convicted murderer rap. "I'll make a deal with you."

"Okay," he said, his voice tainted with suspicion.

"I need to find Reyes as much as you do, or, well, Uncle Bob. You help me and I'll help you."

"Why?" he asked, still suspicious. You'd think I never kept up my side of the bargain. I almost always, nigh 100 percent of the time, tried really hard to attempt to hold up my side of any bargain in any given situation.

Now for the hard part, the yeah-I-know-he-was-convicted-of-murder-and-is-an-entity-who-was-born-of-pure-evil-but-deep-down-inside-he's-really-a-good-guy part. "What all did Uncle Bob tell you about Reyes?"

Garrett's brows knitted in thought, his gray eyes startling against his dark skin. "Well, in a nutshell, he told me Farrow has been a resident of the Penitentiary of New Mexico for the last ten years for the brutal murder of his own father until he was accidently shot in the head trying to save another inmate and was in a coma for a month, only to magically wake up and walk right out of the long-term-care unit without anyone the wiser."

I let that soak in before commenting. "Okay, good start. But there's a lot my uncle doesn't know."

With mouth tilting to the side in doubt, he asked, "Which would be?"

Great. He was reverting back to Garrett the Skeptic Skiptracer. "Reyes Farrow has saved my life on several occasions. And he continues to do so."

"Really?" he said, the sarcasm in his tone undeniable. This was not going to be an easy sell.

"Yes, really." A car behind me wanting the parking space we were standing in honked. I headed toward the street again.

"A man convicted of murder saves you?"

"Yes." When we reached the sidewalk, I stopped and gave him my full attention. "And he's a supernatural being."

His mouth did that tilty thing again, but he decided to humor me. "You mean like ghost supernatural or superhero supernatural?"

Good question. "A little of both, actually."

He sighed and raked his fingers through his hair.

"Look, I don't have time to go into all the details," I said, charging forward. "Can you do something crazy for once in your life that goes against every bone in your body and trust me on this one?"

After a long moment, he offered a reluctant nod.

"Good, because I need to find him ay-sap."

I started for my apartment. Clean jeans were a must for any private investigator. And for said private investigator's sanity.

"Wait."

"Nope. Follow."

"Okay," he said, jogging to catch up. He fell in step beside me. "So, Farrow is supernatural? You mean like you? He's a grim reaper?"

His question surprised me. I didn't think he'd believed a word I told him during our last sit-down. The one where he tried really hard to open his mind and listen to what I had to say instead of mocking me repeatedly. "He's not a grim reaper. He's sort of more."

"How much more?" Suspicion suddenly edged his voice.

"He's a man, Swopes, just like you. Only, like, with superpowers."

"What kind of superpowers?"

I paused long enough to glower at him. "Would you stop with the twenty questions?"

"I just want to know what I'm up against."

"Look, I just need you to put out some feelers. You know, ask around, see if anyone has heard anything, I don't know, strange."

"Fine. I just have one more question."

"Okay."

His gaze intensified. "How do I kill it?" he asked.

Well, that wasn't very nice. All this time, I'd been hoping evolution had eroded the male's thirst for blood. Apparently not. "You don't," I said, turning back to continue my trek. I was brought up short when a dark fog, thick and undulating, materialized into a man in front of me.

Reyes stood blocking my path, a peculiar kind of anger glistening in his mahogany eyes. "What are you doing, Dutch?" he asked, his voice soft, menacing.

Garrett had taken a step then stopped again. He glanced at me and then down the street, trying to figure out what I was looking at.

I decided to ignore both his curiosity and Reyes's anger for the moment. "Are you still alive?"

He took an intimidating step closer, heat radiating from his body in waves. "Unfortunately. What are you doing?"

"Charles, what's up?" Garrett asked, alarmed.

Relief flooded through me with Reyes's admission. He could die at any moment, and I was worried it might already have happened. I tried to breathe easier, but the palpability of his anger made that difficult. I should have known he was still alive. He wouldn't have been so angry if not. Who cares if I find his body once it has passed? The mere thought tightened my chest even more.

My face must have shown my alarm. Garrett leaned into me. "Charley, what's going on?"

Reyes glanced at him then back at me. "Tell it to shut up."

And that was just rude. These boys were not playing well together at all. Reyes had grown jealous of Garrett without reason. There was nothing whatsoever between us. "He's not an it, Reyes," I said, practically inviting him to argue. "He's the best skiptracer in the state, and he's going to help me find you." The gauntlet I threw at him made me sound like a third grader on a playground challenging the school bully to a showdown. Swings. Three o'clock.

A slow smile spread across Reyes's face as he looked back at Garrett, sized him up with one glance, then returned his attention to me. "How's its spine?"

The question took my breath away. It was an open threat, one he knew I would take to heart. He had severed more than one spinal column in my behalf, why not in his own? I eased back and he followed, sustaining a minimum of six inches between us. He was not giving in. He knew how to intimidate me, how to cut with the skill of a veteran surgeon.

"You can't possibly mean that," I said when I stopped, deciding the backing-away thing wasn't working.

"If he even thinks about trying to find me, his last years on this Earth will be . . . fraught with difficulties."

His threat was so hostile, so finite, it ripped at my insides. I had no idea he could hurt so callously. I squared my shoulders and looked up at him, determination raising my chin. "Fine. He won't start searching for you," I said, and the victory shone in his eyes. "But I won't stop."

Just as quickly, the smugness evaporated and he scowled at me once more.

I took a bold step closer, practically wrapping myself into his arms. He let me, welcomed me, letting his guard down for just a moment.

"Are you going to sever my spine," I asked, watching his eyes linger on my mouth, "Rey'aziel?"

It was his turn to be shocked. He stiffened completely, his features unwavering, but I felt the turmoil, the agitation churn inside him. Just as he could read my emotions, I could read his, and right now they could have caused the earth to shake beneath us.

Garrett said something, but I found myself drowning in the apprehension that saturated Reyes's liquid brown eyes. It was almost as if I'd betrayed him somehow, stabbed a knife into his back. But hadn't he just done that very thing to me? And besides, I rarely carried knives.

"How do you know that name?" he asked, his voice soft, dangerous, as if it were more a threat than a question.

I gathered all the bravery I could muster to answer him. "A friend told me," I said, praying I wasn't inadvertently putting Pari's life at risk. "She said she summoned you when she was young, and you almost ripped her leg off."

"Charley, I'm trying here, but maybe we could take this somewhere else."

It was Garrett. He was apparently trying to intervene, to make it look like he and I were having a conversation instead of what it would look like to the casual observer, a psycho girl talking to air. For a split second I focused on my periphery, noticed the odd glance here and the frown of disapproval there. But for the most part, people ignored us. We were on Central in the middle of Albuquerque. It wasn't like the natives hadn't seen such behavior before.

When I felt two hands push me softly, leading me back against the brick wall of a sidewalk café, I refocused on the being in front of me. "Was that you?" I asked, returning to our conversation. "Did you hurt Pari?"

He braced both hands on the wall behind us and pressed his body against mine. That's what he did. When threatened, when intimidated, he pushed. He shoved. And he chose his opponent's weakest point. Went for the jugular every time. Used my attraction against me with the skill of an artist. It was fighting dirty, but I could hardly blame him. It was what he'd grown up with. It was all he knew.

"That was nothing," he said, his tone deceptively calm, "compared to what I could have done."

"You hurt her?" I asked again, unwilling to believe it.

"Perhaps, Dutch," he said into my ear, as if anyone else could hear him anyway, "I don't like being summoned."

And just as his mouth came down upon mine, just as the tingling of his life force lifted me from my body to be enveloped in his warmth, he was gone. The chill of late October slammed into me and I sucked in an icy breath, coming to my senses instantly.

He had hurt Pari. I was just as shocked by that as the fact that he would threaten to hurt an innocent man, namely Garrett, who was in front of me at once, and I realized I had fallen into his arms. I clutched on to him just to be safe as he led me away from the curious onlookers.

"That was interesting."

"I bet," I said, trying my best to figure Reyes Farrow out. Was he angry that I knew his name? His real name? Why would knowing his name make any difference? Unless . . . maybe it gave me some kind of advantage. Maybe I could use it against him somehow.

"So, I take it he doesn't want me looking for him?" Garrett said.

"To put it mildly."

We walked around Calamity's, my dad's bar, to my apartment building behind it. I was still clutching on to Garrett's arm, not quite trusting my legs yet, when we arrived at my second-floor apartment.

Garrett waited while I fished the keys out of my pocket. "I saw his picture," he said, his voice suddenly grave.

I inserted the key and turned. "His mug shot?" I asked, assuming we were still on the subject of Reyes.

"Yes, and a couple other photographs."

That made sense, since he was supposed to be on the lookout for him. "You coming in? I just need to change real quick."

"Look, I get it," he said, stepping in behind me and closing the door.

"You do? Well, thank goodness someone does." I really didn't want to talk about Reyes with him now, his spine being so unsevered and all. "There's soda in the fridge."

I tossed the keys onto the snack bar and headed for my bedroom. "Hey, Mr. Wong."

"He's attractive, right?"

I paused and turned back to him. "Mr. Wong?" I looked at my perpetual roommate, at his utter grayness as he stood in my living room corner. He'd been there since I rented the apartment, and since he did have seniority, I'd never had the heart to kick him out. Not that I'd know how. But I'd never actually seen his face. He hovered 24/7 with his back to me, his nose in the corner, his toes inches from the floor. He looked like a cross between a Chinese prisoner of war and an immigrant from the 1800s.

"Who's Mr. Wong?" Garrett asked. They'd never been introduced.

This was all very new to Swopes, and I figured I should bring him into the fold slowly, let him absorb the new information at a comprehensible rate and save all the bells and whistles for later. Then again, he'd asked to be brought in, insisted on it, so screw him.

"He's the dead guy who inhabits the corner of my living room. But I've never seen his face. Not a full-frontal anyway, so I really couldn't say if he's handsome."

"Not him," he said, "Farrow. Wait, you have a dead guy living in your apartment?"

"*Living*'s a strong word, Swopes, and it's not as if he takes up a lot of space. So, you're talking about Reyes?"

"Yes, Farrow," he said, eyeing the corner I'd greeted, a mixture of curiosity and horror playing on his face.

"Oh, then damn straight he's attractive." I checked messages on my phone. "Wait a minute, are you coming out of the closet?"

A loud sigh echoed against the wall as I traipsed into my room and closed the door. It was funny. "I'm not gay, Charley," he called out to me. "I'm trying to understand."

"Understand what?" I asked, knowing full well what he was getting at. How could a girl like me get mixed up with a guy like Reyes? If he only knew the whole story. Not a good idea, though, since he'd have me committed for falling in love with the son of Satan.

"Look, I get the bad boy thing, but a convicted murderer?"

Surprisingly, the oil hadn't soaked all the way through my pants, so I didn't need another shower. Since my room was still in disaster-zone mode, I rummaged through a lump on the floor and found a pair of jeans that were tolerable, slipped those on with a pair of bitchen boots, and headed to the bathroom to freshen up.

"I think you need to water your plants," Garrett called out to me.

"Oh, they're fake." He was looking at the plants I had along my windowsill. Either that or my mold problem was getting out of hand.

After a long pause, I heard, "Those are fake?"

"Yeah. I had to make them look real. A little spray paint, a little lighter fluid, and voilà! Fake dying plants."

"Why would you want fake dying plants?" he asked.

"Because if they were all thick and healthy looking, anyone who knows me would realize they were fake."

"Yeah, but is that really the point?"

"Duh."

I heard a knock on the bathroom door that exited to my living room and opened it slowly. "Yes?" I asked Garrett as he stood there reading the sign on my door. The one that read *no dead people beyond this door.* This was my bathroom, after all, my inner sanctum. Not that the sign always worked. Mr. Habersham, the dead guy from 2B, completely ignored it on a regular basis.

He reached up and pushed against the door.

I pushed back. "Dude, what are you doing?"

"Making sure I'm not dead."

"Do you feel dead?"

"No, but I thought maybe you had a sign that only dead people could see."

"How on planet Earth would I have a sign only dead people could see?"

"Hey, it's your world," he said with a shrug.

I stepped out of the bathroom ready to face that world again. Or at least a small corner of it. "Look, Reyes is my problem, okay?" I said, grabbing my keys again and heading for the door.

"Right now he's an escaped convict. And he's my problem as well. Did he threaten you back there?"

I needed to steer Garrett clear of anything having to do with Reyes, and I needed to do it fast. As far as I knew, Reyes had never hurt an innocent person—not permanently, anyway—but it simply wasn't worth risking Swopes's spine. "I have a case I need your help on."

"Yeah, well, I'm supposed to be tailing you."

"Our deal's still on." I locked the apartment back up then started down the stairs. "Hi, Mrs. Allen," I called out when I heard the squeaking of a door down the hall.

"Another dead person?" Garrett asked.

I paused and said with a heavy sigh, "Unfortunately, no."

"So, our deal?" he asked as we headed out the front door.

"Like I said, totally on. You check out the origins of a dead guy riding around in Cookie's car, and I'll call you the minute I figure out where Reyes is."

He eyed me with more doubt than I was accustomed to. And I was accustomed to a lot of doubt.

"Well, his body, anyway. The little shit hid it from me."

"Farrow hid his body from you?"

"Yes, he did. The little shit. And we have to find it before it passes."

Garrett scrubbed his face with his fingertips. "I am so confused."

"Good. Stay that way. Your spine will thank you."

On the way to the office, I told Garrett all about Cookie's stowaway and he took down the make, model, and VIN as we passed her car in the parking lot. He could track down its previous owners while I investigated my two missing persons' whereabouts, Mimi and Reyes. I really needed Angel on this, but the least I could do was get Cookie to check the hospitals to see if any injured males—dark, early thirties, super hot—had shown up in the last few hours. Maybe he'd already been found and just didn't want me to know. But I'd have to do it discreetly.

After Garrett took off, I strode up the stairs beside Dad's bar, paused before entering Cookie's office to scan the area, then snuck inside.

Cookie looked up, and I immediately slammed an index finger over my mouth to shush her. Used to the departed showing up willy-nilly, she stilled, glanced around the room warily, then turned back to me, her brows raised in question.

I kept the finger over my mouth, tiptoed over to her—not sure why, it just felt right—and grabbed a pen and paper off her desk. After another quick glance around the room, I scribbled a note, asking her to check the hospitals for Reyes, and handed it to her. That's when I heard a throat clear beside me. I nearly jumped out of my go-gos, scaring the bejesus out of Cook in the process, then turned to see Reyes leaning against the wall beside her desk. Damn he was good.

"Pig latin?" he asked, incredulity lining his handsome face.

I snatched back the note and glared at him. "It's the only foreign language she knows."

"You were hoping to stump me with pig latin?"

I looked down at the note and cringed. It really wasn't the best idea I'd ever had. I turned toward him. "So, what? You gonna sever Cookie's spine, too?"

Cookie gasped aloud, and I pinched the bridge of my nose with my fingertips. She didn't need to hear that, especially with the dead stowaway in her trunk.

Between heartbeats, Reyes dematerialized and rematerialized in front of me, anger clear on his face. "What's it going to take, Dutch?"

"For me to stop looking for you?" I didn't wait for an answer. "You don't know what will happen if your body dies, Reyes. I'm not going to stop."

I could feel frustration rise inside him, simmer and bubble just beneath his perfect surface. He leaned toward me, but before he could do anything, he paused, grabbed his chest, then looked back at me in surprise.

"What?" I asked, but he clenched his jaw shut, his body tensing to a marble-like state, almost as if he were waiting for something. Then I saw it. His image changed. Deep gashes appeared across his face, over his chest, staining his shredded shirt with blood instantly. And he was wet, soaked with a dark liquid I couldn't identify. He grunted through his teeth and doubled over.

"Reyes," I cried out, and lunged for him. Just as our eyes locked, he was gone. In an instant, he vanished. I slammed both hands over my mouth to keep a scream at bay. Cookie rushed around her desk and knelt beside me. The agony of what he was going through shone so clearly in his expression. And he didn't want me to find him?

I would tear apart hell itself to find him.

Chapter Six

After parking my cherry red Jeep Wrangler, also known as Misery, half a block away, I swooped back into *Mission: Impossible* mode to traverse the dangerous domain tucked within the borders of the southern war zone. Gangs proliferated in the poverty-stricken area surrounding the asylum. And the asylum itself, abandoned by the government in the fifties, was now owned by an established biker gang known as the Bandits. For the most part, they were old school, their primary colors reflecting a loyalty to God and country.

I scanned the area, paying special attention to the Bandits' main house beside the asylum, also known as a Rottweiler den of iniquity—the Bandits loved them some Rottweilers—then I started up the fence as fast as I could. Admittedly, it wasn't very fast. In all the years I'd trespassed on Bandit turf, the Rottweilers had been out on patrol only a handful of times. The gang usually kept them inside during the day.

Praying my luck would hold, yet keeping a weather eye, I clawed and slipped my way to the top of the fence, cringing as the metal wire dug into my fingers. Guys made this stuff look so easy. The only things I liked to scale on a semi-regular basis were those same guys who made this stuff look easy.

Dropping to the other side, I had to stop and regroup, partly to wallow in self-pity and partly to take inventory of my throbbing fingers. Fortunately, they were all present and accounted for. Losing a finger in the line of fence scaling would suck.

After another quick glance at the house, I dashed to the basement window I'd been using to gain illegal access to the asylum since I was in high school. Abandoned asylums had always been a particular fascination of mine. I toured them—also known as breaking and entering—regularly after accidently discovering this asylum one night when I was fifteen. I'd also discovered Rocket Man that night, a relic from 1950s science fiction, when spaceships looked steam driven and aliens were as unwelcome as communists. And I discovered that Rocket was somewhat of a savant in the fact that he knew the names of every person who had ever died, millions upon millions of names stored in his childlike mind. Which came in really handy at times.

I scooted through the basement window on my stomach and dropped into a somersault, landing on my feet on the cement slab of the basement. 'Cause that's how I roll.

The times I'd tried that same maneuver only to land on my ass with dirt and cobwebs coating my hair didn't count. I turned to latch the window from the inside. Avoiding Rottweiler jaws always took precedence while visiting Rocket.

"Miss Charlotte!"

For like the gazillionth time that day, I jumped, cutting my finger on the latch. And it was still early. Apparently, this was Scare the Bejesus out of Charley Day. Had I known, I would've ordered a cheese ball.

I whirled around and looked up into the grinning face of Rocket Man. He scooped me up into a hug that was soft and warm despite my assailant's frigid temperature. My breath fogged when I laughed.

"Miss Charlotte," he said again.

"This is like being hugged by an ice sculpture," I said, teasing him.

He set me down, his eyes glistening and happy. "Miss Charlotte, you came back."

I chuckled. "I told you I would come back."

"Okay, but you have to go now." He clutched me around the waist, and I suddenly found myself being stuffed back out the basement window. The same window I had just latched.

"Wait, Rocket," I said, planting my feet on either side of the windowsill, feeling oddly ridiculous. And quite ready for a pelvic exam. I'd been kicked out of asylums before, but never by Rocket. "I just got here," I protested, pushing against the sill. But holy mother of crap, Rocket was strong.

"Miss Charlotte has to go," he repeated, not struggling in the least.

I grunted under his weight. "Miss Charlotte doesn't have to go, Rocket. She promises."

When he didn't budge, just pushed me closer and closer to the window, I lost my footing. Before I knew it, my right leg slipped and I found myself being crammed against the tiny window.

That was when I heard the crack, the chilling sound of glass splintering beneath the force. Damn it. If I had to get stitches, Rocket was so going to pay. Well, not literally, but . . .

I was doing my darnedest to twist and maneuver away from the decades-old glass when Rocket disappeared. In an instant, I dropped to the cement floor, landing mostly on my left shoulder and a little on my head. Pain burst and spread like napalm throughout my nerve endings. Then I realized I couldn't breathe. I hated when that happened.

Rocket reappeared, picked me up off the ground, and stood me up. "Are you okay, Miss Charlotte?" he asked. Now, he was worried.

All I could do was fan my face, trying to get air to my burning lungs. The fall had knocked the breath out of me. The fact that it was a non-life-threatening condition did little to lessen the state of panic I was slipping into.

When I didn't answer, Rocket shook me, waited a moment, then shook me again for good measure. I watched the world blur, refocus, then blur again, wondering if the knock to my head had me seizing.

"Miss Charlotte," he said as I gulped tiny rations of air, none quite large enough to fill the void of imminent suffocation, "why did you do that?"

"What? Me?" I asked, sticking to monosyllabic utterances. I'd work my way up to bigger words in a few.

"Why did you fall?"

"I can't imagine." Unfortunately, sarcasm rarely translated into Rocket language.

"New names. I have new names," he said, dragging me up the stairs. He patted the crumbling walls like they were made of precious metals. That was what Rocket did. Carved name upon name of those who had passed, and while the asylum was huge, I knew he would eventually scrape through the cement-covered walls. He would eventually run out of space. I wondered if the building would fall, if it would crumble to Earth like the people who had been memorialized by Rocket's hand. If so, what would that do to him? Where would he go? I'd invite him to my place, but I didn't know how Mr. Wong would take to an over-sized kid with a scraping fetish.

"I thought I had to leave," I said, my lungs relaxing at last.

He stopped on the top step and looked up in thought. "No, you don't have to go now. Just don't break the rules."

I tried not to laugh. He was such a stickler for the rules, though I had no idea what they were. Still, I had to wonder what all that stuffing-me-out-the-window business was about. He'd never tried to bounce me before.

"Rocket, I have to talk to you," I said, following behind him. He patted the wall on his right as we walked through the crumbling building.

"I have new names. They should not be here. No, ma'am."

"I know, sweetheart, and I'll get to them, but I have to ask you something."

Before I could get hold of his shirt to slow him down, he disappeared again, and it took everything in me not to drop my head into my hands in frustration. Rocket took ADHD to a whole new level.

"Miss Charlotte," I heard him call from down the same hall. "You need to keep up."

I took off toward his voice, hoping the crumbling floors would hold and wishing I'd brought a flashlight. "I'm coming. Stay there."

"All of these," he said when I reached him. "All of these. They should not be here. They have to follow the rules just like everybody else." And Rocket knew it was my job to help them cross. I looked at the wall he'd referenced. It held hundreds of names from dozens of countries. It amazed me how he knew this stuff.

I decided to test him, to see what would pour out of him at the mention of Reyes's otherworldly—for lack of a better term—name. But first I would ask about Mimi Jacobs. I needed to make sure she was still alive. "Okay, but I have some names for you now."

He stopped and turned to me. Nothing on Earth got Rocket's attention faster than the mentioning of a name. His eyes shone eagerly, almost hungrily.

I stepped closer, not wanting to lose him if he took off on one of his quests through the haunted halls of the asylum. "Mimi Anne Jacobs. Her maiden name was Marshal."

He bowed his head, his lids fluttering as if he were a search engine scouring the recesses of his own mind for information. He stopped and looked back at me. "No. Not her time yet."

Relief washed over me, and I braced myself for the next name. I knew it was fruitless to ask Rocket anything else about Mimi, though I suspected he knew more. Now Reyes. After placing a hand on his arm for good measure, I asked, "Rocket, what do you know about Rey'aziel?"

His lips pressed together and he stood motionless for a heartbeat, two, then leaned into me and said quietly, "It shouldn't be here, Miss Charlotte."

Rocket had said that before when I asked about Reyes Farrow. Apparently, he knew they were one and the same.

I squeezed his arm reassuringly and whispered, "Why?"

His face transformed. "Miss Charlotte, I told you." He chastised me with a scowl that looked more like a pout. "He should never have been a boy named Reyes. He's Rey'aziel. He should never have been born at all."

I'd also heard that before. "Rocket, is his corporeal body still alive?"

He bit his lower lip in thought before answering. "The boy Reyes is still here, but he broke the rules, Miss Charlotte. No breaking rules," he said, wagging a finger in warning.

Once again, I breathed a little easier. I was terrified Reyes's body would pass before I could find him. The thought of losing him petrified me.

"Martians can't become human just because they want to drink our water," he continued.

"So, Rey'aziel wanted our water?" I was trying so hard to understand his metaphors, but it wasn't easy. Nothing about Rocket was easy.

His boyish eyes focused on mine. He stared a long moment before answering. "He still does," he said, his fingers brushing over my cheek. "He wants it more than air."

I breathed in softly. Rocket rarely seemed so lucid, so rational. So poetic. "Reyes said once he was born for me, to be with me. Is that what scares you, Rocket? Are you afraid for me?"

"It's Rey'aziel, Miss Charlotte. Of course, I'm afraid for you. I'm afraid for everyone."

Oh. That was probably bad. I squared my shoulders and faced him head-on. "Rocket, do you know where his body is?"

He shook his head with a *tsk*. "He can't break the rules."

"What rules, Rocket?" Maybe the clues were in the rules Reyes had apparently broken. I knew I was grasping at straws, but without Angel's help, I had nothing.

"No playing hide-and-seek in the house."

"Which house?" I asked, a little surprised by his answer. Reyes was hiding his body. Was that the hide-and-seek Rocket was referring to?

He stilled and looked down for a moment as if sensing something. Without warning, he slammed a hand over my mouth and shoved me against the wall. Leaning into me, he glanced around the room, his eyes wide with fear. "Shhhh," he whispered. "It's here."

And in that moment, I felt him. The room became charged with heat and static, like an electrical storm was brewing within its walls. With the fluttering of wings, a darkness exploded in on us, swirled like obsidian clouds in the midst of Armageddon. When he materialized, he stayed ensconced inside his robe, his face shadowed, hidden from view.

Oh, yeah. He was pissed.

I pushed Rocket's hand off me and stepped toward him. "Reyes, wait—"

Before I could say anything, I heard the sing of metal being drawn.

My breath caught when I realized he was going to use his blade on Rocket.

"No, Reyes," I said, jumping in front of Rocket, but the blade was already in full swing. It whirred through the air and stopped a finger-breadth inside my rib cage, on the left side. The sting was instantaneous, but I knew there would be no blood. Reyes killed with the skill of a surgeon, only from the inside out. No external trauma. No evidence of foul play. Just a pristine slice so clean, so sharp, it stumped even the best doctors—or coroners, depending on the outcome—in the country.

Time seemed to stand still as I looked down at the blade, at the sharp edges and menacing angles. It hovered parallel to the floor, an inch inside my body, and glistened with a blinding light.

Reyes jerked the blade back and sheathed it inside his robes as I tipped awkwardly toward the wall, my heart stumbling over its own beats. He pushed back the hood of his robe, concern drawing his brows together, and leaned toward me as if to catch me. I pushed at him and whirled around, but Rocket was gone. Then I turned on Reyes. My anger at his utter stupidity was reaching an all-time high.

"You seem to be very willing to hurt people these days." The realization had me doubting everything I'd come to believe about him. I'd come to believe he was kind and noble and, okay, deadly, but in a good way.

"These days?" he asked, incredulous. "I've been hurting in your behalf for quite some time, Dutch."

That was true. He'd saved my life more than once. He'd hurt people who were going to hurt me more than once. But each and every time, the person had been guilty of something very bad.

"You can't just go around hurting people, killing people, because you want to. I realize your dad didn't teach you—"

With a growl, his robe disappeared and he turned from me, the heat of his anger like the blast from an inferno. "And to which dad would you be referring?" he asked, his tone even, hurt that I would even mention them.

He had been a general in hell. He'd led his father's armies into battle and suffered unimaginable consequences. Then he escaped and was born on Earth. For me. But the life he'd planned—the one where he and I grew up together, went to school and college together, had children together—became nothing more than remnants of a dream when he was kidnapped as a young child and traded to a monster named Earl Walker, the man he'd gone to prison for killing. The life he lived on Earth, the abuse he lived through, defined tragic.

I stepped closer. "I'm sorry. I didn't mean to bring either of them up."

He glanced over a wide shoulder, his muscles rippling under the weight of his memories. "You have to stop looking for me."

"No," I said, my voice a mere whisper.

His mouth formed a smile that didn't quite reach his eyes a heartbeat before he turned away again. "My body will be gone soon enough. It can't take much more."

With a sharp pain, my heart contracted at the thought. "Are they torturing you?" I asked, my breath hitching in my chest.

He stood studying Rocket's work, raised a hand, and ran his fingers along a name, the fluid lines of his tattoo undulating with the movement. "Mercilessly."

I couldn't stop the sting in my eyes, the wetness pooling along my lashes.

He was in front of me at once. "Don't," he said, his voice sharp, menacing. "Don't ever feel sorry for me."

I stumbled back against the wall again. He followed. I liked this better. It was easier to be angry with him when he was being an ass. What I hadn't expected was his probing caress. While he was pretending to fondle, to seduce, he was actually checking the wound he'd just given me, his hand soothing, his caress healing.

"Why did you hurt Pari?" I asked, still amazed that he could be so gentle, and yet hurt so easily.

He pushed away from the wall. "I never hurt your friend. I don't even know who she is."

I blinked in surprise. "But, she summoned you."

"Did she tell you that?"

"Yes. She said she summoned you, Rey'aziel, in a séance."

He chuckled, the sound harsh. "So your friend thinks she summoned me like a dog?"

"No, that's not it at all."

"I can't be summoned by a group of teen nitwits playing urban legend. Only one person alive can summon me," he said, gazing at me pointedly.

Did he mean me? Could I summon him? "So, it wasn't you?"

He only shook his head.

"Then, you didn't hurt her?"

He paused and eyed me for a long moment. "You know what I find most interesting?"

This was a trick. I could feel it. "What?"

"That you honestly believe I am capable of hurting innocent people for no reason."

"You're not?" I asked, hope softening my voice.

"Oh, no, I'm more than capable. I just didn't realize you knew that."

Fine, he was bitter. I got that. "Were you going to kill Rocket? Is that even possible?"

"He's already dead, Dutch."

"Then—"

"I was just going to send him away for a while to cower in fear. He's good at that."

"So, you're cruel, too," I stated, matter-of-fact.

He slid his long fingers around my neck, the heat blistering, and raised my chin with his thumb. "I was a general in hell. What do you think?"

"I think you're trying really hard to convince me how bad you are."

He smiled. "I spent centuries in the underworld. I am what I am. If I were you, I'd take off those rose-colored glasses and think about what it is you're trying to save. Just let my body die."

"Why don't you kill it yourself?" I asked, impatience bubbling inside me. "Just get it over with? Why are you letting them torture you?"

"I can't," he said, dropping his hand, and I stilled to listen. He clenched his jaw in frustration. "They're guarding my body. They won't let me near it."

"The demons? How many are there?"

"More than even you could handle."

"So, then, there're two?" I asked. I couldn't imagine myself *handling* even one.

"If they succeed in taking me, you have to figure out what you're capable of, Dutch, and you have to do it fast."

"Why don't you just tell me?"

He shook his head. Naturally. "That would be like telling a fledgling it can fly before it leaves the nest. It has to do it, to know it can on a visceral level. It's instinct. If I do go back, if I am taken when my body dies, you'll be alone. And yes, they'll find you eventually."

Well, crapola.

Rocket was gone, and there was simply no telling when he would be back. I once went two months without seeing him, and that incident had nothing to do with Reyes. No telling how long he would hide this time.

I strode back to Misery, my mouth still hot from the blistering kiss

Reyes gave me before he disappeared, and called in some backup. Then I checked in with Cookie.

"Nothing yet," she said, filling me in on her findings, or lack thereof.

"That's okay, keep digging. I'm going to see Warren after this. Call me if you find anything interesting."

"Will do."

Taft, an officer who worked with my uncle, pulled up behind me in his patrol car as I closed my phone. A couple of neighborhood kids stood giggling, thinking I was getting in trouble. Kids in these parts rarely saw police as a positive force. It was hard to get past men in uniforms taking your mom or dad away in the middle of the night for a domestic disturbance.

I stepped out as Taft adjusted his hat and made his way toward me, scanning the neighborhood for signs of aggression. He wore a crisp black uniform and military buzz, but he wasn't the one I needed to see.

"Hey, Taft," I said, getting the pleasantries out of the way before looking at the departed nine-year-old girl on his heels, aka Demon Child. "Hey, pumpkin."

"Hey, Charley," she said, her voice soft and sweet, as if she weren't evil.

Much like the devil himself, Demon Child had many names. Demon Child for one, as well as the Spawn of Satan, Lucifer's Love Child, Strawberry Shortcake, or for short, a particular favorite of mine, the SS. She was Taft's little sister and had died when they were both young. Taft had tried to save her from drowning and spent a week in the hospital with pneumonia for his effort. And she never left his side. Until she found me. And tried to claw my eyes out through no fault of my own.

The first time we'd met, she was sitting in the back of Taft's patrol car as he was giving me a ride from a crime scene. When Strawberry thought I was after her brother, she called me an ugly bitch and tried to blind me. It left an impression.

She looked back, her long blond hair falling in disarray around her face, spotted the crumbling insane asylum, and folded her tiny arms in distaste. "What are we doing here?"

"I was wondering if you could do me a favor."

She turned back to me, her nose wrinkled as she considered my statement. "Okay, but you have to do one for me back."

"Yeah?" I asked, leaning against Misery. "What do you need?"

"David is dating someone."

"Oh," I purred, pretending to care. "Now, who's David?"

She rolled her eyes as only a nine-year-old could. "My brother? David Taft?" She hitched a thumb toward him.

"Oh! That David," I said, offering him a conspicuous giggle.

"What's she saying?" he asked.

I ignored.

"She's ugly and she wears too much lipstick and her clothes are too tight."

"So, she's a ho?" I chastised him with a scowl.

He turned up his palms. "What?"

"Deluxe," Strawberry said, confirming my suspicions. She pointed straight at him. "You need to have a talk with him. That ho stayed all night. Really."

I pressed my lips together and jammed my fists onto my hips, hoping I wasn't bleeding internally from Reyes's blade. I hated it when I bled internally. If I was going to bleed, I wanted to see the evidence, revel in the heroics of it all. "I most certainly will." After tossing him a glower of disappointment, one that had him glaring back in annoyance, I explained why I needed her. "While your brother and I have our talk, will you go into that building and look for a little girl?"

Taft and Strawberry both eyed the building with skeptical frowns. "That building looks scary," she said.

"It's not scary at all," I lied. Like a dog. What could be scarier than an abandoned mental asylum where, according to legend, the doctors did *experiments*? "There's a nice man named Rocket who lives there with his little sister. She's even younger than you are."

I'd never seen Rocket's sister, but he told me countless times that she was there with him. She'd apparently died of pneumonia during the Dust Bowl, and from what he told me, I was guessing her age to be somewhere around five.

"His name is Rocket?" The thought made her giggle.

"Yeah, speaking of which . . ." I leaned down to her. "While you're in there, see if you can find out Rocket's real name." I had yet to get any real info on Rocket's origins, though I'd scoured every record I could find on the asylum. Apparently, Rocket Man was not his real name.

"Okay."

"Wait," I said a microsecond before she disappeared. "Don't you want to know why you're going in?"

"To find that little girl."

"Yes, but I need information from her if she has it. I need to know if she can tell me where to find Reyes's body. His human body. Can you remember that?"

She crossed her arms again and said, "Duh." Then she disappeared.

I ground my teeth just a little, certain Strawberry was God's way of punishing me for having one-too-many margaritas last Thursday night that resulted in an ugly, tabletop version of the hokey pokey.

As Taft stood at attention, still eyeing the building with concern, I rested against Misery, propping a booted heel on her running board. "Look," I said, luring his attention my way, "your sister says the chick you're dating is a ho."

He turned to me, aghast. "She's not a ho. Well, yeah, okay, she's a ho, thus my dating her, but she knows?"

I shrugged, incredulous. "Dude, I have no idea if your GF knows she's a ho."

"No, I mean Becky. She knows I'm dating someone?"

I threw my palms up. "Maybe if I knew who Becky was—"

He stared at me, appalled. "My sister."

"Oh! Right!" I said, going for the save. Who knew Demon Child would have such a normal name? I expected something exotic like Serena or Destiny or the Evil One That Comes in the Night to Make Us Chilly.

Taft's radio squawked out something I found completely incoherent. As he strolled toward his patrol car to talk in private, my cell rang out. It was Cookie. "Charley's House of Excruciating Pain," I said.

"Janelle died in a car accident."

"Oh, man, I'm so sorry. Were you two close?"

After an annoyed sigh, she said, "Janelle, Charley. Janelle York? Mimi's friend from high school who died recently?"

"Oh, right," I said, going for the save again. I seemed to be doing that a lot lately. "Wait, a car accident? Mimi told Warren Janelle was murdered."

"Exactly. According to the report, she'd been ill. They think she passed out at the wheel and crashed her car into a ravine off I-25. But it was ruled accidental."

"Then why would Mimi say she was murdered?"

"Something had her spooked," Cookie said.

"And maybe it's connected to our murdered car dealer."

"That would be my guess. I think you need to have that other talk with Warren soon. Find out why he was fighting with a man only days before said man was found dead."

"Great minds think alike, baby. I am so on it."

"Is that Cookie?"

Strawberry had appeared at my side. I closed my phone and looked at her. "The one and only. That was fast. Did you find Rocket's sister?"

"Of course."

Awesome. I never knew if she really existed or if she'd been a figment of Rocket's imagination. I waited for more info. Like forever. "And?"

"She's blue."

Blue? Well, she did die of pneumonia. Maybe the lack of oxygen turned her blue. "Okay, besides that."

She did the crossing-of-her-arms thing. If it weren't so cute, it would be annoying. "You're not going to like it."

"Does she know where Reyes's body is?"

"No. She went to look. But she said Rey'aziel should not have been born on Earth."

"So I've heard."

"He's very powerful."

"Yeah, I figured that out a while ago."

"And if his human body dies, he will become what he was born from the fires of hell to be."

Okay, that was new. "Which is?" I asked, my voice edged with a wary dread.

"The ultimate weapon," she said as if she were ordering an ice cream cone. "The bringer of death."

"Well, crap."

"The Antichrist."

"Damn."

"He is more powerful than any demon or any angel that ever existed. He can manipulate the space-time continuum and bring about the destruction of the entire galaxy and everything in it."

"Okay, I get it," I said, holding up a hand to stop her. I suddenly found myself fighting for air. I just had to ask. It couldn't have been something easy, something non–world destroying. Oh, hell no. It had to be all apocalyptic and ghastly. Well, this sucked ass. I had no idea how to fight that. But finding Reyes's body suddenly became imperative. "You found out a lot in that five minutes."

"I guess," she said with a shrug.

I switched gears, dropped down into neutral, then shifted myself into denial before looking back at Strawberry. "So, did you find out Rocket's real name?"

"Yep," she said, running her fingertips over the sleeve of my sweater. It was disturbing.

I waited. Like forever. "And?"

"And what?"

"Rocket's name?"

"What about it?"

Deep breaths. Deep calming breaths. "Pumpkin head," I said, calmly and deep-breathily, "what is Rocket's name?"

She looked up as if I were insane. "Rocket. Duh."

My teeth slammed together again. If it weren't for her large, innocent eyes, the perfect pout of her bowlike mouth, I would have exorcised her right then and there. Well, if I knew how. I lowered my head instead, played with an errant string on my jeans. "Is Rocket okay?"

She shrugged. "Yeah, he's just a little scared."

Damn it. Reyes could be such a butthead. Freaking Antichrists. A thought emerged. "Hey, so what's his little sister's name?"

Her mouth dropped open before she glared up at me. "Do you even listen?"

What the heck did I do now? "What?"

"I already told you. Her name is Blue."

"Oh, really?"

She nodded.

"Her name is Blue?"

She crossed her arms—again—and nodded, slowly, apparently so I would understand.

"Does she have a last name, mayhap?" Smart-ass.

"Yep. Bell."

I sighed. Another nom de plume. "Blue Bell, huh?" Well, that wouldn't bolster my investigation any. Rocket Man and Blue Bell. Wonderful. No, wait. Now I had a Rocket Man, a Blue Bell, and an alleged Antichrist. Never let it be said that life in Charley Land wasn't interesting.

"So, why won't Blue Bell come out to meet me?" I asked, slightly hurt only not.

"Really?" She eyed me like I was part blithering and part idiot. "Because if *you* had died and wanted to stay on Earth to hang with your bro for all eternity, would you introduce yourself to the one person in the universe who could send you to the other side?"

She had a point.

Taft finished his conversation and strolled back over. "Is she here?" he asked, looking around. They always looked around. Not sure why.

"In the flesh," I said. "Metaphorically."

"Is she still mad at me?" He kicked the sand at his feet.

Had I not been shell-shocked over the pending apocalypse, I would have laughed when Strawberry did the same, her tiny pink slippers skimming over the ground, disturbing nothing. "I wasn't mad," she said. "I just wish he would stop taking ugly girls to dinner." Before I could say anything, she reached up and curled her fingers into mine. "He should take you to dinner."

To say that the mere thought horrified me would have been a grievous understatement. I threw up a little in my mouth then swallowed hard, trying not to make a face. "She's not really mad," I told Taft when I recovered. I leaned in and whispered, "Just please, for the love of God, find a girl good enough to take home to your mother. And do it soon."

"Okay," he said, confusion locking his brows together.

"And stop dating skanks."

Chapter Seven

I STOPPED FIGHTING MY INNER DEMONS.
WE'RE ON THE SAME SIDE NOW.

——T-SHIRT

After presenting my ID at the front, I strolled into the central police station, where they'd brought Warren Jacobs for questioning, and spotted Ubie across a sea of desks. Fortunately, only a couple of uniforms took note of my presence. Most cops didn't take kindly to my invading their turf. Partly because I was Ubie's secret weapon, solving cases before they could, and partly because they thought I was a freak. Neither particularly bothered me.

Cops were an odd combination of rules and arrogance, but I'd learned long ago that both attributes were needed for survival in their dangerous profession. People were downright crazy.

Ubie stood talking to another detective when I walked up to him. At the last minute, I remembered I was annoyed with him for putting a tail on me. Thank goodness I did, because I almost smiled.

"Ubie," I said, icicles dripping from my voice.

Clearly unfazed by my cool disposition, he snickered, so I frowned and said, "Your mustache needs a trim."

His smile evaporated and he groped his 'stache self-consciously. It was harsh of me, but he needed to know I was serious about my No-Surveillance Policy. I hardly appreciated his insensitivity to my need for privacy. What if I'd rented a porn flick?

The other detective nodded to take his leave, humor twitching the corners of his mouth as he walked away.

"Can I see him?" I asked.

"He's in observation room one waiting for his lawyer."

Taking that as a yes, I headed that way, then offered over my shoulder, "He's innocent, by the way."

Just as I stepped inside, he called out to me. "Are you just saying that 'cause you're mad?"

I let the door close behind me without answering.

"Ms. Davidson," Warren said, rising to take my hand. He actually looked a little worse than he had at the café. He wore the same charcoal suit, his tie loose, the top button of his shirt unfastened.

"How are you holding up?" I asked, sitting across from him.

"I didn't kill anyone," he said, his hands shaky with grief. Guilty people were often nervous during interviews as well, but for a different reason. More often than not, they were trying to come up with a good story. One that would cover all the bases and hold up in court. Warren was nervous because he was being accused of committing not one, but two crimes, and he'd committed neither.

"I don't doubt that, Warren," I said, trying to keep my voice firm nonetheless. He didn't tell me everything, and I wanted to know why. "But you had an argument with Tommy Zapata a week before he was found dead."

Warren's head fell into his hands. I knew that Uncle Bob was watching. He'd kept Warren in an observation room, knowing I was coming to see him, but if he was hoping for some kind of confession, he was about to be very disappointed.

"Look, if I'd known he was going to be found dead, I would never have argued with him. Not in public, anyway."

Well, at least he was smart. "Why don't you tell me what happened."

"I did," he said, his voice breathy with frustration. "I told you how I thought Mimi might have been having an affair. She changed so much, became so distant, so . . . unlike herself that I followed her one day. She had lunch with him, a car dealer, and I thought . . . I just knew she was having an affair."

"Is there anything in particular that stood out? Anything that made you feel that way?"

"She was so different toward him, almost hostile. Before their food even arrived, she stood up to leave. He tried to get her to stay. He even took her hand, but she pulled back like she was repulsed by him. When she tried to walk past, he stood and blocked her path. That's when I knew it was all true." The memory seemed to drain the life out of him. His shoulders deflated as he thought back.

"Why?" I asked, fighting the urge to take his hand. "How did you know?"

"She slapped him." He buried his face in his hands a second time and spoke from behind them. "She's never slapped anyone in her life. It looked like a lovers' quarrel."

Finally, I put a hand on his shoulder and he looked up at me, his eyes moist and lined in a bright red.

"After she left," he continued, "I followed him to his dealership and confronted him. He wouldn't tell me what was going on, only to keep an eye on Mimi, that she could be in danger." Moisture dripped over his lashes, and he rubbed his eyes with the thumb and fingers of one hand. The other one balled into a fist on the table. "I'm so amazingly stupid, Ms. Davidson."

"Of course you're not stupid."

"I am," he said, pinning me with a look so desperate, I struggled to breathe under the weight of it. "I thought he was threatening her. Honestly, how thick can one person be? He was trying to warn me that something was happening, something beyond my control, and I yelled at him. I threatened everything from a lawsuit to . . . to murder. God, what have I done?" he asked himself.

I realized immediately Warren was going to need two things when all this was said and done: a good lawyer and a good therapist. Poor schmuck. Most women would kill to have someone so dedicated.

"What else do you know about him?" I asked. Surely he did some kind of investigating into this guy's background.

"Nothing. Not much, anyway."

"Okay, give me what you do have."

"Really," he said, lifting one shoulder in hopelessness, "Mimi went missing right after I confronted him. I just don't have much."

"And you thought she ran away with him?"

His fist tightened. "Told you I was thick."

I could almost hear his teeth grinding in self-loathing. "Did you find out how she knew him?"

After a long sigh, he admitted, "Yes, they went to high school together."

The bells and whistles of a winning spin on a slot machine echoed in my mind. That must have been some high school. "Warren," I said, forcing his attention back to me, "don't you get it?"

His brows furrowed in question.

"Two people who went to the same high school with your wife are now dead, and she's missing."

He blinked, realization dawning in his eyes.

"Did something happen?" I asked. "Did she ever talk about high school?"

"No," he said as if he'd found the answer to it all.

"Crap."

"No, you don't understand. She never talked about her high school in Ruiz before she moved to Albuquerque, refused to. I asked her about it a couple of times, pushed her a little once, and she was so angry, she didn't talk to me for a week."

I leaned forward, hope spiraling out of me. "Something happened there, Warren. I promise you, I'll find out what it was."

He took my hand into his. "Thank you."

"But if I die trying," I added, pointing a finger at him, "I'm totally doubling my fee."

A minuscule grin softened his features. "You got it."

Just as we were wrapping up our conversation, his lawyer walked into the room. As they talked quietly, I excused myself and strolled to the two-way mirror, leaned in, and grinned. "Told you," I said, hitching a thumb over my shoulder. "Innocent. That'll teach you to put a tail on my ass." Payback was fun.

After taking a picture back to the Chocolate Coffee Café to no avail—no one remembered seeing Mimi the night before—I flirted with Brad the cook a little then hustled back to the office, but Cookie had left early to have dinner with her daughter, Amber. Every time her twelve-year-old stayed with her dad, Cookie would insist on taking her to dinner at least once, worried that Amber would be miserable. I suddenly found it odd that in the two years I'd known Cookie, I had never met her ex. I had no idea what he even looked like, though Cook talked about him plenty. Most of it not good. Some not so bad. Some kind of wonderful.

Dad was at the bar when I made it downstairs for a bite. He tossed the towel to Donnie, his Native American barkeep who had pecs to die for and thick, blue-black hair for which every woman alive would sell her soul. But we'd never really seen eye to eye. Mostly 'cause he was much taller than I was.

I watched as Dad wound his way to my table. It was my favorite spot, nestled in a dark corner of the bar, where I could watch everyone without them watching me. I wasn't particularly fond of being watched. Unless the watcher was over six feet with a hot body and sexy smile. And he wasn't a serial killer. That always helped.

Dad's coloring was still off. The normally bright hues of his aura that encompassed him were now murky and gray. The only other time I'd seen him like this was when he was a detective working a brutal series of missing-children cases. It was so bad, in fact, he wouldn't let me get involved. I was twelve at the time, old enough to know everything and then some, but he'd refused my offer of help.

"Hey, pumpkin," he said, plastering on that fake smile that didn't quite reach his eyes.

"Hey, Dad," I said, doing the same.

He brought us both a ham-and-cheese on whole wheat, exactly what I'd been craving.

"Mmm, thanks."

With a smile, he watched while I bit into it, while I chewed then swallowed, while I chased the bite with a swig of iced tea.

I paused and turned to him. "Okay, this is getting creepy."

After an apprehensive laugh, he said, "Sorry. I just . . . You're growing up so fast."

"Growing up?" I coughed into my sleeve before continuing. "I'm pretty much grown."

"Right." He was still somewhere else. A different time. A different place. After a moment, he refocused and grew serious. "Sweetheart, is there more to your ability than what you've told me?"

I'd taken another bite and drew my brows together in question.

"You know, things. Can you . . . do things?"

Last week, I had the murderous husband of a former client try to kill me. Reyes had saved my life. Again. And he'd done it in his usual manner. He'd appeared out of nowhere and severed the man's spinal cord with one lighting flash of his sword. Since that very same thing had happened in the past—criminals' spinal columns being severed with no outside trauma whatsoever, no medical explanation—I feared Dad was beginning to make the connection.

"Things?" I asked, an air of innocence in my voice.

"Well, for example, that man who attacked you last week."

"Mmm-hmm," I said, taking another bite.

"Did you . . . Can you . . . Are you able—?"

"I didn't hurt him, Dad," I said after I swallowed. "I told you, there was another man there. He threw the guy against the cage of the eleva-tor. The impact must have—"

"Right," he said, shaking his head. "I—I knew that. It's just, our forensics guy said that was impossible." He lifted his gaze to mine, his soft brown eyes probing.

I sat my sandwich down. "Dad, you don't really think I have the capability to hurt someone, do you?"

"You have such a gentle soul," he said sadly.

Gentle? Did he know me at all?

"I just . . . I wonder if there's more to it—"

"I brought dessert."

We both looked up at my stepmother. She scooted a chair next to Dad and planted her ass in it, carefully placing a white dessert box on the table. I could tell she'd just had her short brown hair styled and her nails done. She smelled like hairspray and nail polish. I often wondered what my dad saw in the woman. He was just as blinded by her too-polished exterior as everyone else. Anyone who knew her—or thought they knew her—called her a saint for taking on a cop husband with two small children. *Saint* was not the word that came to my mind. I think I gave her the heebie-jeebies. In all fairness, she did the same to me. Her lipstick was always a little too red for her pale skin, her shadow a little too blue. Her aura a little too dark.

My sister, Gemma, followed in her wake, taking the only seat available next to me with an obligatory, albeit strained, smile. Her blond hair was pulled back in a taut wrap, and she wore just enough makeup to look made up yet still professional. She was a shrink, after all.

Our relationship, while never award-winning, had gone nowhere but down since high school. No idea why. She was three years older and had taken every opportunity growing up to remind me of that fact. While Denise was the only mother I had ever known—sadly—Gemma had had three wonderful years with our real mother before she died giving birth to yours truly. I'd often wondered if that was where the strain in our relationship stemmed from. If Gemma subconsciously blamed me for our mother's death.

But the vacancy had been filled only a year later when my dad married the she-wolf. And Gemma had taken to her instantly. I, on the other hand, had yet to reach that apex of the mother–daughter bond. I preferred my bondage stepmother-free and sprinkled with a little sexy.

Oddly, I was almost glad for the interruption. I wasn't sure where Dad had been going with his line of questioning—or if even he was sure where he was going with his line of questioning—but there was still so much he didn't know. And didn't need to know. And would never know, if I had anything to say about it. My being a grim reaper, for one. Still, he seemed so lost. Almost desperate. You'd think twenty years on the police force would have given him better interrogation skills. He'd been grasping at straws, the see-through twirly kind that kids use at birthday parties.

I finished my sandwich in a flash, excused myself to the annoyance of my dad, then hightailed it home, taking note that Denise did not offer me any of the cheesecake she'd picked up at the bakery down the street. I realized on the long, hazardous, thirty-second trek to my apartment building that Gemma seemed as perplexed by Dad's behavior as I was. She kept casting curious glances at him from underneath her lashes. Maybe I'd call her later and ask her if she had any idea what was going on. Or maybe I'd have my bikini area waxed by a German female wrestler, which would be more fun than talking to my sister on the phone.

"Well?" Cookie asked as I walked to my apartment, her head poking out her door. How did she always know I was coming? I was pure stealth. Smoke. Nigh invisible. Like a ninja without the head wrap.

"Crap," I said when I tripped on my own feet and dropped my cell.

"Did you talk to Warren?"

"Sure did." I grabbed my phone then rummaged through my bag in search of my ever-elusive keys.

"And?"

"And that man is going to need medication."

She sighed and leaned against her doorjamb. "Poor guy. Did he really threaten that murdered car salesman?"

"With several employees serving witness," I said with a nod.

"Damn. That's not going to help our case any."

"True, but it won't matter when we find who really did it."

"*If* we find who really did it."

"Did you get a hit on anything?"

"Do cowboys wear spurs?" Her blue eyes sparkled in the low light.

"Oooh, sounds promising. Want to come over?"

"Sure. Let me grab a quick shower."

"Me, too. I think I still smell like an illegally dumped oil slick."

"Don't forget the coffee," she said, closing her door.

I offered a quick shout-out to my roomie, Mr. Wong, before showering. But once again, I wasn't alone. Dead Trunk Guy showed up just as the water got hot. I tried to toss his ass out by bracing myself against the wall and pushing with all my might, but he didn't budge. I totally needed to learn how to exorcise the crazy ones. Afterwards, I threw on some sweats and started a pot of coffee. Hard as I tried, I couldn't keep my mind from straying back to what Rocket's sister had said about Reyes. I mean, the bringer of death? Seriously? Who talked like that?

Just as I pushed Mr. Coffee's button, a fiery heat enveloped me from behind. I paused and reveled in the feel of it a moment before turning around. Reyes had placed both hands on the counter, bracing them on either side of me. I leaned back and allowed myself the rare luxury of just staring. His full mouth was quite possibly the most sensual thing about him. So inviting. So kissable. And his liquid brown eyes, lined with lashes so thick, so dark, they made the gold and green flecks in his irises sparkle by contrast. They were the stuff of every girl's fantasy.

His gaze, unwavering and determined, held mine captive while his fingers grasped one end of the drawstring on my sweatpants and pulled. Then he looked at my mouth, like a kid in a candy shop, and ran his fingers along the waistband to loosen them. As always, his skin was blisteringly hot against mine, and I wondered if it was a product of him being incorporeal yet still alive or of him being born in the fires of hell. Literally.

"I learned some things about you today."

His finger dipped south, causing a quake to shudder through me. "Did you?"

This would get me nowhere fast. With every ounce of strength I had, I ducked past him and stepped to my sofa. "Coming?" I asked when he sighed.

He followed me with his eyes as I plopped down and criss-cross-applesauced my legs. The heat from his fingers still lingered on my abdomen. As badly as I'd wanted those fingers to reach the nether shore, their owner and I needed to chat.

After a moment, Reyes strolled into my living room, which took about two steps, then noticed Mr. Wong in the corner. He turned and studied him with a frown. "Does he know he's dead?"

"No idea. According to rumor, if your corporeal body passes, you'll become the Antichrist."

He paused, clenched his jaw, then lowered his head in a way that had me wondering just how hard I'd hit the nail on the head. I didn't have to wonder long.

"That's why I was created."

The alarm that spiked within me was reflexive, uncontrollable.

He glanced up at me. "You're surprised?"

"No. A little," I admitted.

"Have you ever known a man who wanted to be a professional ballplayer but never quite had the skill?"

My brows furrowed with the sudden shift in direction. "Um, well, I knew a guy once who wanted to play professional baseball. Tried out and everything."

"Is he married now?"

"Yes," I answered, wondering again what he was thinking. "Two kids."

"A son?"

"Yes. And a girl."

"Let me ask you. What does that son do?"

Of course. He had me dead to rights. "He plays baseball. Has since he was two."

He nodded knowingly. "And he will push that kid and push him to be the professional baseball player he could never be."

"Your father could never conquer the world, so he was grooming his kid to do it for him."

"Exactly."

"And how well did he groom you?"

"What are the odds of that kid becoming a professional baseball player?"

"I understand that. You're not like him. But I was told your incorporeal body is like an anchor and without it, you'll lose your humanity. That you'll become exactly what he wants you to be."

"How is it you believe everything you hear about me, yet nothing I tell you?"

"That's not true," I said, clutching a throw pillow to my chest. "You've told me you don't know what'll happen if you die. I'm simply trying to find out."

"Yet everything you hear is negative. Catastrophic." He eyed me from underneath his lashes and whispered, "A lie."

"You just told me why you were created. That wasn't a lie."

"My father created me for one reason. It doesn't make me his puppet. And it damn sure doesn't make me the fucking Antichrist." He turned from me, his anger rising quickly to overtake his frustration. With a loud sigh, he said, "I don't want to fight."

"I don't want to fight either," I said, jumping up. "I just want to find you. I just want you to be okay."

"What part of *trap* don't you understand?" He turned back to me with a glower. "Until you're safe, I'll never be okay."

A knock at the door had both of us glancing that way.

"It's your friend," he said, annoyance edging his voice.

"Cookie?" She never knocked.

"The other one."

"I have more than two friends, Reyes."

"I heard that," Garrett said as I opened the door. His weapon was drawn before my next heartbeat. I totally needed to learn to do that. "Where is he?" He barged past me and scanned the area.

Reyes was still there. I could feel him. I just couldn't see him anymore, and Garrett certainly couldn't see him, not that it would've mattered. That gun would hardly be of benefit in a showdown with the son of Satan. "He's not here."

Garrett turned to me, his jaw clenching. "I thought we had a deal."

"Calm down, kemosabe," I said as I closed the door and strode past him to the watering hole. I needed caffeine. "His corporeal body isn't here. His incorporeal body has scurried off to sulk."

I heard a distant growl as I searched out my favorite mug, the one that said EDWARD PREFERS BRUNETTES.

"You're drinking coffee this late in the evening?"

"It's either this or a fifth of Jack."

"And this whole thing with Farrow's corporeal body, his incorporeal body . . . it's kind of freaking me out."

"Did you get a hit on Dead Trunk Guy?" I asked, just as Cookie walked through the door in her pajamas.

"Oh," she said, surprised we had company. "Um, maybe I should change."

"Don't be ridiculous," I said, frowning at her. "It's just Swopes."

"Right," she said, covering her breasts self-consciously. Like we could see any more than normal in her flannel PJs. A nervous giggle squeaked out of her as she strolled toward the coffeepot.

It was about time those two got to know each other. She'd had a crush on Garrett since the day he sauntered into my office on Uncle Bob's heels. They'd been in the middle of an investigation and Garrett stayed in the waiting room, aka, Cookie's office, so Ubie could ask me in private if I had any info on a murdered elderly woman from the

Heights. That was before Garrett found out the truth about me. I don't know what they'd talked about, but Cookie was never the same. Then again, it could have been the fact that she was alone for a solid ten minutes with a tall, muscular man whose mocha-colored skin made the gray of his eyes shine like silver in the sun.

He grinned, knowing exactly what he did to her, what he did to most women, before settling on the club chair that cattycornered my sofa.

"A kindergarten teacher," he said, apparently answering my question about what he'd found on Cookie's car as I added enough cream to my coffee to make it unrecognizable.

"Swopes," I said, giving Cookie a wink, "we don't care what you want to be when you grow up. We want to know what you found out about Cookie's car."

Her eyes widened. "My car?" she whispered.

"You're funny," he said absently, studying the corner where he knew Mr. Wong stood. Er, hovered. "The previous owner was a kindergarten teacher."

"You mean, the person who owned the car before me?" Cookie asked, taking her coffee black and sitting on the sofa opposite him.

He smiled. I smiled, too, realizing that was probably the most she'd ever said to him at one time.

"Yep. And she's had her fair share of speeding tickets."

I sat next to Cook, realizing that even in her flannel jammies, she made big beautiful.

"Do you think it was a hit and run?" she asked.

"Not if he died in your trunk."

"Oh, yeah." She shook her head. "Wait." Her mouth fell open. "Are you thinking she killed him? Put him in the trunk on purpose?"

"As opposed to accidently?" he asked.

She offered a shrug with an embarrassed giggle.

"She has a DWI," he said. "And was arrested for another DWI that got thrown out of court due to a technicality."

"Okay," I said, thinking aloud, "so she's on her way home from a party when Dead Trunk Guy steps off a curb—only he's not dead yet—and she nails him, freaks out, stops to check on him, then realizes he's still alive. So she stuffs him in her trunk . . . why? So he can't report her?" After a moment, I said, "That makes no sense. If she was so worried about getting caught, why stop at all?"

"True," Garrett said. "Your theory sucks."

I wondered where Dead Trunk Guy was when I wasn't in the shower. Probably back in Cookie's trunk. "You're just going to have to find out more," I said to Garrett.

"Do you know about her fake dying plants?" he asked Cookie.

She pressed her lips together and nodded, twirling her index finger around her ear. Nobody understood the real me.

"So, what did you find out about Mimi?" I asked her.

"Oh, lots." She sat up straight, excited to have the floor. "When Mimi was in high school in Ruiz, she moved to Albuquerque to live with her grandparents."

We waited for more. After a moment, I asked, "That's it?"

She grinned. "Of course not. The class rosters are en route."

Ah, now I understood why she was so proud. The last case we had where we tried to get a class roster from a public school was like trying to get a deadbeat dad to donate a kidney. In the end, I had to recruit Uncle Bob, his rusty badge, and his reprehensible skill at flirting.

"So, how'd you manage it?" I asked, eager to hear what she did.

Her face fell. "I just asked."

Oh. Well, that wasn't very exciting. "But you got them," I said, trying to cheer her up.

"True. And I'm going to bed." She eyed Garrett self-consciously then gave me a furtive look from underneath her lashes. My brows rose in question. She gritted her teeth and widened her eyes. I crinkled my nose, again in question. She sighed and gestured toward the door with a slight nod. Oh! I glanced at Garrett, who was trying to be the gentleman and not notice the exchange between us. He suddenly had an intense fascination with the arm of the chair.

"I'll come with." I hopped up and walked her across the hall, figuring she wanted to talk about Garrett. I hoped she didn't want me to pass him a note. I didn't have any paper on me.

She opened her door then turned back. "So, is he here?"

"Garrett?" I asked, confused.

"What?"

"Wait, who?"

"Charley," she said, annoyed, "the little boy."

"Oh." I'd totally forgotten that while we were traipsing along the streets of Albuquerque at three o'clock this morning—walking in bunny slippers really wasn't much different from walking barefoot—I'd let slip she had a departed child hanging in her humble abode. I needed to learn to keep my mouth shut. I scanned the area quickly. Her apartment was a montage of black and the bright colors of Mexico, her décor a mixture of rustic Southwest and ranch. My apartment, though identical in size and shape to hers, was more a montage of garage sale and leftover college student paraphernalia. "Nope, don't see him."

"Can you check the rest of the apartment?"

"Sure."

After a five-minute search that had guilt eating away at my innards—really, I should never have told her—we were standing back at her front door, no departed kid in sight.

"Okay, I have a question for you," I said, drawing her interest. "If you were the dying son of Satan, where would you stash your body?"

She cast a sympathetic glance my way. "Since you're the one he's hiding from, sweet pea, my guess would be the last place you, of all people, would be likely to look."

"No offense," I said, disappointed, "but that doesn't really help."

"I know. I suck at all of this supernatural stuff. But I fry a mean chicken."

"Oh, good. I hate it when the nice ones get fried."

"Can I have him for Christmas?" she asked.

"Reyes?"

With a lovesick sigh, she said, "No, the other one."

"Ew," I said, realizing she was talking about Garrett. Okay, he was sexy and all, but still, "Ew."

"You're just saying that 'cause you're jealous of our thing."

After an amazingly rude snort, I said, "Your thing needs a good talking to."

"Whatever, girlfriend," she said, showing me a palm before closing her door. I loved it when she got all dramaholic.

When I walked back into my apartment, Garrett had returned to studying Mr. Wong's corner.

"He won't bite," I said, teasing him.

He furrowed his brows in doubt then turned a curious gaze on me. "What was it like growing up with dead people everywhere? Didn't it freak you out?"

I grinned. "It's all I've ever known. And, I don't really get scared like most people. Not much frightens me."

"Well, you are the grim reaper," he said, teasing me with a shiver. Then his eyes traveled slowly over me, apparently taking in the sights.

"Stop gawking at what you can't have," I said, grabbing my cup and heading to the kitchen.

"Just checking out the package deal. You do sweats proud for a girl named Charles."

I couldn't help but laugh as he got up and strode to the door. He opened it then hesitated.

"Is there anything else on your mind?" I asked.

He looked back at me, a mischievous sparkle in his eyes. "Besides the fact that I could make a meal out of you?"

The air crackled with Reyes's anger. I had to wonder if Garrett did that on purpose. Maybe he was figuring out how all this otherworldly stuff worked.

"Cannibalism is frowned upon, buddy."

"Are you going to report me for sexual harassment?"

"No, but I will grade you," I said, rinsing out my cup.

He winked then closed the door.

After a moment, I asked, "Are you going to stay in my apartment and sulk all night?"

In an instant, Reyes was gone. Guess that answered that.

I plopped down at my computer to get a little research in before hitting it with Bugs Bunny. I'd had my comforter-slash-security blanket since I was nine. We'd been through a lot together, including Wade Forester. I was in high school. He was in the school of hard knocks, which taught its students much more about procreation than high school did. Bugs was never the same.

Back to my demon problem. If I couldn't see the darned things, how was I supposed to fight them? Then again, if I *could* see demons, how was I supposed to fight them? I hadn't missed the references Reyes let slip about my going up against evil incarnate. I needed info, the 411 on everything demonic.

I did a search on how to detect demons and received a slew of no help-whatsoever for my effort. Everything that loaded onto my screen was about as useful as dental floss in a plane crash, from demonic possession being the underlying cause of ADHD to video games with scary demon overlords. But a few pages in, I found a site that looked almost relevant. Ignoring the fact that the owner's name was Mistress Marigold, I waded through legend and lore, biblical and historical references, until I came to a page titled "How to Detect Demons." Bingo.

And Mistress Mari was really helpful. She had a list of demon-detecting tricks, from throwing salt in their eyes—which firstly required my seeing them and secondly held the faintest hint of lawsuit when I inevitably blinded some poor schmuck I thought was possessed—to keeping a careful eye on plants when a questionable individual walked into a room. Apparently, a demon's presence would wilt the poor suckers before they knew what hit them. I glanced around my apartment. Damn my love of fake dying plants. Maybe I could get a cactus.

The one thing M&M didn't talk about was the fact that no one could actually *see* demons. In the end, she was about as much help as a BB gun in armed combat.

Just as I went to exit out of the site, two words caught my attention. There, in the middle of a mundane paragraph about a demon's supposed allergy to fabric softener, was a highlighted link that said *grim reaper*. Me! Well, this was exciting. I clicked on the link. The page that popped up had only one sentence just above an Under Construction warning, but it was an interesting sentence.

If you are the grim reaper, please contact me immediately.

Okay. That was new.

Chapter Eight

IS IT SEXY IN HERE OR IS IT JUST ME?

—T-SHIRT

I woke up at four thirty the next morning—also known as five minutes past ungodly—and lay in bed, wondering why in the name of Saint Francis I'd woken up at four thirty in the morning. There were no dead people hovering over me, no global catastrophes looming near or clothes being thrown at my face, yet my reaper senses told me something was wrong.

I listened for the phone. If anyone had the *cojones* to call me before seven, it was Uncle Bob. But no one was calling. Not even nature.

With a sigh, I turned onto my back and stared up into the darkness. With both Janelle York and Tommy Zapata dead, I got the feeling whoever was behind the murders wasn't looking for information. In fact, if I had to take a slightly educated guess, I would say information was exactly what the killer wanted suppressed.

Something happened at Ruiz High twenty years ago, something

other than underage drinking. And at least one person wanted it kept quiet. So much so, he was willing to murder to keep it that way.

Reyes was consuming a good portion of my random access memory as well. Could he really be the Antichrist? 'Cause that would just suck. Maybe he was right. Maybe everyone had it wrong. Admittedly, it was a tad hard to get past the fact that he was the son of the most evil being ever to exist. But that didn't make him evil. Right? Would he really lose his humanity if his corporeal body died? Nobody said he had to follow in his dad's footsteps. But the thought of him dying, now, after all this time.

At some point, I had to stop and ask myself why I was so intent on finding his body, and the answer was ridiculously simple. I didn't want to lose him. I didn't want to lose any chance of having a life with him, which was rather moot, since he'd have to go back to prison and all. But there it was in all its glory. The truth. In many ways, I was as callous and self-serving as my stepmother.

Wow. The truth really did hurt.

Regardless, I had to find a new pool of resources. My dead friends were not really helping. He did have a sister, sort of. And he had a very good friend. If anyone knew where Reyes would stash his body, surely it would be one of them.

I decided to give up on the lure of a decent night's sleep, get some coffee, and contemplate what to do next in my unending quest for the god Reyes. Mayhap I would query Mistress Marigold, ask her WTF?

Having been born a grim reaper, I was quite used to the departed popping in and out of my life at any given moment. I'd grown rather accustomed to the momentary jolt of adrenaline their sudden presence elicited, especially when a fifty-foot-drop-to-solid-concrete popped in for marital advice. But for the most part, my fight-or-flight response tended to hang back, blend into the background, and let me decide for myself if I should resort to fisticuffs or run screaming. So when I dragged my half-asleep body out of bed to seek the elixir of life often referred to as java, the fact that two men were lounging in my living room barely registered on my Richter scale.

I did pause, however, giving them a once-over, then a twice-over—mostly because they weren't dead—before heading for the coffeepot. I definitely needed a kick start before dealing with two men I highly suspected of breaking and entering. A third guy who resembled André the Giant stood barricading the front door. If my best friend Cookie came barreling through it anytime soon, he was going to have one hell of a headache.

I turned on one of the low-wattage lights under my counter so as not to blind myself—thus giving my adversaries an unfair advantage—and headed for my date with Mr. Coffee. André was staring at my derriere. Probably because I was wearing boxers that had JUICY written across the ass. I could have thrown something on, but it was my apartment. If they wanted to enter uninvited, they'd have to deal, same as everyone else who entered my little slice of heaven uninvited.

I scooped coffee into the filter as my guests watched, pushed the ON button, then waited. My new maker brewed much faster than my old one, but it would still be an awkward three minutes. I rested my elbows on the snack bar to study my visitors.

One of the men—I assumed he was the higher-up—sat on my club chair, his jacket off, gun in plain sight. He looked about fiftyish with graying brown hair, a crisp cut neatly combed, and dark eyes to match. He was busy studying me with a genuine curiosity lining his face.

The man beside him, however, the dangerous one, didn't seem to have a curious bone in his body. He was about my height with black hair and the youthful, sand-colored skin of his Asian ancestry. He stood on guard, almost at attention, his muscles taut, ready to strike should the need arise. I couldn't tell if he was a colleague or a bodyguard. He wore no shoulder holster like his friend, which meant he didn't need a gun to protect himself or his colleagues. A fact I found oddly disturbing.

André just looked like a big bear. I was certain he needed a hug, but he had a gun as well. All this muscle and metal for little ole me. I felt important. Illustrious. Majestic. Or I would have, had my ass not said "Juicy."

In contrast, my visitors were quite the dapper gentlemen. Dressed for success, and well suited to charcoal gray. I thought about suggesting they steer clear of anything in a rouge, but not everyone took kindly to fashion advice from a chick in a T-shirt and boxers.

After lacing my coffee with just enough cream and sugar to turn it the color of melted caramel, I strolled to the overstuffed sofa across from boss man, sank into it, then leveled my best death stare on him.

"Okay," I said after taking a slow, gratifying sip, "you got one shot. Make it good."

The man tipped his head in greeting before allowing his eyes to drop to the letters on my T-shirt. I hoped the saying didn't give him the wrong impression of me. NERDY didn't quite encompass the image I wanted to project. Had it said BADASS INCARNATE . . .

"Ms. Davidson," he said, his voice sure, calm. "My name is Frank Smith."

That was a big fat lie, not that it mattered. "'Kay, thanks for coming. Come back when you have more time to catch up." I rose to show them out. The deadly one tensed, and I had a sneaking suspicion he wasn't only there to protect boss man. Damn. I hated torture. It was so torturous.

"Please sit, Ms. Davidson," Mr. Smith said, after staying his man with a gesture.

With an annoyed sigh, I obeyed, but only because he said please. "So, I know your name and you know mine. Can we get on with this?" I took another slow sip as he studied me.

"You have an amazing sense of calm." His expression turned serious. "I have to admit, I'm a bit impressed. Most women—"

"—have enough sense to lock themselves in their bedrooms and call the police. Please don't mistake an underactive sense of self-preservation with intelligence, Mr. Smith."

The deadly one worked his jaw. He didn't like me. Either that or my use of big words intimidated him. I decided to go with that.

"This is Mr. Chao," Smith said, noting my interest. "And that's Ulrich."

I glanced over my shoulder. Ulrich nodded. All things considered, they were quite cordial. "And you're here because?"

"I find you quite fascinating," he answered.

"Um, thanks? But really, a text would have sufficed."

With a slow grin, he took note of every expression, every gesture I made. I got the distinct feeling he was studying me, assembling a baseline so he would later be able to tell if I was deceiving him or not.

"I've done quite a bit of research on you," he said. "You've led an interesting life."

"I like to think so." I decided to hide behind my cup, to obscure part of my response to his questions. While the eyes gave away a lot, the mouth betrayed even the best liars. This way, he would only be able to tell if I was half-lying. That'd teach him.

"College, the Peace Corps, and now a private investigations business."

I counted on my fingers. "Yep, that about sums it up."

"And yet everywhere you go, things—" He looked up, searching for the right words before returning his gaze to me. "—tend to happen."

I consciously stilled, tried to dilute my response, to muddy the waters, so to speak. "That's the thing about things. They tend to happen."

An appreciative smile crept across his face. "I would expect nothing less from you, Ms. Davidson. As you, by now, would expect nothing but brutal honesty from me."

"Honesty is nice." I glanced at Mr. Chao. "Though brutality is un-necessary."

With a soft laugh, he crossed his legs and sank farther into his chair. "Then honesty it is. It seems you and I are looking for the same person."

I let my brows arch in question.

"Mimi Jacobs."

"Never heard of her."

"Ms. Davidson," he said, casting a shameful glance from under-neath his lashes. "I thought we were being honest."

"You were being honest. I was being professional. I can hardly talk about my caseload. PIs have this weird code-of-ethics thing."

"True. I commend you. But might I add that we're on the same side?"

I leaned forward, making sure my point was clear. "The only side I am ever on is that of my clients."

He nodded in understanding. "So, if you did know where she was—"

"I wouldn't tell you," I finished for him.

"Fair enough." He inclined his head to the side, indicating average, dark, and deadly with a nod. "But what if Mr. Chao were to ask?"

Damn. I knew it would come down to torture. I tried not to clench my teeth, tried not to let my eyes widen even that fraction of a milli-meter that constituted an involuntary reflex, but it happened anyway. He had me dead to rights. He knew I was concerned. But I also had a few tricks up my sleeve if it came to that. If nothing else, I would go down swinging.

I looked at him and said, matter-of-fact, "Mr. Chao can bite my ass."

As if made of stone, Mr. Chao's expression remained utterly blank. I got the feeling he would enjoy torturing me. And call me sentimental, but damn it, I liked bringing joy to the world.

"I've upset you," Smith said.

"Not at all. Not yet, anyway." I thought about Reyes, about how he seemed to show up anytime I was in danger, but would he now? He was mad at me, after all. "If there is one thing I can promise you, it's the fact that you'll definitely know when I'm upset." I eyed him a moment then asked, "Am I lying?"

Smith studied me a long moment then raised his palms in surrender. "I told you, Ms. Davidson. I've done my research. I was hoping we could be friends."

"So you break into my apartment? Not a good start, Frank."

He pinched the bridge of his nose and chuckled. I was really beginning to like him. I would probably go for the groin, bring him to his knees before Chao got to me. Then I'd be toast, but like I said, I would go down swinging.

After he sobered, he leveled a pointed gaze on me. "Then may I insist that you drop your investigation? For your own safety, of course."

"You certainly may," I said, flashing my biggest, brightest smile. "Not that it'll do you any good."

"The organization I work for will not take your sparkling personality into consideration should you get in their way."

"Then perhaps I should show them my darker side."

He seemed almost regretful as he watched me. "You are a unique creature, Ms. Davidson. I just have one more question." It was his turn to lean in, a mischievous grin widening across his face. "Are you nerdy or juicy?"

I needed a new wardrobe.

A loud thud had us all turning toward Ulrich. But he turned as well and looked over his shoulder. The door swung open again and slammed into his rock-solid back, eliciting another loud thud. Then another, and another, on and on until Cookie finally stopped and shouted, "What gives?" Then we heard grunts as she tried to push past the obstacle that was blocking her entrance.

Ulrich looked back at Smith in question. Smith, in turn, looked at me.

"It's my neighbor."

"Ah, Cookie Kowalski. Thirty-four. Divorced. One child, female," he said, his way of letting me know he had indeed done his homework. "Let her in, Ulrich."

Ulrich stepped to the side, and Cookie came barreling through the door, her momentum too great to stop on a dime. After a near head-on collision with my snack bar, she screeched to a halt and looked around.

"Hey, Cook," I said cheerfully. When she only glanced from man to man, I added, "These are my new friends. We're really hitting it off."

"They have guns."

"Well, there is that." I rose and took the coffee mug out of her hands to fill it. Our mutual admiration for that little jolt of heaven every morning had helped us bond the moment we met three years ago. Now it was a staple. "I have to admit," I said, looking at Smith, "I'm not convinced our relationship will be a lasting one."

Cookie had yet to take her eyes off them. "Because they have guns?"

"We were just leaving," Smith said, rising and shrugging into his jacket.

"Do you have to go? For realsies?"

He smiled, apparently choosing to ignore the sarcasm dripping from my every word, and nodded as he strode past.

"You forgot to mention who you're working for, Frank."

"No, I didn't." He offered an informal salute before closing the door.

"He was nice looking," Cookie said, "in a James Bondy kind of way."

"That's it. I'm getting you a male blowup doll for Christmas."

"Do they have those?" she asked, intrigued.

I had no idea. But the thought made me giggle. "Why are you here at this hour?" I asked, slightly appalled.

"I couldn't sleep, and I saw your light on."

"I guess we'll get an early start, then." We clinked our coffee mugs together, toasting God knows what.

Since we'd once again hit the showers before the butt crack of dawn—separately, of course, though I did have the company of Dead Trunk Guy, which was getting really, really old because it was difficult to shave my legs with goose bumps—Cookie and I found ourselves strolling to the office with the sun just barely peeking over the horizon. Oranges and pinks burst across the sky, winding around smoky clouds to herald the arrival of a new day. And it was going to be beautiful. Until I tripped and spilled coffee on my wrist.

"Mistress Marigold?" Cookie asked as I bit back a curse. She seemed intrigued and a little repulsed.

"I know, but she knows something. I know it. And when I know what she knows, we'll all know a little more. Knowledge is power, baby."

"You're doing that weird thing you do."

"Sorry. I just can't seem to help myself. My brain is freaking out. Two predawn mornings in a row. It doesn't know what to think, how to act. I'll have a talk with it later. Perhaps get it into counseling."

"Hopefully, we'll have those class rosters this morning and I can start searching Mimi's classmates, see if any of them have met with similar fates."

"You mean death?"

"Pretty much," she said.

We took the outside stairs to the office. While I made a beeline for the coffeepot to prep for the day, Cookie checked the fax machine.

"They're here," she said excitedly.

"The class rosters? Already?" That was fast.

Cookie turned on her computer and plopped down in front of her desk. "I'm going to do some hunting, see what I come up with."

The front door to Cook's office opened, and a hesitant head popped in. "Are you open?" a man asked. He looked about sixty turned sideways as he was.

"Sure," I said, inviting him in with a wave. "What can we do for you?"

He straightened and entered, followed by a woman about the same age. He wore a dark blue blazer and reminded me of a sportscaster, his gray hair perfectly combed. And she wore an only-slightly-out-of-date khaki pantsuit that matched her light hair. A cloud of grief, thick and palpable, followed in their wake. They were hurting.

"Are either of you Charley Davidson?" the man asked.

"I'm Charley."

He gripped my hand like I was humanity's last hope. If that were the case, humanity was in a lot of trouble. The woman did the same, her fragile hand a shaking mass of nerves. "Ms. Davidson," the gentleman said, his expensive cologne wafting toward me, "we're Mimi's parents."

"Oh," I said, surprised. "Please, come on back." I gestured for Cookie to join us, then led them to my office. Ever efficient, she grabbed a notepad to take notes.

"You must be Cookie," the man said. He took her hand.

"Yes, sir, I am, Mr. Marshal." She took the woman's in turn. "Mrs. Marshal. I'm so sorry about everything."

"Please, call me Wanda. This is Harold. Mimi has told us all about you."

Cookie's smile wavered between appreciation and horror before she gestured for them to sit. I'd have to get the lowdown later.

I pulled up a chair for her, then settled behind my desk. "I don't guess you know where she is?" I asked, taking a wild-assed shot.

Harold's eyes met mine, his gaze sad but knowing. I could feel the helplessness roll off him, but he had a sense of hope as well, one that Mimi's husband, Warren, didn't. I had a sneaking suspicion he might know more than the average bear. "I'll pay anything, Ms. Davidson. I've heard good things about you."

That was different. People rarely had good things to say about me, unless "certifiable nutcase" had finally shed its bad rep. "Mr. Marshal—"

"Harold," he insisted.

"Harold, I read people pretty well—it's part of what I do—and you seem more than just hopeful that Mimi is all right. You seem almost expectant, as if you know something no one else does."

The couple glanced at each other. I could see the doubt in their eyes. They were wondering if they could trust me.

"Let me see if I can help," I offered.

With a hesitant nod, he gave me the go-ahead.

"Okay. Mimi started acting strange a few weeks ago, but she wouldn't tell you what was bothering her."

"That's right," Wanda said, clutching her handbag in her lap. "I tried to get her to open up when she came for her visit—she brings the kids for an overnight stay on the first of every month—but . . . she just . . ." Her voice cracked, and she paused to dab at her eyes with a tissue before looking back at me. Her husband covered her hands with one of his.

"But she told you something. Maybe it seemed strange at the time, but when she disappeared, you put it together."

Wanda gasped. "Yes, she did, and I didn't understand . . ." She'd trailed off again.

"Can you tell me what she said?"

She lowered her lashes, reluctant. I could feel a desire to trust me radiate out of her, but whatever Mimi had said had her doubting everything. Everyone.

"Wanda," Cookie said, leaning forward, her expression filled with concern, "if there is any one person on this planet I would trust with my life, it is the woman sitting across from you right now. She will do everything humanly possible—and even a little inhumanly—to get your daughter back safely."

That was about the sweetest thing Cookie had ever said about me. We'd have to talk later about the inhumanly comment, but she meant well. She totally needed a raise.

"Go ahead, sweetheart," Harold coaxed.

Wanda's breath hitched and she swallowed hard before speaking. "She told me she'd made an awful mistake a long time ago and that she did something horrible. I argued with her, told her it didn't matter, but she insisted that all mistakes had to be paid for. An eye for an eye." She looked up at me, her expression one of such desperation, it broke my heart. "I don't want her to get into trouble. Whatever she did, or thinks she did, it was a mistake."

"That's why we're hoping she disappeared of her own accord," Harold added. "That she planned this and that she's safe."

"But she would never leave Warren and the kids without an extremely good reason, Ms. Davidson. If she did so, it's because she felt she had no other choice."

Harold nodded his head in unison with his wife's. I was glad they didn't suspect Warren. They seemed to trust him implicitly. But I felt they should know what was happening. "I'm sorry to have to tell you this, but Warren is being questioned."

Wanda pursed her lips sadly as Harold spoke. "We know, but I promise you, he had nothing to do with this. If anything, Mimi was trying to keep him out of it."

"Cookie and I think this might stem back to something that happened in high school."

"High school?" Harold asked, surprised.

"Did she have any enemies?"

"Mimi?" Wanda scoffed softly. "Mimi got along with everyone. She was just that kind of girl. Warmhearted and accepting."

"Too accepting," Harold said. He glanced at his wife before continuing. "We never really cared for her best friend. What was her name?"

"Janelle," Wanda said, her expression hardening slightly.

"Janelle York?" I asked. "They were best friends?"

"Yes, for a couple of years. That girl was wild. Too wild."

After a quick glance to give Cookie a heads-up, I scooted forward and said, "Janelle York died in a car accident last week."

Their shocked expressions confirmed they'd had no idea. "Oh, my heavens," Wanda said.

"And did you know Tommy Zapata?" In small towns, everyone seemed to know everyone. Surely they'd known our dead car dealer.

"Of course." Harold nodded. "His father worked for the city for years. Landscaping and whatnot, mostly at the cemetery."

This was going to sound bad, but again, I needed them to know. I needed to find out what was going on. "Tommy Zapata was found dead yesterday morning. Murdered."

Their shock morphed into disbelief. They were genuinely stunned.

"He was a year older than Mimi," Harold said. "They went to school together."

"I don't understand what's happening," Wanda said, her voice laced with despair. "Anthony Richardson died last week, too, Tony Richardson's boy. He committed suicide."

Cookie scribbled down the name as I asked, "Did he go to school with Mimi as well?"

"He was in her class," Harold said.

Someone was cleaning house, tying up loose ends, and Mimi was obviously on his radar. Surely the Marshals knew something. Surely something had happened in high school that would pinpoint the root of all of this.

"Mr. and Mrs. Marshal, when Mimi was in high school, she moved from Ruiz to Albuquerque to live with her grandmother. Why?"

Wanda blinked back to me, her brows furrowed in thought. "She'd had a fight with Janelle. We just figured she wanted to get away."

"Did she tell you they had a fight?"

"No," she said, thinking back. "Not really. They were best friends one day and enemies the next. They just seemed to drift in different directions."

"We were not upset by that fact," Harold added. "We'd never approved of Mimi's friendship with her."

"Did anything happen in particular to cause the rift?"

They glanced at each other and shrugged helplessly, trying to think back.

"Whatever happened," Wanda said, "it caused Mimi to go into a deep depression."

"We would catch her crying in her room," Harold said, his voice despondent as old memories, painful memories, resurfaced. "She stopped going out, stopped eating, stopped bathing. It got to the point where she would claim to be sick every morning, beg us not to send her to school. She missed almost three weeks straight at one point."

Wanda's face saddened with the memory as well. "We took her to a doctor, who suggested we schedule an appointment with a counselor, but before we could arrange it, she asked to move to Albuquerque with my mother. She wanted to go to Saint Pius."

"We were thrilled that she was getting interested in her studies again. She was always a straight-A student, and Saint Pius is an excellent school." Harold seemed to need to justify his letting her move away. I was sure they didn't take the decision lightly.

Wanda patted his knee reassuringly. "Quite honestly, Ms. Davidson, as bad as this will sound, we breathed a sigh of relief when she left. She completely turned around when she got here. Her grades improved, and she excelled in extracurricular activities. She was her old self again."

Cookie was scribbling notes as the Marshals talked. Thank goodness. My handwriting sucked.

"From what you've told me," I said, "it sounds like her worries in Ruiz were based on more than a falling-out with her best friend, like Mimi was being bullied, possibly even threatened. Or worse," I added reluctantly. Rape was a definite possibility. "Did she mention anything? Anything at all?"

"Nothing," Wanda said, alarmed with my conclusion. "We tried to get her to talk about what was bothering her, but she refused. She started to turn hostile every time we brought it up. It was so unlike her."

Warren had used those exact words to describe Mimi's behavior before she disappeared. *So unlike her.*

"We should have been more diligent," Harold said, his voice brimming with guilt. "We just assumed it was Janelle. You know what high school is like."

I did indeed.

Chapter Nine

UPON THE ADVICE OF MY ATTORNEY,
MY SHIRT BEARS NO MESSAGE AT THIS TIME.

—T-SHIRT

Two hours later, Cookie and I sat in her office, marveling at what we'd found via the class rosters and the Internet. In the last month, six former students of Ruiz High had either died or gone missing. The casualties included a murder, a car accident, two apparent suicides, an accidental death by drowning, and a missing person: Mimi.

"Okay," Cookie said, studying her list, "every one of these people not only matriculated from Ruiz High, but they had all been within one or two grades of one another."

"And we could be missing someone. We don't have any married names on the women."

"I'll have to run a check on those," she said.

"Considering there were only about a hundred students in the entire high school, the odds of something like this happening by chance are astronomical. There has to be another connection. I doubt our guy is out to just kill every kid he went to high school with. If he were a serial killer, there would be a pattern, similar deaths in a contained area, most likely. Whoever is behind this is trying to make them look like accidents or suicides, for the most part."

"Maybe Warren's threatening Tommy Zapata offered the guy an opportunity to kill two birds with one stone, Tommy and Mimi, while shifting the suspicion to Warren," Cookie said.

"And since the others were ruled accidental, someone is getting away with murder."

"You know," Cookie said, studying the roster again, "Mimi's name isn't on here. This roster must be from after Mimi moved."

"Okay, let's do this," I said, thinking aloud. "You search the Ruiz police records for anything amiss from the time Mimi moved, working backwards to about a month or two prior. Although the odds are against it, something could have landed on the sheriff's radar."

"Got it. I'll also run a check on the married names of some of these women, just in case."

"And while you're at it," I said, piling on the work, "you might call and see if you can get an earlier roster."

"Yep, already have that down. Hey, what are you going to do?"

Reyes had a sister in a screwed-up, kidnapped kind of way. When Kim was two, she had been dumped on Earl Walker's doorstep by a drug-addicted mother mere days before the woman died of complications due to an HIV infection. I could only hope that had Kim's mother known what kind of monster Earl Walker was, she would never have left her daughter with him, suspected father or not. And while Walker didn't sexually abuse her as I'd feared, he did the next best thing. He used her to control Reyes. He starved her to get what he wanted out of him. And what he wanted from Reyes was all kinds of evil.

"I'm going to go talk to Reyes's sister, Kim."

Cookie's expression transformed to one of hope. "Do you think she knows where he might be?"

"Sadly, no, but it's worth a shot."

"Are you going to contact Mistress Marigold?" she asked with a teasing grin. " 'Cause that if-you're-the-grim-reaper thing is just too weird."

"Tell me about it. And I haven't decided yet."

"How about I do it for you? Holy cannoli," she said, glancing at the roster again.

"What?" I hopped up to read over her shoulder.

"Mimi went to high school with Kyle Kirsch. I just made the connection."

"The congressman? The same congressman who recently announced his plans to run for a seat in the U.S. Senate?"

"Yes. His first name is Benjamin. It's listed as Benjamin Kyle Kirsch. The *Benjamin* threw me. He must go by his middle name."

I leaned in, leveled a pointed stare on her. "The same congressman who announced his plans to run for the U.S. Senate *one month ago*?"

Cookie's jaw fell open. "Holy cannoli," she repeated.

She had a way with words.

A congressman. A freaking congressman. Somebody, and I wasn't naming any names, but somebody had at least one major-ass skeleton in his closet. Like King Kong major. A skeleton he didn't want to escape. Possibly 'cause nothing was scarier than giant skeletons running amok. And my money, all forty-seven dollars and fifty-eight cents, was on Kyle Kirsch. Congressman. U.S. Senate hopeful. Murderer.

Then again, it could all be some wild coincidence, some bizarre chain of events that just happened to revolve around a group of teens from

Ruiz, New Mexico, and a man who just happened to announce his candidacy around the same time his classmates started dropping like fruit flies in September. And I could be crowned Miss Finland before the year was out.

Now, thanks to Kyle Kirsch, I had one more conundrum wreaking havoc on my innards. What the bloody heck did this guy do? Unless he'd partaken in ritualistic sacrifice to a dark overlord or had been an Amway rep at any point in his life, I really couldn't justify his murdering innocent people.

He had to go down. Preferably hard.

I pulled into Kim Millar's Pueblo-styled apartment complex and knocked on her turquoise door.

"Ms. Davidson," Kim said when she opened the door, her eyes wide with worry. She grabbed my wrist and pulled me inside. "Where is he?" Her auburn hair was pulled back into a harried ponytail, and dark circles lined her silvery green eyes, making them look large and hollow. She'd looked fragile the first time I met her. Now her porcelain exterior seemed on the verge of shattering.

I took her hand into mine as she led me to a beige sofa.

"I was hoping you could tell me," I said when we were settled.

The glimmer of hope she'd been hanging on to tooth and nail fled, placing a hairline fracture in her aura. A grayness descended, a misty overcast darkening her eyes.

I didn't know how much to tell her. Would I want to know if my sibling were essentially committing suicide? Damn straight I would. Kim had a right to know what her pigheaded brother was up to.

"He's very mad at me right now," I said.

"So, you've seen him?"

I realized how hard their arrangement must be on her. They had a zero-contact contract. Reyes didn't want her hurt because of him ever again, and she refused to be the leverage that got Reyes hurt in turn.

No one, not even the state, knew what she was to him. Though not actually blood related, they were siblings through and through, and I had a feeling Reyes would come un-superglued if he knew I was talking to her.

"Kim, do you know what he is?"

Her brows worked themselves into a delicate knot. "No. Not really. I just know that he's very special."

"He is," I said, scooting closer. Not that I was about to tell her who he really was. What he really was. "He is very special and he can leave his body."

She swallowed hard. "I know. I've known for a long time. And he's very strong. And fast."

"Exactly. And when he leaves his body, he's even stronger and much faster."

With a gentle nod, she let me know she was following.

"For that reason," I told her, hoping I wasn't about to break her heart, "he has decided to let his corporeal body pass away."

Her red-rimmed eyes blinked in stunned silence before my meaning sank in. When it did, a hand shot up to cover her mouth and she stared at me in disbelief. "He can't do that," she said, her voice airy with grief.

I squeezed the hand still nestled within mine. "I agree. I need to find him, but he won't tell me where his body is. He's . . . injured," I said, sidestepping the truth. She didn't need to know how dire the situation was. How much time he didn't have.

"What? How?"

"I'm not sure," I lied. "But I have to find him before it's too late. Do you have any idea where he might be?"

"No," she said, her voice breaking as tears ran freely down her face. "But the U.S. marshal said he's in a lot of trouble."

My blood turned cold in my veins. Nobody, not even the state, knew Kim was Reyes's pseudo-sister. She was completely off the grid. No contact. Reyes had insisted. And there were absolutely no records whatsoever that would connect the two. None that I knew of, anyway.

"And now this," she continued, unaware of my distress. "Why? Why would he just leave me like this?"

Either that marshal was very good at his job, or he had inside information. I was going with the inside information because nobody was that good.

I wrapped her hand into both of mine. "Kim, I promise I will do everything possible to find him."

She pulled me into a hug. I squeezed gently, afraid she would break in my arms.

I zigzagged through traffic on I-40, wondering how the bloody hell a U.S. marshal found out about Kim. The thought left me boggled. She was not easy to track down, and I had known about her beforehand. There just weren't many people on Earth who did.

My phone sang out in the ringtone version of "Da Ya Think I'm Sexy?" I opened it, knowing Cook was on the other end. "Charley's House of Ill Repute."

"You need to pick me up," she said.

"Are you trying to sell your body on the street again? Haven't we talked about this?"

"A few weeks before Mimi moved to Albuquerque, a girl from her class disappeared."

I downshifted and eased Misery into the right hand lane to exit. "What happened?" I asked above the honking and shrill screams. "Need therapy much?" I yelled back.

"Nobody knows. They never found her body."

"That's interesting."

"Yeah. It's really sad. According to a five-year-old news article, her parents still live in Ruiz. They've lived in the same house for twenty years, hoping their daughter would find her way home."

That was quite common, actually. When parents had no closure, they were often afraid to move for fear of their child returning to find them gone. "Closure, good or bad, is not overrated."

"And guess what her name was."

"Um—"

"Hana Insinga."

Ah. The *Hana* part of Mimi's message on the bathroom wall at the diner. "Be there in two," I said before hanging up.

"Here's the address," Cookie said, climbing into Misery.

"Who's going to man the phones?" I didn't really care, but somebody had to give Cook a hard time, damn it. It may as well be me.

"I'm forwarding all the calls to my cell." She had a stack of papers, file folders, and her laptop with her as well.

"It's a good thing. I'm not paying you to tour the country like a rock star."

"Do you pay me? I feel more like a slave."

"Please, you're way cheaper than a slave. You provide your own shelter, pay your own bills."

Ever the multitasker, she stuck her tongue out and clicked her seat belt at the same time. Show-off. I saw an opening and floored it onto Central. Timing was everything. The files flew off Cookie's lap. She grabbed for them then yelped. "Paper cut!"

"That's what you get for sticking your tongue out at me."

Sucking on the side of her finger, she cast a vicious scowl before pulling her hand back to get a good look at her injury. "Does workman's comp cover paper cuts?"

"Do chickens lay snowballs?"

Just over two hours later, we were sitting in a charming living room in Ruiz with a lovely woman named Hy who served us Kool-Aid in tea-cups. Hy looked part Asian, most likely Korean, but her husband had been a blond-haired, blue-eyed pilot in the navy, and they'd met when he was on leave in Corpus Christi, Hy's hometown set in the deep south of Texas. And she had the twang to prove it. She was tiny with a round face and graying black hair cut in a bob along her jaw. The white blouse and khaki pants she wore helped her seem younger than her years, though she looked as delicate as the teacups she handed us.

"Thank you," I said when she offered me a napkin.

"You want cookies?" she asked, her Texas accent at odds with her Asian features.

"No, thank you," Cookie said.

"I'll be back." She rushed off to the kitchen, her flip-flops padding along the carpet as she walked.

"Can I just take her home with me?" Cookie asked. "She's adorable."

"You can, but that's called kidnapping and is actually frowned upon by many law enforcement agencies." I chuckled into my teacup when she offered me a scowl. Apparently, paper cuts made her grumpy.

Hy trod back with a plate of cookies in her hands. I smiled as she handed it to me. "Thank you so much."

"Those are good cookies," she said, sitting in a recliner opposite us.

After placing one on my napkin, I handed the plate to Cook. "Mrs. Insinga, can you tell us what happened?"

We'd told her we were here to ask her about her daughter when we introduced ourselves on her doorstep. She was kind enough to let us in.

"That was so long ago," she said, withdrawing inside herself. "I can still smell her hair."

I put my cup down. "Do you have any idea what happened?"

"Nobody knows," she said, her voice faltering. "We asked everybody. The sheriff interviewed all the kids. Nobody knew anything. She just never came home. Like she disappeared off the face of the Earth."

"Did she go out with a friend that night?" The pain of her daughter's disappearance resurfaced, emanated out of Hy. It was disorienting. It made my heart pound, my palms sweat.

"She wasn't supposed to leave. She snuck out her window, so I have no idea if she was with anyone."

Hy was struggling to control her emotions, and my heart went out to her.

"Can you tell me who her closest friends were?" I asked. Hopefully we would at least leave with a few contacts.

But Hy shook her head in disappointment. "We'd lived here only a few weeks. I hadn't met any of her friends yet, though she did talk about a couple of girls from school. I'm not positive they were close—Hana was painfully shy—but she said one girl was very nice to her. After Hana disappeared, the girl moved to Albuquerque to live with her grandmother."

"Mimi Marshal," I said sadly.

She nodded. "Yes. I told the sheriff they were friends. He said he questioned all the high school children. Nobody knew anything."

I couldn't ethically bring up Kyle Kirsch's name. We had no evidence that he was actually involved in any of this. But I decided to approach it from a different angle. "Mrs. Insinga, were there any boys? Did she mention a boyfriend?"

Hy folded her hands in her lap. I got the feeling she didn't want to think of her daughter in that way, but the girl was at least fifteen when she disappeared, possibly sixteen. Boys were very likely a big part of her thought process.

"I don't know. Even if she had liked someone, she would never have told us. Her father was very strict."

"I'm so sorry for your loss," I said when she mentioned her husband. She'd told us he died almost two years ago.

She bowed her head in gratitude. After steering the conversation to greener fields, asking about her hometown and what she missed most about Texas, Cookie and I stood and walked to the door.

"There is something else," she said as she led us out. Cookie was already headed toward the Jeep. "We began getting money deposited directly into our account every month about ten years ago."

I stopped and turned to her in surprise.

"I didn't want to believe it had anything to do with Hana, but I have to be honest with myself. Why would anyone give us money for no reason?"

That was a good question. "Is it transferred from another account?"

She shook her head. Of course not. That would have been too easy. "It's always a night deposit," she added. "One thousand dollars cash on the first of every month. Like clockwork."

"And you have no idea who it is?"

"None."

"Did you talk to the police?"

"I tried," she said with a shrug, "but they didn't want to waste the resources to stake out either bank location when there really wasn't a crime being committed. Especially since we refused to file any charges."

I nodded in understanding. It would have been a hard point to argue with the authorities.

"My husband and I had tried a few times to see who was doing it, but if we were staking out one location, the deposit was made at the other. Every time."

"Well, it's certainly worth looking into. May I ask you one more question?" I asked as Cookie turned at the end of the sidewalk to wait for me.

"Of course," she said.

"Do you remember who the sheriff was at the time of Hana's disappearance? Who the lead investigator was?"

"Oh, yes. It was Sheriff Kirsch."

My heart skipped a beat, and a soft gasp slipped through my lips. Hoping my surprise didn't alarm her, I said, "Thank you so much for your time, Mrs. Insinga."

After we left, Cookie and I sat in Misery—the Jeep, not the emotion—a stunned expression on both our faces. I'd told her who the sheriff on the case had been.

"Let me ask you something," I said to Cookie as she stared into space. "You told me Warren Jacobs is wealthy, right? He writes software programs for businesses all over the world."

"Mm-hmm," she hummed absently without looking at me.

"Then why does Mimi work?"

She turned to me then, her expression incredulous. "Just because her husband is wealthy, she can't have a job? A little independence? An identity of her very own?"

I held up a palm. "Cook, can we put the feminist movement on hold for a moment? I'm asking for a reason. Hy told me someone has been making night deposits, putting a thousand bucks into her banking account on the first of every month for the last ten years. Harold and Wanda said Mimi visits them religiously. She brings the kids and stays the night with them on the first of every month. Cook, Mimi is making those deposits."

She took a moment to think about what I said, then lowered her head and nodded in resignation. "But that would mean she feels guilty about something, wouldn't it?"

"It would seem that way. But people feel guilty for different reasons, Cook. It doesn't mean she did anything wrong."

"She told her mom she'd made a mistake. Charley, what happened?"

"I don't know, sweetheart, but I'll find out. And I'd bet Garrett's left testicle, it has something to do with our Senate hopeful."

I turned the ignition key. Misery roared to life as Cookie stared out her plastic window.

"Do you have any idea what this means?" she asked.

"Besides the fact that Kyle Kirsch is most likely a murderer?"

"This means that we are about to bring felony charges against a United States congressman. A man who is hoping to be our next senator. A hometown hero and pillar of the community."

Was Cookie having second thoughts because he was a bigwig? Bigwigs had to follow the constructs of the law just like medium-sized and little wigs.

She turned a starry-eyed expression on me, her aura brimming with a fiery passion. "God, I love this job."

Chapter Ten

By the time we stopped at the Mora County Sheriff's Department, Cookie was on fire. She was taking charge of the investigation and doing a pretty good job of it, too. If you didn't count the dropped calls, the slow Internet access, and the lashing from an eighty-year-old woman claiming she was Batman when Cookie dialed a wrong number. Cook was getting a little annoyed with my repeated impersonation of the woman. She really shouldn't have put her on speakerphone if she didn't want to reap the consequences.

After we climbed out of Misery, she pushed past me and said, "You're messing with my flow."

I tried not to giggle—well, not real hard—and asked, "Didn't you have surgery for that?"

Unfortunately, the current head honcho was out on business. The clerk told us the former sheriff, Kyle Kirsch's dad, was now living in

Taos with his wife, working in security, so we didn't get to chat with him this go-around. But the clerk did give us copies of everything they had on the Hana Insinga case for the low cost of a round-trip ticket to a dark and dank basement and the shuffling of a few file boxes.

The clerk herself was too young to remember the case, which was a bummer. But I was sure with all the hoopla going on underneath all the hoopla going on up top, we would ruffle a few feathers just for the asking. If nothing else, we would get Kyle's attention, and fast. Of course, between the fake FBI agents and my new friends from this morning, we may already have revealed our secret hideout and nefarious plans to stop Kyle Kirsch from taking over the world.

I sort of got off on making bad guys sweat. Which was not unlike my love of making good guys sweat, just by very different means.

On the way back, we had to pass through Santa Fe, which gave me the perfect opportunity to have a one-on-one with Neil Gossett, a deputy warden at the prison there. Actually, he'd called while we were en route and pretty much insisted that I stop and see him. He had his assistant schedule us an appointment, as prisons were big on appointments.

"Do you think Neil will give you access to that kind of information?" Cookie asked when she got off the phone with her daughter, Amber. From the sound of things, Amber was having a good time at her dad's, which seemed to ease Cookie's concerns. "I mean, aren't visitation records kind of confidential?"

"First things first," I said as we drove to the prison. I took out my cell and called Uncle Bob.

"Oh," Cookie said, tapping keys on her laptop. "Your Mistress Marigold just answered my e-mail."

"Really? Did she mention me?"

She chuckled. "Well, I asked her what she wanted with the grim reaper, and she said, and I quote, 'That is between me and the grim reaper.'"

"She did mention me! She's nice."

Cookie nodded as Uncle Bob answered, his tone brusque. "What have you got?"

"Besides great boobs?" I asked.

"On the case."

He was so testy. "Do you want the whole shebang or just a partial?"

"All of it, if you don't mind."

Thus I spilled our entire case for the next ten minutes while Cookie did some research on her laptop. She barked out a few details from time to time, apparently dissatisfied with my rendition of *Kyle Kirsch Takes Over the World: The Musical.*

After a long pause that had me wondering if he'd finally succumbed to his blocked arteries, I heard some huffing and puffing and a door squeak just before he whispered, "Kyle Kirsch?"

"Where are you?"

"I'm in the freaking john. You can't go around saying shit like that out loud in public. Kyle Kirsch?"

"Yep."

"*The* Kyle Kirsch?"

His synapses must have been misfiring. "I have to go to prison now. Let me know when your software has been updated, and we'll chat."

"Okay, wait," he said just before I hung up, "let me look into the missing-girl case. Don't do anything rash."

"Me?" I was only a little offended.

"You stir up more hornets' nests than a twelve-year-old boy with a baseball bat. You're like Lois Lane on crack."

"Well, I never. So, do you have anything else for me?"

"No."

"Darn."

"Are you going to stay out of trouble?"

"What? K-shhhhhh. You're breaking up." I hung up before he could say anything else. If I was Lois Lane, then Reyes Farrow was definitely my Superman. I just had to find him before the kryptonite demons finished what they started. The fact that I hadn't seen him all day did not escape me. Did he die? Was he already gone? The mere thought caused a crushing weight to push against my chest. I breathed in deep, calming breaths as we pulled up to the main gate of the prison.

"According to the write-up in the paper, Janelle York is survived by a sister, but she lives in California now," Cookie said.

"Wow, that's a bit far to drive. We're here to see Neil Gossett," I told the guard.

He scanned a clipboard, his posture like a soldier at attention. "Do you have an appointment?"

"Sure do," I said, letting a flirtatious smile slide across my face. "My name is Charlotte Davidson, and this is Cookie Kowalski."

A grin threatened the corners of his mouth. He was too young to be jaded and too old to be naïve. A darned good age, in my book. "I only have you down, Ms. Davidson. Let me call up," he said.

I widened my smile, which in my experience could open more doors than an AK-47. He forced his mouth to stay grim, but his eyes smiled right back before he turned and strode to the guardhouse.

"Maybe Janelle's sister came down for the funeral," Cook added. "I'll call the funeral home, try to get the contact information."

As she typed in a search for the number, the guard walked back to us, the grin still trying to push past the harsh line of his mouth. "You're clear. If you'll just follow this road around," he said, pointing to the right, "it'll take you right to his building."

"Thank you."

Ten minutes later, I found myself once again in the state pen. Well, in Neil Gossett's office in the state pen, anyway. Cookie stayed in the outside office to do some more research and make a few calls. She was so productive. I heard Neil coming. He greeted Cookie then stopped to speak with Luann, his administrative assistant, the one who met us at the entry and eyed me like I was out to kill her puppy every time I visited. She had pale skin that revealed every bit of her forty-plus years and contrasted starkly with her short black hair and dark eyes. I'd always wondered why she glared at me every time I came in. Never enough to ask, but still. All I got in the way of emotion was distrust, but thinking back to the first time I'd met her, I didn't even feel that until she found out I was there about Reyes. She seemed almost protective of him, and I suddenly wondered why.

Neil thanked Luann, then started toward his office. He and I went to high school together, but our paths had rarely crossed. Mostly 'cause he was a jerk. Thank goodness prison life had matured him. And because of an incident that happened when Reyes first arrived here ten years ago, which involved the downfall of three of the deadliest gang members the prison population had to offer in about fifteen seconds flat, Neil knew a smidgen about Reyes. Whatever Neil saw left an impression. And he knew just enough about me to believe anything I said, no matter how crazy it sounded. That had not been the case in high school, where I had been called everything from schizoid to Bloody Mary—which was odd 'cause I was rarely covered in blood. But now I could use his newfound faith in my abilities to my advantage, and I was counting on that trust to make my case.

He stepped into the office and cast a knowing glance my way before settling behind his desk. Neil was a balding ex-athlete who still had a fairly nice physique despite his obvious fondness for libation.

"Have you seen him?" he asked, getting right to the point. He was going to be all business for the time being. That worked. And it made sense that he wanted to know where Reyes was, him being the deputy warden of the prison Reyes essentially escaped from and all.

"I was going to ask you the same thing."

"You mean, you don't know where he is?" He sounded agitated.

"No." I tried to sound agitated right back.

He breathed a weary sigh, dropping his deputy warden persona, and his next statement surprised me more than I wanted to admit. "We have to find him, Charley. We can't let the U.S. marshals get to him first."

Alarm spiked within me. "What makes you say that?"

"Because it's Reyes Farrow," he said, his tone sardonic. "I've seen what he's capable of. I've seen what he can do with pure skill. God only knows what he could do with an actual weapon in his hands." He scrubbed his face with his fingers, then added, "You know better than I do what he's capable of."

He was right. I knew a hell of a lot more than he did. If Neil was anywhere near the town of Clued In, he'd really be freaking.

"They won't be able to stop him," he continued, his expression dire. "And when they can't stop him, they will use any means necessary to bring him down."

The thought of Reyes being taken down by a group of marshals clamped and glued my teeth together for a long moment, squeezed the chambers in my heart shut. Reyes said it himself. In human form, he was vulnerable. He could be taken down. I wasn't sure how far Neil would go to help me help Reyes, but I was about to find out. And if I wanted him to trust me, I'd have to trust him. Though the truth, the whole truth, and nothing but the truth would be too much and could do more harm than good, Neil had seen enough to know Reyes was a different animal. I would use that knowledge to reel him in while leaving those pesky little facts that incorporated words like *grim* and *reaper* and *son of Satan* for another day.

"I don't know where he is," I said, taking a gargantuan leap of faith, "but I do know he's being hunted and he's hurt."

What I said startled him. While his expression remained impassive—a true connoisseur of the ever-popular poker face—his emotions lurched at my statement, and I knew in that moment I'd found a true ally. He wasn't angry with me for having such knowledge about Reyes or hungry for the hunt that would bring his prisoner down. No visceral lust shimmered in his eyes at the thought of the accolades he would receive for capturing an escaped convict.

No, Neil was afraid. He seemed to genuinely care for Reyes. The realization surprised me. Neil worked with hundreds of convicts on a daily basis. Surely compassion fatigue played a big role in his profession. One would think frustration alone would keep any feelings of true concern at bay. But I could feel it. I could feel the connection he had with Reyes. Maybe he'd formed an attachment after having Reyes as a prisoner for so long, knowing all the while he was something more, something not entirely human. Either way, I could have kissed him on the mouth right then and there if he hadn't been such a jerk to me in high school. Relief at having Neil on my side through this, on Reyes's side, eased the tension in my stomach, if only minutely.

"How do you know he's hurt?" he asked, and I could literally feel the emotions warring within him. Concern. Empathy. Dread. They pushed forward and swirled through me like a suffocating smoke.

I blinked through it and concentrated. "I'm going to tell you something," I said, hoping that leap of faith wouldn't come to a crash landing in a cactus patch. 'Cause that shit was painful. "And you know that whole open-minded thing you've got going here?"

He hesitated, wondering what I was up to, then offered me a wary nod.

I leaned forward, softened my voice to hopefully lessen the blow. "Reyes is a supernatural entity." When he didn't react, didn't even blink, I continued. Mostly 'cause I really, really needed his help. And a little because I was curious how far I could go. How far he would go to learn the truth. "I mean, I have a little supernatural mojo myself, but I'm nothing like him."

After a long, thoughtful moment, he covered his face with his palms and looked at me through his splayed fingers. "I'm losing it," he said. Then, rethinking his verb tense, he added, "No. I take that back. I've lost it. It's a done deal. There's no hope for me now."

"Okey dokey," I said, shifting in my seat. I figured I'd just go along with it. No judging. No jumping to conclusions. No buying him a straitjacket for Christmas.

He pressed a button on his speakerphone.

"Yes, sir?" came the immediate response. She was good.

"Luann, I need you to have me committed ASAP. Yesterday, if possible."

"Of course, sir. Any particular program?"

"No," he said with a shake of his head. "Anything will do. Just use your best judgment."

"I'll get on it immediately, sir."

"She's a good egg," he said when Luann disconnected the call.

"She seems like it. And you're having yourself committed because?"

He scowled at me like his mental breakdown was my fault. "As much as it pains me to admit this, I believe you."

I fought to keep a relieved grin from surfacing.

"No, I mean, I *believe* believe you. As if you'd just told me you had a flat tire or it was cloudy out. Like what you said is just an everyday thing. Nothing out of the ordinary. Nothing to get worked up about."

Man, he had changed a lot since high school. And I didn't just mean the beer pooch and receding hairline. "And that's bad?"

"Of course it's bad. I work in a prison, for God's sake. Things like this just don't happen in my world. And yet, every bone in my body is accepting the fact that Reyes is a supernatural entity. I'd sooner doubt the weatherman, at this point."

"Everybody doubts the weatherman, and you're in my world now," I said with a grin. "My world is supercool. But I told you that for a reason."

He refocused on me and raised his brows in question.

"I need your help. I need to know who's been visiting Reyes."

"And you need that information because?"

"Because I need to find his body."

"He's dead?" Neil shouted in alarm. He jumped up and walked around to me.

"No, Neil, calm down." I held up my palms in surrender. "He's not dead. Or, well, I don't think he's dead. But he will be soon. I have to find his body. Like I said, he's hurt. Bad."

"And you're thinking someone might be harboring him? Someone who's come to visit."

"Exactly."

He turned and punched a button on his speakerphone again. "Luann, can you get me the names of everyone who's visited Reyes Farrow in the last year? And I need to know who he's requested be put on his visitation list, whether they were approved by the state or not."

"Would you like that information before or after I have you committed, sir?"

He pursed his mouth in thought. Making a decision, he said, "Before. Definitely before."

"I'll get them immediately."

"I just love her use of the word *immediately*," I said, vowing to introduce the concept to Cookie. "So, visitors have to be approved?"

"Yes." He sat back down behind his desk. "The inmate has to turn in anyone's name he wants to receive visitations from; then that person has to fill out an application, which is submitted to the state for approval before he or she can visit. So let's get back to this supernatural thing," he said, a tinge of mystery in his eyes.

"Okay."

"Are you psychic? Is that how you know Farrow is hurt?"

Always with the PS-word. "No. Not especially. Not in the way that you mean. I can't predict the future or tell you about the past." When he eyed me doubtfully, I said, "Seriously, I can barely remember last week. The past is a blur, like fog only blurrier."

"Okay, then what do you mean by supernatural?"

I thought again about telling him the truth, but just as quickly decided against it. I didn't want to lose him, but I didn't want to lie to him either. This was a guy who'd worked with convicted felons for over a decade. Deceivers one and all.

I studied the speckled pattern of his carpet, trying to figure out what to say. I hated the uncertainty of how much to tell someone, how much to hold back. The problem with telling people the truth was that by my doing so, their lives were forever altered. Their perspective forever skewed. Since most people would never believe a word of it anyway, I was rarely put in such a precarious position. But Neil had seen things. He knew Reyes was more powerful than any man he'd ever met. He knew I could see things others couldn't. But there was a line, a limit to what the human mind could accept as reality. If I crossed it, I would lose his cooperation and his friendship. Not that I really gave a crap about his friendship, but still.

"Neil, I don't want to lie to you."

"And I don't want to be lied to, so this whole thing should be pretty cut and dry."

With a deep sigh, I said, "If I tell you the truth . . . let's just say you won't sleep well at night. Ever again."

He tapped a pen on his desk in thought. "I have to be honest, Charley, I haven't slept all that well since your last visit a couple of weeks ago."

Damn. I knew it. I'd already screwed up his world.

"I could be wrong," he continued, "but I'm certain I would sleep better if I knew the whole story. It's the bits and pieces that are kicking my ass. Nothing is solid anymore. Nothing fits. I feel like the foundation of everything I've ever believed in is crumbling beneath my feet and I am losing my grip on what's real and what's not."

"Neil, if I tell you more, the last thing that knowledge will do is help you get a stronger grip on reality."

"Can we agree to disagree?"

"No."

"So we *are* disagreeing?"

"No."

"So we're in agreement?"

"No."

"Then let me put it this way." He leaned forward with an evil, evil grin. "If you want a gander at those visitation records, I want to know everything."

Did he just use the word *gander*? "I don't think I can do that to you," I said with regret.

"Yeah? Well, maybe I didn't tell you everything either."

My brows snapped together. "What do you mean?"

"Do you honestly think that one little story I told you about Reyes was everything?"

The first time I'd visited, Neil told me the most amazing story. He had just started working at the prison when he witnessed Reyes, a twenty-year-old kid at the time, take down three of the most deadly men in the state without breaking a sweat. It was over before Neil could even call for backup. That's when he knew Reyes was different.

"Do you think that was all there was to tell?" he asked. I half expected an evil laugh. "I have dozens of stories. Things that . . . things that are impossible to explain." He shook his head as he contemplated what I could tell was a plethora of unexplainable phenomena. I tried not to drool. "And quite honestly, Charley, I need an explanation. Call it the scientist in me," he added with a shrug of his brows.

"You sucked at science."

"It's grown on me."

He wasn't giving up. I could see the determination in his eyes. That same determination that took our high school football team to state three years in a row. Damn it.

"Tell you what," I said, slipping into negotiation mode. "You show me yours, and I'll show you mine."

"So I have to go first, is that what you're saying?"

I smiled in affirmation.

"Damn it. I always have to go first, then half the time, you girls chicken out and run away before showing me yours."

He'd clearly had too much experience in that area. "You don't trust me?" I asked, trying really hard to be appalled.

His mouth thinned. "Not even a little."

I indicated our surroundings with turned-up palms. "Dude, we're in a prison. If I don't hold up my part of the bargain, you can put me in solitary until I do."

"Can I get that in writing?"

I wanted more, needed more as much as I needed air. My appetite to learn as much as possible about Reyes was insatiable. "You can get it in blood."

After a long, thoughtful sigh, he said, "I guess blood won't be necessary. I'll give you one of the highlights." He worked his lower lip a moment before choosing. "Okay, there was this one time when I was still a guard, we'd received word that a fight was going to break out. A bad one between South Side and the Aryans. The tension was so thick that by the third day we knew something was going to happen. The men gathered in the yard, eyed each other, inched closer and closer until the shot caller of each gang was nose to nose. And right in the middle of it stood Farrow. We were surprised."

"Why were you surprised?" I asked, certain my eyes were wide with wonder.

"Because he had no affiliation. It's rare, but every once in a while, an inmate will go it alone. And he did. Quite successfully."

"So, he's in the middle of this fight?" Even though I knew Reyes was okay, my heart still stumbled at the thought.

"Smack dab. We couldn't believe it. Then men started dropping. As Farrow wound his way through the inmates, man after man fell to the ground. They just passed out." He paused, lost in thought.

"What happened next?" I asked, my voice full of awe.

"When Farrow got to the shot callers, he spoke to them. By that time, most of the others were backing off, a look of astonishment on some of their faces, fear on others. The shots glanced around, realized what was happening, then the one from South Side showed his palms and backed off. But the Aryan grew furious. I think he felt Farrow was betraying his race or something."

"They're so testy about that sort of thing."

Neil nodded. "The Aryan got in Farrow's face and started yelling. Then, before anyone knew what'd happened, he just crumbled to the ground."

I flew to my feet and laid my palms on Neil's desk. "What did Reyes do?"

He looked up at me. "We didn't know at first, but he touched them, Charley. Surveillance showed him walking through the crowd and touching them on the shoulder. And they dropped like flies."

I stood with my mouth agape probably much longer than was appropriate.

"The guards rushed in, found their weapons, searched everyone else, and put the whole place on lockdown." Neil shook his head as he thought back. "There's no telling how many lives were saved that day. Including mine."

That surprised me. "Why yours?"

He studied his hands a moment before answering. "I'm not as brave as I pretend to be, Charley. The Aryans had made a promise to come after me. I'd pissed one of them off when I put him in lockdown after he threw a tray at another inmate." Neil stared hard. "I would never have made it out of there alive. I know that. And I was scared shitless."

"That's nothing to be ashamed of, Neil." I chastised him with a glare then stated the obvious. "So, he saved your life, too."

"And I'm eager to return the favor."

"Let me ask you something," I said, a suspicion niggling the back of my mind. Reyes's best friend from high school had also been his cellmate. "His cellmate Amador Sanchez didn't happen to be affiliated with South Side, did he?"

He thought back. "Yes, actually, I think he was."

Interesting. I wondered had that not been the case would Reyes have done anything.

"I think Farrow would have stopped the fight nonetheless," Neil said, as if reading my mind.

"Why do you say that?"

"When we stormed onto the yard, I went straight for him. I wanted to make sure nobody else went after him. Partly because I didn't want him hurt and partly because I knew a little of what he was capable of. I didn't want any of my coworkers hurt either. I ordered him down and kneeled beside him as the tactical team launched tear gas into the yard. I had a gas mask on, but I leaned down to him. . . . I just had to know."

"Know what?"

"I asked him why he stopped the fight."

"What did he say?"

"At first he denied it. Said he didn't know what I was talking about, then refused to say anything else, but that could have been the tear gas."

"Then later?"

"When we were marching the men inside for lockdown, he leaned into me as he waited his turn to be searched and told me he'd seen enough war to last a thousand lifetimes."

Knowing exactly what Reyes had been talking about, I swallowed hard.

Neil fixed a curious gaze on me. "What did he mean? He's certainly never been in an actual war, and I figured you might be able to answer that one." He laced his fingers together. "I believe it's your turn."

Okay, I had to be honest with him, but I couldn't tell him everything. That wouldn't be fair to Reyes. I would tell him only what I had to. "I'm not sure how to say this," I offered hesitantly, "but Reyes has definitely seen war, tons of it." I watched Neil, studied him to gauge his reactions. "He was a general in an army for centuries, just not an army from this world."

"He's an alien?" Neil almost shouted.

"No," I said, trying not to laugh. "He's not. I can't tell you everything. . . . He's just a supernatural entity."

"That's it," he said, rising from his desk. "You're going into solitary."

He grabbed my arm and lifted me out of my chair, albeit carefully. "What? I'm telling you shit."

"No, you already told me that shit, I need new shit, shinier shit. And you're holding out."

"I am not. I just—"

"Do you know how many people I've told that story to?" He leaned down, his voice a harsh whisper, as if someone might hear. "Do you know how crazy it sounds?"

We were headed to the door. "Wait, you can't actually put me in solitary."

"Watch me."

"Neil!"

"Luann," he said when he opened the door, "get the restraints."

Cookie had been sitting in Luann's office and glanced up from her laptop, frowned in mild interest, then went back to her research.

"Okay, I give." I showed my palms in surrender. When he eased his grip, I jerked my arm out of his hand then said through gritted teeth, "But don't blame me when you start wetting your bed at night."

He smiled at Luann congenially, then closed the door. "You got one chance. If you don't make it good, you will never see the light of day again."

"Fine," I said, jabbing his chest with an index finger, "you want to play it rough, we'll play it rough. Reyes Farrow is the son of Satan." The moment I said it, the moment the words slid through my lips, I went into a state of shock. My hands flew over my mouth, and I stood for a very long time staring into space.

Reyes was going to kill me for letting a secret like that slip out. He was going to slice me into tiny pieces with his shiny blade; I just knew it. No, wait. I could fix this. I let my horrified gaze land on Neil. He seemed undecided on the solitary thing.

I dropped my hands and laughed. Or tried to laugh. Unfortunately, I sounded like a drowning frog, but I was rattled, discombobulated. "Just kidding," I said, my voice straining under the pressure of certain death. I socked him on the arm. "You know how it is when you're facing solitary confinement. You'll say the craziest things."

As I turned to sit back down—and to drop my jaw open to gawk at my own stupidity without him seeing—he said, "You're not kidding."

"Pffft," I *pffft*ed, turning back to him. "I was so kidding. Really? The son of Satan? Pffft." I chuckled again and sat down. "So, where were we?"

"How is that possible?" He walked back to his desk in a daze. "I mean, how?"

Damn it. I totally gave myself away by floundering like a carp on dry land. I stood again and leaned over his desk. "Neil, really, you can't tell anyone."

The desperation in my voice brought him back to me. He blinked up and furrowed his brows in question.

"If there was ever anything in your life that you could not tell another living soul, Neil, this is it. I don't know what Reyes would do if he found out that you knew. I mean—" I turned and paced away from him in thought. "—I don't think he would hurt you. I really don't, but there's just no way to be certain. His behavior has been . . . erratic lately."

"How is that possible?" he asked again.

"Well, he's been under a lot of stress. And torture."

"The son of Satan?"

"Are you listening to me?" I asked. Holy cow, talk about screwing the pooch. I screwed the whole litter. "You can't breathe a word of this to anyone." I'd already made the mistake of telling Cookie before I even considered the consequences. And now Neil? Why not just take out an ad in *The New York Times*? Put up a billboard on I-40? Have it tattooed on my ass?

"Charley," Neil said, coming to his senses before me. "I understand. Not a word. I know what he can do, remember? I'm not about to incur his wrath. I promise you."

With a huge sigh of relief, I sank back into the chair.

"But how is that possible?" he asked for the third time.

I offered a helpless shrug. "Even I don't have all the details, Neil. I'm so sorry I told you. It's not as bad as it sounds, really."

"Bad?" he said, astonished. "How is that bad?"

"Ummm—" I gave it a moment's thought. "—is that a trick question?"

"I happen to know he's a good person, Charley. Just because his father is, well, broiled evil on toast. Do you know what true evil is?" he asked.

I shrugged my brows.

"When Americans talk of evil, they mean it in a malicious way, cruel and brutal. But that's not what evil is. That's simply our take on it."

"What are you getting at?"

"Evil is simply the absence of good, the absence of God."

I'd never thought of it that way. "So, you know that Reyes is not evil? That he's a good person."

"Of course." He said it like I was a nincompoop. "But, seriously, he really is? You know, his son?"

"Yes," I said, regret filling me. "He really is."

"That is the coolest thing I've ever heard."

"Cool?"

Neil grinned. "Yes, cool."

"I don't understand. How is that cool?"

He reclined in his chair and steepled his fingers. "From the moment you arrived last week . . . No, I take that back. From the moment Reyes arrived in my life ten years ago, I've questioned things. I've asked myself if there really is a higher power. If heaven exists. If God exists. Part of that, I'll admit, is seeing day after day the atrocities man is capable of. But then knowing, having a glimpse of this other world, this other reality and not knowing what it was, where it came from.

But now . . ." He fixed an appreciative gaze on me. "In a word, you have reaffirmed my belief in God, Charley. I mean, think about it. If there's a son of Satan, you can be damned certain there's a Son of God."

I shook my head. "You're absolutely right. I'm just a little surprised at how well you're taking all of this."

"Think about it. Jesus loves me."

Chuckling in relief, I leaned forward and whispered, "Jesus may love you, but I'm his favorite."

He started to laugh, then paused. He studied me. For, like, a really long time.

"What?" I said, becoming self-conscious.

"If Farrow is the son of Satan, then what are you?"

"Uh-uh," I said, wagging a finger. "You gave me one; I gave you one."

He continued to study me, suddenly very curious, when Luann knocked. "Come in."

She walked in and handed him some papers.

"This is it?" Neil said in astonishment as he settled a pair of glasses on his nose.

Luann had brought him the visitation records he'd asked for. "Yes, sir. He refuses all the others."

"Thank you, Luann." After she left, he said, "Farrow has only one person on his approved-visitors list. No attorney. No advocate. Just one guy."

"Let me guess: Amador Sanchez."

"That's right. They were cellmates for four years."

"They were friends in high school as well."

"Really?" he asked, surprised. "How the hell did they end up cellmates? And remain cellmates for four years?"

How *did* Reyes manage that? He grew more intriguing by the heartbeat. "What did Luann mean, he refuses all the others?"

"Oh, the women, you know." He waved the idea off with a hand as he studied the records. "Okay, Amador Sanchez visited him the week before he was shot. He seemed to visit fairly regularly."

"What women?" I asked as he flipped through the pages.

"The women," he said without looking up. "He doesn't allow any of them to visit, so we probably don't have any records. But God knows they try. At least one or two a month." He glanced at the ceiling in thought. "Come to think of it, they usually fill out an application, try to see him regardless. We might still have copies. I'll have to check." He refocused on the papers.

"Yes, you said that. What women?" I asked again, trying to rein in the hot streak of jealousy that ripped through me.

After a long moment that had me plotting his assassination in various ways—I was up to seventeen—he glanced over the rim of his glasses. "All those women from the Web sites." His tone successfully conveyed the fact that he suddenly found me idiotic.

I began leaning toward a slow death. With lots of pain. Perhaps number four. Or thirteen. "What Web sites?"

He laid the papers on the desk and stared, his expression incredulous. Which was just rude. "Aren't you an investigator?"

"Well, yeah, but—"

"And you've been investigating Farrow for how long?"

"Hey, I just found out who he was about a week ago. Less if you go by Saturn's calendar."

"First, remind me never to hire you."

I changed my mind. It was definitely going to be number twelve. I almost felt sorry for him.

"And second, do yourself a favor and Google him."

"Google Reyes? Why?"

He laughed softly and shook his head. "Because you're in for one hell of a surprise."

I scooted forward in my chair. "Why? What are you talking about? Do women write him?" I'd heard of women who wrote to prisoners. Without conjuring any of the thousands of adjectives I used to describe those women, I asked, "Does he have pen pals?"

Neil pinched the bridge of his nose while fighting a grin. "Charley," he said, looking back at me, "Reyes Farrow has fan clubs."

Chapter Eleven

YOU CAN OBSERVE A LOT JUST BY WATCHING.
—YOGI BERRA

"You never just Googled him?"

"Well, you didn't either," Cookie said when I'd asked about Reyes. We were driving back to Santa Fe. "I just browsed official databases to find his arrest record and conviction information. And I went to the *News Journal*'s site for articles about the trial."

"And you never just Googled him?"

"You didn't either," she repeated, distressed. She was typing away on her laptop.

"Fan clubs!" I said, more than slightly appalled. "He has fan clubs. And mountains of mail."

A sharp pang of jealousy slashed through my chest, ripping a hole in it. Metaphorically. Hundreds of women, possibly thousands, knew more about Reyes Alexander Farrow than I did.

"Why would anyone create a fan club for an inmate?" Cookie asked.

I'd asked Neil that very thing. "Apparently, there are women out there who become obsessed with prisoners. They scour news articles and court documents until they find prisoners who are attractive, then they make it their mission in life to either prove that prisoner is innocent—as they all profess to be—or they just admire him from afar. Neil said it's almost like a competition for some women."

"That's just so wrong."

"I agree, but think about it. The pickin's are pretty slim for these men. Maybe women do it because they know they'll almost surely be accepted by the prisoner. I mean, who's going to reject a woman sending you love letters or going to the prison to visit? What do these women have to lose?"

Cookie cast a worried glance my way. "You seem to be taking all this exceptionally well."

"Not really," I said, shaking my head. "I think I'm in shock. I mean, holy cow, they tell stories."

Cookie seemed to be in a state of shock as well. She was surfing a site on her laptop as I drove to one Elaine Oake's house. Her eyes were wide and slightly lovestruck. "And they have pictures."

"And they tell stories. Wait, what? They have pictures?" I decided, in the interest of transportation safety, to pull to the side of the highway. I hit the hazard lights then looked over at Cookie's screen. Holy mother of banana cream pie. They had pictures.

An hour later, we stood at the doorstep of the woman I could refer to only as Stalker Chick. I mean, really? Paying guards and other inmates to get information on Reyes? To steal from him? Not that I wouldn't do the same, but I had good reason.

A tall, thin woman opened the door. Her blond hair was cut short and styled to look messy, but I doubted that a single hair on her head was not exactly where she wanted it to be.

"Hello, Ms. Oake?"

"Yes," she said, her voice holding the slightest hint of annoyance.

"We're here to ask you about Reyes Farrow."

"I have hours posted." She pointed to a sign over her doorbell. "Can you come back then?"

I fished my PI license out of my back pocket. "Actually, we're on a case. We'd really like to talk to you now, if you have a minute."

"Oh. Well . . . okay." She led us inside her humble abode, if a multimillion-dollar house with something like twelve gazillion rooms could be considered humble. Which, how could it? "I was just getting so many visitors, I had to post hours. Never a free minute." She led us to a small sitting room. "Shall I call for tea?"

Was she serious? Is that what rich people did? Called for tea? "No, thank you. I just had thirty-two ounces of sugar-free nirvana on ice."

She brushed a knuckle under her nose as if my uncouth behavior was . . . well, uncouth. "So," she said, recovering from my impudence, "what has that rascal done now?"

"Rascal?" Cookie asked.

"Reyes," she said.

Jealousy caused my muscles to spasm with her casual mentioning of Reyes's name. It was uncharacteristic of me. I rarely spasmed, and in my book, it was every woman for herself. May the best flirt win. I'd always assumed I didn't have a jealous bone in my body. Apparently, when it came to Reyes, I had 206.

I tamped the emotion down with teeth gritted and fists balled. "Have you been in contact with him any time over the last month?"

She laughed. Apparently, peasants amused her. "You don't know very much about Rey, do you?"

Rey? Could this get any worse, I thought as my eyelid twitched. "Not really," I said with my teeth still clamped together, so it was kind of difficult.

When Elaine stood and walked to a door, Cookie placed a hand on mine and squeezed. Probably to remind me there'd be a witness should I murder the woman and bury her lifeless body under her azaleas. I didn't even know azaleas could grow in New Mexico.

"Then maybe you should come with me." She opened a set of adjoining doors that led into what could only be described as a Reyes Farrow museum.

I stood with a gasp as a huge mural of Reyes met my eyes, teased me, caressed me with a fiery gaze that left me weak kneed and breathless.

"I thought you might like this," she said as I drifted out of my chair and walked aimlessly forward.

I floated into Reyes heaven, and the rest of the world fell away. The room was large with lighted display cases and framed pictures lining the walls.

"I was the first," she said, pride swelling in her voice. "I discovered him even before he was convicted. All the other Web sites followed in my wake. They know nothing about him except what I tell them to know."

Or what guards at the prison tell her to know. Neil informed me they had fired four guards over the years for selling information and pictures to this woman, all featuring Reyes Farrow. And from the looks of her house, I'd be willing to bet Elaine could have afforded a lot more. Most of the framed pictures were the same ones featured on the Web site, candid shots that guards had taken when Reyes wasn't looking. I wondered what she'd paid them to risk their jobs. And knowing Reyes, their lives.

There were even a couple of grainy ones of him in the shower. And grainy or not, that boy was hot. I leaned in to study the steely curve of his ass, the fluid lines of his muscles.

"Those are a personal favorite of mine as well."

I jumped at the sound of Elaine's voice and continued on with my perusal, calculating the odds of my getting away with breaking and entering here later to steal those. In the display cases were different items that had supposedly belonged to Reyes. From prison uniforms, a comb, and an old watch to a few books and a couple of postcards he'd apparently received. I looked closer. There was no return address on either of the postcards. Drifting farther down the case, I noticed several handwritten pages splayed along one shelf. The writing was crisp and fluid and reportedly Reyes's.

"He has gorgeous handwriting," Elaine said, her tone a little smug. She seemed to be reveling in the fact that she'd floored me. "We're still unraveling the mystery of Dutch."

I froze. Did she just say Dutch? After a long moment, I recovered, straightened, and placed my best look of nonchalance on her. Thankfully, Cookie stood behind her and off to the side, so the woman couldn't see the wide-eyed expression on her face.

"Dutch?" I asked.

"Yes." She sauntered forward and pointed. "Look closely at the script."

I bent back down and read. *Dutch*. Over and over. Every line, every word, was simply *Dutch* repeated again and again. So, what looked like a letter was actually my nickname en masse. The last page was a little different. It was an actual drawing, word art, again with the Dutch insignia. My heartbeats tumbled into each other, as if racing for a finish line.

"Do you know how old these are?" I asked after a few calming breaths.

"Oh, several years. Once Rey figured out a guard was stealing them for me, he stopped writing them."

A photograph sat at the end of the case and was quite possibly the most compelling of them all. It was a black-and-white of Reyes sitting on the cot in his cell, an arm thrown over a bent knee. He'd laid his head back against the wall, closed his eyes, and had the most forlorn expression on his face.

My chest constricted. I could understand why he didn't want to go back to prison, but I still couldn't allow him to die. Especially with what Blue had said, and Pari.

This place, this museum, was simply overwhelming. Here I thought Reyes was all mine, my little secret, my treasure to have and to hold till death did us part, and all this time he'd had hordes of women pining after him. Not that I could blame a single one, but the sting bit hard nonetheless. Cookie remained stock-still, wondering what I was going to do.

"So, you don't know who Dutch is?" I asked, fishing for more information.

"One of the guards tried to find out for me. I'd offered him a hefty sum, but by then Reyes had caught on to me and the guard was fired. Reyes is very intelligent. You know he has two degrees. Earned them in prison."

"Really? That's amazing," I said, feigning ignorance. If she figured out I knew more about Reyes than I was letting on, she would likely become a pit bull to get at it. Or she would offer me a lot of money that I wasn't sure I could turn down. Especially now that Reyes was doing his darnedest to get on my bad side. "You couldn't possibly give me the name of your current informant?"

"Oh, no. That would be a breach of confidentiality. And I've already been warned to cease and desist my exploits. I can't risk getting this person fired or myself arrested."

Did she not realize what a private investigator did? "Why did you ask me if I knew Reyes well?"

She chuckled, completely oblivious of the fact that deep down inside, I wanted her dead. "Reyes doesn't see anyone. Ever. And trust me, dozens of women have tried over the years. He gets more mail than the president. But he never reads a single one."

That made my innards happy.

"Really, this is all on the site. I try to warn newbies who visit that he won't see them or read their letters. But each and every fan thinks she will be the one he falls in love with. They have to try, I suppose. I certainly can't blame them. But of all the women who've tried, I'm the only one he's ever seen."

I could feel the lie all the way to my marrow. She'd never laid a naked eye on the man. That made my innards happy, too.

"So, how did you find out about Reyes?" she asked, finally growing suspicious of my presence.

"Oh, I'm on a case, and his name came up."

"Really? In what capacity?"

I tore my eyes off him and turned to her. "I can't really say, but I do need to ask you a few questions."

"Questions?"

"Yes. For example, do you know where he is at the moment?"

She offered a patient smile. "Of course. He's in a long-term-care facility in Santa Fe."

"Oh," I said. Cookie cast a sideways glance in my direction, encouraging me to put the woman in her place. Just a little. "Actually, he was scheduled to be taken off life support last week."

This time, she froze. I'd surprised her, and it took her a moment to recover. "I'm sorry, but that's not what my resources have told me," she said, blinking those false eyelashes repeatedly.

"Well, then, you need to find new resources. He was scheduled to die, Ms. Oake. Instead, he woke up and hightailed it out of the medical facility."

"He escaped?" she asked, her voice a high shriek. This was much more fun than I'd expected it would be. And her surprise was genuine. She had no idea where Reyes had absconded with his body. I was torn between relishing that fact and despising it. We were no closer to finding him than we were before. I'd turned back to look at his writings again as Elaine sought a chair, her legs apparently weak.

The drawing, the one that looked like art but still said my name, was actually a sketch of a building. I stepped closer and breathed in softly.

"Oh, that's an old building," Elaine said from behind me. "We don't know where it is, but we think it's somewhere in Europe."

I turned back to Cookie, gestured her my direction with the hint of a nod. Her brows slid together and she inched closer, casting cautious glances over her shoulder. When she stood beside me, she studied the drawing and gasped softly as well.

"I'll bet you're right," I said. "It looks European." Except it was in Albuquerque, New Mexico, and both Cook and I lived in it.

My gaze traveled back to the postcards. "Can I see where those postcards are from?" I asked.

Elaine was busy fanning herself. She forced her body out of the chair and went around to the other side of the display case to open it. "Do you think he'll come after me?" she asked as she handed them over.

"Why would he do that?" I asked, only slightly interested. Both postcards were from Mexico. They had Reyes's prison address, but no return address and no message whatsoever. Which was way more interesting than Elaine's sudden need to jump into panic mode.

"H-he knows who I am," she said. "He knows I've paid money to get information on him. What if he comes after me?"

"Can I keep these?"

"No!" She snatched them back.

Okay. Possessive much? "Look, here's my card," I said, handing it to her. "If he comes after you, call me. I really need to take him in." Cookie and I turned to leave.

"Wait, no, that's not what I meant." She followed us, her heels clicking along the Spanish tile. "What if he comes here to kill me?"

I stopped and eyed her suspiciously. "Is there a reason he would want you dead, Ms. Oake?"

"What? No." She was lying again. I wondered what she'd done, besides paid people to spy on him for years.

"Then I really don't see a problem." I turned again to leave.

She rushed around us and blocked our paths. "It's just, I . . . everyone . . ."

"Really, Ms. Oake, I have a case to solve."

"Here," she said, handing over the postcards. "I'll give you these. I have them scanned into my computer anyway. I just need you to call me the minute he's found."

I glanced at Cookie, my face the epitome of reluctance. "I don't know. That would be kind of like your breach of confidentiality."

"Not if my life is in danger," she squeaked. "I'll hire you."

My earlier conclusions were wrong. This was totally interesting. "First, I already have a client. I could hardly take on another concerning this case. That would be a conflict of interest. And second, why would your life be in danger? Are you afraid of Reyes Farrow?"

"No," she said with a nervous grin. "It's just that, well, we're married."

Cookie dropped her purse and tried to catch it midair. In the process, she knocked over a vase. When she lunged for the vase, she slipped on the tile and overturned an entire table. A lovely handblown piece of glass flew in my direction, and all I could think as I caught it was, *Really? Again?* We were going to have to practice muscle control.

"Married?" I asked after the table crashed to the ground. Cookie righted it and replaced the glass orb, a sheepish expression on her face. "You're going to have to be completely honest with me, Ms. Oake. I happen to know Reyes is not married."

Elaine eyed Cookie a long moment before answering. "It was a silly argument," she said, refocusing on me, "and, well, I sort of let people believe that we were married. One of the other site owners said she and Reyes were writing each other, which was a lie and I knew it, then another said they were dating—dating!—so, I upped the ante, so to speak. They think we've been married for six months."

After a melodramatic rolling of my eyes, I refocused on her. "Why would they even believe you?"

"Because, I . . . well, I sort of forged a wedding license. It's all on the Web site. Well, not the fact that I forged it."

Now that I had a bargaining tool—namely, her desire to live—I turned back to the display cases. "Just what are you offering in exchange for my services?"

"John Hostettler," I said into the phone as Cookie and I drove into Santa Fe to grab a bite to eat.

Neil Gossett was on the other end. "He's one of my guards."

"And he's one of Elaine Oake's informants."

"No shit?"

"No shit." He would, of course, need some kind of proof, but that wasn't my problem. "And I forgot to bring up something else odd."

"Besides you?"

"You're funny. I ran into Owen Vaughn the other day. He's a city cop now. What the hell did I do to him?"

He sighed. "You mean when he tried to maim you with his dad's SUV?"

"Yes."

"I'd always wanted to ask you the same thing. He never told us. Just got really weird."

"You mean weird like you?" I asked.

"You're funny."

Cookie and I ate at the Cowgirl Café before leaving Santa Fe. We ate in silence, studying the papers and pictures we'd obtained from Elaine—especially the grainy ones—both of us stunned speechless. We drove home the same way.

"I'm going to go through these files on the Hana Insinga case," Cookie said when we pulled into the apartment complex.

"Okay, I'm going to run to the office and check messages and, I don't know, do something productive."

"Okay." We were both in another world, both worried about Mimi and Reyes.

As I crossed the lot to Dad's bar, I realized I had slipped into a bit of a depression. Who needed PMS when I had RAF? Mood swings apparently came with the job. But I couldn't get past the fact that I had not seen Reyes all day. Not once. And his wounds, from what little I saw, were mortal, even for a supernatural being.

Had he died in the night while I slept in the warmth and comfort of my bed? It had been a fitful sleep, but still, I wasn't being tortured. Or maybe he'd died while I was having coffee with the Three Stooges this morning, or while I was having tea and crumpets with Stalker Chick.

Seriously, how long could he have lasted? He healed faster than the everyday human, but I couldn't imagine him surviving even a few hours with those wounds, much less days.

I cut through the bar to get to my office. Dad was nowhere in sight. I thought about seeking him out, but a couple of guys turned my way the minute I stepped inside, frosty mugs in hand, so I ducked into the stairwell before they could act on their nonexistent chance to hit on me. I checked messages and e-mail before typing in the words that had brought me so many sleepless nights, so many heated dreams and illicit fantasies. I clicked on SEARCH, and approximately three seconds later, a list of Web pages loaded, each resplendent with the name *Reyes Farrow.*

I needed to find out how much they knew. Did they know what he was capable of? Did they know his background? Did they know what his idea of the perfect date was?

The hours passed in a fog.

In the end, I came to two conclusions. One, none of them had a clue who or what Reyes really was. And two, there were some lonely-ass women in the world. I went from being consumed with jealousy to simply incredulous and even a little sympathetic. It's not as if I could blame them. Reyes was nothing if not magnetic, his gaze in each and every picture hypnotic, a born heartbreaker. No wonder hordes of women desired him, craved him despite his criminal record.

Remarkably, there was one tidbit of information that pretty much stunned me speechless. It was a good thing Mr. Wong didn't talk much. Or, well, ever. I felt astonished beyond the ability to converse. Under a tab on Elaine Oake's Web site titled "Unconfirmed Rumors" was one section that explained a lot.

> It is an unconfirmed rumor, and quite frankly we here at Reyes Farrow Uncensored are skeptical, that our beloved Rey has a little sister. A thorough search of state and county records would indicate to the contrary, but we all know what a secretive man our guy is. As always with Reyes Farrow, anything is possible.

She sounded like a gossip columnist. Surely that was how the U.S. marshals found out about Reyes's sister, Kim, but how the hell did Elaine get that information?

I was actually a little surprised that none of the stories Neil told me had leaked onto any of these sites. I was certain Elaine would have paid a small fortune for such things. Maybe Neil had covered it up as much as possible. I'd have to ask him about that.

Before I knew it, the clock struck three. Metaphorically. I hadn't stayed up this late since that *Twilight Zone* marathon a few weeks back. I shuddered to think about how many cups of coffee I'd drowned my sorrows in over the last few hours. Which would explain the uncontrollable shaking I was experiencing.

Hoping sleep would not evade me completely, I decided to see if Dad was still downstairs before I hit the sack. He usually went home between midnight and two, but it never hurt to check. Either way, I could raid the kitchen. A quick bite might help me sleep.

Maybe it was that fifth cup of coffee, or even that sixth, but I had a strong sense something was not quite right at Calamity's when I got downstairs. The place was pitch black, as it should have been, but a light filtered into the room from underneath Dad's office door. My stomach was a little queasy as I weaved around tables and barstools. Maybe I'd just hunt down some soup when I got home instead.

I opened the door. Dad's light was on, but he wasn't there. As mundane as that sounded, a jolt of adrenaline rushed straight to my heart. Because now I could feel a twitch of fear emanating from the kitchen. I could feel disorientation and dread as well, but the fear overrode everything else. I ducked behind the bar and grabbed a knife before making my way around to the kitchen door. The closer I got, the more overwhelming the fear became. With the warmth that surrounded the emotion, the texture and scent of honey-lemon cough drops, I knew it was Dad. And he was doing it all on purpose. Almost as if he were warning me to stay away. But he didn't know I could feel other people's emotions. Did he?

I had no choice but to ease as quietly as I could through the swinging doors that led into the pitch-black kitchen. Once inside, I inched into a corner to allow my eyes to adjust. Why I didn't carry night-vision goggles on my person twenty-four/seven, I would never know.

Before I could get my bearings, the lights flickered on and I suddenly found myself just as blind as I'd been before. I raised a hand to block the blast of light and squinted into a stark whiteness. That's when a beefy arm came into view with a knife much longer than my own. It rocketed toward me so fast, my one and only thought consisted of probabilities. If my calculations were correct, taking into account the weight behind the swing, and the length and glistening sharpness of the blade thrusting toward me, this was going to hurt.

Chapter Twelve

YEAH, BUT WHAT IF LIFE HANDS ME PICKLES?
—BUMPER STICKER

At the very moment I was supposed to die from a razor-sharp blade rushing toward my heart, a spike of adrenaline coursed through my veins, and the world seemed to slow around me. I looked at the knife as it inched closer. I looked at the man's face, thick and furious, a snarl twisting his features. Oh yeah, he wanted me dead. Which sucked, 'cause I didn't even know him. Then I glanced to the side. My father sat gagged and bound on the kitchen floor. Another dose of adrenaline spiked when I saw the blood streaming down the side of his head, his eyes wide with fear, but not for himself. For me.

The knife was closing in. I looked back just as the tip broke the skin over my heart. Before I could second-guess myself, I ducked and the world came rushing back. The man, unable to stop his forward momentum, flew toward the wall behind me. As he flew past, I raised my own knife, and between his own lumbering weight and the force of my upward thrust, I sliced into his throat.

He stumbled over some boxes and launched headfirst into the wall, knocking himself senseless and dropping the knife. I kicked it under the stainless steel prep tables and rushed to my father's side, all the while keeping a wary eye on my would-be murderer. The man grabbed his throat as blood spewed through his fingers. He made gurgling sounds, too.

I felt kind of bad, but he started it.

About that time, I heard sirens. Maybe Dad had been able to trip the silent alarm before the man disabled him. I tried to get the gag off, but there were just so many layers—the man liked him some duct tape— and I realized I was coming down off an incredible high when the world darkened and I lost my balance, falling into the cabinet beside me. I took in a lungful of air, righted myself onto the balls of my feet again, then went in search of the end of the duct tape, which was apparently as elusive as the end of a rainbow. It didn't help that my fingers were shaking uncontrollably.

I heard a couple of uniforms burst in through the back door. "We're in here," I called out, studying my attacker. He was flailing like a fish on dry land, trying to squirm over the boxes and hold on to his severed jugular at the same time.

The cops entered the kitchen cautiously before one of them rushed to my side to help. The other one called for backup and an ambulance.

"That man tried to kill me," I said to the cop, appalled. I didn't know the officer. He was young, probably a rookie.

He glanced over his shoulder as he unwound the duct tape from my father's head, then back at me. "I think you won," he said with a wink.

For a moment, pride swelled within me. "Yeah. I did win." I refocused on Fish Man. "Come at me with a really pointy blade, will ya."

The other cop had handcuffed the man and was now applying pressure to his neck with a dish towel. I hoped he wouldn't bleed to death. I'd never been the direct cause of someone dying.

The rookie managed to get the tape unwound.

"I'm so sorry, sweetheart," my dad said, his voice hoarse.

I hugged him to me as the cop continued his quest to release my dad. Duct tape galore decorated almost every inch of him. Dad and I were both shaking and teary eyed.

"Are you hurt?" I asked him just as Uncle Bob stormed into the room, an EMT team on his heels.

"Leland," he said as he knelt down. He leveled a long, cold stare on Fish Man, then turned back to us. "We didn't get the signal."

"What signal?" I asked, becoming very wary.

My dad glanced at the floor as Ubie explained. "Caruso has been threatening your dad for a couple of weeks now, which is pretty much in direct violation of his parole. We'd placed men to keep watch, but we'd also worked out a signal if he should show up."

"He sort of surprised me," Dad said, his voice sarcastic.

"Oh, me, too," I said, confirming Dad's statement. "He totally surprised me, too."

"I knew you would come out of this okay," Dad said as the rookie cut his arms free. His expression turned to one of a wary awe. "How did you do that?"

I glanced at Ubie self-consciously. "Do what?"

"The way you moved," he said, his voice airy, "it was . . . inhuman."

"Okay, let's get him something to drink, shall we?" Uncle Bob said to the rookie.

"Absolutely, sir." The rookie glanced at me with a frown as he left. Great. Half the police force already thought I was a freak. I guess it was time to recruit the other half as well.

"Leland," Ubie scolded as he helped him to a chair, "you can't say shit like that in front of other people."

"You didn't see it," Dad said, and I suddenly felt like the ugly duckling again. I thought I had shed that persona years ago. Apparently not. "The way she moved, it was like—"

"—like a well-trained private investigator?" Ubie offered.

Dad blinked, tried to focus on something else, but his gaze kept coming back to mine, a million questions in his eyes.

The EMTs were already pushing Fish Man out, their movements precise but quick—he must not have had much blood left—and a second team surrounded Dad and me. I realized when one of them started to poke around Danger and Will Robinson, I had a long gash in my chest from when I had ducked with a knife protruding from me. Next time, I would dislodge the knife before ducking.

"That's going to need stitches," said the EMT.

Fortunately, Cookie charged through the police barrier about that time and drove me to the hospital. What did Dad mean, he knew I would be okay? His frightened expression as I was being attacked would never have led me to believe such a thing. But it was the way he said it, like he'd been calculating the odds long before the actual event. And the look on his face. He'd never looked at me that way before. It was disturbingly similar to the way my stepmother looked at me every time we saw each other.

Still, that wasn't the only thing niggling at me. For the first time in my life, Reyes didn't show up to save it. Which meant he was either really pissed or dead.

After a long wait, I sat in the ER with superglue holding me together, though the attending actually called it SurgiSeal. The cuts seemed to already be fusing, surprising more than one doctor and several nurses to boot. Thus, no stitches. Just superglue.

"I smell supergluey," I said to Cook as she waited beside me. The freaking paperwork took way longer than the two minutes it took for them to glue me back together.

"I just can't believe this," she said, upset that Dad hadn't told me about the parolee threatening his life. "If nothing else, he should have warned you for your own protection, instead of trying to keep you blissfully unaware that a madman was out to kill him and his entire family."

Uncle Bob walked over to us. "How are you feeling?"

"Oh, don't even," Cookie said, her mouth a thin line of disappointment. "You are just as much a part of this as that man." She pointed to Dad, who lay asleep on the other side of the emergency room, his head bandaged. He had to stay the night for observation. Probably a good thing. Cookie was on a rampage.

My stepmother looked up when Cookie started in on Uncle Bob. Really. The man didn't stand a chance.

"You of all people should have warned her." Cookie poked him in the chest to emphasize her point, and I just knew Ubie would come unglued. I glanced around for the tube of superglue just in case.

Instead, he bowed his head in regret. "We just didn't think—"

"Exactly," she said and took off in search of coffee.

"Dude, could you hold it down?" the man on the bed next to me asked. "I got me a nine in my head and it's pounding like a son of a bitch."

I didn't doubt it. I'd never had a nine-millimeter in my noggin, but it probably hurt. I looked back at Uncle Bob. "Is that why you had Garrett following me?"

He pursed his mouth. "That was the number one reason."

"And the other was just in case Reyes Farrow happened to show up."

"That would be number two."

I stood, disgusted with men at the moment. "So, you could tell Swopes but not me?"

"Charley, we didn't know if this guy would ever show or if he was just full of shit. He blamed your dad for the death of his daughter. She died when Caruso crashed his car during a police chase. Your dad was the one doing the chasing. When he got out of prison, he started calling your dad, telling him he was going to kill his entire family, so we put tails on all of you. Your dad didn't want you to worry."

He may as well have ended that statement with *your pretty little head.* That was the most chauvinistic thing I'd ever heard come out of Ubie's mouth.

I stood toe to toe with him, furious that every man I was even remotely close to had been lying to me for the past two weeks. I tiptoed and whispered, "Then fuck you all."

Paperwork or no paperwork, I left to look for Cookie, also known as my ride home. As I walked past the elevators, the doors opened, and there stood my sister. She sighed and stepped out. "So, are you going to live?" she asked.

"As always."

"How's Dad?"

"The doctor said he'll be fine. He has a concussion and a few bruised ribs, but nothing's broken. He's going to be out for a good while."

"Fine. I'll come back in the morning." She turned and strode down the hall slightly ahead of me, as if she didn't want to be seen with me in public. In that case, I'd give her good reason.

With a gasp, I grabbed my chest, collapsed against the wall, started hyperventilating. Trying to fake hyperventilation without actually hyperventilating was not as easy as one might think.

Gemma turned back and glared. "What are you doing?" she asked through clenched teeth.

"It's all coming back to me," I said, throwing a hand over my head in agony. "When I was in the hospital getting my tonsils out, I tried to escape. The fluid leaking from my severed IV led them right to me and I was recaptured."

Worried someone might be watching, she did a quick perimeter check before refocusing on me. "You've never had your tonsils out. You've never even been in a hospital overnight."

"Oh." I straightened. That was embarrassing. "Wait! Yes, I have, when Aunt Selena died. I stayed with her, held her hand all night."

She rolled her eyes. "Aunt Selena is a missionary in Guatemala."

"Seriously? Then who was that old lady?"

After a loud and lengthy sigh, she started for the exit again and spoke over her shoulder. "Probably your real mother, because we cannot possibly be related."

I smiled and trotted after her. "You're just trying to make me feel better."

Chapter Thirteen

DON'T GO BUYING TROUBLE.
IT'S FREE AND IT KNOWS WHERE YOU LIVE.

—T-SHIRT

The next morning, I slept until nine, which was understandable since I didn't go to bed until well past five. My mental state was still leaning toward fluffy when I searched out the coffeepot.

"Morning, Mr. Wong," I said, my gravelly voice sounding as sleep-deprived as I felt. As I was reaching for the coffee can, I noticed a note lying on Mr. Coffee. He was so romantic. I paused to open the first fold.

What do you call a PI who doesn't give up?

Hmmm. Several options came to mind. Aggressive. Dependable. Stalwart. Somehow I doubted any of those would be the answer they were looking for. I opened the last fold of the note.

Dead.

Dang. I should have stuck with monosyllabic guesses. Criminals weren't keen on big words.

As enlightening as that was, I had work to do—so many lives to destroy, so little time—and new locks to buy. Having approximately three minutes to spare after I turned the pot on to brew, I decided to pee. But as I walked past my front door, someone knocked. I stopped, looked around, waited. After a moment, another round of raps echoed in my apartment.

I tiptoed toward the door, vowing that if they were already there to kill me, I was going to be really pissed. I peered out the peephole. Two women stood there, Bibles in hand. Please. That was such a bad disguise. They were probably expert assassins, sent to put two in my head before noon.

But there was only one way to find out. I slid the chain on my door into place and cracked it open. The older woman smiled and started in right away. "Good morning, ma'am. Have you noticed how the world is plagued with bad health right now?"

"Um—"

"That disease and illness have spread to every corner of God's green earth?"

"Well—"

"We're here to tell you that it is not always going to be that way." She opened her Bible and thumbed through it, giving me an opportunity to speak.

"So, you're not here to kill me?"

She paused, crinkled her thin brows at me, then glanced at her friend before saying, "Excuse me? I don't think I understand."

"You know, to kill me. To assassinate me. To put a gun to my head—"

"I think you have us confused with—"

"Wait! Don't leave." I closed the door to unchain it. When I swung it open, they took a wary step back. "So, you're not assassins?"

They both shook their heads.

"You're Jehovah's Witnesses?"

They nodded.

This could be a good thing. Maybe they knew something I didn't. "Perfect. Let me ask you," I said as the younger one in back let her gaze wander over my attire, which consisted of a Blue Oyster Cult T-shirt that advised people not to fear the reaper and a pair of plaid boxers, "as Jehovah's Witnesses, what exactly have you witnessed?"

"Well, if you'll take a look . . ." The older one was rifling through her Bible again. "As a witness, it is our obligation to separate ourselves from wrongdoers, to purge evil persons from among us, and—"

"Right, right, that's great." I interrupted her with a wave of my hand. "But what I really need to know is, can you see, or *witness*," I said, adding air quotes for effect, "demons?"

They glanced at each other. The younger one spoke this time, her shoulders straightening in confidence. "Well, demons are simply fallen angels who sided with Satan, the ruler of the world in these end times. It is our responsibility to remain chaste and faithful—"

"But have you ever seen one?" I said, interrupting again. At this rate, I would never get invited to a service.

"Seen one?" the older woman asked hesitantly.

"Yes. You know, in person?"

They shook their heads. "Not physically, no. But if you'll look at this passage—"

Man, she liked that Bible. I'd read it and could definitely understand its appeal, but I didn't have time for this. My three minutes were probably up as it was. "No offense, but—and I mean this in the most respectful of ways—you're not helping." I closed the door, a little saddened by the confusion on their faces. I just thought that maybe they had happened upon a demon or two on their treks through the city. If I was alone in this, if Reyes was really gone, I needed a way to detect them. But surely Reyes wasn't gone. He couldn't be.

I continued my trek to the outhouse and realized the old saying was right: Denial really wasn't just a river in Egypt.

After dragging my boneless body into the office an hour later, I stood studying Cookie's attire. She was wearing a purple sweater with a red scarf thrown around her neck. I tried not to worry.

She looked up from her computer. "Okay, I got a hold of Janelle York's sister. She was on her way home, but she was kind enough to answer a few of my questions."

Cool. "And?" I asked, pouring myself a cup. Because sometimes three just isn't enough.

"She said that Janelle got heavily into drugs after Mimi moved to Albuquerque. Her parents thought it was because they'd had a falling out, but when I asked about Hana Insinga, the sister said she'd tried to talk to Janelle about the disappearance when Hana went missing. Janelle, Mimi, and Hana were in the same grade. But Janelle was outraged when she asked, told her never to mention Hana's name again."

"Wow, that's a volatile response to such an innocent question."

"That's what I thought. And Warren's cousin Harry who always asks for money?"

"Yeah."

"Dead end. He's been in Vegas for over a month, working at a gambling casino."

"As opposed to a nongambling casino?"

"I also spoke to our murdered car salesman's wife," she continued, ignoring me.

"You've been busy."

"She had the exact same story as Warren. Her husband started to withdraw, to get depressed. She said he worried constantly and told her the oddest thing."

I raised my brows in question.

"He told her that sometimes our sins are too great to be forgiven."

"What the hell did they do?" I asked, thinking aloud.

Cookie shook her head. "Oh, and she thought the same thing that Warren did. She thought her husband was having an affair. She said large sums of money went missing from their savings. I assured her he wasn't having an affair."

I cast her a teasing glance. "Just because he wasn't having an affair with Mimi doesn't mean he wasn't having one at all."

"I know, but that woman was a wreck. No need to make her suffer more. He wasn't having an affair. I'm sure of it. Speaking of wrecks, how are you doing?" she asked, concern drawing her brows together.

"Wreck?" I balked, feigning offense. "I'm good. The sun is shining, the superglue is holding. What more could a girl ask for?"

"World domination?" she offered.

"Well, there is that. Have you talked to Amber today?"

She sighed heavily. "It seems my daughter is going camping with her dad this weekend."

"That's cool. Camping's fun," I said, careful to keep my tone light. I knew why the thought upset her, but chose not to mention it. When Amber stayed with her father, Cookie went into a kind of depressed state. Come Friday, that would have changed. Now her happy fix would have to wait until after the weekend. I felt for her.

"I guess," she said, her voice noncommittal. "You look tired."

I picked a couple of file folders off her desk. "So do you."

"Yeah, but you were almost murdered last night."

"*Almost* being the pertinent word in that independent clause. I'm going to do some research and then I'll probably go talk to Kyle Kirsch's parents in Taos. Can you call and make sure they'll be home?"

"Sure." She dropped her gaze and started thumbing through some papers. "He lived," she said as I turned to go to my office. "Your attacker. After five pints of blood." I paused midstride, restrained the emotion that threatened to surface, then continued into my office. "Oh, and I'm going with you to Taos."

I figured she'd want to go. Just before I closed the door, I leaned out and asked, "You didn't happen to leave me a note, did you? On Mr. Coffee?"

Her brows furrowed. "No. What kind of note?"

"Oh, it's nothing." I didn't figure Cookie would threaten my life, but I had yet to find out if she was a black widow. She did have a dead guy in her trunk, and one could never be too certain these days.

I sat down at my desk, my thoughts cloudy with a chance of rain. He lived. That was good, I supposed, but he would always be a threat. I almost wished Reyes had been there, had taken him out, or at least incapacitated him so he would never be able to hurt anyone again. An age-old question surfaced despite its uselessness. Why did monsters like that get to live when good people died every day?

A soft knock brought me out of my musings as Cookie poked her head into my office. "Somebody's here to see you," she said, as though annoyed.

"Male or female?"

"Male. It's—"

"Does he look like a Jehovah's Witness?"

She blinked in surprise. "Um, no. Do we suddenly have a problem with Jehovah's Witnesses?"

"Oh, no. Not at all. I closed the door on a couple this morning. Thought they might send their homies after me."

She shook her head. "It's your uncle Bob."

"Even worse. Tell him I'm out."

"And who do you suppose he's going to think I've been talking to all this time?"

"Besides," Uncle Bob said, pushing past Cookie, "I heard your voice." He leveled a chastising glare on me. "Shameful, asking Cookie to lie for you. What did you do to those Jehovah's Witnesses?"

"Nothing. They started it."

He sat across from me. "I need your statement about last night."

"No worries. I typed it up."

"Oh." He brightened and took the paper I handed him. His face fell as he read. "I heard a sound. A bad guy swung a knife at me. I ducked and cut his throat. The end." He breathed in a heavy sigh. "Well, that needs some work."

"But I'm just a girl," I said, a bitter edge to my voice. "It's not like I've solved dozens of cases for you and my father both. It's not like I should have to worry my pretty little head with nasty things like details. Right? God forbid I know anything about anything."

He worked his jaw a long moment, probably calculating his odds of getting out of my office unscathed. "How about we do this later?" he asked, tucking my statement into a folder.

"How about?"

Just as Uncle Bob stood, Cookie buzzed me on the speakerphone. "Yes?"

"You have another visitor. It's Garrett. I'm not sure if he's a Jehovah's Witness or not."

Oh, the other traitor. Perfect. "By all means, send him in."

As Garrett and Uncle Bob passed each other, Ubie must have tipped him off with a warning expression. His brows shot up in curiosity just before he strode over to pour himself a cup of java and folded himself into the chair across from me. I sat tapping my fingernails on my desk, waiting for the opportunity to tear into him.

He took a long draw then asked, "What'd I do?"

"You knew about the guy threatening my dad?"

He paused, shifted in his chair, so freaking busted, it wasn't funny. "They told you?"

"Why, no, Swopes, they didn't. Instead, they waited until the guy knocked the fuck out of my dad and readied him for spaceflight with duct tape then tried to kill me with a butcher's knife."

He shot out of his chair, cursing when he spilled coffee in his lap. Apparently nobody had called him. "What?" he asked, swiping at his jeans. "When? What happened?"

"I can print my statement out for you, if that would help."

He sat back down, eyeing me warily. "Sure."

I printed my statement, happy that all the work I'd put into it wouldn't go unnoticed. He took it, read my four sentences for a really long time that had me wondering if he was dyslexic, then looked back at me. "Wow, that's a lot to take in all at once."

"It was for me, too," I said, the sarcasm dripping from my tongue unmistakable.

"You cut his throat?"

I leaned toward him, my voice menacing as I said, "I do things like that when I'm angry."

He worked his jaw a moment. "How about I come back later?"

"How about?"

As he strode out the door, he paused and turned back. "We need to interview the previous owner of Cookie's Taurus. She's going to be home late this afternoon. You in?"

I unglued my teeth to answer. "I'm in."

"I'll leave the info with Cookie. Right now, I have a phone call to make."

When I gave myself a minute to calm down, I realized that an anger had come over Garrett just before he left. An explosive kind of anger one would be wise to steer clear of. I'd have to find out who'd rained on his parade later.

"Mr. Kirsch is expecting us this afternoon," Cookie called out from her office, since the door separating our offices was open. "His wife is out of town, but he said he'd be happy to talk to us about the Hana Insinga case."

I stood and walked to the doorway. "It's almost three hours from here. We should probably get on the road."

"He asked that we bring the case file."

"Of course."

We packed up and headed out the door for our journey to one of the most beautiful places on Earth: Taos, New Mexico.

"I handed Garrett Mistress Marigold's e-mail address and gave him the short version," Cookie said when we jumped into Misery. "He's going to e-mail her, try to get her to spill about why she wants the grim reaper to contact her. But for now, I could tell you dirty jokes on the way, if that would help cheer you up."

I turned the key with a smile. "I'm okay. Just annoyed."

"You have every right to be. I'm annoyed and I wasn't attacked. Or slashed open with a butcher's knife. Stevie Ray Vaughan?"

We both looked down at my stereo, slow grins coming over our faces. "This should be a good trip," I said, turning it up. Any trip starting out with Stevie Ray was good.

Most PIs would simply call the former sheriff of Mora County instead of driving three hours, but I could tell much more about a person with a face-to-face. There would be no question as to what

Mr. Kirsch knew about the case by the end of the day. If he knew his son was involved in something illicit, I'd know. Maybe not the finer points, but I'd have a good idea if he was involved in any kind of cover-up.

Cookie worked the entire way, gathering intel and making calls. "And you worked for Mr. Zapata seven years?" she said into her phone. Mr. Zapata was our murdered car dealer, and she was speaking to one of his former employees. "Mm-hm. Okay, thank you so much." She closed her phone and cast me a weary gaze. "I hope when I die people only remember good things about me as well."

"Another testament to Zapata's pending sainthood?"

"Yep. Same story, different day."

"Whatever they did back in high school," I said, taking a right on Mr. Kirsch's block, "nobody but nobody is talking about it. At least we know one thing about this group of kids."

"What's that?" she asked, making notes on her laptop.

"They were all really good at keeping a secret." I pulled into Mr. Kirsch's drive. "Where did you say his wife is?"

Cookie closed her laptop and looked up. "Wow, nice house." Most houses in Taos were nice. It was an expensive place to live. "She's up north visiting her mother."

"You know what?" I asked, climbing out of my Jeep. "When this case is over, I vote we join her. I mean, north is a good direction."

"We should go to Washington State."

"Sounds good."

"Or New York," she said, changing her mind. "I love New York."

I nodded my head. "I only like New York as a friend, but I'm in."

Congressman Kyle Kirsch's father looked as though he had been a force to deal with in his day. He was tall and lanky, solid muscle even now.

He had graying sand-colored hair and sharp cerulean blue eyes. Retired or not, he was a law enforcement agent through and through. His stance, his mannerisms, every unconscious habit pointed to a long and successful career bringing down criminals. He reminded me of my own father, which forced a pang of sadness to surface. I was so angry with him and yet so concerned. I decided, for the good of all present, to focus on the concern. We were going to have a long talk, the two of us. But for now, I needed to know if Mr. Kirsch was involved in Hana Insinga's disappearance.

"I remember the case like it was yesterday," Mr. Kirsch said, his eyes scanning the file like a hawk eyeing a meal. I doubted much got past him. "The entire town banded together to find her. We sent search parties into the mountains. We had flyers and bulletins in every town for a hundred miles." He closed the file and settled his startling gaze on mine. "This, ladies, is the one that got away."

Cookie and I glanced at each other. She sat beside me on a leather sofa, her pen and notebook at the ready. The Kirsches' home was decorated in the blacks and whites of Holstein cows and the subtle tans of the New Mexico landscape. The décor was a charming mix of country and Southwest.

I could feel the pain in Mr. Kirsch's heart, even after all this time. "The report said you talked personally to every single high school student. Did anything stand out? Anything you didn't think important enough to put in your report?"

His mouth thinned into a solid line. He unfolded his towering frame and stepped to a window overlooking a small pond. "Lots of things stood out," he admitted. "But try as I might, I just could not put my finger on what any of it meant."

"According to witnesses," I said, taking the file folder and opening it on my lap, "Hana may or may not have been at a party that night. She may or may not have left early and alone. And she may or may not have walked to a gas station down the road from her house. There are so many conflicting testimonies, it's hard to put the pieces together."

"I know," he said, turning toward me. "I tried for two years to put them together, but the more time went by, the more vague everyone's stories became. It was maddening."

Situations like these always were. I decided to go for the gold. At that point, my gut told me the former sheriff had nothing to do with any cover-up, but I had to know for sure. "In your report you say that you interviewed your son, that he had been at that party, yet he was one of the students who said he never saw her there."

With a heavy sigh, he sat across from me again. "That's partly my fault, I think. His mother and I were on vacation that weekend, and we basically threatened his life if he left the house. At first, he said he didn't go to the party for fear of getting in trouble. But when I had several kids tell me he'd been there, he finally admitted he'd gone. However, that was about all I could get out of him. Just like several of the others, I was getting mixed signals. Odd mannerisms I couldn't get a handle on."

Mr. Kirsch was telling the truth. He was no more involved in Hana's disappearance than I was. "Sometimes kids are covering up other things they think they will get in trouble for that have nothing to do with our case. I've run into that several times in my own investigations."

He nodded. "Me, too. But adults do the same thing," he said with a grin.

"Yes, they do." We stood to leave. "Congratulations on your son's vie for the Senate, by the way."

Iridescent rays of pride emanated from him. The warmth surrounded me and my heart sank just a little. If I was right, his son was a murderer. He was not going to take the truth well. Who would? "Thank you, Ms. Davidson. He's speaking in Albuquerque tomorrow."

"Really?" I asked, surprised. "I had no idea. I don't always keep up with these things like I should."

"I do," Cookie said, raising her chin a notch. I tried not to giggle. "He's going to be giving a speech on the university campus."

"That he is," Mr. Kirsch said. "I can't go, unfortunately, but he's speaking in Santa Fe in a couple of days. I hope to make that one."

I hoped he would make that one, too. It might well be his last chance to see his son shine.

After grabbing a bite in Taos then driving the three hours it took to get back to Albuquerque, Cookie and I went straight to the address Garrett had left us. He was already there, waiting down the street in his black pick-'em-up truck. We pulled in behind him as he stepped out.

"How'd your phone call go?" I asked in reference to the call he suddenly had to make when leaving my office that morning. I was curious whom he'd called and why.

"Wonderful. I now have one less employee."

"Why?" I asked, a little startled.

He turned a mischievous grin on me. "You made me promise not to follow you. You didn't say anything about me having you followed."

I gasped. Aloud. "You slime."

"Please," he said, going around my Jeep to help Cookie out. Admittedly, Misery was not the easiest vehicle to maneuver oneself in and out of.

"Thank you," Cookie said, surprised.

"Not at all." He led us down the street toward a small white adobe in serious need of a weed whacking. "I've been keeping a man on you twenty-four/seven." He glanced down at me as I walked beside him. "Or at least I thought I was keeping a man on you twenty-four/seven. Apparently, the one from yesterday evening felt he needed to break for a late-night snack without waiting for his relief. Around three in the morning?" he asked. I nodded, my teeth clamped together in anger.

"Your life was in danger, in case you didn't get the message." He fished out a paper from his back pocket.

"I got the message loud and clear when I was stabbed in the chest." I glanced to my side. Cookie totally had my back with a determined nod.

He rolled his eyes. It was very unprofessional. "You weren't stabbed. You were sliced. And I heard back from your Mistress Marigold—speaking of which, really? Mistress Marigold?"

"What did she say?" Cookie asked, enthralled. It was funny.

"Well, I told her I was the grim reaper, like you said—" He hitched his head toward Cookie. "—and she told me that if I was the grim reaper, she was the son of Satan."

I tripped on a crack in the sidewalk. Garrett caught me as I glanced back at a wide-eyed Cookie.

"I tried to e-mail her back," he continued, eyeing me warily now, "but she'll have nothing to do with me."

"Can you blame her?" I asked, faking nonchalance. Holy cow, who was this woman?

"This woman's name is Carrie Lee-ah-dell," he said, struggling with the pronunciation.

"Mistress Marigold?" How the hell did he know that?

He frowned. "No. This chick." He pointed to the house. "She's a kindergarten teacher."

Oh, right. I drew in a deep breath, then glanced at the paper, at the name Carrie Liedell, and giggled. "It's pronounced Lie-dell."

"Really? How do you know?"

I stopped my trek up the sidewalk and pointed to the paper. "See this? This *i-e*? When two vowels go walking, the first one does the talking."

He furrowed his brows at me. "What the fuck does that mean?"

I started for the door again, casting a humorous glance underneath my lashes at Cook, and at that very moment in time, I realized how ultracool the click of my boots on the concrete sounded. "It means that you never learned to read properly."

Cookie hid a giggle behind a cough as Garrett met me at the door. He waited while I knocked. Just as the doorknob turned, he asked in a low voice, "Where does that leave freight?"

He had a point.

"Or said."

A thirtyish woman with a short, dark bob that squared her already square jaw to a harsh extreme cracked open the door.

"Or, I don't know, blood."

Now he was just showing off.

"Yes?" she asked, her tone wary. She probably thought we were selling something. Vacuum cleaners. Magazine subscriptions. Religion by the yard.

Before I could say anything, Garrett leaned down to whisper in my ear. "Or should. And yes, Charles, I can do this all day."

I was fully prepared to beat him to death with serving tongs. "Hi, Ms. Liedell?" I held up my laminated PI license. Mostly 'cause I looked cool doing it. "My name is Charlotte Davidson, and these are my colleagues Cookie Kowalski and Garrett Swopes. We're investigating a hit-and-run that happened about three years ago."

Having no idea what actually happened to Dead Trunk Guy, I was taking a huge risk. If she was involved with his death, any number of things could have happened. But since he probably died in the trunk, a hit-and-run made the most sense. I figured she was driving home late one night and just didn't see him. Fearing she would get in trouble, she coaxed him into her trunk? It was thin, but I had nothing else.

My gamble paid off immediately. I felt a surge of adrenaline rush through her, a sharp spike of fear as guilt descended like a dark cloud, though her face showed only the slightest hint of distress. Her eyes widened ever so slightly. Her mouth pursed the tiniest degree. She'd practiced this moment, which made her a murderer.

I decided to push forward, to deny her system a chance to recover. "Would you care to explain what happened, Ms. Liedell?" I asked, my voice knowing, accusing.

A hand closed the collar of her blouse self-consciously. Or it could have been the sudden chill of having a dead homeless man standing over her, staring down with a spark of recognition coming to light in his green eyes. I'd never had a departed hurt a living human—I didn't even know if they could—but I was really hoping I wouldn't have to tackle the guy. He was huge. And since I was the only one who could see him, it would look odd.

"I—I have no idea what you're talking about," she said.

Noting the telltale quiver in her voice, I said, "You hit a homeless man, locked him in the trunk of your 2000 white Taurus, then waited for him to die. Does that about sum it up?"

Garrett's jaw clenched in my periphery, and I honestly couldn't tell if he was concerned about my line of questioning or if he was angry at what she'd done.

"It was on Coal Avenue," Dead Trunk Guy said, his deep voice clear and sharp. It startled me at first, but even crazy people had their lucid moments. He turned to me then, pinning me to the spot with his fierce gaze. "In a parking lot, believe it or not."

"You hit him in a parking lot?" I asked, my pitch high with surprise. Garrett shifted beside me, wondering where I was going with this. I was wondering, too.

This time when her eyes widened, the guilt on her face was undeniable. "I—I never hit anyone."

"She was wasted," the guy said, memories lining his face, "falling down drunk, and she told me to sit on the back of her car, that I would be fine."

"You told him to sit on the back of your car," I said, dissecting her with an accusing scowl. "You'd been drinking."

Ms. Liedell looked around, as if making sure she wasn't on *Candid Camera*.

"I must have had a concussion. I couldn't focus. I was talking to her one minute, then dying in her trunk the next. She hit me again, only with a brick that time."

"What the hell did you say to her?" I asked him, no longer worried about appearances.

His bitter gaze traveled back to me. "I told her I was a cop and that she was under arrest."

"Holy fuck," I said in full freak-out mode. "Are you serious? You were a cop? Like undercover?"

He nodded, but Liedell gasped, covered her mouth with both hands. "No, I didn't know he was a cop. I thought he was a crazy homeless guy. H-he was filthy. I thought he was lying to get money out of me. You know how they are." She was panicking. Under more normal circumstances, it would have been funny. "You're not cops," she said to us. "You can't do anything."

Just then, Uncle Bob pulled his SUV to a screeching halt in front of her house, followed by two patrol cars, lights flashing. His timing, though impeccable, had me stumped.

"No," I said, unable to wipe the astonishment from my voice, "but he is." I hitched a thumb over my shoulder toward Ubie, aka Man on Fire. He was walking toward us with a purpose. A mission. Or hemorrhoids. Or both.

"Carrie Liedell?" he asked as he barreled toward us.

She nodded absently, her whole life most likely flashing before her eyes.

"You are under arrest for the murder of Officer Zeke Brandt. Do you have anything in your pockets?" he asked just before he turned her about face and frisked her. A uniform quoted the Miranda as Liedell started bawling.

"I didn't know he was a cop," she said between sobs. "I thought he was lying."

When the uniform took her away, Ubie turned to me, his expression dire. "Officer Brandt has been missing for three years. Nobody knew what happened to him. He was investigating a drug ring that used homeless people to sell for them."

"But, how did you know?" I asked, still stupefied.

"Swopes told me what you were investigating, the case you'd put him on while he was supposed to be watching you."

I scowled at Garrett. "Is nothing sacred?"

He shrugged.

"I take it you dealt with that little problem?" Ubie asked him.

"I have one less employee, but I'll get by," Garrett said, referring to the employee who was supposed to have been keeping an eye on me when I was attacked.

"Wait a minute," I said, raising a palm for a time-out. "How did you know Carrie Liedell killed your officer?"

Uncle Bob moved closer, not wanting anyone to hear. "When Swopes told me about your departed homeless guy in the back of Cookie's white Taurus, I remembered that during the investigation of his disappearance, one of the surveillance tapes we'd acquired from a local video store had footage we thought could have been a hit-and-run. But it was so grainy, and almost all of it occurred slightly off camera, we couldn't pinpoint what happened. We revisited the tape, figured out it was probably our guy as he'd checked in that night from that very video store, and had the footage enhanced to show this woman's license plate."

Ubie reached over and took Garrett's hand in a firm shake. "Good work," he said before taking Cookie's. "Nice work. Sorry about your car. We won't keep it long."

She gazed at him, still in stunned-speechless mode.

Then he turned to me. "Are we friends again?"

"Not even if you were the last hero cop on Earth struggling with hemorrhoids."

He chuckled. "I don't have hemorrhoids." Then the butthead leaned down and kissed my cheek nonetheless. "This guy meant a lot to me, hon," he said, whispering into my ear. "Thank you."

As Uncle Bob hoofed it to his SUV, Cookie stood with mouth agape. "Did that just happen? 'Cause that was really unexpected. I mean, I thought kindergarten teachers were nice."

"If we stay in this business long enough, Cook, I think we'll find every profession has its bad apples." I grinned and elbowed her. "Get it? Teachers? Apples?"

She patted my shoulder without so much as a glance my way then walked to Misery.

"I totally owe you one," I called after her. I turned to Dead Trunk Guy, or, well, Officer Brandt. "So, you're not nuts?"

A grin as wicked as sin on Sunday slid across his face, and he was suddenly handsome. I mean, he still had matted hair and crap, but dang those eyes.

"And the showers?" I asked, almost in fear.

His grin widened, and I was torn between lividity and admiration. I'd never been duped like that by a dead guy.

"You can cross through me," I said, still playing nice.

"I can?" He was being sarcastic. He already knew. He stepped toward me. "Can I kiss you first?"

"No."

With a soft laugh, he reached around my waist, pulled me to him, and bent his head. I breathed in softly as his lips touched mine; then he was gone.

When people crossed through me, I could feel their warmth, sense their fondest memories, and smell their auras. After he disappeared, I lifted the collar of my sweater to smell him again. His scent was a mixture of cotton candy and sandalwood. I breathed deep, hoping never to forget him. When he was twelve, he risked his life to save a neighborhood boy from a dog attack, resulting in twenty-seven stitches for himself. The fact that neither he nor the boy died was slightly miraculous. But that's all he'd ever wanted to do. To help people. To save the world. Then along came a drunk kindergarten teacher named Carrie Liedell to rob us of one of the good guys.

And he had been lost. For three years, he'd lost who he was, what he'd grown up to be. Until Cookie opened that trunk and my light found him, he lay in confusion and darkness. Somehow, according to his memories, my light had brought him back. Maybe there was more to being a grim reaper than myth would have me believe. I totally owed Cookie a margarita.

"Do you kiss dead people all the time?" Garrett asked.

I'd forgotten he was there. "I didn't kiss him," I said defensively. "He crossed through me."

"Yeah, right." He shouldered me as he walked past. "Remind me to cross through you when I die."

Chapter Fourteen

SOME GIRLS WEAR PRADA.
SOME GIRLS WEAR GLOCK 17 SHORT RECOIL
SPRING-LOADED SEMIAUTOMATIC
PISTOLS WITH A LOADED CHAMBER INDICATOR
AND A NONSLIP GRIP.

—T-SHIRT

For a short, blissful moment, I'd almost forgotten that Reyes could be dead, that I might never see him again. The moment I climbed back into Misery and started home, the weight of sorrow resettled around me. I focused on breathing and passing every car possible just because I could. It was after six when we got back to the office. I didn't bother going to see my dad. The hospital released him and he was home, which would mean a tedious drive to the Heights, and the four hours of restless sleep I'd managed the night before had worn off around noon. I figured I'd go see him on the morrow. After a long night's sleep.

Cookie was going to do a little more work and was checking messages as I headed out. Ubie had left one, explaining where Cookie's car was and still wanting his statement. Didn't I give him a statement? It was never enough with that man.

"Will you make it home?" Cookie asked me, frowning in doubt.

"Don't I look like I'll make it home?"

"The truth?"

"I'll make it home," I promised with a grin.

" 'Kay. How about that Mistress Marigold?"

"No kidding." I shook my head in astonishment. "How on Earth did she pull the son of Satan out of her bag?"

"I wish I knew. I just signed you up for a fake e-mail address and e-mailed her. You need to check it from time to time." She handed me a scrap paper with the username and password on it. Her face softened then. "He's okay, Charley. I'm sure of it."

The mere thought of Reyes siphoned the breath from my lungs. I decided to change the subject before I turned blue from lack of oxygen. Blue was not my best color. "Mistress Marigold's a nut. And I think Mimi's in hiding."

She acquiesced with a smile. "I think so, too. On both accounts. I think Mimi knew what was happening and went underground on purpose."

"We'll find her." After a promising nod, I went home to a bowl of cold cereal and a shower. A hot one, now that Dead Trunk Guy had crossed. The rascal.

I barely remembered landing on my bed when I was awakened by a familiar texture sliding over my skin. A warmth. An electricity. My lashes fluttered open, and I looked over at one Mr. Reyes Alexander Farrow sitting on the floor underneath my window. Watching.

He was incorporeal, so despite the darkness that drenched the other objects in the room, every fluid line of his being was visible, each one tempting, luring my eyes, like the hypnotic waves of the ocean. I followed them, drifted over the plains and plummeted into the valleys below.

I turned over to face him, burrowing farther into the folds of my comforter. "Are you dead?" I asked, my voice a groggy echo of its real self.

"Does it matter?" he volleyed, evading the question.

He was sitting as he'd been sitting in the black-and-white photograph stalker chick Elaine Oake had—one leg bent, an arm thrown over it, his head back against the wall. The intensity of his gaze held me captive. It was hard to breathe under the weight of it. I wanted nothing more than to go to him, to explore every solid inch of his hard body. But I didn't dare.

As if aware of the exact moment I decided not to go to him, he smiled, tilted his head. "Little girl grim," he said, his voice like butterscotch, smooth and sweet and so tempting, my mouth literally watered. "I used to watch you for hours on end."

I battled down the elation that thought evoked. The thought of him watching me. Staring. Studying. I'm sure he felt it anyway. He had to know how easy I was when it came to him.

"I used to watch the way you ran through the park to get to the swings, the way your glistening hair spilled over your shoulders and fell in tangles down your back. The way your lips turned red when you ate Popsicles. And your smile." A heavy sigh slid through his mouth. "My God, it was blinding."

Since he was only about three years older than I, that statement wasn't nearly so perverted as it might've sounded. I could feel the summoning in the deep timbre of his voice, the coaxing energy, luring me to him, seducing me like an incubus, and every part of me shivered in response, quaked with a need so visceral, so consuming, it stole my breath.

"And when you were in high school," he continued, as though he were reliving a dream, "the way you carried your books. The arch of your back. The flawlessness of your skin. I craved you like an animal craves blood."

I grew weaker with each word, with each heartbeat that reverberated toward me. I knew I would give in if I let him continue. I didn't have the superhuman strength it would take to resist him for long. There simply wasn't much super in me, human or otherwise.

"So, what exactly is brimstone?" I asked, hoping to douse the flames. And I wanted to remind him where he came from, to cut him just a little, because he was cutting me. By not trusting me, by tossing my wishes and concerns to the wind, he was cutting. Just like every other man in my life of late.

A slow, calculating smile spread across his face. "If you ever bother my sister again, I'll slice you in two."

I guess it worked. I cut him. He cut me. I could live with that. "If you're not going to tell me where you are, if you're not going to trust me to help you, then why are you here? Why bother?"

After the room reverberated with a soft growl, I felt him leave. I felt his essence drain from the room, the cold stillness that lingered in his wake. A split second before he vanished completely, he brushed past me, whispered in my ear. "Because you're the reason I breathe."

With a sigh, I burrowed into my blankets even farther and lay there a long while, contemplating . . . everything. His words. His voice. His stunning beauty. I was the reason he breathed? He was the very reason my heart beat.

With a gasp, I bolted upright. His heartbeats. I could feel his heartbeats. Rumbling toward me as he spoke, strong and even. He was alive!

I jumped out of bed, stumbled a bit when a sheet plagued with separation anxiety attacked my foot, then hopped to the bathroom to sit on my porcelain throne and tinkle. I had one more shot to find out where he was. I hoped Reyes's best friend, Amador Sanchez, didn't mind crazy female private investigators visiting him in the middle of the night. I might should take my gun, just in case.

After throwing on some clothes, pulling my hair back, and accessorizing with a Glock, I ran to the office and got everything Cookie had on Reyes's BFF from both high school and prison. Mr. Amador Sanchez. It was touching that they'd stayed close and could spend so much time together over the years. Snort.

I cut through light traffic—it being three in the A.M.—and landed in the Heights a little over fifteen minutes later, a tad surprised I was going to the Heights in the first place.

Amador Sanchez had been a fair-to-poor student in high school, had been arrested a couple of times for petty crimes, then was arrested and received four years for assault with a deadly weapon resulting in great bodily harm. It didn't help that he'd also hit a police officer. Never a good decision. And yet he lived in one of the wealthiest neighborhoods in the city. I needed to remember to ask him who his broker was. Mr. Wong and I could do with some nice digs ourselves.

The house I pulled up to wasn't exactly what I'd been expecting, despite the address. I'd conjured something from the South Valley, low-income housing, or even a halfway house. A stunning trilevel Spanish-tiled adobe with a stained glass entryway hardly fit my image of an ex-convict who'd done time for assault.

Feeling almost bad, I hurried through the frigid air and rang the doorbell. Maybe this wasn't Amador's house? Maybe he lived in a care-taker's house or something out back. But according to Cook's notes, he lived here with his wife and two kids. I couldn't help but hope this was the right place. An ex-convict who'd made it past all the stereotypes to forge a successful—and hopefully legitimate—career would make my day.

I pulled my jacket tighter around me and rang again, letting the occupants know I was not going away. A porch light blazed on, and a blurry figure gazed out the stained glass window at me. I finally heard the turning of a lock, and the door opened warily.

"Yes?" A Latino in his early thirties stood rubbing one eye and studying me with the other.

I held up my license and set my jaw. "Reyes Farrow. Where is he?"

He dropped his hand and stared at me like I was part lunatic and part escaped mental patient. "I don't know any Reyes Farrow."

I crossed my arms. "Really? That's how you want to do this? Did I mention that my uncle is an APD detective and I can have him over here in about twenty minutes?"

He got defensive at once. "You can call your aunt while you're at it, too. I haven't done a fucking thing." He was so testy.

"Amador." A woman walked up behind him, a scolding edge to her voice. "Stop being so rude."

He shrugged sheepishly and stepped aside as she took hold of the door.

"What can we help you with?"

I flashed my license again. "I'm so sorry for the hour."

"She didn't apologize to me for the hour," he told his wife.

I glowered at him. Tattletale. "I'm here about Reyes Farrow, and I'm hoping your husband knows his current whereabouts."

"Reyes?" She closed the collar of her robe, worry lining her pretty face. "They haven't found him?"

"No, ma'am."

"Please, come in. It's freezing."

"You're just going to invite her in?" Amador asked. "What if she's a serial killer? Or a stalker? I have lots of stalkers, you know."

The woman smiled at me apologetically. "He doesn't have any stalkers. He just says that to make me jealous."

I couldn't help but grin as she led me to a gorgeous living room sprinkled with toys of every color.

"Please excuse the mess," she said as she began picking up. "We weren't expecting anyone."

"Oh, please don't." I felt bad enough.

"Of course we weren't expecting anyone," Amador said. "It's three thirty in the freaking morning. Cut that out."

With a sigh, she sat down beside her husband, and I had to admit, they were as stunning as their house. An absolutely beautiful couple.

"You probably know who Amador is," she said, "and I'm Bianca."

"Oh, I'm sorry." It would have been nice of me to introduce myself. "My name is Charlotte Davidson. I need to find Reyes Farrow immediately. I—I . . ." I stuttered to a stop when I realized they were staring at me with mouths agape.

Bianca recovered first. "I'm sorry, you were saying?" She elbowed her husband.

Okay. "Um, it's just that . . ."

Amador was still staring. Bianca reached over and closed his mouth. "We really were raised better," she said with a nervous giggle.

"Oh, no, that's okay. Is it my hair?" I smoothed my hair self-consciously.

"No, it's just that, we're a little surprised to see you."

"Right. So, have we met?"

"No," Amador said. They looked at each other and shook their heads before turning back to me and continuing to shake their heads.

Okeydokey. "Well, I'll just get down to business, then." I stabbed Amador with another glare. "Where is Reyes Farrow?" I was serious, damn it. But when the only emotion that came over him was pleasure, I had to admit I was stumped.

"I don't know where he is. I swear."

They were both back to shaking their heads in unison. This was getting ridiculous.

"That's it," I said, showing my palms, "what is going on?"

Even Bianca was almost giggling now, so much so that I jammed my fists onto my hips. "Did I miss something? I mean, you guys seem really . . . I don't know, happy. May I remind you that the hour is much too ungodly to be happy?"

"Oh, we're not happy," Bianca said happily.

Then it hit me. Well, punched me in the gut. They knew who I was. "Holy cow, did Reyes tell you about me?"

Their heads almost vibrated, they shook them so fast. And they were lying.

Unable to believe he would do such a thing, I stood and paced their living room, tripping twice on a Transformer. I was a slow learner. "I can't believe it," I said through gritted teeth. I turned on them. "Did he tell you what *he* is? Huh? Huh? Of course he didn't." He wouldn't tell his best friend that he was the stinking, low-life son of Satan. Oh, hell no.

After a moment, I realized they were laughing. I stopped and stared a moment before folding back into the seat. "Okay, no offense—but, like, what?"

The smile that overtook Amador's face was charming. "It's just that, we never—" He looked back at his wife. "—we didn't know if you were real."

"What do you mean?"

"You're Dutch," Bianca said.

My heart leapt at the sound of my nickname. Reyes was the only one who'd ever called me that.

"You're the girl from his dreams."

"The one made of light," Amador said.

The girl from his dreams? Did they not know I was the grim reaper? Probably not. I doubted they would be so happy to see me if they'd gotten a hold of that golden nugget.

"Wait," I said, inching closer, "what dreams? He dreams about me?" This was getting good.

Bianca covered her mouth and laughed as Amador spoke. "You're all he's ever talked about. Even in high school, when every girl there wanted him more than air, you were all he talked about."

"But he said he'd never seen you, not in real life, so we just didn't know if you really existed or not."

"I mean, c'mon," Amador said, "a beautiful girl made of light? Which, by the way, I'm not really getting that part. I mean, you're white and all."

Bianca hit him on the shoulder, then turned back to me. "The more Amador and I found out about him, the more we realized you probably did exist."

"So, he called me beautiful?" I asked, zeroing in on that one word.

Bianca grinned. "All the time."

Wow. That was about the coolest thing I'd heard all day. Of course, it was still early, but I was there for a reason. After a heavy sigh, I blinked back and said, "I really and truly need to know where he is. I'm sorry to have to tell you this, but if I don't find him soon, he'll die."

That brought the festivities to a screeching halt. "What do you mean?" Amador asked.

"Okay, look, exactly how much do you know about him?" I needed a gauge of how much I could and could not tell them.

Bianca bit her lower lip before answering. "We know that he can leave his body and go places. He has an amazing gift."

"He used to do it in prison. He'd learned to control it better by then, instead of it controlling him."

I never knew it did control him. That was interesting. Their knowledge and openness to Reyes's ability would help me explain what was going on. "Reyes has decided that he no longer needs his corporeal body."

Bianca's lovely brows slid together in concern. "I don't understand."

I scooted to the very edge of my seat. "You know how he can leave his body?"

They both nodded.

"Well, he wants to be out of his body all the time. He wants to rid himself of it. He thinks it slows him down, makes him vulnerable."

A delicate hand covered Bianca's mouth.

"Why would he think that?" Amador asked, angry.

"Partly because he's a butthead." I left out the other partly. No reason to tell them the whole truth. The knowledge that demons really existed could ruin their day. "He doesn't have much time." I looked at Amador pleadingly. "Do you have any idea at all where he might be? Anything?"

Amador dropped his head in regret. "No. I haven't heard a thing. When he woke up and walked out of that hospital, I thought for sure he would come here."

Bianca laced her fingers into his.

"The cops thought that as well," he continued. "They had the place staked out, and I realized he wouldn't risk us by coming here after all."

He wasn't lying, and I still had nothing. I wanted to cry. And kick and scream a little. I was going to kill Angel when all this was said and done. My only investigator and the only person I could trust to scour the streets incorporeally, and he hadn't shown up in days. I was seriously considering firing him.

"Can you think of anything, Amador?"

He closed his eyes in contemplation. "He's clever," he said, his eyes still closed.

"I know."

"No, he's really clever. He's a stone genius like I've never seen." He opened his eyes again and looked at me. "How do you think we got this house?"

I stilled, his question piquing my interest.

"He studied the market while I was in prison with him, stocks and bonds, and he passed info through me to Bianca on what to invest in, when to pull it, and when to buy something else."

"He took my one thousand dollars," Bianca said, "and made us millionaires. I was able to go back to school, and Amador opened his own welding and fabrications business when he was released."

"He's everything to us," Amador said. "And not just because of this." He indicated his surroundings with a gesture. "You've no idea how many times he's saved my life. Even before we were in the pen together. He's always been there for me."

I was suddenly having a hard time seeing Amador assaulting anybody. He had a kind spirit, and I was willing to place a bet that he got into trouble protecting one of his own.

"And he's clever," he repeated, suddenly deep in thought again. "He's not going to hide from just anybody. He's going to hide from *you*. He's going to hide where he wouldn't expect *you* to look."

"Charlotte," Bianca said, her voice sad, "would you like some coffee?"

Amador nodded in approval. "We were going to have to be up in an hour anyway."

"In that case . . ."

Like dangling a carrot in front of a donkey. We sat in their kitchen and talked for the next hour about Reyes, about what he was like in high school, what his hopes and dreams had been. And shockingly, they all centered around me. Amador didn't know much about Earl Walker, the man who had raised Reyes, abused him mercilessly, because Reyes refused to talk about him. But he did say Reyes didn't kill anyone, including Earl. I wanted to believe that.

Our conversation eventually wandered around to the Web sites. I told them about meeting Elaine Oake. Bianca giggled and cast curious glances at Amador.

"Tell her," he said at last with a smile.

Bianca focused on me. "I didn't have any money to invest when Reyes was studying the market, right? So he told me to call this woman who'd been trying to see him and who'd been offering the prison guards money to get information on him. And I did. I told her that my husband was his cellmate and that I could get her anything she wanted. She bought every ounce of information I had. Literally. With money. We were actually running out of things to tell her." She laughed aloud. "That's how I got the original thousand to invest."

"You sold information?" I couldn't help but laugh with her.

"Yes, but mostly insignificant details, nothing that could come back to haunt him. Every once in a while, Reyes told me to feed her something important from his past to keep her on the line. Still, there were a few things he didn't want getting out that leaked through the guards. We had no idea how they were getting some of their information."

Ah, I think I knew one. "Was one of those about his sister?"

Bianca cringed. "Yes. We have no idea how that leaked to a guard."

"Reyes never talked about her," Amador confirmed.

I was certain the U.S. marshals found out about Kim from one of those Web sites. Still, Amador was right. Reyes was ridiculously clever. Not that I didn't already know that, but . . . Wait a minute. I studied him warily. "So, what about the pictures of Reyes in the shower?"

"How do you think we got the down payment for this house?"

My jaw dropped open. "Did Reyes know?"

He laughed out loud. "It was his idea. He knew she'd pay big bucks for them, and he wanted us to have this house."

I sat stunned. He did it all for his friends. And yet he would have me believe he went around hurting innocent people? I doubted that now more than ever. But what if he died? Would he really lose his humanity? Was that even possible?

I'd been hoping to gather some kind of hint as to where Reyes might be during our conversation, something that the Sanchezes were

perhaps unaware they even knew, but nothing struck me as being particularly salient. I gave them a card and rose from the kitchen table.
Amador rushed off to hit the showers as Bianca walked me to the door.

"So, what did he say about me?" I asked her.

She giggled and shook her head.

"No, really. Did he mention my ass?"

I entered my apartment building, my head filled with all things Reyes
and my heart filled with hope. I wasn't sure why. Maybe just knowing
he was still alive was enough to raise my spirits. I'd never realized I
could hear his heartbeat, but thinking back, I'd always heard it, mostly
in the twilight between awake and asleep, when semi-lucid dreams
skated across the surface of my consciousness. The heartbeats would lull
me deeper into oblivion.

As I slid my key into the lock, I heard Mrs. Allen down the hall.

"Charley?" she said, her voice weak.

Lord of the Rings, what now? The only time Mrs. Allen spoke to
me was when her poodle PP ran off and she needed a licensed PI to find
him. Prince Phillip was a menace, if you asked me. I highly suspected
that whoever came up with the concept of poodles in general had sold
his soul to the devil. Because, really? Poodles?

I turned toward her. If nothing else, I should get a plate of homemade
cookies out of the deal, as Mrs. Allen considered homemade cookies
payment enough for spending hours hunting down America's Most
Menacing. Which actually worked for me.

"Hey, Mrs. Allen," I said, starting toward her. In the very next moment, I heard an odd thump. Then a flash of pain exploded inside my
head as the floor came rushing toward my face, and all I could think
before darkness swallowed me whole was, *No freaking way.*

Chapter Fifteen

A jolt knocked my head—the same head that had just been traumatized by a blunt object—against the side panel of the interior of a trunk. It startled me awake. But I quickly started losing ground, slipping back into oblivion with each beat of my heart. A rich, warm darkness threatened to overcome me, forcing me to push, to bite and claw back to awareness.

I focused on the sharp pain throbbing in my head, the fact that my hands and feet were bound, the hum of an engine, and the whir of tires on pavement beneath me. If this was Cookie's way of finally getting me into the trunk of a car, she was getting a year's supply of bikini wax treatments for Christmas.

"So, like, what are you doing?"

I forced my eyes open to the grinning face of a thirteen-year-old gangbanger named Angel. Thank goodness. Surely, he could get me out of this. He was leaning in through the backseat. At that moment, I would have killed a woolly mammoth to be incorporeal as well.

"I'm dying," I croaked, my parched throat making me hoarse. "Go get help."

"You're not dying. Besides, do I look like Lassie?" His smart-ass smirk faltered for a split second, just long enough for me to see the concern on his face. That was bad.

"Who is it?" I asked, closing my eyes against the layers of pain throbbing in harmony against my skull.

"It's two white men," he said. Worry strained his voice.

"What do they look like?"

"White men," he said with a vocal shrug. "You guys all look alike."

I tried to release a loud sigh but couldn't get enough air in my constricted lungs. "You're about as helpful as a spoon in a knife fight." I felt my shoulder holster for my gun, but it was gone. Naturally. And my shaky grip on consciousness was ebbing as well. "Go get Reyes," I said, losing ground much faster than I could keep up.

"I can't find him." His voice sounded like an echo in a cavern. "I don't know how."

"Then let's hope he knows how to find me."

What seemed like moments later, the trunk lid opened, waking me for the second time, and a rush of light filled the cramped space. I suddenly felt an odd kinship to vampires as I squinted against the harsh brightness.

"She's awake," one of them said. He seemed surprised.

"No shit, Sherlock," I said, receiving a sharp stab of pain at the base of my skull for my effort.

Of all the times for me to be scared, now would be a good one, but I was getting nothing. No rush of adrenaline. No fear coursing through my veins. No panic-induced sweats or stomach-turning anxiety attacks. Either they gave me something in the form of illegal drug use or

I had turned into a zombie. Since I had no desire to eat their brains, I was leaning toward the narcotics rap.

"You hit me," I said as they dragged me out of the trunk and toward what looked like an abandoned motel. With infinite rudeness, neither of them answered, and I realized then that I wasn't talking clearly. And walking with my feet bound was proving darned near impossible, too. Luckily, I had an armed escort. It made me feel oddly important. I totally needed bodyguards of my own. The implementation of a maximum-security program would not only deter future kidnappings, but it would also boost my self-esteem, and an esteemed self is a happy self.

"What do I do?" Angel asked, bouncing around like a grasshopper in a skillet. He was hard enough to see as it was. I couldn't seem to focus on anything beyond the thickness of my tongue.

"Get Ubie," I answered in a flurry of slurs.

"Don't you think I've thought of that? I tried to get him when you were channeling a coma patient, Rip Van. He's freaking out, trying to call you right now. He thinks he's being haunted by your great-aunt Lillian."

My escorts hefted me over the threshold of a crumbling single occupancy. A chair sat at the near end of the room along with a variety of blurry torture devices on the dresser next to it. Needles, knives, disturbing metal appliances designed with one thing in mind. At least my escorts had put some effort into this, had done their homework and prepped the area. I wasn't just some random chick they were going to torture and bury in the desert. I was specially chosen to be tortured and buried in the desert. The self-esteem had already jumped a notch.

"So, why does Ubie think he's being haunted by Aunt Lil?" I asked as they plopped me into the chair before tying me to it.

"Who is she talking to?" one of my escorts asked.

The other one grumbled. It wasn't hard to distinguish which was

Riggs and which was Murtaugh, though they were clearly the evil versions. And I figured out why I couldn't place their faces. They were wearing ski masks, which really didn't coordinate well with their suits.

I soon discovered that being bound to a chair was far less comfortable than one might think. The ropes cut into my wrists and upper arms and squished poor Danger and Will Robinson to no end. They would never be the same.

"Well, I tried the sugar trick," Angel said, still jumping about, trying to see exactly what they were doing. "You know, like you told me before, but his cat kept licking at it until it looked less like 'Charley needs help' and more like 'Lil likes ass.' "

"Ubie has a cat?"

I saw a flash of movement, so fast, it hardly had time to register before I was looking toward the rusted sink at my right. Only then did a sharp pain shoot through my jaw, and I was beginning to realize how much this was going to suck. Grrrr, I hated torture.

"You hit me again," I said, growing oddly annoyed.

"Ya think?" Evil Riggs said. Smart-ass.

"Part of my brain hurts. I demand to know what that part of my brain is called and what its job is."

Evil Riggs paused. "Lady, I don't know what that part of your brain is called. Do you know?" He turned toward his BFF.

"Are you kidding me?" Evil Murtaugh asked, though I felt his inquiry insincere.

I did my best to identify the men I highly suspected of kidnapping, but I just couldn't focus. Whatever they gave me was great. I'd have to get the recipe.

Their voices sounded like a recording played too slow, and I couldn't quite zero in on their eyes to assess the color. I pretty much couldn't zero in on anything that would have me tilt my head any direction but down. They had nice shoes.

"We're running out of patience and time, Ms. Davidson," Evil Murtaugh said. His voice wasn't particularly deep, and he had small hands. Definitely not my type. "You're getting one chance and one chance only."

One chance was better than none. I'd have to give it my best shot. Go for the gold on the first try. Beginner's luck, don't fail me now.

"Where is Mimi Jacobs?"

Shit. Well, when all else fails, lie. "She's in Florida."

"Where's Floyd?" Evil Riggs asked his partner.

"Florida," I repeated. Geez. I tried again. "Flo-wi—"

My head whipped to the right again, and pain shot all the way from my jaw down my spine in white-hot waves. Still, I had a feeling Evil Murtaugh's love taps would've hurt a lot worse had I not been drugged out the ass. Now I had to regain my bearings all over again. I sighed in annoyance.

Evil Murtaugh kneeled before me and lifted my chin so I could look at him. It really helped. I could almost make out the color of his crystal blue eyes. And I would've bet my last nickel the other one might have had crystal blue eyes as well. I knew they'd creeped me out for a reason. Freaking fake FBI agents sucked.

"This is going to hurt you a lot more than it hurts me," said Evil Murtaugh, aka Special Agent Powers.

I smiled. "Not if the guy standing outside that window has anything to say about it."

Both my kidnappers whirled around. Before they could do anything, Garrett Swopes put two into Evil Riggs, his draw so quick, it barely registered. Of course, nothing was registering clearly for me, but still. Evil Murtaugh drew his gun and shot back, forcing Swopes against the outside wall. It was all quite loud. I tried to give Swopes some help by head-butting Evil Murtaugh, but all I managed to do was to lop my head down for a good view of his shoes again.

"Woohoo!" Angel said, whooping and hollering and jumping around. I couldn't take him anywhere.

There was some more gunfire, and someone kicked the door in. He had nice shoes, too. Shiny. Suddenly, Garrett was untying me. He was wearing dusty boots and jeans. And Evil Riggs might or might not have been dead at my feet. I mean, he looked dead with his eyes open and unseeing like that. But I didn't want to jump to any conclusions.

"He went out the back," Garrett said to the guy with nice shoes. Who knew he kept such good company?

I managed to raise my head long enough to identify Deadly Ninja Guy of the Three Stooges. He hadn't changed much since he and his cohorts had broken into my apartment the other morning. "Mr. Chao," I said, utterly surprised. "How did you guys find me?"

"Mr. Chao and I traded numbers a while back when I busted him tailing you," Garrett said, struggling with the ropes. He gave up and brought out a wicked-looking knife.

"You mean, when *you* were tailing me, too?"

"Yeah. He'd been tailing you for days."

"Mr. Chao," I said, my voice admonishing. "I do have a nice ass, though, huh?"

"Should we go after him?" Mr. Chao asked, a soft Cantonese accent flowing from his tongue.

Garrett cut me free, and I fell forward into his arms like a ragdoll. "Where the hell did my bones go?" I asked. This whole upright thing had me stumped.

"You and your buddy can," Garrett said, answering Chao. My question had been fairly rhetorical anyway.

I looked up to see Frank Smith, Mr. Chao's boss, his charcoal suit impeccable. He had a grin on his face, as though he lived for such events.

"I just want to get Charles to safety," Garrett continued.

"You wearing your Juicy underwear?" Smith asked, clearly humored.

"How did you find me?"

Smith gestured with a nod. "Mr. Chao noticed two men loading something large into their trunk in the alley behind your apartment building."

"Large?" I asked, suddenly offended.

"He called me," Garrett said, trying to help me stand, "to come check out your apartment while he followed the vehicle, just in case. Sure enough, you weren't home."

"By the time we figured out they had kidnapped you, Mr. Chao had called me as well, and we all met behind that hill over there." Smith pointed out the shattered window. All I saw was a stark brightness.

"The cops are on their way," Garrett added.

"Charley," Angel said with a startled voice, a split second before a shower of bullets rained down on us.

Garrett shoved me to the ground behind a rather disgusting mattress and box spring, and both the other men took a dive as well. The sound was bizarre. Gunfire from a fully automatic weapon echoed and zinged around us as bullet after bullet punctured the Sheetrock, the paltry furniture, and dinged against the ancient sink. Then it stopped for what I assumed was a reloading. Mr. Chao grunted in pain. He'd been shot, but I couldn't tell how bad.

"We have to get help," I said to Garrett as I tried to stand.

"Charley, damn it." He jerked me back down behind the broken and rusted bed. "We have to figure out what to do first."

"We could, I don't know, take Mr. Chao and get the fuck outta Dodge." The spike in adrenaline must have de-fuzzed my tongue. I was suddenly having no problem articulating my opinion.

Garrett wasn't even paying attention to me. For real? We were pulling this shit again? "If we wait it out, the cops will be here any minute," he said.

"If we grab Mr. Chao and head for that back window, we could get the fuck outta Dodge and wait for the cops out there."

Another round of gunfire blared around us. "Son of a bitch," Garrett said as bullets ricocheted in every direction. "Who the fuck is that, anyway?"

"Oh, yeah, I forgot to mention that he told me his name. It's Let's-Get-the-Fuck-Outta-Dodge Redenbacher."

"Here, take this." He reached behind his back.

"Is it a get-the-fuck-outta-Dodge-free card?"

He placed a small pistol in the palm of my left hand.

"Dude, I'm totally a righty."

"Charley," he said, exasperation filling his voice.

"I'm just sayin'."

"You stay here," he ordered. He climbed onto his knees, apparently readying himself to do something heroic.

The first bullet that found its mark inside Garrett's body sent me into a state of shock. The world slowed as the sound of metal meeting flesh hit my ears. He stared at me, his face a mask of disbelief. When a second bullet convulsed through him, he looked down at his side, trying to find the entry point. By the time the third bullet hit him, I knew what I had to do.

As a line of rounds paraded across the wall behind us, the gunman's spray stopped and reversed, careening back in my direction as he did a standard sweep pattern.

So, I climbed to my feet, locked my knees, and waited.

Garrett collapsed against the wall, his jaw clenched in agony as each incoming round ripped chunks of Sheetrock out of the threadbare walls, ricocheted against the metal sink, and slashed through the rickety furniture as though it were paper. The room looked like the hapless victim of a Friday-night pillow fight.

Where was a son of Satan when you needed one? Maybe he was still mad at me. Maybe he wouldn't be there this time—he didn't show up when the parolee intent on cutting out my heart attacked, a first—but it was a risk I was willing to take, for Garrett.

I waited for one of two things to happen. I would either be shot dead right then and there, or Reyes would come. He would save the day. Again. And all of this, all the noise and chaos, would end. I felt the concussion of gunfire ripple over my skin, the heat of an object moving faster than the speed of sound vibrate along my nerve endings.

I closed my eyes and whispered softly, unable to hear myself over the gunfire. "Rey'aziel, I summon you."

The reverberation of a round thundered past me. And another. They were getting closer. The next one would hit me in the neck, possibly severing my jugular.

I opened my eyes, braced myself for the impact, and watched in astonishment as the world slowed even more. The debris hung in midair like ticker tape frozen in time as a line of bullets pushed slowly through the atmosphere toward me. I studied the one closest. The one that had my name on it. The metal was white hot, the friction of traveling so fast heating the metal instantaneously. Then the world came crashing back as a powerful force threw me to the ground, knocking the breath out of me. The bullets I'd been watching sank into the wall over my head with popping sounds.

And everything darkened, starting with my periphery and closing in around me until I fell into a beautiful black oblivion.

What seemed like seconds later, my eyes fluttered open and I found myself floating toward a crumbling ceiling I didn't recognize. I looked back at my body, at the pool of blood growing in an arc around my head. Then I looked up at the dark figure lifting me toward the heavens and I ground my teeth together, curled my hands into fists.

Freaking Death. I was so going to kick his ass.

I jerked my arm out of his grip and fell back to Earth. Reyes was in front of me at once, his dark robe undulating around him. But I had already been in full swing and clipped him on the jaw.

"What the hell was that for?" he asked, lowering his hood to reveal his perfect face.

"Oh." I shrugged sheepishly. "I thought you were Death."

A grin slid across his face, bringing to light his charming dimples, which in turn caused a shiver to dance along my spine. "That would be you," he said, eyebrows raised teasingly.

"Right, I'm Death. I knew that." I looked down at my body sprawled unappealingly across the floor. "So, am I dead?"

"Not hardly." He inched closer, placed his fingers underneath my chin, and turned my head side to side to check out the damage from Evil Murtaugh. "You should have summoned me earlier."

"I didn't even know that I could. I just took a chance."

His brows furrowed. "Usually you don't have to. I can feel your emotions before they surface."

"They drugged me. I was really happy."

"Oh. Next time summon me earlier."

I lowered my head, hesitant.

"What?" he asked.

"I was attacked the other night by a guy with a knife, and from what I remember, my emotions were pretty strong then. You weren't there."

"Is that what you think?"

I blinked up at him in surprise. "You were?"

"Of course I was there. You were doing just fine by yourself."

I couldn't help but snort. "Apparently, you went to some other chick named Charley's attempted stabbing, 'cause I was almost killed, mister."

"And you dealt with it. Told you, by the way."

"Told me what?"

"You're capable of more than you think." A most sensual grin tipped the corners of his mouth, and he closed the distance between us. "Much more."

"Garrett!" I shouted, and woke up an instant later beside him. Back in my body, I scrambled up and looked around for Reyes. Had I dreamt all that? It would be just like me, really. But the gunfire had stopped. "What happened?" I asked Smith.

"The gunman is dead," he said, helping Mr. Chao. "And the cops are almost here, so we're leaving."

"Wait, did you stop him?"

He pulled a groaning Mr. Chao to his feet and wrapped his arm around him. "Not me."

"Wait, Garrett," I said as he wrestled his colleague out the door. An SUV pulled up with André the Giant, aka Ulrich their third man, at the wheel.

"The cops are almost here. Apply pressure."

"Thanks," I said at his back. Turning to Garrett, I realized the blood I saw in an arc around my head was not mine but his. I sought out the worst of his wounds and, well, applied pressure.

Chapter Sixteen

NATIONAL SARCASM SOCIETY:
LIKE WE NEED YOUR SUPPORT.
—BUMPER STICKER

It was late when I slipped into Garrett's hospital room. He was still asleep, so I decided to help myself to his tray. I'd been admitted for a concussion and he'd been admitted for three gunshot wounds. So he won. This time.

"What are you doing?" he asked, his voice gravelly from fatigue and medication.

"I'm eating your ice cream," I said through a huge mouthful of vanilla delight.

"Why are you eating my ice cream?"

Really, he asked the silliest things. "Because I already ate mine. Duh."

He laughed then cringed in helpless agony. He'd been in surgery for-like-ever, then in recovery, but they put him in a room because, despite the amount of blood loss, his wounds were no longer life threatening. "You here to get in my pants?" he asked.

"You're not wearing any pants," I reminded him. "You're wearing a girly gown with a built-in ass ventilator." I was in a similar outfit, but Cookie had brought me a pair of sweats to wear underneath.

My doctor was reluctantly dismissing me after making Ubie and Cookie promise not to let me fall asleep for twelve hours. He was doing the paperwork now. It was late, but really there was no reason for me to sit in a hospital when my computer was clearly in my apartment and I could just as easily sit there. And pass the time looking at pictures of Reyes on the Web.

I put the ice cream down and crawled into bed with Garrett. "You're not a blanket hog, are you?"

I could feel Reyes close. I could feel him tense when I climbed into bed with Garrett. Was he jealous? Of Garrett? I was there for a friend. Period. To console and comfort him.

"I'm very uncomfortable," Garrett said with a groan.

"Don't be ridiculous. My presence alone is comforting."

"Not especially."

I reached an arm over his head and pulled it onto my shoulder.

"Ouch."

"Please," I said, rolling my eyes.

"I got shot in the shoulder you're leaning on."

"You're on pain meds," I said, patting his head roughly. "Suck it up."

"Sanity's not really your thing, is it?"

I let go of his head with a loud sigh and scooted away from him. "Better?"

"It would be if I could fondle Danger and Will Robinson."

Ignoring the surge of anger that crackled in the room like static electricity, I covered the girls protectively. "You certainly may not," I said, thumping him on his IV'ed hand.

Garrett chuckled again, then grabbed his side in pain. After a moment of recovery, he asked, "Do any other body parts besides your breasts and ovaries have names?"

I'd introduced him just last week to Danger, Will Robinson, Beam-me-up and last but not least, my right ovary, Scotty. "As a matter of fact, my toes were recently christened in an odd game of Spin the Bottle and one-too-many margaritas."

"Could you introduce me?"

I hefted myself upright and wrestled off my socks, wiggling the bed just enough to elicit soft gasps of agony from Garrett. "You're such a whiner," I said, lying back beside him and lifting my feet. "Okay, start-ing with my left pinkie toe, we have Dopey, Doc, Grumpy, Happy, Bashful, Sneezy, Sleepy, Queen Elizabeth the Third, Bootylicious the Patron Saint of Hot Asses, and Pinkie Floyd."

After a thoughtful moment, he asked, "Pinkie Floyd?"

"You know, like the band, only not."

"Right. Did you name your fingers?"

I turned an incredulous look on him. I was a master of incredulity. "That is the most ridiculous thing I've ever heard."

"What?" he asked, all offended like.

"Why on planet Earth would I name my fingers?"

He looked at me with a drug-induced glaze. "It's your world," he said, his consonants slightly slurred, and I knew that last bit of mor-phine was kicking in.

I leaned into him and kissed his cheek just as his lids closed. I ex-pected another blast of anger from Reyes, but I realized he was gone. His absence left an emptiness in the general vicinity of my upper torso.

After a night of hospitals, uniforms, and questions, I was finally re-leased on my own recognizance. Since I had no idea what recognizance meant, I felt it would be unfair to hold me accountable later should

I screw it up. Garrett was in stable condition, and I was once again superglued back together. Or, at least my head was. A dull ache pounded continually to remind me what getting knocked out felt like.

When the cops arrived at the abandoned motel, the gunman was dead. His neck had been broken when he apparently slipped off the back of his car while shooting at us. Okay. That worked for me. I told them that Garrett, worried they might have taken me, had followed the men out there. When he realized they had, he called the police and came in with guns blazing, shooting one of the kidnappers dead. Evil Riggs.

But the dead gunman outside did not have crystal blue eyes. Thus, he was not who I suspected Evil Murtaugh to be. Namely one of my fake FBI agents. The one Garrett shot was apparently the supposed Agent Foster. He turned out to be a petty criminal from Minnesota. So then, where was my other fake FBI guy? Special Agent Powers? He must've gotten away. And the gunman was new. I'd never seen him.

I had yet to hear from my Juicy fan Mr. Smith and hoped Mr. Chao was okay. I couldn't tell Uncle Bob to check the hospitals for him without letting him know there were more people on scene than I'd let him believe. Hey, if they didn't want to be identified, who was I to blab?

As Cookie and Ubie walked me to my apartment, I stopped off at my neighbor Mrs. Allen's place and knocked. It was late, but she crept around her apartment all hours of the night, and I needed to make sure they hadn't hurt her when they took me. She cracked her door open.

"Mrs. Allen, are you okay?"

She nodded, her expression heavy with fear and regret. I found out that she'd called the police after they took me, but she couldn't describe the car or the men. At least she'd tried.

"All right. If you need anything."

"Are you okay?" she asked, her voice quivering with age and worry.

"I'm fine," I said. "How's PP?"

She looked over her shoulder. "He was so worried."

I offered her the biggest, most reassuring smile I could conjure. "Tell him I'm just fine. Thank you so much for calling the police, Mrs. Allen."

"They found you?"

"They found me." I promised never to take that woman or her poodle for granted again as Uncle Bob and Cookie escorted me to my apartment.

"Okay, looks like it's going to be a lot of coffee for us."

"Oh, no, you don't," I said as Cookie headed for the maker. Well, not *the* Maker, not like God, but the coffeemaker. "You get some rest. I won't fall asleep, I promise, and you are not staying up one more minute on my account." It was almost midnight, and this week had been the most chaotic of my life, if I didn't count the time I was investigating a missing tourist during Mardi Gras.

She and Uncle Bob eyed each other doubtfully.

"How about I take the first watch?" he said to her. "You get some rest, and I'll wake you in a few."

She pressed her lips together then headed to the pot anyway. "Okay, but I'll put some coffee on to brew. It'll help. And you have to promise to wake me up in two hours."

He grinned at her. Like grinned. Like flirty-grinned. Ew. I had a concussion, for heaven's sake. I was already a bit queasy.

And she grinned back! Calgon!

"What is this?" Cookie asked, her voice suddenly razor sharp.

"What?"

"This note. Where did this come from?"

Oh, it was the threatening note from that morning. "I totally told you about that," I said, my face a picture of innocence.

She gritted her teeth and strode toward me, note in hand. "You asked me if I left you a note. You never said anything about it being a death threat."

"What?" Uncle Bob jumped up from the sofa he'd just sat on and took the note from her. After reading it, he cast me an admonishing scowl. "Charley, I swear if you weren't my niece, I'd arrest you for obstruction of justice."

"What?" I sputtered a little to make it look good. "On what freaking grounds?"

"This is evidence. You should have told me about this the moment it arrived."

"Ha," I said. I had them now. "I have no idea when it arrived. It was on my coffeepot when I woke up."

"They broke in?" he asked, flabbergasted.

"Well, it's not like I invited them in."

He turned to Cookie. "What are we going to do with her?"

Cookie was still glaring at me. "I think I should turn her over my knee."

Uncle Bob brightened. Would Cookie never learn? "Can I watch?" he asked under his breath. Like I wasn't standing right there.

Cookie giggled and headed back to the pot.

Oh, for the love of Godiva chocolate. This was unreal.

A knock sounded on the bathroom door. "Charley, honey?"

"Yes, Ubie, dear?"

"Are you awake?"

He was funny. "No," I said, rinsing soap off my back.

An annoyed sigh filtered to me before he spoke. "I've been called to the station. It looks like we might have something on the Kyle Kirsch case." He whispered the words *Kyle Kirsch,* and I almost giggled. "I have two men posted downstairs. I'm sending one up."

"Uncle Bob, I promise to stay awake. I have some research to do." In the form of one Mr. Reyes Alexander Farrow and his hot Boys

Gone Bad photo shoot. I would have paid a fortune for those ass shots as well. "I'll be fine."

After a long moment of thought, he said, "Okay. I should be back in no time. I'll tell them where I'm off to, so if you need anything. And don't fall asleep."

I snored. Really loud.

"You're hilarious," he said, though I felt his admiration insincere.

Hoping the superglue would hold, I washed my hair with the gentlest of ease. Concussions freaking hurt. Who knew? I had to sit on the shower floor to shave my legs. The world kept tilting to the right just enough to tip me off balance. Getting back up was a bitch.

Just as I was about to cut the water off, I felt him. A fiery heat drifted toward me and the air charged with electricity. The earthy smell of him, like a lightning storm at midnight, wafted around me, encircled me, and I breathed deep. I could hear his heartbeat. I could feel it reverberate through the room and pound against my chest. The sound was glorious, and I couldn't wait for the day I would once again get to meet him in person. The flesh-and-blood Reyes. The real deal.

He didn't make a sound, didn't make a move toward me, and I began to wonder if he had another kind of superpower. "Can you see through this shower curtain?" I asked, only half-kidding.

I heard the zing of metal a split second before he slashed through the plastic liner. It floated down and pooled on the floor. "I can now," he said, a lopsided grin tilting his full mouth, and I felt my own heart tumble in response.

He sheathed his blade under the folds of his robe; then it disappeared to reveal the hills and valleys of his solid body. He was wearing the same T-shirt, only no lines of blood streaked across the torso. But I knew if he faltered, if his human self reawakened, he would be reduced to the shredded man his corporeal body had become. My stomach contracted at the thought, and I forced it aside. I had another chance staring me in the face. Another opportunity to convince him to tell me where he was. And I was not above bribery in any way, shape, or form. Nor stone-cold blackmail.

I turned off the water and reached for a towel. He reached over and took it out of my hand, leaving me naked and dripping wet. Which I used to the best of my ability.

"Is this what you want?" I asked, opening my arms, exposing myself to him completely, and hoping he didn't mind the superglue. That shit was hard to get off.

With a look of hunger, he stepped forward and took me into his arms. But he paused, hesitated, his gaze boring into mine a long moment, as if in wonder. He ran his fingers along my jaw, brushed his thumb over my lips, his eyes the color of coffee in sunlight. Gold and green flecks shimmered like glitter until his thick lashes lowered and he pressed his mouth against mine. The kiss was blisteringly hot as his tongue separated my lips and dived inside. He tasted dark and dangerous.

A wayward hand dipped, cupped my ass as his mouth left mine in search of my pulse. Pleasure shuddered through me, and it took every ounce of strength I had to whisper into his ear. "You can have me, all of me, after you tell me where you are."

He stilled, waited a long moment to get his breathing under control, then stepped back and narrowed his eyes on me. "After I tell you."

"After."

The room cooled significantly in a matter of seconds. I had angered him, and in the blink of an eye we were back to our impasse. I was worried about whiplash at this point, the back-and-forth nuances of our relationship so finite, so unmovable.

"You would use your body to get what you want?"

"In a heartbeat."

He was hurt. I could feel it echo through him. He stepped closer again, leveled his face inches from mine, and whispered in the softest of voices, "Whore."

"You can leave now," I said, unable to quell the sting his statement elicited.

He vanished, a void of bitter emptiness churning in his wake. Then it hit me. The whore, or, um, prostitute. The silver screen star. What had I been thinking?

"Cookie, hurry, get up." I shook her hard enough to make her teeth rattle, then made a beeline for her closet.

She bolted upright and tossed up her dukes like a cartoon character. I would have doubled over laughing if my concussed head had not been throbbing.

But I did giggle. "You have some serious bed-head, girlfriend."

She smoothed her hair self-consciously and squinted at me. "What's going on?"

"I have an idea."

"An idea?" She glowered a solid minute until a pair of sweats smacked her in the face. I couldn't help it. I sucked it up and doubled over in laughter. Mostly 'cause revenge was a dish best served cold. Or at least a little chilly.

"You need to work on your aim," she said, peeling off the sweats and offering me a sleepy frown.

"My aim is perfect, I'll have you know."

My head felt on the verge of a nuclear disaster as we sneaked out the back and around to Misery in a shameful attempt to avoid the cops on watch. I felt bad, but if I showed up with a police escort, I doubted I would get anywhere fast. When we pulled up to the Chocolate Coffee Café, Cookie cast a hopeful gaze my way. "Did we miss something? Did you find more evidence?"

"Not exactly." I turned to her before we got out. "I have an idea. It's just going to look odd to Norma and Brad and anyone else who might be in there, so I need your help."

"As long as it doesn't involve pole dancing."

We stepped into the café and scanned the area. Norma was indeed on duty, but we couldn't see who was cooking. And there were two customers sitting in a very inconvenient spot. But I'd deal with that later.

I gestured toward the bar with a nod, and Cookie and I strolled forward. My silver screen star was standing at it, leaning on his elbows, legs crossed at the ankle. His tan fedora and trench coat came straight out of the forties, the Humphrey Bogart look undeniable. And the entire picture left me a little breathless. Cookie and I loved us some Humphrey.

I sat on the stool right beside him as Norma strolled up. "Hey, sweethearts, did you find who you were looking for?"

Cookie sat beside me, but on the wrong side. I grabbed her jacket underneath the counter and steered her around me. "No," I said sadly. "We're still looking."

Norma *tsk*ed and poured us two cups without even asking. I was actually a little worried about drinking coffee with my head throbbing like it was, but still, saying no to coffee would be like saying no to world peace. Everyone involved would benefit from a resounding yes. The moment someone came out with a way to mainline it, I was so in.

Cookie sat down, then cast me a nervous look underneath her lashes.

"Do you remember your lines?" I asked her.

Her brows slid together, but she played along and nodded.

I smiled. "Good, we have to get them down before tomorrow night's dress rehearsal."

"Oh, right," she said with a shaky giggle. "The dress rehearsal."

"You two in a play or something?" Norma asked, passing us menus.

"Yeah, at the Stage House. Nothing special."

"Wonderful," she said, going back to wiping down the counters. "I did some acting in high school. Let me know when you're ready."

"Thanks," I said before looking back at Cookie.

Bogart was between us. He cast me a sideways glance.

"Hi," I said, hoping to come across innocuous.

He turned toward me, a grim line thinning his mouth. "Of all the cafés in all the towns in all the world, she walks into mine."

My heart skipped a beat. He was so much like Bogart. It killed me that Cookie couldn't see him.

"You here to collect my soul?" he asked.

I was a little surprised he knew my job description. "If you don't mind," I answered. I fished out the picture I had of Mimi Jacobs and held it up. "Have you seen this woman?"

He turned back to stare through Brad's pass-out window. "Don't look around much."

I smiled. "You looked at me."

"You're kinda hard to miss."

Fair enough. "Why don't you want to cross?"

He shrugged. "Do I have a choice?"

"Of course. I take the *grim* out of being a grim reaper. I can't force you to cross."

He looked back at me in surprise. "Sweetheart, you're the only one who can."

I wasn't going to argue with him. "Well, I won't. If you don't want to cross, I'm not going to make you."

I looked past him at Cookie. She sat staring at me, nodding, as if critiquing my performance. I snorted, and she glanced around self-consciously.

"Are you laughing at me?" she asked through her teeth, pretending not to be talking.

"No," I promised before focusing on Bogart again.

"Babe!"

I turned and grinned at Brad as he stuck his head through the pass-out window. "You came back to me."

"Naturally," I said. "And I'm hungry, handsome."

A confident grin slid across his face. "You just said the magic words, baby."

He ducked back in and started cooking God only knew what. But I was fairly certain his creation would be nothing short of a work of art.

"Sometimes," I said to Bogart, "our memories are hidden, buried. And when people cross, I can see them. I was hoping you might have seen Mimi, taken note of something everyone else missed. If you cross through me, I can scan your memories, look for her. But I won't make you cross." I didn't bother to mention that I couldn't do that anyway.

He shook his head. "Don't really have anyone waiting on me."

"Nonsense. Everyone has somebody waiting. I promise, you might not know it, but you have someone."

"Oh, I got people." After a heavy sigh, he said, "I think I'll pass, if it's all the same."

My heart broke a little. He did have people waiting, he knew that, but he didn't feel worthy to cross. He'd done something in his past, something that caused a rift, most likely in his family.

I was hoping I could talk him into it. He didn't realize what he was missing by remaining earthbound. But he had his reasons. I wasn't going to push.

"When you're ready," I said, placing a hand on his arm. He looked down, picked up my hand, and raised it to his cool mouth. After placing a soft kiss on my knuckles, he disappeared.

I glanced at Cookie in defeat. "He didn't buy it."

"You can see their memories?" she asked in awe. Why anything should awe her at this point was beyond me.

"I can, but I've never tried to scan them, to look for anything in particular. I think I could, though. I have to try. And I have one more person to talk to."

I gestured for her to pick up her cup and follow me into the dining area. About a dozen tables peppered the large room that was lined with booths along the walls. The lights were low, and a young couple sat whispering by one of the large plateglass windows that overlooked the intersection. At a table farther back sat the woman who looked like she'd been a drug-addicted prostitute. From the look of her skin, she'd done her fair share of meth.

I eyed the chair, then Cookie. "You'll be cold," I told her, regret filling my voice. But we were already getting odd looks from Norma. I really needed her in front of me while I talked to the woman.

As if walking on eggshells, she took a careful step forward then sat down, curling inside herself. The woman filtered through her, completely oblivious of the fact that her personal space had been invaded. "This is disturbing on so many levels," Cookie said.

"I know. I'm sorry."

"No," she chastised, "for Mimi, I'd do this all day. Just wiggle your fingers, do your magic, and find out where she is."

I grinned and sat across from her. "You got it."

The woman's arms were on the table as she stared out the window. She kept rubbing her wrists together, and I suddenly realized she'd cut them. But the wounds had healed, scarred up, so that wasn't how she died. Whatever did her in, she looked like she'd had a rock-hard life.

"Sweetheart," I said, reaching out and touching an arm.

She paused her OCD behavior and leveled an empty gaze on me.

"My name is Charlotte. I'm here to help you."

"You're beautiful," she said, raising a hand to my face. I smiled as she ran her fingers over my cheeks and mouth. "Like a million stars."

"If you want to cross through me, you can."

She jerked her hand back and shook her head. "I can't. I'm going to hell."

I reached over and took her hands into mine. "No, you're not. If you were going to hell, honey, you'd already be there. I have no jurisdiction, and hell is pretty hell-bent on taking care of its own."

Her mouth trembled as tears pooled in her lashes. "I'm . . . I'm not going to hell? But . . . I just thought that since I didn't go to heaven . . ."

"What's your name?"

"Lori."

"Lori, I have to admit, even I don't always understand why someone doesn't cross. Oftentimes it's when the departed has been the victim of a violent crime. Can you tell me how you died?"

Cookie hugged her arms to her, fighting off the chill.

"I don't remember," Lori said, leaning forward and wrapping her fingers around mine. "Knowing me, I probably OD'd on something." She cast me a shameful look. "I was not a good person, Charlotte."

"I'm sure you did the best you could. Obviously someone thinks so, or like I said, you would have gone the other direction. But you're here. You're just confused, maybe." I took out the picture of Mimi and showed it to her. "Have you seen this woman?"

She narrowed her eyes, shook her head in memory. "She seems familiar. I'm just not sure. I don't always pay attention to people. They're so far away."

"When you cross, if you decide to, can I have permission to look through your memories and see if I can find her in there?"

She blinked in surprise. "Of course. Is that possible?"

"I have no idea," I said with a chuckle.

She smiled. "So, what do I do?"

I stood up. "You walk through me. The rest just seems to happen."

After a long intake of breath, she stood. The air around us danced with excitement. I was happy for her. She'd seemed so completely lost.

Maybe this is what Rocket was always talking about. Maybe many of those who stay behind are lost and need me to find them instead of them finding me. But I didn't know how, short of traveling around the country nonstop.

I had to concentrate, to focus on searching her memories. Just as I took a deep breath, Lori took a step forward, and I heard her whisper, "Oh, my god."

Her life came rushing at me full-force. From the time she was a child and her mother sold her to a neighbor for the afternoon to get her fix to the time she was in high school and a group of girls pulled her hair as they walked past in the locker room. But the heartbreak was quickly overshadowed when I saw a poem of hers win a contest. It was published in a local paper along with her picture. She had never been so proud. She cleaned up and went to college a semester, but she quickly fell behind, and the heavy weight of failure took root again. She went back to the life she knew, life on the streets peddling herself for her next high, and died of an overdose in a dirty hotel room.

I had to push past the salient parts, to scan her memories before she was gone completely. I found the first time she walked into the café. She sat down and never got up again, remaining locked inside herself for years. I crawled forward, saw patron after patron, too many to look through, so I forced Mimi's image to the forefront, and I saw a woman stumble in the front door, her face full of fear, her eyes wide and searching.

She sat down and waited, but as car after car pulled up, her nerves got the better of her, and she grabbed an unopened Sharpie off the register and hurried to the bathroom. About a minute later, another woman entered the bathroom, and Mimi rushed out the door, the darkness of night enveloping her.

With a gasp of air, I opened my eyes and clutched at my chest as if emerging from a pool. I filled my lungs and eased back into the chair, blinking in surprise. I'd done it. I'd searched her memories. It took a moment for me to absorb everything I saw. I fought down the sadness that threatened to overwhelm me. Lori's life had been anything but easy. But she was most definitely in a better place, as hokey as that sounded.

And I found her. I found Mimi.

I glanced back at Cookie, a tiny grin tugging at my mouth. "Let me ask you a question," I said breathlessly.

"Okay."

"If you were the wife of a very well-off businessman with a humongoid house and gorgeous children whom you loved more than life, where is the last place anyone would look for you?"

Cookie's expression changed to hope. "Did it work?"

"It worked." I glanced over my shoulder and pointed across the street.

"That homeless shelter?" she asked, her voice brimming with disbelief.

I looked back at her with a shrug. "It's perfect. I can't believe I didn't think of it before. She was right under our noses the whole time."

"But . . . oh, my god, okay, what do we do now?" She patted her palms on the table, her enthusiasm barely containable.

"We go say hi."

Chapter Seventeen

YOU KNOW THOSE BAD THINGS THAT
HAPPEN TO GOOD PEOPLE? I'M THAT.

—T-SHIRT

I dropped a twenty on the counter as we ran past. "Brad, can you make our orders to go?"

He stuck his head through the pass-out window, his palms raised in question.

"We'll be right back."

We raced across the street to a brick building with bars on the windows and a large metal door. It was starting to sprinkle.

"I don't think they're open," Cookie said, panting behind me.

I pounded on the door, waited a moment, then pounded again. After a long while, a sleepy-eyed Hulk opened up.

I decided to smile. Mostly 'cause I didn't want to incur his wrath. "Hi." I held up my license. "My name is Charlotte Davidson, and this is Cookie Kowalski. I'm a private investigator on a case for the Albuquerque Police Department," I half lied. "Can I talk to you?"

"No." Hulk was grumpy when awakened in the middle of the night. The show never mentioned that aspect of his character. I'd have to write the producers.

And clearly he was not impressed with my license. I held up a twenty instead. "I just want to ask you a couple of questions. I'm looking for a missing woman."

He snatched the twenty then waited for my Q&A session.

"Oh." I took Mimi's photo out of my bag. "Have you seen this woman?"

He studied it, like, forever. With a heavy sigh, I handed over another twenty. If this kept up, I'd have to find an ATM PDQ or we'd be SOL.

"Maybe," he said. He took it from my hands and looked closer. "Oh, yeah. That's Molly."

"Molly?" Molly made sense, considering her name was Mimi. It would be semi-easy for her to get used to answering to as opposed to something like Guinevere or Hildegard.

"Yeah, I'm pretty sure. But they're all asleep right now."

"Listen, you know how, like, if a nuclear bomb were going to drop on our heads any second, kissing our asses good-bye couldn't wait until morning?"

He chuckled. Who said the Hulk didn't have a sense of humor? "You're funny."

"Yeah, well, think of me as an armed nuclear warhead. I really can't wait until morning."

"So, you want to see her now?"

Damn, he was fast. "Speed of light, buddy. Are you a stone genius?"

He frowned at me, trying to figure out if I was making fun of him.

I leaned forward. "And afterwards, maybe you and I could hoof it to the café over there and have a cup?"

"You're not my type."

Damn. It happened. What was a girl to do? "Fine, will you just let us in?"

"My type is more . . . green."

"Oh-Em-Gee, mister." I took out my last twenty. "You're breaking me here."

He plucked it out of my fingers and opened the door. "You'll have to sign in, and I need a copy of your PI license, then I'll take you to her."

Five minutes later, Cookie was nudging a sleeping woman wrapped in a gray blanket on one of dozens of cots scattered throughout a huge gymlike room. "Mimi?" she said, her voice an airy whisper. To help Mimi understand that we came in peace, Cookie borrowed the Hulk's flashlight and held it under her face. I didn't have the heart to tell her she looked like the Ghost of Christmas Past. "Mimi, honey?"

Mimi stirred, looked up through heavy lids, then let rip the loudest, most bloodcurdling scream I'd ever heard in my life. From a human being, anyway. The homeless people around us did everything from jump out of their skins to continue snoring.

"Mimi, it's me!" Cookie said, shining the light straight on her face. Which really only made her look more like the Ghost of Christmas Present as it smoothed the fine lines of age and gave her skin that soft, nuclear-irradiated glow.

Mimi's legs had shot up in the air, and I had to admit, as a fight-or-flight response, it just didn't make much sense. Then she scrambled to the side of the cot and fell to the floor.

A man tapped my leg from behind. "What the hell is going on over there?"

"Exorcism. No need to worry, sir."

He turned over with a harrumph and went back to sleep.

Mimi poked her head above the mattress. "Cookie?" she asked, her voice much softer than before.

"Yes." Cookie hurried around to help her back onto the cot. "We came to help you."

"Oh, my god, I'm so sorry. I thought——"

"You're bleeding," Cookie said as she fished a napkin out of her bag.

Mimi touched her upper lip, then dabbed at her bleeding nose with the napkin Cookie handed her. "This happens when my life flashes before my eyes." She paused and stared straight ahead a moment. "And I may or may not have peed my pants."

"Come on, sweetheart." Cookie helped her stand, and I rushed to Mimi's other side. For the low cost of a twenty spot—this time from Cookie's wallet—we borrowed one of the offices in which to talk to her.

"You got a set of lungs, girl," I said as I raided a small fridge for a water. I handed it to her when her nose stopped bleeding.

"I am so sorry about that," she said, waving a hand in front of her face. "I was disoriented. I just didn't know who you were."

"Well, it didn't help that Casper the Flashlight Ghost was all up in your face."

Cookie scowled. "Mimi, this is Charley," she said.

"Oh, my gosh." She tried to stand, but her legs didn't hold and she toppled back into the chair.

I reached a hand over and took hers. "Please don't get up. I'm not that special."

"From what I hear," she said, holding my hand in hers, "you're every bit that special. How did you find me?"

Cookie grinned. "That's what Charley does. Are you okay?"

After a few minutes of introductions and the lively tale of how Mimi ended up in a homeless shelter that involved a drunken taxi driver and a small but containable fire, we moved onto the more important part of the story, *why* she was in a homeless shelter.

"I just thought no one would look for me here. I thought they wouldn't find me."

"Mimi," Cookie admonished, "Warren and your parents are worried sick."

She nodded. "I can live with that. Better worried sick than dead."

She had a point. It was late and my head was on the verge of exploding. I decided to fill her in on our suspicions and go from there. "Stop me if you've heard this one."

She frowned up at me.

"One night in high school, there was a party. A girl named Hana Insinga snuck out of her house and went to this party, and the next day she was reported missing by her parents."

Mimi looked down when I said Hana's name.

I continued. "Some people remembered seeing her there, some didn't. Some said she might have left the party with a guy, some said no way, she didn't leave with anyone."

A soft hitch in Mimi's breath had me thinking I might be on to something.

"And now, twenty years later, everyone who saw Hana leave the party with a boy is dying one by one. Does any of that ring a bell?"

Mimi lowered her head as if unable to face us. Cookie put a supportive hand on her shoulder.

"You're almost there, but Hana didn't leave the party with just a boy. She left with several of us."

Cookie stilled. "What do you mean?"

"She means," I said, fighting through the sorrow that suddenly consumed her, that pushed against my chest, "that several kids took her body out of the house that night. She was already dead, and they went together to bury her. Am I right?" It was the only explanation that made sense.

She wiped at a tear with the blood-soaked napkin. "Yes. Seven of us. There were seven."

Cookie tried to stifle a gasp behind her hand.

I kneeled down to Mimi's eye level. "Someone at that party killed her. And you saw it, perhaps? Did they threaten to do the same to you?"

"Please stop," she said, sobbing openly now.

"Did they bully you at school? Push you in the halls? Knock books out of your hands? Just to remind you. Just to keep you on their leash."

"I can't . . . I—"

I decided to begin with Tommy Zapata, to leave Kyle Kirsch for my grand finale. "Did it have anything to do with the car dealer you had lunch with, Tommy Zapata?"

She gasped and looked up at me. "How did you know that?"

"Tommy was found dead three days ago."

Her hands flew over her mouth.

"They're bringing murder charges against your husband if we don't prove he didn't do it soon."

"No!" She jumped up and headed for the door. "No, he didn't do anything. They don't understand."

I followed suit and clutched on to her arm. "Mimi, stop. We can help, but I have to know what happened."

"But—"

"You have to sit down and explain this to me so I can get both you and your husband out of trouble. What happened that night?"

She hesitated, wavered, then with a shaky sigh folded herself into the office chair once more. "We were at the party, and I'd went to an upstairs bathroom with a friend. I wasn't feeling well."

The friend was most likely Janelle York.

"We were at Tommy Zapata's house. His parents were out of town." She turned a desperate gaze on me. "We were having fun. You know, just messing around and listening to music. But my friend and I went into the bathroom off Tommy's parents' bedroom. I guess we were in there awhile, just talking. Then we heard voices, so we turned out the light and cracked open the door to look. We figured someone was making out on his parents' bed, and we were going to scare them. As a joke."

Cookie found a clean tissue and offered it to Mimi. She took a moment to blow her nose.

"But it was three of the boys. Three of the football players. They had Hana on the bed. They were having sex with her." She sobbed into the tissue.

"Was one of them Tommy?" I asked.

"No, he was making out in the corner."

So he had definitely been there, and now he was dead.

After taking a moment to recover, she continued. "I don't think it was actually consensual. Hana was so drunk. Then she threw up on one of the boys. He got off her and started yelling. He scared her. She stumbled to her feet and tried to walk to the door. That's when it happened. I'm not sure if the boy pushed her or what. It was hard to see. But she fell into the corner of the Zapatas' dresser and busted her head open. Tommy tried to stop the bleeding, but she was dead in moments."

I found the fact that she wasn't telling us Kyle's name interesting. Was she that afraid of him?

She looked up at us beseechingly. "It was an accident. It could have been explained, but the boys freaked out. For, like, half an hour they paced and cursed and tried to figure out what to do. Tommy's dad worked at the cemetery, and one of them came up with a plan. So, the guys were going to wrap her in some towels, and that's when they found us. I was crying really hard. The guys freaked out even more."

"Did they hurt you?" Cookie asked, her expression almost as desperate as Mimi's.

"No," she said, "not really. They wrapped Hana in some towels and cleaned up the blood, and after everyone left the party, they carried her to Tommy's truck. After throwing two shovels into the bed, they made us get in the back with them. Then they drove us to the cemetery."

"Of course," I said, having a V8 moment. "The numbers you wrote on the bathroom wall by Hana's name. I knew they looked familiar. They're plot addresses. They buried her in a fresh grave."

"Not just in one. Underneath one." When my brows furrowed in question, she said, "The mortuary had already dug a grave for a funeral that was to be held the next day. The guys dug down some more while we watched." Her voice cracked with the memory. "We just watched. We didn't even try to stop them. If ever there was a time to do the right thing . . ."

Cookie took both her hands into her own. "This wasn't your fault, Mimi."

"But they said it was," she argued. "They said that we helped, that we were accomplices, and that if we said anything, they would kill us. Oh, my god, we were so scared."

The fear that had consumed her for twenty years reared up and took hold of her again. It washed over me in suffocating waves. I fought it, filled my lungs with air to keep it at bay as she continued.

"We thought for sure they would kill us, too. But they didn't. They put Hana's body in and covered her up. The next day, they buried Mr. Romero right on top of her. And nobody knew."

The fact that it was somewhat of an accident and not a planned murder was the only reason in my mind Mimi and Janelle survived. If those boys had been true killers, utterly remorseless, I doubted I would ever have met Mimi.

"I was shaking so hard, I could barely breathe," she said, shaking almost as hard right then. "And you were right about the bullying."

She looked up at me. "They got more and more brazen, and it just became unbearable. I stopped going to school and then finally begged my parents to let me live with my grandmother here. I just couldn't live there any longer. I couldn't look at Mr. and Mrs. Insinga any longer, knowing what they must have been going through."

"Did they offer Janelle the same treatment?" I asked.

She looked up at me, confused. "Janelle?"

"Janelle York."

Her face morphed from sadness to disgust. "She became nothing more than their lapdog. She was a part of it, a part of them."

"I don't understand." I rose to my feet. "You two were hiding—"

She frowned at me. "I wasn't hiding with Janelle in the bathroom," she said, almost appalled that I would even think such a thing. "She'd been in the room with them, making out with Tommy on a beanbag in the corner. She would've done anything for him. When he freaked out about his parents finding out what happened, it was her idea to bury Hana underneath that grave."

I turned up my palms. "Then who was hiding with you? And who was having sex with Hana?"

She swallowed hard. I could tell she didn't want to tell us. "It was Jeff. Jeff Hargrove was . . . on her."

"Wait, Jeff Hargrove was having sex with Hana?"

"Yes, well, at that time. I think . . . I think they took turns."

"And who were *they*?"

She thought back with a helpless shrug. "Besides Jeff, there was Nick Velasquez and Anthony Richardson."

What the hell? "Mimi, who was in the bathroom with you?"

She lowered her head. "This is confidential, right?"

I kneeled down and peered into her eyes. "I can't promise this won't get out, Mimi, but we need to know who was there."

With a heavy sigh, she said reluctantly, "Kyle Kirsch."

Her answer knocked the wind out of me. "You mean, Kyle had nothing to do with Hana's death?"

She seemed surprised. "No, not at all. They treated Kyle almost as badly as they treated me. Only he was the son of the sheriff, so they didn't go quite so far with him." She gripped my arm, her fingernails sinking into my sleeve. "You would have to know Jeff Hargrove. He's crazy. Sheriff or no sheriff, he would have killed us both."

I fell back on my heels. "Okay, so then what?" I asked, thinking aloud. My incredulous gaze landed on Cookie. "Kyle, what? He didn't want all of this surfacing, so he's killing everyone?"

"What?" Mimi almost screamed, her fingernails digging in, setting up shop. "Kyle would never do that. He would never hurt anyone."

"Mimi," I said, my voice sympathetic, "everyone started dying about two seconds after Kyle Kirsch announced his intention to run for a seat in the Senate. That's a little hard to explain away."

"I know everyone started dying, but nobody knows who's doing it. Even Kyle. He's scared shitless." She glanced at Cookie. "Hired all kinds of bodyguards." After a moment lost in thought, she shook her head. "It has to be Jeff Hargrove. He was always nuts."

Cookie leaned forward. "Mimi, Jeff Hargrove drowned in his swimming pool two weeks ago."

Pure, unadulterated shock overtook Mimi's features. She was just as confused as the rest of us. And I was utterly lost.

"And Nick Velasquez allegedly committed suicide three weeks ago."

"I knew that. Anthony Richardson did, too, but I didn't know about Jeff."

"Sweetheart, they're all dead, everyone who was in that room, except for you and Kyle. There's no other explanation."

"No," she said, shaking her head in denial, "that's just not possible. If you knew Kyle."

"Were you two involved?" I asked her. Love was not only blind, it often careened into Blithering Idiotsville as well.

She cast me another one of her looks of incredulity. She was really good at those. "No, we weren't . . . You don't understand." She stopped and bit her bottom lip, then said with an acquiescent sigh, "Nobody knows this, nobody, but Kyle is gay. We were in the bathroom talking about boys."

Oh, for the love of hush puppies. This just got better and better. "Okay, let me think," I said, rubbing my forehead. "Tell me again, why did you have dinner with Tommy Zapata the other day?"

Her brows crinkled. "He asked to meet with me. I was kind of scared not to. He said he was being blackmailed and he just couldn't live with himself any longer."

Blackmail tended to convince people they could no longer live with what they'd done. It was amazing.

"He said he'd met with Kyle and told him he was going to step forward and confess everything, take responsibility for his part in all of it. He asked me if I would back him. He was going to tell the authorities how they threatened Kyle and me, how they forced us to go with them."

This was still not making a lick of sense. "Kyle's family has money and you are married to a wealthy man, yet neither of you were being blackmailed?" I asked, incredulous.

"No, but we think we know who was doing it."

"Really?"

"Tommy thought it was Jeff Hargrove."

"Wait, the guy voted most likely to go to prison for rape and murder? That Jeff Hargrove?"

"Yes. Tommy thought he'd gotten into some financial trouble and decided Tommy, who owned a car dealership, would be an easy target. And Tommy was right. I checked into Jeff's financial records—"

Dang, she was good.

"—and he'd made deposits on the same days as Tommy's drops. Three of them."

Wow, and yet both Tommy and Jeff were dead.

"Kyle called me later," she continued. "He told me Tommy had actually apologized because he was likely going to ruin his political career."

"That's a pretty good reason to kill, Mimi," Cookie said.

"No, Kyle didn't care. He was going to step forward with Tommy. He was going to give a speech today with Tommy by his side and announce what happened."

Gutsy. "Maybe he changed his mind."

She sighed in frustration. "You would have to know Kyle. What you're implying is so against his character, it's unreal. He felt like he was living a lie anyway, hiding his homosexuality."

I ran a hand down my face. My head hurt and not entirely because of the concussion. I thought I had this thing figured out. That's what I got for thinking. "Okay," I said, my voice airy with frustration, "so after you left for Albuquerque, what did Kyle do? Did they ease up on him?"

She shrugged, her mouth a grim line. "Kyle's a good actor. He eventually convinced Jeff he was on their side. Then when school was out, he did the same thing I did. He left and spent the whole summer with his grandmother."

"So, after you met with Tommy Zapata, did someone threaten you? Is that why you ran?"

"It wasn't long after that I realized everybody was dying. I knew that my family was in danger. As long as I was a target and they were around me, they would not be safe. So I just got in a cab one day and ran. If not for that fire, I'd be in Spokane right now."

"You kept yourself alive," Cookie said. "Now we need to get you to safety."

Yeah, while I figure out what the hell is going on.

The lights flickered out, and an eerie silence fell over us. I shushed everyone, then squatted down and peeked out the office door. An emergency light down the hall showed a large body, most likely belonging to Hulk, sprawled on the floor.

"Son of a bitch," I said, unable to quite believe it. "They followed us?" I totally needed to pay more attention to who was on my ass. This was getting ridiculous.

"Who?" Mimi asked, her high-pitched whisper traveling down the hall.

Cookie shushed her with a finger over her mouth. I took hold of Mimi's hand while Cookie took the other and we rushed out of the office toward a back exit I'd spotted on the way in. We weaved around boxes and bags as quietly as we could until we came to the back door. Thankfully, the rain pelting the roof offered us some cover. There was an emergency release on the door, but it would set off an alarm, so I was hesitant to go through it. Then again, maybe an alarm was exactly what we needed.

I led everyone to a darkened corner near the door, and we huddled there as I tried to decide if I wanted to draw that kind of attention.

"Hey, boss," Angel said, appearing at my side.

I jumped, startling Cookie and Mimi, then scowled at him. "Again? Really?" I whispered.

"What are you doing?"

"Running from bad guys. What else do I do on a regular basis?"

"Who's she talking to?" Mimi asked.

"Um . . ." Cookie panicked a moment, then said, "She's rehearsing for a play."

"Now?"

"So, I should just leave you to it?" Angel asked with a husky giggle.

I rolled my eyes and turned to Cookie. "Okay," I whispered, "have your phone ready. You two run through that door and don't stop for anything. I'll close it and try to barricade it from the outside."

"With what?" Cookie asked, her whispery voice squeaking in fear.

"Cook," I said, wrapping a hand around hers, "have I ever let you down?"

"I'm not worried about you letting me down. I'm worried about you letting you down. These people are cold-blooded killers, Charley."

"I think I'm going to be sick," Mimi said. They were both shaking so bad, I had serious doubts they would make it to safety without collecting at least a couple of fractures from a fall. "Cook, you have to get Mimi out of here. She's counting on us. You can do this."

She took a deep breath. "Right. Okay. I'll do it. But hurry. You're a much better shot than I am." She took out a .380 from her bag.

"Holy cow," I said. I had yet to get my Glock back from the abandoned motel crime scene. Cookie rocked like a rock star. But, judging by the weight of it . . . "So, do you have bullets to go with it?"

"Oh!" She dug in her bag again and brought out a fully loaded clip. She handed it over with a smile. "Hurry," she said as I locked the clip into place and chambered a round. The clicking sound echoed loudly, and I cringed. The rain seemed to muffle it a bit, but anyone within a stone's throw would have heard it and been clued in to the fact that I had a gun.

"Do you know how many there are?" I asked Angel.

"Just one. The mean one from the motel."

"Evil Murtaugh?" I asked.

"Okay," he said with a shrug.

"Damn him," I said, scanning the area. "Damn him to hell."

"She's really good," Mimi said. "Dramatic."

"Aw." I turned to her with a smile. "Thank you."

It was Cookie's turn to roll her eyes. After an exasperated sigh, she took Mimi's hand and charged toward the door, slamming into it really hard. Her second attempt was much more productive. When the door opened, as expected, it set off a shrill alarm that reminded me a lot of Mimi's scream, and as I followed them through it, two things happened simultaneously: Cookie stumbled down the steps outside, and a wicked, wicked knife sliced across my back.

Chapter Eighteen

IF AT FIRST YOU DON'T SUCCEED,

FAILURE MAY BE YOUR THING.

—T-SHIRT

For some odd reason, people wanted to carve me up like a jack-o'-lantern this week, probably because Halloween was just around the corner. As a general rule, knives hurt. I fell forward, stumbling on Mimi, who had stumbled on Cookie, and prayed to God I wouldn't shoot anyone.

In Cookie's defense, it was raining wildcats and rabid dogs. As we tumbled into a heap at the bottom of the steps, Angel pushed at the door with all his might—God bless his freaky little gangbanger soul—basically slamming it in Evil Murtaugh's face. The door hit with a loud thud, and the knife clattered down the steps.

"Woohoo, Angel! That was awesome!" I said, knocking Cookie in the knee with my concussed head. That'd teach her.

"Run!" Angel said, annoyed. He was irritable all of a sudden.

My heart jumped into overdrive as we scrambled to our feet and ran down the alley, where it was darkest. If he happened to have a gun, which I suspected he did, he would be able to pick us off easily if we ran for the street. The lights were too bright to offer any cover. The way I saw it, we could run around the building and hightail it for the café. I prayed Norma had a key to lock the doors. And hopefully that alarm would bring the cavalry.

Cookie's gaze darted wildly about as she ran. That woman could move pretty darned fast when she had to. But before we got twenty feet, the door swung open and crashed against the brick exterior of the building. Mimi screamed really helpfully. In case someone didn't hear the earsplitting alarm.

"Run," I told them as I turned and aimed the gun. Which was much harder than I'd anticipated with rain cascading in rivulets down my face. I fired one shot, and he ducked back into the building, allowing Cookie and Mimi time to get the heck outta Dodge. I quickly joined them.

"What do I do?" Angel asked, reanimating his grasshopper-in-a-skillet routine.

"Whatever you can, sweetheart." I sprinted ahead and checked out the easement between the shelter and a candy-making factory next door. There were some crates and boxes, but it looked like we could make it through and the obstacles might make decent cover should the need arise.

Unfortunately, the need arose too soon. A shot sounded out, and Mimi fell to the ground with a squeak. She covered her head. I took aim and fired again, but not before he got off two more rounds.

For the first time in my life, I was in a shoot-out. A real, honest-to-goodness shoot-out with a bad guy. And apparently, we both sucked. I aimed for his head and shot the light above it. And I had no idea what the hell he was aiming at, unless he was taking out the windows at the candy-making factory as part of some strategic maneuver to outwit us. Cookie and Mimi were close to a Dumpster and they headed that way for cover. Evil Murtaugh was racing toward us when Angel tripped him. His gun crashed to the ground and went sliding.

"Get his gun!" I yelled to Angel as I bolted across the alley to join Cookie.

He glared at me and threw his arms in the air. "It doesn't work that way."

Oh, geez. There were rules?

"Are either of you shot?" I asked breathlessly as I took position behind the trash bin.

"I don't think so," Mimi said. "How long do you think it'll take the cops to get here?"

"Longer than we have," I said truthfully. Angel had kicked the man's gun away, but it took him mere moments to track it down and head in our direction.

Now we were stuck behind a Dumpster with nowhere to run. I scrambled past the women to see if there was an opening in the fence bordering us. No such luck. It had to have been ten feet high. And since it was cinder block, I doubted my ability to crash through it without a really long running start. If we could climb onto the Dumpster, we could scale it, but that would mean exposing ourselves to Evil. And he probably had more bullets left than I did.

"I'm sorry, Mimi," I said. She'd been hiding for a freaking reason, and we led the bad guy right to her. Way to go, Charlotte.

"No, please don't be sorry." She started crying and shaking uncontrollably, and my heart clenched in response. "None of this is your fault. It's mine and mine alone."

I did a quick sweep of the perimeter. Evil Murtaugh was almost upon us, gun raised and at the ready. I might could actually shoot him if he got within arm's reach and stood really still.

"If I had just done the right thing twenty years ago."

"Mimi," Cookie said, wrapping an arm around her.

Before I could change my mind, I raised the .380 and stepped from behind the Dumpster, feeling more exposed than I'd ever felt before. Discounting that one time in Mexico City. Freaking tequila.

"You hit me!" I shouted through the pounding rain. I had no choice but to summon Reyes. I hated to bug, since he was being tortured and all, but . . .

An evil grin spread across my opponent's face, making me realize why he was known 'round these parts as Evil Murtaugh.

"Rey'aziel—"

Without another thought, Evil Murtaugh squeezed.

Wait. I wasn't finished.

But the world slowed and the bullet came to a rest in front of me.

"Didn't we discuss your timing issues earlier?"

I glanced to my right as Reyes looked on, his robe undulating around him in glorious waves as if he were an ocean unto himself. Then I turned back to the expression of rage lining Evil Murtaugh's face, to the raindrops hanging in midair, to the bullet as it trailed through the atmosphere toward me, splashing playfully through a drop. I could almost see the concussion of air as it propelled forward. It hovered mere inches from my heart. If time slipped, if it skipped a microsecond into the future, the bullet would hit home.

"How is this possible?" I asked Reyes.

I saw him shrug in my periphery. "That's what happens when someone shoots at point-blank range," he explained, his deep voice soothing despite my predicament.

"No, this. Everything just stops. Or, well, slows down a lot."

"It's the world we live in, Dutch." He looked down at me, his robed head tilted as if in curiosity. "Well? Do you want me to take care of him for you?"

I did. I really did. But that one nagging issue still hung between us like a loose string on a sweater. I wanted to pull at it, but I knew if I did, I'd risk unraveling everything. For some reason that ranked right up there with Chihuahuas and weapons of mass destruction, I just couldn't let it go. "Are you going to tell me where you are?"

"You're going to bring that up now?"

"Yes."

"Then no."

"Then I can take care of this myself."

The moment I said it, the moment the words slipped from my mouth, I realized there might be more to the rumors of my lack of mental stability than I'd allowed myself to believe. Wasn't the fact that I needed his help the reason I summoned him in the first place?

"Sure about that?"

"Abso-freaking-lutely."

It was official. I was psychotic.

With that growl thing he did that sent shivers down my spine, he turned from me in anger. "You are the most stubborn—"

"Me?" I asked, incredulous. "I'm stubborn?"

Oh, yeah. Just lock me up and throw away the key.

He was in front of me at once. "As a mule."

"Because I don't want you to commit suicide? That makes me stubborn?"

He leaned down, his face inches from mine, even though I couldn't actually see it. "Abso-freaking-lutely."

He totally stole that. I set my jaw. "I don't need your help."

"Fine. But you might want to just . . ." He put a finger on my shoulder and eased me to the left out of the bullet's path. "Next time, duck."

The feeling each time the world rushed back was comparable to a speeding freight train crashing into me. The force sucked the air out of my lungs, and the sound reverberated against my chest, echoing in my bones as the bullet picked up where it left off and flew harmlessly past.

I stumbled to the side and had just enough time to look back at Evil Murtaugh as he blinked in surprise and aimed again.

If I had been paying attention, if the roar of the thunder and rain had not been so deafening, I might have heard the car speeding up the alley. And so might've Evil Murtaugh. As it stood, we were both a tad surprised when a black SUV came barreling toward us. The driver slammed on the brakes and skidded into a spin that swept Evil Murtaugh up like a tornado and threw him against the candy-making factory while leaving me untouched.

I stood a long moment, blinking against the rain pelting my face as the SUV screeched to a halt and Ulrich of the Three Stooges jumped out of the backseat. He strode to Evil Murtaugh as the passenger's-side glass rolled down. Mr. Smith sat grinning at me.

"I swear, Juicy, you get into more trouble than my great-aunt May, and she's senile," he said.

I looked over at Ulrich. He checked Evil Murtaugh's pulse, then belted him one, I was guessing for good measure. Angel fell to his knees in relief and then collapsed onto the ground in a dramatic rendition of *Death of a Salesman*.

"How did you find us?" I asked Smith.

"We've been looking for this guy for quite a while. You were the most logical person to follow."

"Are you cops?" I asked.

"Not hardly."

Then what the heck? I heard sirens in the distance and knew they would leave soon. I looked over at Mr. Chao, aka Stuntman Dave. "Are you sure you should be driving with your injuries?"

Ulrich belted Evil again. "Now he's just being obtuse," Smith said.

"I'm out of here." Angel sat up and saluted me before he disappeared. I liked the saluting thing. That might have to become standard operating procedure at the office.

"Charley, are you okay?" Cookie asked from the shadows. I doubted she saluted me.

"Super-duper, stay there." I still had no idea who these men were. They could want Mimi just as dead as Evil Murtaugh did.

Mr. Chao climbed out of the driver's side and came around. I headed him off, blocked the opening between the Dumpster and cinder block fence. If he wanted Mimi Jacobs, he was going to have to get through me. Which should take him about five-sevenths of a second. Give or take.

He leaned to the side and looked over my shoulder. Satisfied, he looked back at me, his hair already dripping wet. When he raised a hand to my face, I flinched, but only 'cause I thought he was going to break my neck or something. Stuff like that tended to happen to me. Instead, he ran his fingers over my brows, pushing my dripping wet bangs out of my eyes. Then he bowed slightly and headed back to the driver's side.

"She's alive," he told Smith, and I realized he was talking about Mimi.

"I don't suppose you're going to tell me who you work for?" I asked him.

"You might say we work for the big guy."

"God?"

He fought a grin. "Come down a step, as in commander in chief."

"Then this does have something to do with the seat in the Senate."

"Something, yes."

"Damn, they don't mess around. Wait, so, Kyle Kirsch did this after all?"

He squinted his eyes and shrugged. "Look farther north."

"Oh, come on. That's all you're giving me?"

"We did just save your life," he said, brows raised.

I snorted. "Please, I totally had that."

Smith chuckled and shook his head. "I have to say, this was the most interesting assignment I've ever been on." He leveled a regret-filled gaze on me. "I'll miss you. And your boxer shorts." He looked past me into the shadows. "Get that woman to the police. She has quite a story to tell."

After one more solid pounding, Ulrich strode past me with a nod and climbed in the backseat. I had a sneaking suspicion I would never see them again. As they drove off, Cookie and Mimi tackled me from behind, and I was soon ensconced in the most suffocating group hug I'd ever been ensconced in.

Blue and red lights undulated over the buildings as a plethora of police and emergency vehicles cordoned off the alley. Two EMTs loaded a handcuffed Evil Murtaugh into the back of an ambulance while another EMT was seeing to a concussed Hulk. He moaned a lot. I knew how he felt. I stepped over to watch them load Evil just as two men in crisp suits walked up to me. There seemed to be a lot of crisp suits around lately. Dillard's must have had a sale.

"Ms. Davidson?" one of them asked.

I nodded. Now that all the excitement was over, my back was stinging. Evil Murtaugh had ruined a perfectly good jacket and left a bit of a fissure across my spine. I squirmed in my jacket, trying to ease the discomfort.

"I'm Agent Foster with the FBI." He held up his ID. "And this is Special Agent Powers."

"Yeah, right," I said with a snort. "I've heard that before."

Agent Foster's expression didn't change. "So we were told. That's why we'd like to talk to you before we question this man."

I looked into the ambulance at Evil. "Sucks when the real deal shows up."

"I can't leave you alone for a minute," Uncle Bob said as he strode toward me.

"I think I'm probably off to the station," I told the agents.

"We'll meet you there."

"Are you injured? How's your head?" Uncle Bob asked. He was such a softy.

"Better than yours. Have you considered electroshock therapy?"

He blew out a long breath. "You're still mad at me."

"Ya think?"

As it turned out, Evil Murtaugh and Evil Riggs were related. Cousins or something. Big surprise. They both hailed from Minnesota and had been in and out of trouble their whole lives. But nothing like murder. At least, not that we knew of.

The station was like a melting potty of old and new cases by the time we arrived. Morning was burning its way across the horizon as Cookie sat with Mimi in an interview room for support while Mimi gave her statement. They'd both been wrapped in blankets and given hot chocolate. All things considered, they looked pretty comfy. Mimi's parents had shown up and were in there with her as well. Her father couldn't let go of her and kept her in his embrace, which made it difficult for her to drink her cocoa, but I doubted she minded. One was never too old to revel in the embrace of your dad. From what I could tell, a lot of old baggage was being unpacked, dirty underwear and all.

Uncle Bob was working on getting Warren's charges dropped, and he'd called in Kyle Kirsch, who was due any moment.

"I don't think they were paid enough," Ubie said as he walked up, a pile of papers in his hands. I was pouring creamer into a cup of coffee while trying to keep a blanket around my shoulders, mostly to hide the slice across my back. I didn't think I could stand another round of superglue. "The Cox cousins' bank accounts show cash deposits of fifty thousand each."

"So, who are the Cox cousins again?"

He sighed. It was funny. "The men who kidnapped you? One of them just tried to kill you in a dark alley? Art and William Cox? Any of this ringing a bell?"

"Of course. I just wanted to make you say *Cox* again. And as determined as they were," I said, taking a sip, "they were probably promised a lot more once the job was done."

"I'm sure. But we can't trace the deposits. And the dead gunman from the motel was a jailhouse chum of theirs. We're still looking into his financial records, too."

I looked over as Kyle Kirsch hurried into the station, two bodyguards on his trail. I recognized him from his campaign posters. He stopped to ask the desk sergeant a question, and Mimi came barreling out of the interview room toward him. She ran into his arms.

"Are you okay?" she asked, and he gaped at her.

"Me? Are *you* okay? What happened?" he asked, hugging her to him again.

"This man came after me and Cookie and her boss, Charley, saved my life."

I cringed. It was nice of her to leave out the part where we were the reason she almost got killed in the first place.

Uncle Bob strolled up to him and offered a hand. "Congressman," he said.

"Are you Detective Davidson?" he asked, shaking his hand.

"Yes, sir. Thank you for coming in. Can I get you anything before we start?"

Kyle had agreed to give a statement, insisting he had nothing to hide. He hugged Mimi again, a sad smile on his face. "I guess this is it," he said to her.

"We had to do this sometime."

"That we did."

I wondered if they would be arrested for not coming forth earlier. I hoped not. They were victims in all of this as well.

"This is Charley Davidson," Mimi said when she saw me hovering.

Kyle took my hand. "I owe you everything."

"Warren!" Mimi ran into her husband's arms as he practically stumbled into the station, looking as harried as usual.

I spoke to Kyle under my breath. "I hate to have to tell you this, but I thought you were the one behind these murders for quite some time."

He smiled sadly in understanding. "I don't blame you, but I promise," he said to Uncle Bob, "I had nothing to do with them. I'm not exactly innocent, but I'm not guilty of murder." He took out his cell phone. "I know we have an interview, but would you mind if I called my mother? I couldn't get a hold of my dad. I think he went fishing, and he never carries his cell. I just want to let them know where I am and what's going on before they see it on the news."

"Not at all," Ubie said.

"Thank you." He spoke over his shoulder as he walked away. "She's visiting my grandmother in Minnesota."

Uncle Bob and I both froze. I stepped up and placed a hand on Kyle's, lowering the phone from his ear.

He frowned and closed it. "Is something wrong?"

"Kyle . . . Congressman—"

"Kyle is fine, Ms. Davidson."

"The murder suspects were hired henchmen from Minnesota. Did you tell your mother or grandmother what was going on? What happened in Ruiz? Or even that Tommy Zapata wanted to step forward and confess what he did?"

Kyle blinked in surprise, contemplated what I'd said, then turned from me, his face a mask of astonishment.

"Kyle, everyone who was in that room with Hana Insinga is dead except for you and Mimi. And trust me, Mimi was not going to see another day if those men had anything to say about it." I touched him gently on the shoulder. "That leaves you."

He covered his eyes with a hand and breathed deeply.

"Your mother didn't happen to borrow a hundred thousand dollars from you recently, did she?"

"No," he said, facing me with a resigned expression. "My mother comes from money. She would never have had to borrow any from me."

That explained the ritzy house in Taos that she lived in with a retired sheriff.

"Do you think she's capable of—?"

"My mother is more than capable, I promise you." A bitterness suddenly edged his voice, cold and unforgiving. "I told her everything that happened that night twenty years ago. She made me swear not to tell my father. She said I would be arrested, that people would say I was just as much to blame as anyone. The minute school let out for the summer, she sent me to my grandmother's."

"She knew all along?" Uncle Bob asked.

He nodded. "When I told her I was going to step forward with Tommy Zapata, she went ballistic. She said nothing mattered more than the Senate. And eventually, the presidency." He laughed, a harsh, acidic sound. "It would never have worked, anyway. They would have found out about my past, my lifestyle. People like me don't get to be president, but she insisted that I try, beginning with a seat in the Senate." He leveled a hard gaze on me. "That woman is nuts."

"Maybe we should get that statement now," Uncle Bob said.

He led him to a separate interview room while I hung back. My head was still pounding out a symphony, but it had moved from Beethoven's Fifth to Gershwin's "Summertime." I did feel better about one thing.

My stepmother may be nuts, but she wasn't a murderer. Not that I knew of, anyway.

I took two ibuprofen and sat on one of the chairs in the waiting room. My lids grew heavier than I would have liked, but I wanted to wait on Cookie and see what Uncle Bob came up with. I was pretty sure we just solved a murder mystery. Still, my lids didn't care. The world blurred, dipped, spun a little, did the Hokey Pokey and turned itself around. Then my dad came in. I figured he'd heard what happened and came to check on me.

"Hey, Dad." I pried my body out of the chair and gave him a groggy hug. I hadn't seen him since the night of the attack, which made me a very bad daughter.

"What are you doing here?" he asked, holding me tight.

"Um, what are you doing here?"

"I still have to give my statement on the attack."

"Oh." Duh.

"Why are you wrapped in a blanket? What's going on?"

"Dad, I'm fine. Just the usual. PI stuff and all that."

"Charley," he said, exasperated, "you need to find another job."

I scoffed as Denise and Gemma walked in. I was surprised to see the old ball and chain with him as well as my sister.

"What are you doing here?" Denise asked. "I thought she wasn't coming." She glanced at Dad questioningly.

He gritted his teeth. Sucks when the old hag spills the beans. Gemma raised a cordial hand in greeting, then yawned. She looked as exhausted as I felt.

"And why wasn't I coming?" I asked Dad.

He shook his head. "We're just going over some things. I didn't think you'd want to be here," he said, stumbling over his tongue. This was interesting. "You have to give a statement from your perspective later. I didn't want to take up your time or influence your testimony."

"Well, I guess we're in luck," I said, a humongous smile brightening my face, "I'm already here. I'd love to join in the fun."

Dad worked his jaw as Uncle Bob joined us. "The congressman is writing everything down," Ubie said to me. "I think he's going to be a while. We can go over those tapes now."

"Tapes?" I asked, all innocence and virtue.

"Yes, the tapes of Caruso when he was calling your dad. Leland started recording them. But I have to admit, bro," he said to Dad, "I'm not sure Denise and Gemma will want to hear these."

"Certainly, we do," Denise said, strolling past them toward the conference room. My Dad was so whipped, it was embarrassing.

"This is awesome," I said, following her with a new bounce in my step, "killing twenty-seven birds with one stone. Who knew a visit to PD would be so darned productive?"

"She's still a little miffed," Ubie explained to Dad.

Apparently, this was a community event. We, meaning the family and a couple other detectives, sat around the conference table while cops of every size and shape, mostly nice and really nice, lined the walls. Even Taft showed up. It was interesting, but for the life of me, I couldn't figure out why everyone was so fascinated with these tapes, especially Denise and Gemma.

"Who should I kill first, Davidson?" the speaker on the recording, Mark Caruso, asked. For the most part, he had good vocal projection, decent pronunciation. He just needed to tweak his tone to better reflect his mood. "Whose death will bring you to your knees?" That was a great opening. He'd really thought out these little speeches of his. "Whose death will send you spiraling down a pit so deep and dark, you'll never be able to claw out of it?" I felt his question was more rhetorical than inquisitive.

Everyone in the room took turns slashing furtive glances in Dad's direction, wanting to see what pent-up emotions Caruso could stir in him. This situation nailed why reality TV was such a hit. The human appetite to witness tragedy, to observe the subtle difference between pain and anguish, to see each emotion twist the features of a normally smiling face, was irresistible. It wasn't their fault. A certain amount of morbidity was innate in each of us, part of our biological makeup, our DNA.

"Your wife, Denise?" Caruso said as though asking permission.

My stepmother gasped softly and tossed a hand over her mouth at the mention of her name. Dutifully, tears sprang to her eyes. But I had mad skill at reading people, and I could tell she was getting off on the sympathetic gazes sliding her way. Even more than that, however, I could feel the relief that swallowed her as she glanced toward me, because Caruso had come after me, not her. I supposed I couldn't blame her for that, really, but I could have done without her fix for attention at my expense.

Caruso waited for a reaction. "No," he said, his voice resigned. "No, you need to lose a daughter, just like I did. How about Gemma? The pretty one?"

Though Gemma had hardly moved an inch the entire time, she stilled. Her face paled, and her breathing stopped for what seemed like a full minute before she looked up at Dad. Denise wrapped an arm into his and leaned into him to offer support in her superficial way, but he neither looked up at Gemma nor acknowledged his wife's ministrations. He was lost inside himself, a shell where my father had once been. Oddly enough, he was sweating nine millimeters. Why now? It was said and done. The guy was back behind bars.

And still, he did not answer the man.

Then everyone waited, knowing what was coming next. Who was coming next.

"Or how about that pistol of yours?" Caruso asked, his gravelly voice enjoying the moment. "What's her name? Oh, yes . . . Charlotte."

He said my name slowly, as though he relished every sound, every consonant as it rolled off his tongue. I felt each gaze present snap in my direction, but I lowered my eyes and kept them down. I could especially feel Uncle Bob's, for some reason. He had always had such a soft spot for me. One that I took advantage of every chance I got.

But then Dad spoke, his voice crystal clear in the recording, each note strained, each syllable forced. He hadn't said a word when Caruso mentioned Denise or Gemma, but when my name came up, he broke.

"Please," he said, his voice hoarse with the emotion he held at bay, "not Charley. Please, not Charley."

My heart stopped. The air in the room thickened until I thought I would suffocate on it. The truth of what was happening washed over me in waves of such shock, I sat utterly stupefied for a solid minute before glancing up. Now, everyone had cast gazes of sympathy toward my father. They saw a man in anguish. I saw a man, a veteran cop and detective, who had made a decision.

My father lowered his head and, from underneath his lashes, cast furtive, sorrowful glances at me. To say I was taken aback by his plea would be the understatement of the century. The whisper of emotion he fought tooth and nail to control was not the pain of fear, but the pain of guilt. His eyes locked on to mine, a silent apology dripping from each lash, and the agitation that overcame me pushed me out of my chair like a bully on a playground.

I stumbled to my feet, the blanket and the rest of the recording forgotten, and scanned the faces around me. Denise was appalled that her husband was begging for my life when he hadn't begged for hers. Her shallow sense of reality simply didn't run deep enough to grasp the truth. It must've been nice to see the world so one-dimensionally.

But Uncle Bob knew. He sat with mouth agape, staring at Dad like he'd lost his mind. And Gemma knew. Gemma. The one person on planet Earth I didn't want or need sympathy from.

Thankfully, any tears that might have surfaced from the knowledge that my father had practically painted a target on my forehead stayed behind a wall of bewilderment. My lungs were still paralyzed, as if the air had been knocked out of me. They started to burn, and I had to force myself to breathe as I stared in utter disbelief.

My father, a twenty-year veteran of the Albuquerque Police Department, was way too smart to do something so incredibly stupid. And my Uncle Bob knew it. I could see the shock and anger mingling behind his brown eyes. He was just as stunned as I was.

The look on my father's face was reprehensible. The clueless look on my stepmother's as her gaze darted back and forth between the two of us was almost comical. But there were three other people in the room who'd figured it out. Uncle Bob I could understand, but I couldn't believe that even Taft had figured it out. He had planted a surprised look on me that bordered on apologetic.

But the look of incredulity on Gemma's face was more than I could bear. She stared hard at our father, her face a picture of stupefaction. Her Ph.D. in psychology was paying off. She knew that our father had chosen her over me. Had chosen our stepmother over me.

My feet carried me back until I felt a door handle nudge my hip. I reached behind me and turned the knob just as my father stood up.

"Charley, wait," he said as I rushed out the door. The hall opened up to a sea of desks with phones ringing and keyboards clicking. I hurried through them.

"Charley, please stop," I heard my dad call behind me.

And let him see the drooling mess I'd become? Absolutely not.

But he was faster than I'd given him credit for. He caught my arm in his long slender hand and pulled me around to face him. It was then that I realized my tears had broken free. He was blurry, and I slammed my lids shut and wiped my face with the back of my free hand.

"Charley—"

"Not now." I jerked out of his grasp and started toward the exit again.

"Charley," he called out again and caught me just as I was heading out the door. He pulled me back inside, and in my attempt to get free, I jerked my arm out of his grip. He grabbed me again and I jerked again, over and over until my palm whipped across his face so hard, the sound echoed throughout the precinct. A silence fell over the room, and every eye was suddenly focused on us.

He touched his cheek where I slapped him. "I deserve that, but let me explain."

We stood in the hall as a prickly kind of betrayal and humiliation kept me from hearing anything he had to say. I shut down. His words bounced back as though I had an invisible force field protecting me, and after delivering the best glare I could conjure, I turned and tried to walk away again, mostly because I saw Gemma and Denise coming. The thought of dealing with their indifference made me physically ill. I swallowed hard, fighting the bile in the back of my throat.

Dad didn't grab me this time. He just braced an arm on the wall, blocking my path. He bent down to me, whispered in my ear. "If I have to handcuff you and carry you kicking and screaming back to that room, I will."

I glowered at him as Denise hastened up to us in a huff. "Did she just hit you?" she asked, appalled.

More than any other time in my life, I wanted to belt her as well. Where was Ulrich when I needed him?

"What are you going to do about it?" she asked my dad. *My* dad. She glanced around the room, embarrassed that the other officers had seen my tantrum. "Leland—"

"Shut up," he said, his voice so quiet, so menacing, it left her speechless. For once.

She raised a hand to cover her throat self-consciously. By law, any police officer who saw me hit him was duty bound to arrest me. None stepped forward.

Dad towered over me, his frame thin but rock solid, and I knew beyond a shadow of a doubt that if he wanted to wrestle me back, he could. But he would be grabbing a cat by its tail. He would have a fight on his hands, one he would not soon forget.

"Fine," I said, my voice just as soft as his, "cuff me, because I am not going back into that room so that everyone can feel sorry for me because my father sent a madman to kill his own daughter."

He sighed, his shoulders crumpling. "That's not what I did."

"Isn't it?" Gemma asked, her voice hard as she stepped forward. "Dad, that's exactly what you did."

"No, I mean—"

"She's so special. She's so unique," Gemma said, her words stealing my breath. "She's so much more than even you know. And you sent him to her?"

"Gemma," Denise said, and I could feel the betrayal wafting off her, "what are you talking about? He begged that man not to hurt Charley."

Gemma seemed to be struggling for patience. She closed her blue eyes a long moment, then turned to her. "Mom, did you not hear him?"

"I heard every word." Denise's voice was suddenly edged with bitterness.

"Mom," Gemma said, placing her hands on Denise's shoulders, "open your eyes." She said it softly, not wanting to hurt the hag's feelings.

I had no such qualms. "That's impossible."

Denise's jaw clenched in anger. "See?" she asked Dad, pointing at me just in case he didn't get it.

I was still floored by Gemma's reaction. Quite frankly, I didn't think she gave a crap.

Uncle Bob had been standing back, but he stepped forward now. "Maybe we can take this to my office."

"I'm leaving," I said, so exhausted, I thought I was going to be sick. I started out the door again.

"I knew he would lose," Dad said quietly after me.

I stopped and turned around. Waited.

"I knew he would end up like the others."

What others? How many did he know about?

He stepped closer to me, leveled a beseeching gaze on me. "Sweetheart, think about it. If he had gone after Gemma or Denise before we found him, they would be dead right now."

He was right. But that didn't make what he did hurt less. A twisting pain like I'd never felt in my life burrowed a hole in my chest, blocked off my passageway until I was gasping for air. And then it happened again. The fucking waterworks. God, could I be any more lame?

Dad put a hand on my face. "I knew you would be okay. You always are, my beautiful girl. You have, I don't know, a power or something. A force that follows you. You're the most amazing thing I've ever seen."

"But, Dad," Gemma said in admonishment, "you should have told her. You should have prepared her." Gemma was crying now, too. I couldn't believe it. I had entered the Twilight Zone. No more science fiction marathons for me. Gemma stepped to my side and hugged me. Like, really hugged. And damned if I didn't hug back.

The bitterness and frustration from years of being the fuckup, the odd girl out, the ugly duckling surfaced and I could not, with my most concentrated effort, stop the sobs from racking my body. Dad joined in, whispering airy apologies as we embraced.

I glanced up at Denise. She stood looking around, confused and embarrassed, and I almost felt sorry for her. Only not. Then I motioned for Uncle Bob to join us. He stood with a dreamy smile on his face, but when he saw me motion him toward us, he frowned and shook his head. I stabbed him with my laserlike death stare and motioned again.

He blew out a long breath, then walked up and encircled us in his arms.

So there we stood, in the middle of an APD precinct, hugging and sobbing like celebrities in rehab.

"I can't breathe," Gemma said, and we giggled like we used to in high school.

Chapter Nineteen

JUST BECAUSE I DON'T CARE DOESN'T MEAN
I DON'T UNDERSTAND.

—T-SHIRT

"No offense, but you've been a stone bitch to me for years." I blinked toward Gemma as we sat at a table in Dad's bar. Sammy was making us huevos rancheros and Dad was filling our drink order. Denise had followed us there as well, and even Uncle Bob excused himself from work for a bite to eat.

"The congressman can wait," he'd said with a grin. Right before he said, "Care to explain the slice across your back?"

And then I patted his belly and said, "You know, if you keep eating like you do, I might have to start calling you Uncle Blob."

And he said, "That wasn't very nice."

And I said, "I know, that's why I said it."

And he said, "Oh."

And then we came here.

Gemma shifted in her chair. "I'm working on that, okay? I mean,

do you know what it's like growing up with the amazing Charley Davidson as a sister? *The* Charley Davidson?"

I'd taken a sip of the iced tea Dad handed me and promptly choked
on it. After a long and arduous coughing fit, I gaped at her as best I
could. "Are you kidding? You were always the perfect one. And you
had issues with me?"

"Duh," she said, rolling her eyes. We were much more alike than I
remembered. It was creepy.

"You don't even say hi to me," I argued. "You don't even look up
when I walk into a room."

"I didn't think you wanted me to." Her gaze dropped self-consciously
along with my jaw.

"Why would you think such a ridiculous thing?"

"Because you told me never to speak to you again. Not even to say
hi. And never, under any circumstances, was I to ever look at you
again."

What? I totally didn't remember that. Well, there was that one time.
"Dude, I was nine."

She shook her head.

Okay, there was that other time. "Twelve?"

Another shake.

"Well, whatever, it was a long time ago."

"You didn't mention a time limit. You obviously don't remember,
but I do, like it was yesterday. And besides that, you were always so
secretive. I wanted to know so much more, and you wouldn't tell me."
She lifted her shoulders. "I always felt so left out of your life."

It was my turn to shift uncomfortably. "Gemma, there are just some
things you're better off not knowing."

"And there she goes again," she said, tossing her arms into the air.

Dad had sat across from us, and he laughed. "She does the same thing
to me. Always has."

"Really, guys. I'm not kidding," I said.

"Charley is right," Denise said. "She needs to keep that stuff to herself." We were venturing into Denialville again, which was not nearly as fun as Margaritaville. There was nothing Denise liked less than talking about Charley.

"Denise," Dad said, placing a hand over hers, "don't you think we've insisted on that long enough?"

"What do you mean?"

"I mean, you've always pushed her aside, refused to acknowledge her gifts, even when the evidence was staring you in the face."

She gasped. "I have never done any such thing."

"Mom," Gemma said. She genuinely liked the woman. It boggled my mind. "Charley is very special. You know that. You have to know that."

"And that's why I did it," Dad said, his face turned down in shame. "I knew that if Caruso came after you, sweetheart, you'd make it through unscathed. You always do."

I wouldn't say I'd come through the ordeal unscathed. I did have superglue holding my chest together. Well, for a few minutes. The cut healed almost immediately, but I didn't have the heart to tell the doctor. Which was another aspect of me my family didn't know, how quickly I healed.

"Dad, why didn't you just tell me about him?"

A deep and sorrowful shame swallowed him whole, and I reached over and took his hand, afraid he would disappear. "I didn't want you to know anything about Caruso if it could be helped. About what I did. We were hoping to find him before he could act on his threats."

"Dad, you can tell us anything," Gemma said.

"But you don't understand. He was right." Dad's face fell in disgrace. "I was the reason his daughter died. We were in a high-speed chase, and I fishtailed him. He skidded into the guardrail, bounced off, and careened down a short embankment on the other side. His car rolled, and his daughter was thrown out."

"Dad—oh, my gosh," I said, exasperated with him. "That makes it his fault. Honestly, he's in a high-speed car chase with children in the car?"

After a long sigh, he nodded. "I know, but it didn't make it any easier to stomach." He glanced back at me. "I just couldn't tell you. But I did. Your turn."

"Oh, man, that was totally a setup."

Uncle Bob snorted.

"He's right. You gotta give us something."

Holy macaroni, if they knew I was the grim reaper . . . No. No way was I going there.

"For starters," Dad said, "how did you do that thing the other night?"

"Do what?" I asked as Donnie, Dad's Native American bartender, brought us our food. I took a moment to gaze at his chest; then I snickered when I caught Gemma doing the same. We high-fived under the table. "Hey, Donnie."

He looked up and frowned. "Hey," he said, his tone wary. He'd never taken to me.

"That thing," Dad said when Donnie left. "The way you moved." He leaned in close and said under his breath, "Charley, there was nothing human about the way you moved."

Gemma's eyes grew to the size of saucers. "What? How did she move?"

Even Denise suddenly became very interested as she mashed her eggs and red chili together.

As Dad explained what I did, *how I moved* to everyone, I looked over at Strawberry Shortcake. She had appeared at my side. I scooted Gemma over with my hip and made room for her.

"Hey, pumpkin," I said as she climbed onto the bench seat with me.

When Dad stopped and the whole table stared, I rolled my eyes. "Okay, really, everyone here knows I can talk to the departed."

"We know," Gemma said. "We just want to eavesdrop."

"Oh. Well, okay, then."

Denise feigned an extreme interest in her food. I half expected her to snort or throw a fit, but I think she was realizing she was outnumbered. For once in her life.

"What's up?" I asked Strawberry. "Is your brother dating ho's again?"

"Charley," Gemma admonished.

"No, he really does," I explained. "He might need an intervention."

"I don't know." Strawberry shrugged, her blond hair spilling over her shoulders. "I've been at Blue's house. That old building. It's really fun. And Rocket's so funny."

My heart kick-started when she mentioned Rocket. "So he's okay?"

"Yep. Says he's good as gold."

With a sigh of relief, I wondered if Blue might have found Reyes's body. I hated to say it out loud, but . . . "Did she find him? Did she find Reyes?"

Uncle Bob stilled. He was the only one at the table who knew anything about Reyes and the fact that he had escaped from prison, so to speak.

Strawberry shrugged. "No, she said only you can find him. But you're looking with the wrong body part."

My gaze darted to my crotch before I caught myself. "What does that mean?"

"I have no idea."

"Well, did she tell you—" I leaned in and whispered. "—which body part I should use?"

Everyone at the table had leaned in as well.

"She just said to listen."

"Oh." I sat back, confused. "Did she tell you what I should be listening for?"

"I don't know. She talks funny."

"Okay, well, tell me exactly what she said."

"She said to listen for what only you can hear."

"Oh," I said again, my brows furrowing.

"We're going to play hopscotch."

"Okay."

"Oh, yeah, she said to hurry."

"Wait!" But Strawberry was already gone. "Freaking dead people."

"What?" Gemma asked, her interest utterly piqued.

It was kind of nice to be so open. I glanced at Uncle Bob knowingly. "She said that if I was going to find Reyes, I had to listen for what only I could hear. I don't know what that means."

"Charley," Gemma said, "I know what you are."

My jaw started to drop open before I caught myself. I glanced around self-consciously. "Gemma, nobody at this table knows what I am."

"And why is that?" Dad asked.

Gemma grinned. "I know you're in love with someone," she said. Then she offered a conspiratorial wink, and I realized she was covering. She did know what I was. When the hell did that happen? "And I know you have abilities you've never told us about."

Dad leaned back and eyed us both. He wanted answers I simply wasn't willing to give. Not just yet.

"Would it help to know I use my powers only for good?"

His mouth slid into a thin line.

"What does your heart tell you to do?" Gemma asked.

I plopped my chin into a cupped palm and started stabbing my side of hash browns with a fork. "My heart is too in love with him to think clearly."

"Then stop and listen," she said. "I've seen you do it. When we were little. You would close your eyes and listen."

I would. My shoulders straightened with the memory. She was right. Sometimes when I would see Big Bad in the distance—who later turned out to be Reyes—I would stop and listen to his heartbeat. But he was near me at the time. That was why I could hear it. Or was it?

Gemma chastised me with a frown. "Close your eyes and listen." She leaned in and whispered into my ear. "You're the grim reaper, for heaven's sake."

I kept my surprise hidden behind a mask of reluctance. "How did you know that?" I whispered.

"I heard you tell that kid Angel when you first met him."

Holy cow, I'd totally forgotten.

"Now concentrate," she said, eyeing me like she had all the faith in the world.

Drawing in a long breath, I let it out slowly and closed my eyes. It came to me almost immediately. A faint heartbeat in the distance. I focused on it, centered everything else around the sound. It grew louder the harder I concentrated, the rhythm so familiar, the cadence so comforting. Was it really Reyes's? Was he still alive?

"Reyes, where are you?" I whispered.

I felt a warmth, a rush of fire and heat; then I felt a mouth at my ear and heard a voice so deep, so husky, the low vibration curled over me in sensual waves. "The last place you will ever look," he said almost teasingly.

I opened my eyes with a gasp. "Oh, my god, I know where he is."

I scanned the faces around me. They all sat waiting expectantly. "Uncle Bob, can you come with me?" I asked as I jumped up. He slammed another bite into his mouth and got up to follow. So did Dad. "Dad, you don't have to come."

He offered a sardonic gaze. "Try to stop me."

"But this might be nothing, really."

"Okay."

"Fine, but your food's going to get cold."

He grinned. I looked back at Gemma, unable to believe that she knew what I was. But the thought of Dad knowing crushed my chest. I was his little girl. And I wanted to remain that way for as long as possible. I leaned toward her just before I ran out the door. "Please, don't tell Dad what I am," I whispered.

"Never." She leaned back and smiled at me reassuringly.

Wow, this was nice. In an Addams Family kind of way.

Where was the one place I would never look for Reyes? In my own house, naturally.

I raced across the parking lot as fast as my killer boots would carry me, not waiting for Dad or Uncle Bob, and practically stumbled down the basement stairs. It was the only logical explanation. All the apartments were rented with college in session. Reyes had to be in the basement.

When I finally skidded to a halt on the cement floor, the door up top had closed, and I realized I'd forgotten one thing. Light. The switch was at the top of the stairs. I turned to go back up but stopped. An odd kind of anxiety skimmed along the surface of my skin, like static electricity rushing over raw nerve endings. The first thing that registered was an odor. A pungent aroma hung thick in the air. The acidic scent burned my throat and watered my eyes.

I covered my nose and mouth with a hand and blinked into the darkness. Geometric figures started taking shape. Sharp angles and protruding joints materialized before my eyes. When my sight had time to adjust, I realized the shapes were moving, crawling one over the other like giant spiders, dripping off the ceiling, crushing each other for a spot up top.

I stumbled back before I realized they were everywhere. I turned in a circle, completely surrounded.

"They sent two hundred thousand."

I spun around and saw Reyes, fierce, sword drawn, so savage, so breathtaking, I shuddered.

"*In numeris firmatis,*" he said. Strength in numbers.

They wanted him so badly, they were drooling. Literally. Dark fluid dripped from their razor-sharp teeth to form puddles on the floor. That's when I saw his corporeal body, a shredded shell of what he was before, and my knees gave beneath me. I clutched at the stair rail to stay upright, fought back a dizzy spell with a shake of my head, then refocused. He was unconscious, soaked in a mixture of his own blood and the thick, black saliva of demons.

"This is all that made it through," he continued.

All? The basement was hardly small and now held two, maybe three hundred of them. Demons. Like black soot and ash with teeth.

The light flickered on, and in that instant, I understood. They had been banished from the light. And in it, they disappeared. "Turn the light out!" I screamed, because I could no longer see them.

"What?" Uncle Bob asked from the top stair.

"Turn off the light out and stay out."

"No, keep the light on," I heard Reyes say. "If you can see them . . . ," he said, repeating his earlier warning.

But Uncle Bob obeyed.

Reyes growled in annoyance. He stood fully robed, the black mass rolling in waves around him, his blade glinting even in the dark depths of the basement. They were closing in on him, and they just kept coming, crawling over themselves, oozing out of cracks and crevices and dropping from the ceiling, fighting for a front position among legions.

My heart thundered in my chest as I scanned the beings around me. And just as Reyes had warned, they saw me. One by one, their skeletal heads turned in my direction. They seemed—in a nightmarish, optical illusion kind of way—to smile, their wide mouths and razor-sharp teeth forming an upturned crescent as they lowered their heads in preparation for attack.

"Turn on the light," Reyes repeated, his voice strained as he swung his giant blade when one got too close. "It'll blind them, give you time."

"Charley, what's going on?" Ubie called from the other side of the door. I looked up. The stairs were completely blocked now, packed with dozens upon dozens of real-life, state-of-the-art demons.

It took a moment to absorb the reality of my environment. I stood transfixed, utterly stunned.

Then Reyes was in front of me, the warning in his voice so desperate, so determined, it sucked the already fleeting breath out of my lungs. He held his blade at the ready, leaned in, and said, "Don't make me kill you."

They were advancing. Reyes stood in front of me, ready to swing. Angel appeared at my side, his eyes wide with terror. And I realized between heartbeats just how much I had utterly and completely fucked up. I should have listened to Reyes. I should have heeded his warning.

Then again, no. If I had listened to him, if I had stayed away, how long would this have gone on? How long would they have tortured him? How many pieces could they rip him into before he died?

"Dutch," Reyes said in warning. He raised his blade. "Please."

Wouldn't they have found me eventually anyway? Wouldn't I face this fight regardless? Unfortunately, it was a fight I couldn't win. There were simply too many of them. Reyes was right. If they got through, if they found a way into the heavens, another war would begin, and it would be my fault. I could not be the catalyst for war. The portal had to be closed.

I let my lashes drift shut for the last time, and Reyes didn't hesitate. I heard the swing of the blade slicing through the air as if it were splitting atoms. And again, the world slowed. My heart stilled, and I decided to face my fate head-on. I opened my eyes just as a demon jumped, his gaze zeroed in on my jugular. The air rippled around me as Reyes's sword swung full force. A microsecond later, I stood whole and uninjured, while the demon lay in pieces. Reyes had decapitated the demon in midair.

Then time came crashing back as demon after demon attacked. Reyes turned and thrust as he sliced through each one, his skill with the blade undeniable. And somewhere in the back of my mind, I reveled in the fact that he didn't kill me, that he was fending them off, fighting them for me. One by one they went down, but they still advanced. They still closed in. And they knew Reyes's weak point.

One demon stood in the midst of the turmoil. Watching the battle unfold. It seemed smarter than the rest, more determined. It studied Reyes, the way he fought, the cleanliness of his kills, then it looked down at the corporeal body beneath its feet and struck. Its long serrated fingers sliced through Reyes's chest and the god before me stumbled. The robe that offered him protection evaporated and he grabbed his chest as dozens of demons descended like vultures, taking complete advantage of the moment.

By sheer will, he crawled to his feet, shook them off, swung his blade, and persevered. His robe enveloped him once more, weaving around the hard contours of his muscles, linking over the expanse of his chest.

But the moment it materialized, the demon struck again, burying its talons in his shoulder. The robe vanished again and he fell onto his palms. The sight of such a powerful entity being brought to his knees shattered me from the inside out. I shot forward, but he turned and pinned me to the spot with a glare, his shoulders hunched, the beast in him unleashed.

"Leave," he growled as he disappeared beneath a sea of demons. My lungs seized at the sight, and this time, my knees gave completely. I sank to the floor in shock, watching the pile of spider demons grow. Regret flooded every molecule of my being. Then the others turned toward me in unison. Dark fluid dripped from their teeth as they closed in, taking their time, their only obstacle clearly busy.

"Charley, run," Angel said, pulling me to my feet. I wobbled up and eased one foot behind the other only to be brought up short by the sting of breath on the back of my neck.

Fear gripped me so hard, the world spun, the edges of my periphery darkened, and I realized one thing that was enough to bring tears to my eyes. I was about to die.

Chapter Twenty

My eyes drifted shut as the creatures closed in. I was the grim reaper, for heaven's sake. Literally. Reyes said I could fight them, but how? I didn't even own a sword. But I was bright, damn it. I had that going for me. So bright, the departed could see me from continents away. Or so I'd been told. If the demons had been banished from the light, why could they get close to me? Why were they not banished in my light?

My eyes flew open.

The moment I thought it, the moment the idea popped into my head, a visceral force sparked inside me, vibrated with energy, shook with need, churned and grew, building and building until I could no longer contain it.

"Angel," I said, unable to control the energy swirling within me, "run."

Three things happened simultaneously. Angel's hand left mine, the prickly points of razor-sharp teeth pierced the skin around the back of my neck, and light exploded out of me in every direction, flooding the room with brilliance, saturating and swallowing every shadow. The roar of raw energy consuming everything in its path drowned out the screams of demons. They burst into flames, burned like paper into ashes, and when the light returned to me, tucking itself safely inside the core of my being, I stood for a long while contemplating the utter coolness of what had just happened.

"Charley," Uncle Bob said, bursting into the room, "what was that sound?" Dad was on his heels as they rushed down the steps.

"Wait," I called to them, holding up a hand. "Just stay there a minute."

"Is that Farrow?" Uncle Bob asked.

"Call an ambulance." I inched closer and realized that Reyes's incorporeal self was nowhere around. My heart seized until I heard his voice echo off the walls.

"It's still vulnerable."

I swung around to see him crouching on a shelf, balancing on the balls of his feet, one hand raised, gripping the hilt of his sword. The tip of the blade was at rest on the ground in front of him. It was almost as tall as I was. His robe billowed around him, up and over his head to fill every corner of the room. It swelled and receded, and I felt like an ocean of dark mass had swallowed me. He was the most magnificent being I'd ever seen.

And he was here. He was alive. "I thought I had vanquished you, too."

He turned his head, but I couldn't see his face. "I'm no demon. I was forged in the light."

"The light from the fires of hell," I reminded him. He didn't respond. Suddenly I was angry. Why did everything about being a grim reaper have to be so difficult? "Why didn't you just tell me I could do that?"

"As I said, it would be like telling a fledgling it could fly. You have to know you can do it on a visceral level. Had I told you, I would've been doing you no favors."

"What if I hadn't figured it out, Reyes?"

His hooded head tilted to one side. "Why question such things? You did it. You succeeded. End of story. But that is still vulnerable," he said, eyeing his corporeal body, the tattered, shredded shell of the man he used to be.

"You'll be fine when we get you to a hospital."

"To what end?"

I turned back to him. "What do you mean?"

"Do you think that was it? Do you think my father will just give up? That was a win for him. He now knows a portal walks the Earth. He'll stop at nothing, and he'll find a way to take you down. To rip you apart limb from limb to get at your core, your essence. And he now knows your weakness." He glanced back at his body. "You don't understand what will happen if my father gets ahold of me. There's a reason I need to ditch my corporeal self, Dutch. It's a chance I can't take."

"Charley, I need to get to him. He's dying."

I could hear the sirens of an ambulance growing louder. "Just one moment," I said to Uncle Bob. I didn't know what Reyes would do if Uncle Bob got near him. "What do you mean? What reason?"

Reyes toppled from the shelf to land effortlessly in front of his physical body. "They can find me. They can track me through this body," he said.

"You already told me that. But there's another reason. What is it?"

He shook his head. "You cleared the path. Now I can finish this."

The realization of what I'd done stunned me to my toes. I stepped closer. "Why didn't you just kill me when you had the chance? Why do this?"

"Charley," Dad said in warning, "what's going on?"

Reyes raised a gloved hand to my face. The heat that emanated from him caressed me like hot silk. "Kill you?" he asked, his velvety voice winding its way to my core. "That would be like smothering the sun."

I blinked in helplessness as Reyes turned and raised his blade, both hands on the hilt of the massive weapon. As he brought it down with a lightning-quick strike, I bolted through time, ducked under his arms, and covered his body with my own. The blade came to a stop millimeters from my spine.

He lifted it with a growl. "Move," he said, his voice edged with a hard warning.

"No." I couldn't stop the evidence of emotion from bursting forth, from stinging my eyes. I ground my teeth as I lay on Reyes. Soaked with blood, his body was still like an inferno, hot, vital and alive. His heart beat underneath my palms. His pulse roared in my ears. "I'm not letting you do this."

He took a menacing step forward and lowered his hood so I could see the hard lines of his face. "You don't understand what will happen if they find me, if they take me."

"I do understand," I said, my voice pleading. "They'll torture you. They'll use the key to get onto this plane. But—"

"It's not that simple."

That was simple? "Then what? Just say it."

He worked his jaw, reluctance radiating off him. Finally, he said, "I'm like you. I'm the key."

"I know. I understand that."

"No, you don't." He rubbed his forehead with a gloved hand. "Just like you're the portal into heaven—" He dropped his head as though ashamed. "—I'm the portal out of hell. If they get ahold of me, legions will come through, and they will not have to piggyback to get onto this plane."

I took a moment to absorb his meaning. It was hard to believe. We were so much more alike than I'd ever imagined. Both keys. Both portals. One to heaven and one to hell. Like a mirror.

"They would have direct access through me, just like the departed have direct access to heaven through you. And the first thing they'll do is hunt you down. They'll have a way out of hell, and with you, they'll have a way into heaven. Now, move, or I'll move you."

He would do it, too. He would move me, throw me across the floor to get to his body. I felt such desperation when I looked up at him, such agony. So I raised my hand and spoke.

"Rey'aziel, *te vincio*."

He stopped, his eyes widening in disbelief.

"That's right," I said when he gazed at me in question, "I bind you."

He stepped back, the shock plain on his face. "No," he said, grabbing at his robe as it disintegrated around him. His blade fell and seemed to shatter and disappear when it hit the floor, and he looked back at me, his eyes pleading. "Dutch, no."

The guilt that stabbed through my heart felt a hundred times worse than anything he could have done to me with his sword. The accusing stare, the betrayal in his eyes. Then he was gone. In an instant, his corporeal body came to life with a loud gasp. He seemed to seize, his teeth welded together as he writhed in pain, the agony on his face so evident, so absolute.

"Uncle Bob!" I screamed, and he and Dad barreled toward me. "Please, help him."

They loaded Reyes into the back of an ambulance. He'd already been fitted with oxygen and an IV. His steely body looked so vulnerable, so childlike. I wanted nothing more than to wrap him in my arms and make everything bad that had ever happened to him go away. But that would involve the magic of fairy tales. Even with my abilities, or possibly in spite of them, the last thing I believed in was magic.

Uncle Bob, Dad, and I had rehearsed our story before the ambulance arrived. The three of us had been heading to my apartment, so the story went, for some paperwork on a case when I heard a sound in the basement. We found Reyes there unconscious and called an ambulance. It sounded good if one didn't look too close. But after I'd told it about twenty thousand times, it got kind of old.

I sat in the waiting room at the hospital, still wrapped in my dad's jacket to cover my blood-soaked clothes and hoping for word on Reyes's condition as another doctor drilled me with questions. "Look, that's all I know. I have no idea how he was injured or what happened, and I'm sorry some of the injuries look days old. I just found him like that."

Neil Gossett, after dismissing the physician with a scowl, sat down next to me, two coffees in hand.

"Thanks for that," I said.

"Where's your uncle?"

"He had to go back to the station. We just solved a pretty big case, and he's taking statements." He was also going to let Cookie know what happened. She'd be glad we found Reyes.

"Well," Neil said, handing me a cup and frowning at the blood still on my hands, "the way I see it, Reyes woke up in that long-term-care unit with amnesia. He was in a coma, after all, with a head wound. Didn't know who he was, much less where he was. Can't possibly be held accountable for escaping when he had no idea he was doing it."

I gaped at him. With a grin, he reached over and closed my mouth.

"You would do that?" I asked, appreciation evident in my voice.

"I would do that."

I sighed a breath of relief. "Neil, thank you so much."

"Don't mention it," he said, taking a sip. "No, really, don't mention it. I like my job."

I smiled. "Oh, hell yeah. Now I have something to blackmail you with. Hmmm," I said, taking a long sip of hot java, "what do I need?"

"Your head examined?" he asked. "Which, by the way, you don't have to resort to blackmail to get. I know some people who know some people."

"If I want my head shrunk, I'll talk to my sister."

"Oh, dude, your sister is so hot." He sat back, his expression full of reminiscent thought.

"Ew." She was beautiful, but still. Neil Gossett? With my flesh and blood? Not likely. "I have to tell you something."

He straightened. "Sounds serious."

"It is. I bound him."

"What?"

With a heavy sigh, I said, "I bound him, like tied him."

He leaned toward me and asked under his breath, "Should you be telling me this?"

"Not like that." After a backhand to his shoulder, I lowered my eyes, ashamed at what I was about to tell him. "I bound his incorporeal self to his corporeal body. He can't leave it. He's bound to it."

"You can do that?"

"Apparently. It just kind of came to me."

"Wow."

"No, what I mean is, he's mad."

He paused and leveled an astonished stare on me. "What?"

"He's kind of furious," I said, shrugging one corner of my mouth.

Neil worked his jaw a moment, as if trying to figure out what to say. "Charley," he said, apparently decided, "I've seen Reyes furious once, remember? It left an impression."

"I know and I'm sorry. He was going to essentially commit suicide. I didn't know what else to do."

"So you infuriate him then send him back to prison?" he asked, his voice a harsh whisper.

I cringed. He made it sound so bad. "Pretty much."

"Holy shit, Charley."

"What'd she do now?"

We both looked up. Owen Vaughn, the guy who tried to maim me in high school, stood over us in his black police uniform. Shiny badge and all.

"Vaughn," Neil said by way of a chilly greeting.

Owen tapped his badge. "Officer Vaughn," he corrected. "I need to know what happened in that basement."

Oh, for the love of Pete's Dragon. "I gave my statement to Detective Davidson," I said, challenging him with my eyes.

"Don't you mean Uncle Bob?"

"That's the one."

Owen looked down the hall each way, then leaned down to me. "Would you like to know what I think of you?"

"Um, is that a trick question?"

"Never mind," he said, straightening. "I'll save it for a more appropriate time." He smirked in anticipation. "Like the day I haul your ass to jail."

As he stormed off, Neil asked, "Seriously, what the hell did you do to him?"

"You were his danged friend," I said, throwing a palm up. "You tell me."

Neil stuck around awhile; then Cookie showed up with food and a change of clothes. She tried to get me to go home, but I just couldn't leave, not before knowing Reyes's condition. Dad came and went. Gemma came and went. A doctor finally came out, his eyes weary. Reyes was in ICU, but he was doing remarkably well, all things considered. Still, I couldn't leave. Angel showed up around dark and stayed the entire night with me. He sat on the floor beside my head as I laid claim to a small padded bench and slept as well as could be expected on a small padded bench.

Uncle Bob came back early the next morning, a little annoyed. "Why didn't you go home?"

"'Cause." I rubbed my eyes then my back, glancing over at Angel. "Did you stay here all night, babe?"

"Of course," he said. "That guy over there was eyeing you the whole time."

"Who, that man?" I asked, pointing to the guy asleep across from me. "I think he just sleeps with his eyes open like that."

"Oh. That's just wrong."

"Yeah. So what's up?" I asked Ubie.

"We're going to Ruiz. We were granted a permit to exhume the body of one Mr. Saul Romero."

"Oh, good. Who's Saul Romero?"

"The guy Hana Insinga is allegedly buried under."

"Oh, right. I knew that."

"So, you in?"

I offered a weak shrug. "I guess. The state won't let me see Reyes anyway."

"Then why the hell did you stay here all night?"

I shrugged again. "Glutton. I need a shower."

"Come on, I'll take you. We have to pick up Cookie, anyway, and meet the sheriff up there."

We pulled into the Ruiz Cemetery right behind Mimi and Warren Jacobs. Kyle Kirsch was already there with his father. From the crimson lining their eyes, I'd say neither got much sleep. Kyle's mother had been picked up in Minnesota and was awaiting transport back to New Mexico. And, sadly, Hy Insinga was there as well, her face the definition of agony. My heart ached for her.

"It's that one," Mimi told the Mora County sheriff, pointing to Mr. Romero's grave. "The second one on the left."

Two hours later, a team from the Office of the Medical Investigator from Albuquerque was lifting out the twenty-year-old remains of Hana Insinga. The pain on her mother's face was too much to bear. Grateful she had a friend with her, I went back to Ubie's SUV and watched as Hy Insinga walked up to a trembling and sobbing Mimi, worried what the outcome of that reunion would be. They hugged each other for a very long time.

Three days later, Reyes Farrow, after showing remarkable and unexplainable improvement, was released into the care of the Penitentiary of New Mexico's medical team. I drove to Santa Fe to see him, literally quaking in my boots as I stood in line with the other visitors, waiting my turn to be ION scanned for drug residue. But a guard pulled me out of line and told me Deputy Warden Gossett wanted to talk to me first.

"How you holding up?" Neil asked when the guard showed me into his office.

I was getting used to the organized clutter and sat across from him. "I'm good," I said with a shrug. "Taking a little break from the PI business at the moment."

"Is everything okay?" he asked, alarmed.

"Oh, yeah. Just nothing too pressing. So what's up? Can I see him, or is he still in the medical unit?"

Neil glanced down before answering. "I wanted to tell you this myself instead of them telling you in the visitation area."

My heart lurched in my chest. "Did something happen? Is Reyes okay?"

"He's fine, Charley, but . . . he refuses to see you." He tilted his head in regret. "He had the state deny your application."

I sat in stunned silence a full minute and absorbed the meaning of what he said. A vise locked around my chest and was inching closed.

My periphery darkened. I could barely breathe, and I needed out of there. "Well, I'll be going, then." I rose and headed for the door.

Neil rounded his desk and caught my arm. "Charley, he'll change his mind. He's just angry."

I offered a smile. "Neil, it's okay. Just . . . take good care of him?"

"You know I will."

I walked out of the prison with a smile on my face and drove home fighting the suffocating weight of sorrow tooth and nail. Wetness slipped past my lashes nonetheless. It was pathetic. I contemplated my future on the way. What would life be like without Reyes Farrow in it? He could no longer separate from his body. He could no longer come to me, talk to me, touch me, save my ass every other day. After a lifetime of having him practically at my beck and call, I was alone.

By the time I pulled into my apartment complex, I realized in a most deplorable and humbling way that I was now one of those women, one of the hundreds of women who tried to see him, who tried in vain to get close. I was Elaine Oake.

I was nobody.

After trudging to my apartment, I fired up my computer and skimmed a few e-mail messages marked urgent, two from Uncle Bob. Deciding they could wait, I exited and checked my fake e-mail while making up excuses to hit the sack at 11 in the A.M. I wanted to be productive, but lethargy sprinkled with traces of depression was calling to me. A message from Mistress Marigold popped onto the screen. It was probably the exact same message she'd sent Cookie and Garrett. Barely interested at that point—and wondering if I really needed to ever take another breath again—I clicked on the link and read it.

I've been waiting a long time to hear from you.